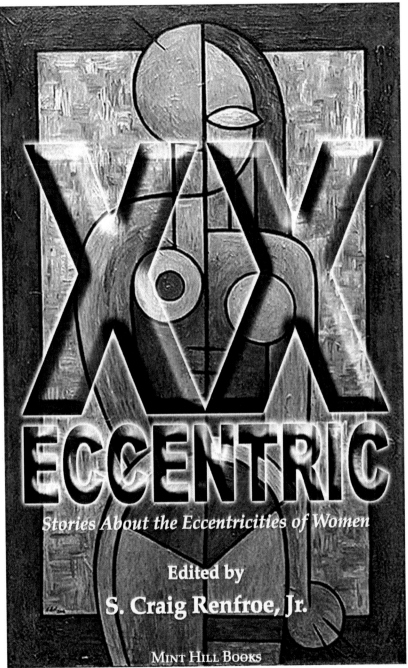

ECCENTRIC

Stories About the Eccentricities of Women

Edited by

S. Craig Renfroe, Jr.

MINT HILL BOOKS

MAIN STREET RAG PUBLISHING COMPANY
CHARLOTTE, NORTH CAROLINA

Acknowledgements:

"Shimmy Twins" first appeared in *Crab Orchard Review*.
"Against the Wall" was first published by *Short Story
    Review.*
"My Wife, the Porn Star" was first published in the book
    Fracture City (Main Street Rag, 2008).
"Rhoda" in *The Falcon* (Mansfield State College).
"Small Business" was first published in *Nidus* (University
    of Pittsburgh).

Library of Congress Control Number: 2009928576

ISBN 13: 978-1-59948-187-6

Produced in the United States of America

Mint Hill Books
Main Street Rag Publishing Company
PO Box 690100
Charlotte, NC 28227
www.MainStreetRag.com

CONTENTS

Introduction

D ear reader, you may recall from basic biology that women have the *XX* sex chromosomes, as opposed to the male *XY*. Is that little letter, that one *X* instead of a *Y*, is that what explains the mysteries of the woman. Maybe.

Here in this short story collection we have sterling fiction that brings to emotional life women and not just biology. These stories are about women, but not your ordinary women—if there is such a thing. These women are eccentric, which can too often be just another euphemism for weird or annoying. Some of the women here are weird and annoying. Mostly they are eccentric as in: not following convention; finding their own path.

We've all known the mothers and the daughters and their endless struggle. We've read about the grandmothers cooking and the teenagers experimenting. We wanted to see other sides of women, beyond the normal roles ascribed to them.

The women in this anthology give us what we want, but maybe not in the way we knew we wanted it. They pay their way through college by selling themselves to ice fishermen, they obsess over George Harrison or Abe Lincoln, they find a dead monkey, they think about walking on all fours in a past life, they have bad instincts for relationships, they have really bad instincts for relationships, they get stuck on a giant crucifix, they embalm pets—that sort of thing.

Whatever the form of their distinct path, these characters raise our expectations and our understanding. They challenge our definitions of what women should be and can do. We can fall in love with them, be frustrated by them and be betrayed by them. We can live their lives for a short moment and in doing so, experience the world anew.

Dear reader, we invite you to enjoy the eccentricities of these women.

—S. Craig Renfroe, Jr., Editor

LIFE WITHOUT FORELEGS

Melody Clayton

His return was nearly imperceptible from the day he left. Same blue sky, same warm air, same spring blossoms, and the same old song and dance about who owns what. Only differences worthy of notice are a new set of birds chirping and a different girlfriend waiting impatiently, possibly nervously, in the car outside. I peek through the heavy drapes at her. She sees me then turns meekly away, dare I say slouching low into her seat as if hiding. Obviously he's told her horror stories about me.

Primarily he has come for Seamus and a few other things he suddenly found dear. He's working from a list written on a slip of pink paper he holds crumpled in his hand. I wonder if he had to put Seamus on the list or if he would remember him out of true affection? Seamus is only a goldfish with no ability to express his feelings. Yet, I'm certain he doesn't want to go. Seamus knows how difficult he can be. Nevertheless, he feels entitled to take Seamus with him.

We had little to say to each other. The house was quiet except for his frantic movements from room to room. The tick of a clock in the next room could be heard when he was out of sight, fading away once he returned. If love makes a death rattle when it passes away, then the refrain of that clock must be the sound it makes. It groaned away with its steady gauge many times in the hostile silences between us. We failed to hear it then.

In a cold metal chair on the far wall I sit watching him buzz around in search of things, opening and closing drawers, searching bookshelves, referring to the list.

Impatiently he moves from room to room.

I notice he has the Italian espresso maker. He doesn't drink coffee. But I suspect it was a gift from her and she must want him to retrieve it.

I remain silent until he begins swirling the little green net around in the fish tank, poor Seamus dodging him at ever turn.

"I have distinct memories of being a camel," I finally say. "From my recollections I am almost certain that I was a wild two-humped Bactrian camel indigenous to Mongolia."

"Ummm," he says. He's not paying attention. He never did.

I keep most of my memories to myself. No one could really understand how disappointing life without forelegs can be. As a camel I had bony toes with leathery skin between the soles like webbed feet so that I wouldn't sink into the sand. My human feet, of which there are naturally only two and a disadvantage in and of itself, have no webbing and sink quickly. They burn easily on hot asphalt. They cramp when I've walked too long. If one is injured then I am left unbalanced and teetering.

"I remember being Napoleon," he says without turning.

"That makes sense."

"What makes sense?"

"Good question."

Once he dumped the fish into a bag and sloshed it around a bit he headed for the door. Seamus peered frantically at me through the plastic, wiggling his little body from side to side trying to readjust to his new, smaller existence inside of a bag.

There were no inside jokes left to exchange and no words of well wishes. Not even words of disgust and accusations. Those were all used up and so it was final and that was that.

"Thanks," he says.

Ten years and that's how it ends. Thank you.

I guess that's civil.

At first I was overwhelmed by the silence, the closed door so final, the fish tank empty with just a shipwreck left buried in the blue gravel. I leave the water in the tank. I keep the lights and heaters on for weeks after Seamus is gone. At night I pull up a chair and stare into the abyss because it seems there is nothing to do but sit alone wandering through my thoughts, classifying my reality as either life with or life without forelegs.

I entertained the idea of getting another fish but decided against it.

I've taken on a second job cleaning beach rentals to fill the time. Lola and I stand on the balcony of a four story mansion overlooking white sand and greenish ocean. We're having a smoke break, peacefully watching the sun glitter over the water and vacationers bake their skin blazing shades of red. Overhead a pelican spreads its wings beautifully, and then suddenly tucks them back, dive bombs head first into the ocean. It emerges with a fish.

Lola claps. She was cheering for the pelican.

I didn't want to take a side.

She flicks her cigarette into the swimming pool below. "That's Juan's department."

"Sure," I say.

"So tell me the rest of the camel story. What happened after the male camel left her. No, I mean, after he left you," she says. Lola believes in my previous existence as a camel. She says she was Marie Antoinette and can distinctly recall the guillotine blade cross her neck. She claims to have seen her headless body for a second. I really don't believe Lola's stories. They're too far fetched. Besides, I know about ten people personally who think they were Marie Antoinette. How can everyone have been someone famous? Why was I merely a wild camel? It doesn't seem fair.

"Once he left me I easily found another lover."

"Ooh. Tell me who is this lover?"

"This is the camel story, Lola."

"Oh, sorry. Go on."

"My camel lover stayed by my side most of the winter. He readily did battle with any male contender, his mouth always lathered in white, his legs tense, and his tail whipping."

"Sounds very sexy."

I give her a puzzled look. She smiles, waiting.

"Once in a while one of the domesticated camels owned by a local villager would escape, adorned with silver and beaded saddles."

"Ooh. Rich one's. I like that. That's sexy."

Again the look. Again the smile.

"They were no match for my lover."

"Of course not."

"Their necks tangled and rubbed together until the dandy camel ran away in fear. My lover and I were never domesticated and used for wool or milk. We were much too stubborn and could see that in this false security of the Mongolian herder we would be rewarded for our efforts by being slaughtered for meat."

"Sounds like marriage," Lola says.

"It wasn't the life for me because in my camel mind I wanted to live free and die happy."

"Is that not true of this life too?"

"Sometimes. It's complicated."

There persists a body of literature which sets out to illustrate mankind's inability to communicate. Some do it with comedy. Some use drama or tragedy. But I'm wondering: since I read the story and I see the message of our failure to communicate and I laugh in all the right places, haven't we thus communicated something?

Lola doesn't think so. She thinks no one has ever really connected with another human being and our attempts to communicate, to bridge a connection from one human to another is wasted efforts. Lola likes to envision a world where no one speaks except to communicate a present need such as ordering coffee or asking for help.

I tell Lola she is welcome to move in with me and stare into the empty abyss of Seamus's tank. She chuckles and lights another cigarette.

D octor Barrett is a middle-aged man with tiny silver glasses and a dark mahogany desk. His office is in a shabby part of town and I suspect the high price I pay to see him is funding his future, more prestigious, location complete with a Starbucks around the corner and exceptional parking.

"I have distinct memories of being a camel," I tell him at the start of our session. He writes it down. I'm excited to see that he's searching for a cure.

"Go on. Tell me what you remember." He's interested. He is not shocked.

"Mostly I remember swaying from side to side when I walked. I had two legs on one side moving forward together and then the other two legs on the other side moving forward. There was great power in those movements. I could run very fast, too."

"Run?"

"I ran across desserts, sometimes dusted with snow like pastries. I would never get tired from running. It was invigorating. I could go anywhere without worries. I had nothing to plan. Nothing to prove. There was nowhere that

I had to be. Just wide open spaces and I could go in any direction forever and ever if I wanted."

"Then why run? You have time and space. No need to hurry, right?" I think he's mocking me a little.

"I'm sure camels don't think that way."

"Don't you know how they think?"

"I can't recall."

"But you can still run with human legs."

"I can't run as fast. Not as much power and grace. I get tired."

"Tired?"

"Well, maybe lazy is a better word. I just don't care to make the effort."

"Would you prefer your camel life over your human one?"

"Yes."

"Why?"

"I miss my forelegs. I feel severed. Though arms are nice. Arms create responsibility."

"Explain."

"Have you ever asked a camel to pass the salt or give you a hug?"

We end our session with some talk about my methods for relaxing. I tell him cleaning toilets is a form of meditative therapy for me. He's not convinced. Doctor Barrett is a nice man but by professional default an incredible skeptic. He writes me a prescription but I have no intention of ever having it filled. I crumple it and toss it on my way out.

A hand reaches from underneath a bus stop bench where I sit waiting. I clutch my purse closer to my body. I have no cash. Like a good American I only have credit. The homeless can't deal with credit.

"I have no money," I tell the hand touching my foot. "It would be the drowning saving the drowning if I did."

"I don't want your money," he says. He sounds drunk or toothless. Maybe both. "Do you have the time? Is the bus late?"

"It is late," I say after glancing at my watch. I decide to walk to the next stop, away from the strange man underneath the bench.

As I walk I think it best to put on a more hurried expression and a more determined gait as if nothing mattered as much to me in this world as my arriving at my destination; as if the person waiting for me is not Lola, but someone who owes me a large sum of money or an explanation.

The heel of my shoe catches in a crack on the sidewalk. I stumbled forward. I curse human legs and their failings. I curse shoes that bind. Mostly I just keep walking. I don't look back even though the heel is broken. I drag it along, scraping the sidewalk until I reach the other bus stop. Luckily there were no homeless men sleeping under the bench and the bus was on time. You have to count your blessings where you can find them.

"What happened to you?" Lola asked. She slides me a drink. "You're late."

"Don't ask."

The music is loud. It's too crowded to move.

Lola unapologetically invited Alley who is her friend but not mine. I dislike Alley immensely and Lola knows so she decided not to tell me that she would be joining us for drinks. Alley thinks she was once Don Quixote.

"Nora was a camel from the Bible," Lola interjects.

"Not from the Bible."

"Really," Alley says, "I always think of camels as conceited, the way they walk with their heads so high and their noses in the air. Not to say that you are conceited, of course."

"You realize Don Quixote never existed," I tell her. "You couldn't have been someone fictional."

"Haven't you ever heard of a muse, Nora?" she asked. "I think I was the original Don Quixote. The one who inspired the story."

Alley is too emotionally retarded to navigate reality.

"Hey," calls a man's voice. Then there is a tap on my shoulder.

I turn around.

"Would you like to dance," he asks.

I take him in. Cowboy hat. Tight jeans. Nice build. Not too young. Not too old.

Count me in.

"Sure," I say.

"Sorry, but camel's can't dance," Alley shouts. She starts to laugh.

"Yeah, but this is life without forelegs."

I follow the cowboy to the dance floor. I begin to feel something odd happening to my face. For the first time in months I think I'm actually smiling. The thought of it makes me nervous. I have to keep my head down, my eyes on the floor.

Recently I Googled camels and discovered a small group of wild camels living in a protected area of the Great Gobi. I think I recognized a photo of my former camel self sneering into the camera. In the background I can see my camel family surrounding me with their frozen expressions of bewilderment. My lover stands just to my left with that familiar expression of determination and strength in his eyes.

The one who left me never returned. After his mating with a Mongolian herder's prize camel, he was slaughtered.

Such is life with forelegs.

As a camel I didn't grieve.

It wasn't part of my nature.

SMALL BUSINESS

William Borden

If you gaze long into an abyss,
the abyss will gaze back into you.
—Nietzsche

Julia Cathcart, in her thirties, divorced, childless, majoring in communications and hoping someday to be a news anchor, gazed out her dormitory window at frozen Lake Betawigosh and the two or three hundred fish houses sprinkled across the lake's cold whiteness. Roads had been plowed from the lakeside to the houses. She could see pickups, snowmobiles, cars, snuggled beside the houses like faithful pets awaiting their owners. Smoke drifted from a few houses, where a wood or charcoal brazier warmed the interior. Most of the houses were warmed by bottled gas. Most of the houses, smaller than a prison cell, were of wood, and a few were of light-weight but durable plastic, easy to move to a better fishing spot; here and there sat a larger enclosure, built for company, card-playing, and the comforts of home. She watched a pickup wind its way through the spontaneous alleys and pull up beside a large bright blue fish house. A man climbed out of the pickup and stepped into the house, pulling the door closed behind him.

Because Julia was also taking psychology in hopes that it would help in interviewing and understanding people, the fish houses seemed to her like a speckled Rorschach blot, patternless yet inviting some interpretation, some projection of the observer's unacknowledged desires. The thought, oddly enough, brought to mind her grandmother, Grace, who had been a self-employed entrepreneur of the region, servicing first the lumberjacks and, later, after the timber had been clear cut, the Civilian Conservation Corps that had moved through the area, constructing buildings for state and county parks. Grace had outfitted a school bus with a bed and hot and cold running water and driven from camp to camp, covering, with an enviable reliability, a several-county territory extending from St. Cloud north into Manitoba and west to North Dakota. Julia remembered a white-haired, buxom matron who made sugar cookies and wild blueberry pies and sang popular songs of the '30's and '40's. Her grandmother passed on when Julia was still a child, a year after her husband, Julia's grandfather, a gregarious former tavern owner who had not held Grace's profession against her but rather had admired her for her initiative and self reliance, her grandfather recognizing that to fulfill a need, to meet a demand, whatever it might be, was in the truest American tradition of Emersonian self-reliance, Dale Carnegie initiative, and Rockerfellerian intrepidity.

Julia was also thinking—or rather it was her next thought, although it came so quickly, as thoughts do, that it seemed coincident with the first—that her job as a waitress at the Calistoga Café made her feet sore and her back ache and didn't pay enough for her to keep up with her bills for tuition, books, dormitory, and incidentals. The Calistoga patrons were mostly working class and retired and believed that even a ten per cent tip was asking a lot. Julia had tried to get a job at the upscale Lakeside Resort, but they seemed to hire only young women, who were cute and flirtatious.

Not that Julia wasn't good looking. She had what a mature man might call an interesting face—high cheek bones, arched eyebrows, straight nose, dark eyes, and black hair which she had let grow since her divorce until it flowed lushly to her shoulder blades. She was slim but not thin; waitressing kept the weight off, and she watched what she ate. She walked, too, and swam sometimes, and in the winter she liked to cross country ski. Her legs looked good, even in sensible shoes, and her breasts were ample and firm. Her voice was husky, even though she had quit smoking.

Julia had not grown up in Betawigosh. Her mother had married a salesman who thought there were more opportunities in the Twin Cities, and Julia had grown up on the south side of Minneapolis. When she married Justin, just out of high school, he took her to Brainerd, where he sold boats, then cars, then snowmobiles, then electronics, then appliances, until he finally went into rehab and joined AA and met Marjorie, who, he said, understood him.

Justin ice fished, and so Julia had an understanding of the psychology of men who ice fished. It was, in the first place, almost entirely men who ice fished. It seemed to be something coded in their DNA—the hunt, the solitude, the escape from the mysterious female presence. Just as South Sea tribesmen went off to live in male-only long houses, just as Aboriginal adolescents proved their manhood with year-long solitary walkabouts, just as anchorites retired to mountaintops or caves to plumb the vagaries of God's dispensations, so, it seemed, men in Minnesota retired each winter to their small ice-bound huts—to catch fish, to meditate, to escape. Some men brought old easy chairs or abandoned sofas or even cots. They might stay out on the ice for days.

Rafe, 60, living on his disability check after the chain saw slipped from his hands and nearly severed his foot, sat on his folding chair peering into the green luminescence of his fish hole. His spear rested lightly in his hand. His lure hung listlessly in the water. He was in his long underwear. The fish house was warm from the propane heater. His mind was blank. He had ice fished every winter for over forty years. The one thing he could count on was that he would not be disturbed. It was better than being a Trappist monk.

So when he heard the knock he thought it was the wind rattling the plywood door. When the door opened, and the afternoon's pale light fell into the darkness, he thought the door had simply come unlatched. When the shadow fell into the light, and the figure appeared in his peripheral vision, he figured it was maybe Carl Osterholm, who had a fish house a few yards away and maybe wanted to borrow a lure or a beer.

But the figure, face hidden by the fur-trimmed parka, didn't seem to be Carl. It was slipping its boots out of cross country skis and stepping inside and leaning the skis against the wall before a mittened hand pulled back the parka's hood to reveal a woman's face and tousled black hair.

Rafe didn't have any money with him—what was he going to buy in the middle of a frozen lake?—but said he would have some tomorrow, if she'd come back. She gave him a three-by-five card on which were printed the various prices, so he could decide ahead of time what he wanted, or what he could afford. She told him she was working her way through college, and she knew it could get lonesome out here in a fish house, and it was private, no one would know, it was their business strictly, and she could provide a variety of services, for different prices, and it was all up to him what he might want or might want to afford. She understood that different men had different inclinations, and different abilities. She could, she said, for just five dollars, take off her sweater and her flannel shirt and let him look at her breasts. In fact, as a kind of sample, or free preview, she whipped off her sweater and unbuttoned her red and green flannel shirt and let him gaze at her breasts, which, he thought, were not bad at all, the nipples sticking out from the sudden change in temperature. For ten dollars he could feel them, she said, and for fifteen he could suck on them, for up to five minutes.

He said that seemed kind of steep.

Here, give it a shot, she said, stepping into him, being careful not to step in the hole in the ice, her breast suddenly right in his face, the nipple seemingly drawn like a magnet to his lips, already open in astonishment. She let him suck for almost a minute, let him squeeze her breast. She said her philosophy—she was taking Introduction to Western Philosophy from Professor Jens Andreesen and thought this was the idea behind Kant's categorical imperative—was that a fellow should know what he was paying good money for, and that she would get more business in the long run, more paying business, if she gave out samples, the way they do Saturdays at Olson's Supermarket—the little chunks of summer sausage speared by a pretzel, the little wedge of Northern Star pepperoni pizza, the little paper cup of Johnson's New Orleans coffee—because, she said, "Once you have a taste of something really good, you definitely want to come back for more."

"You definitely want to come back for me," was what Carl thought she said, not "for more," but he wasn't sure, because he didn't seem to be thinking clearly, with her nipple, larger, it seemed, than his wife's, although it had been so long he couldn't be sure, hard against his tongue.

She didn't protest, either, when his hand found her buttock and rested there for a moment. Finally, though, she stepped gently away and buttoned her shirt. "Tomorrow?" she asked. He nodded. "Same time?" He nodded.

Rafe wasn't a bad-looking man. His gray hair was disappearing from the top of his head, but he sported a rakish walrus mustache. He was a sturdy man, having worked outdoors most of his life, although since his injury his pants had gotten smaller just hanging in the closet. He took his current disability as he took most of life—philosophically, he liked to say, although he had never studied the subject, never gone to college, but everyone at the Next Door Bar, where he sometimes went on Friday afternoons in the spring and fall, when there wasn't any fishing to be done, seemed to understand what "philosophical" meant. It meant simply to take what life threw at you, without complaint or even much surprise, whether what hit you was a chain saw gone wild, a wife who preferred Jay Leno to sex, an enlarged prostate, or the final long cold sleep.

Rafe was so used to taking disappointment with a shrug, he didn't know how to take sudden good luck. After his free sample from Julia he was disoriented. He tried to maintain his usual aplomb, but he found he couldn't sleep that night, and his mind kept replaying those few minutes of surprising nurturance as if his brain had a film loop that couldn't be turned off. When he did sleep, his dreams were vivid and chaotic, images of women with huge breasts chasing him across the ice, women with pendulous breasts rising like mermaids from his fish hole in the ice and pulling him down and dragging him deep, where they made love in green water and he didn't have to breathe or come up for air.

In the morning his wife, Gert, asked if he had had nightmares, he had been moaning and gasping for air.

With the winter-spring semester that began in January Julia was able to schedule all of her classes—Advanced News Reporting, Public Relations II, Public Speaking, Psychology of News Gathering, and Controversies in Ethics (Professor Andreesen's specialty, using the book he had written in which famous ethicists such as Plato, Aristotle, Spinoza, Hume, Kant, Russell, Confucius, Jesus, Moses, Moses Maimonides, Henry Ford, and Dr. Seuss meet to discuss various moral topics)—in the morning and early afternoon, leaving later afternoons and evenings, and weekends, free for business.

Of course, she had to have time to study, but she soon developed a regular clientele whom she could visit by appointment, reducing the time wasted in door-to-door solicitation. She had her appointment book, and her pencil (the ballpoint wouldn't write in the cold), and the client's requests, so she could estimate how much time she should allot for each appointment, and she could have a pretty good idea of her weekly income, and so know when she could give more time to her studies. She also developed a more efficient wardrobe, one that was warm, for skiing between ice houses, but which could be removed and restored in mere seconds, snaps and zippers replacing buttons.

Rafe's disability check wasn't large, but then he didn't have a lot of expenses. Gert worked as a nurse's aide at the rest home. Their modest house was paid for. Their car, with over a hundred thousand miles on the odometer, was good for another hundred thousand. He was a cautious man, though, and so the first time Julia came back he opted for the breast sucking she had let him sample the day before. He liked it that she was mature, not too young. She didn't make him feel so old. She had a frank, saucy way about her that he appreciated, and she had a sense of humor. When he had finished with her breast, she glanced down and blurted out a spur-of-the-moment variation on the old Mae West line, *Is that a Northern pike in your long johns or are you just glad to see me?* Rafe said he was glad to see her. She said she was glad to see him, too, and she impulsively gave him a playful little squeeze. Then they both had the same idea at the same time.

She admitted she hadn't thought of putting this on her card. How much? he asked. She let her hand slide back and forth as she thought. Forty dollars, she said. Rafe hadn't brought any extra. But she could tell they were too far along to stop without grave disappointment, so she told him he could bring it tomorrow, she would trust him, and he said okay, and he did.

She received an A on her paper for Professor Andreesen's class. She argued in her paper that prostitution was like any small business and could be ethically justified—not, perhaps, by the Old Testament Moses, but by Moses Maimonides, who took a more Talmudic approach than his ten-commandments namesake, and it was clearly in keeping with Jesus' befriending Mary Magdalene and his golden rule. She quoted *The Oxford Companion to Philosophy* to the effect that Spinoza believed that "our primary aim should be joyous living in the here and now." And she found Spinoza himself stating, "There cannot be too much merriment, for it is always good; but on the other hand, melancholy is always bad."

Professor Andreesen, a boyishly handsome man in his forties who felt himself misplaced by Fortune to be in a two-member philosophy department in a small midwestern college, believed that he should by rights be at a prestigious university on the east or west coast, and that if he just had a stimulating intellectual environment and a lighter teaching load he could do the research and writing that would, he was sure, make his as formidable a name as Rorty or Nussbaum.

As it was, he encouraged Julia to major in philosophy, even though it could lead nowhere, vocationally speaking, because she had a gift for incisive argument, and he had to agree that prostitution was a victimless crime and the Europeans were more sophisticated about it and that, yes, temple prostitution might prove the essential sacredness of the profession.

Julia almost confessed her after-school small business, but she wasn't sure Professor Andreesen would accept the material reality of an idea as readily as the abstract concept. Sometimes it seemed as if he lived mostly in his head, and that the nitty gritty of life could throw him for a loop.

Rafe didn't talk much, which was all right with Julia. She liked to keep things moving, the way she had as a waitress—take the orders, bring the dishes, clear the table, bring the check—get the work done and go home. But she was discovering that the men on the ice were like the men at the Calistoga Café; they were lonely, and they wanted to talk. They seemed to need conversation as much as physical discharge. They talked about their wives and pulled out photos of their children. They revealed their fears, admitted their failures, volunteered their hopes, listed their troubles, and confessed their misdeeds. She even wondered briefly if she should give up broadcast journalism and go into psychology, but she soon realized that these outpourings of confidences were, to Julia's way of thinking, unseemly. She didn't want to be kneeling between a man's legs as he told her how wonderful his wife was, even though she had certain inhibitions; and she didn't want to waste valuable time listening to stories of how a son scored the winning goal last night in peewee hockey when the fellow should be dropping his drawers and getting himself ready.

Sometimes, when a customer was rattling on about how his wife wouldn't try this or that, or he was taking a tediously long time to get to where he wanted to go, Julia found herself staring at the greenish glow of the ice hole, gazing idly at the languid mosaic of light and water, imagining that the ripples formed themselves into spider webs or maps of Europe or Jackson Pollock drip paintings (she had taken Modern Art last year) or even into faces, some strange and disfigured, others familiar, like Robert Redford or Katherine Hepburn.

So Rafe's taciturnity came as a pleasant relief. He didn't even mention Gert until Julia asked him one day if he was married. She was pulling on her parka and unaccountably felt a curiosity for something personal, after the personal things they had been doing to one another for the past hour. She had guessed he was a widower, he seemed so solitary, so accustomed to loneliness, so resigned to a kind of persistent, low-grade sadness.

Her question, however, opened up something in Rafe. The next time she came he asked her questions about herself. He asked what foods she liked, if she went to the movies, what courses she was taking. He became especially curious about her philosophy courses. He hadn't known there was such a smorgasbord of opinion and argument when it came to philosophy.

He listened attentively as she summarized the courses. Once she left, he did his best to think through the things she had talked about, and how her readings seemed to tie ideas into knots. Things that before had seemed to him clear and plain now lurked in shadows and skittered away along twisted passageways. The next time she came he would raise some new question, he would stop her—sometimes at a particularly sensitive stage of their professional engagement—for clarification.

Sometimes Julia brought him books—*The Varieties of Religious Experience, Thus Spake Zarathustra, The Apology*— but Rafe wasn't one for reading. The words swam before his eyes. Like Socrates (Julia assured him), Rafe was a creature of dialectic, of the spoken give and take of the pursuit of truth.

He wanted her to explain what Plato meant by love and what Spinoza meant by God and why logic and metaphysics had so much trouble talking to each other. Sometimes, after Julia left, Rafe felt as if his head was exploding. What did

William James mean by a pluralistic universe? Why would somebody as smart as Aristotle think slavery was okay? Could a person really be an *Ubermensch*, or was that merely big talk, the kind he heard at the Next Door Bar when a fellow had too much to drink?

Truth to tell, Julia enjoyed these fish house seminars, as she called them. They gave her a chance to try out ideas before she had to expose them in Professor Andreesen's class. They stimulated her thinking. They sharpened her mind.

As winter dragged itself frigidly on, Rafe found himself, despite his better judgment, succumbing to an escalating appetite. It was as if, deprived for so many years, an overwhelming hunger had been created, and it seemed to be insatiable. He was not satisfied with her breast. He was impatient with her hand, expert though it was. Her oral solicitations satisfied him only momentarily. Intercourse became old hat.

He drew money out of his savings account. He started going for the Grand Slam Special. He asked for things that weren't on the card. He took out a loan. He wanted her to come twice a day.

Julia had seen addiction before, with Justin and alcohol, with her father and alcohol. She realized Rafe had gone off the deep end. She hadn't worried about it at first. She assumed he had plenty of money, until he mentioned one day that he'd tried to mortgage his house but needed his wife's signature and of course that was a problem. Still, she thought things would wind down soon. The weather was warming up, and the houses would have to be off the ice before long.

Not so. Rafe wanted her to come to his house. Or he could visit her in her dorm room. Or maybe he would buy a trailer somewhere in the woods. He could withdraw money from his retirement account. It was a sure source of income, but Julia had principles. The question was, how to help Rafe with his unforeseen addiction? Cut him off, cold turkey? Or find a suitable rehab—which would bring unwanted notoriety, and perhaps marital discord?

What Julia failed to realize was that even though Rafe could admit that he was in the thrall of an addiction, he was also convinced that he was—well, there was no other word for it—he was in love. The trouble had begun, Rafe realized, and Julia concurred, when Rafe started asking her about herself. When they started talking about philosophy. When it became clear to Rafe that no matter what a fellow set out to do, he could make a convincing argument for it. And why shouldn't he, after all these years, feel the visceral implosion of love? Sure, Socrates thought love should be only in the head, but hadn't Lucretius written an entire book singing Love's praises? Didn't Pericles think enough of Aspasia, the most famous courtesan of all, to love her and marry her?

"But Rafe," Julia had to admit, "I don't love *you*."

Rafe didn't care. He said all he wanted was to keep feeling the overwhelming love he felt for her, experience the hot thrill pumping through his veins. He had never felt this alive, he said. He'd even been to the doctor, and his arthritis was gone and his cholesterol was down. She didn't have to reciprocate. Not with love, anyway. And he would continue to pay her, just as before. He had gotten several credit cards in the mail in the past few weeks, and he was activating all of them. He would get cash advances. He would do anything, but he loved her, and he had to have her.

Which made Julia wonder what difference there was, really, between an addiction and love.

The next day was Sunday, when many of her clients were in church and, later, watching the Vikings on TV. She went out anyway, not for business but to clear her head, to try to find a way to cure poor Rafe's addiction, or love, if there was a difference. She skied straight out, skirting the houses, some of which had already been removed. She skied until she found herself shivering, a sudden chill wind whipping snow off the ice and pelting her face. She headed for the one solitary fish house that was nearby. She didn't see a vehicle parked outside, so she assumed the house was empty. She would go in and warm up and wait out the storm. She unstrapped her skis, pulled the door open, and stepped into the dim refuge.

"Professor Andreesen?"

Jens Andreesen sat hunched over the square opening in the ice, the water casting an eerie green glow on his face. Julia thought it was merely the strange light that made his face look so anguished. Then she saw that he was holding, not a spear or a line, but a rifle. Was he shooting at the fish? That was illegal, of course, as well as pointless. But he was holding the barrel toward his face, not the hole.

"What are you doing?" she demanded.

"Julia?"

"Give me the gun."

"You don't understand."

She understood enough. Besides, she was cold, and she was tired, and, she just realized, she was tired of her small business. She was tired of the men who hadn't bathed or brushed their teeth, who smelled of beer and cigarettes and fish and old socks, men with rough hands and stubbled faces and rude words, men whom she had told herself were likable, or unfortunate, or not well brought up but who were actually oafs and creeps and insensitive slobs, except for Rafe, and she didn't know what she was going to do about Rafe. So all she could think to say to Professor Andreesen was not something understanding and sympathetic, as her psychology course had taught her, but, "I'm counting on an A in your class. If you blow your head off now, what's going to happen to my grade point? Don't you think of anybody but yourself?"

"Julia—"

"No, really, I'm out here on the ice every day working my way through school, and all you can do is—what's wrong? Did you reread *Nausea*? *The Stranger*? Heidegger? You can't take that stuff seriously. I mean—don't you have children? What will they think?"

She reached for the rifle. He let her take it. She unloaded it and set it against the corner. It was cold in the house. She could see their breaths. She lit the propane stove. He put his face in his hands and began to weep.

She watched him. Really, she was out of sympathy for men. She hadn't realized it before. It must have been the long hours, the interminable winter, the unrelenting cold, the pressure of studying, everything piling up, like the snow outside. All she said, as he continued to sniffle, was, "Oh, stop it. Really."

She had to admit, she was surprised to see this side of Professor Andreesen. But she wasn't surprised that he had this side. All winter she had listened to self-pitying confessions, to paroxysms of guilt, to tales of inexhaustible unhappiness. She knew that even professors were human. She understood that philosophy had its uses, but it didn't cure everything, at least not for most people.

"You don't understand," Jens Andreesen sniffled.

"Blow your nose."

She handed him a tissue from her pocket. He blew. He stared into the luminescent water. "My God," he said. "You—" He looked at her. "You're the answer to my unspoken prayers. You're a gift. A miracle. An angel."

"Don't be silly."

"What other answer is there?"

"Luck. Coincidence. Extrasensory perception."

"I was so sure," he said, gazing again into the cold water.

"Of what?"

"Nothingness. The abyss."

"You get used to it." She cupped her cold hands and blew into them.

"You, too?" he asked, looking at her. "You stared into the abyss?"

"It's not pretty." She rubbed her hands together.

"But how do you—?"

"Go on?"

He nodded.

"One day," she said, "I noticed that the abyss was staring back at me. It was laughing at me."

"The abyss?"

"It was one of these holes in the ice."

He glanced at the water, then looked away quickly.

She slipped her hands between her thighs. "It looked like a cartoon face. It was laughing at me for taking it so seriously."

"A cartoon face?"

"It looked like...Sartre."

"Sartre?"

"It had that funny eye he has, that looks off to the side, as if he's looking at both sides of a question at once."

"Sartre laughed at you?"

"He said it was all a joke."

"Life?"

"Everything. The whole caboodle."

Jens Andreesen glared at the water. "It's a bad joke then," he muttered. He glanced at the rifle.

"Sartre was laughing," Julia went on, "and then he started singing. It's an old song. You probably know it." She began to sing.

Life is just a bowl of cherries
Don't take it serious
Life's so mysterious...

Andreesen stared at her as if she were crazy. She kept on singing, not paying any attention to him. He started humming. He sang along with her. They sang together, over and over, until they were both laughing, laughing so hard they couldn't stop, and Julia was thinking that Rafe would just have to go cold turkey and learn that life was hard, she might send him a copy of Epictetus to help him over the rough spots, she couldn't be everything to everybody, she had her own life to live, and they sang and laughed, and she tossed the bullets from the rifle into the abyss, and she tossed the rifle into the abyss, and she tossed her appointment book into the abyss.

SHIMMY TWINS

Nicole Louise Reid

One is Pride. And one is Honor. And neither is either. Two shimmy twins. Two blind twins, of which only one is. Corner musicians, corner tooters. Pride's got the guitar; Honor sways a standup bass. Each wears a hat just for passing: a felt cap with dangly fringe and beads, making music making time on Honor's head.

Their mama got them all wrong. Honor lies streaks every color there is. Pride sees fit to blame herself. Pride's the blind one, can't see a stitch held right up to her nose. Honor's got eyes, but nobody knows it. Their mama cooked it up, the number, their set. She bet on that money 'til they were five, walked them down to Lexington and Park. The twins clung to her, and she'd say *curb*, and *lamppost*, and they made it there all right. Pride on harmonica, Honor singing hymns, folks walked on past. So their mama stopped telling them *curb*, *lamppost*, and the crowds were there every day, panting for the stumbling parade.

The parade is nothing less now, though each is full woman at nineteen. Pride with her guitar case. Honor wheeling a bass taller than she. Both with red-tipped canes *tap tapping* the walks. Somehow they manage. On sunny days, Pride might trip through the heat; Honor lets her cane get stuck in a sewer grate: momentary delays that set the crowd's collective heart aflutter. Few even notice the only difference between the two blind twins: one's eyes wander up and some to the side; the other's drift and scan, cannot steady from flicking this way and that when a pretty boy runs past. But then Honor tips her head, brings her eyes back to just tucked up slightly under her eyelids, making a production of the whole thing.

So they wiggle and twist. They strum and they pluck. They hoof for pennies. They pass a felt cap making its own music. And they thrust out their hands groping for each other, to grab hold and bow. One is Pride, and one is Honor, but their mama had them all wrong.

Now Honor's light and coppery as the number two chestnut horse last Wednesday, the one that lost her week's cut of shimmy shake. And Pride's dark as the bay number nine: velvety dark, all sorts of plush look to her—though she'd never know it, and she won't bet at all. Honor tells Mama she's off window-shopping, but everyone knows she's off to Pimlico. She leaves her bass at home, tucks her cane up into her underdrawers, and doesn't care if Pride won't come, and so Pride manages the bus steps, knows the hoofy rumble of the track's stop—even if Honor clamps down all her beads to shimmy the bus aisle in silence. Honor shoots for trifectas every time. And Pride *tap taps* right on behind her sister, who tries to lose her in the crowds.

Even so, Honor's got a whole system dependent on Pride. She chooses riders' silks by the color of Pride's shoe leather, or the green or red feather pinning back a hank of her hair. Honor likes handicapped entries the best; she's simpatico with a horse made to drag twelve extra pounds in its saddle. And entry numbers are always decided by where her finger falls on the program or how many taps and shimmies Pride makes between the pretzel stand and the only man for miles without spats. And if Honor weren't so set on picking the one, two, and three each and every time, there'd be a handsome stash in the shimmy shake fund, and Pride and Honor could shimmy and shake at home.

But Honor can't seem to appreciate degrees of winning, so it's all or nothing for her. She placed three horses once, had a real feel for that race and put everything down on it. "Second race, fifteen dollar trifecta on the two, eleven, and eight, please," she said. The two because Pride had found Honor on the bus right quick; the eleven whose jockey looked like a peppermint lollipop, was for Pride in her green tapping shoes and pink roll-top stockings; and the eight because Pride cried out her sister's name that many times when she lost her checking track conditions railside.

But Pride stood behind her shaking her head. "Honor," she whispered, "Honor, I heard someone call a filly Bonnet Strings. Pick her."

Honor hesitated.

"You got to be sure, girl," the pink-nosed man in the window who ought to have recognized Honor by now, looked down over his half-frames at the shimmy twins: "Ain't that a lot to you? Better know what you're up to."

Betting fifteen dollars was too much, a month of corner hoofing, but she had it all figured: if she won she'd rake home $168, enough to kick the *tap tapping* routine. But, Honor supposed, she could have miscounted Pride's calls to her. "Change the eight for Bonnet Strings," she consulted her program, "the seven."

She placed her bet, took her ticket, and let Pride follow her back to the rail. The bell rang, gates yanked open, the horses shot out like heart attacks, and Honor's own heart about sat on the floor next to her. Her fingers wrapped the railing like hairbands snapping down. Her view wasn't of the start and wouldn't be of the finish, but she'd see them come down for the first turn. Pride laid her palms to the rail, losing herself in the spectacular clapping of hooves right down to her core, a clapping that shimmied her right in to her shake: her feet were going, her arms swinging, her hips knocking side to side.

Honor's horses weren't anywhere good. The field had bunched up with too many entries, and locked in her favorites. But the eleven broke clean and tight to the rail. The two filly wove tight then wide until she was on the outside and could move. But there was no hope for the seven, whose nose was penned in on all sides and stuck to fourteen's croup. Eleven still had it by four lengths. The two, travelling the outside, was covering too much distance to make up. At the first turn, Honor bit her lip to see her picks: Pride was wearing a red feather, and Honor was sure she should have kept the sorrel eight horse now easing up out of the pack. Pride licked their wind from her lips and went on shaking.

Honor lost sight and stuffed her claim stub in her dress pocket along with yesterday's and the rumpled remains of that of the day before. She watched the distant cloud of kicked-up mud promising to herself, her mother, and Pride never to come back. She swore it secretly, knowing she couldn't stick to it; too much of her mama in her. She didn't even hear the announcer trumpet the two's digging strides to overcome the eleven, the glorious eight's snapped tarsal, the track's fanning out around him and the seven's cutting through the pack just quick enough to place. Honor did not even hear the winners called, she was already planning her speech to Mama, her plan to earn it all back on the corner with her cane and her tripping here and there. But Pride heard and grabbed her sister's wrist dragging her this way and that to the betting window to collect, where Honor kissed Pride square on the lips.

Honor counted and recounted her take: frontwards, backwards, by sight, and by feel. They didn't ride all the way home on the bus, but got off at Fulton and Orleans so the sisters could hoof it home, shimmy-shaking all the way there. And with her roll of cash tucked up under her skirt, Honor pulled out her cane and rattled and swung, and tripped and slipped, and swore up and down she'd stop while ahead. Pride still felt the track in her, still licked the gales of such speed nettling her lips, and *tap tapped* her cane in one hand, passing Honor's hat with the other. The beads, their skirts, their green and black shoe leathers scuffing along, made their music, and the crowds followed them down Parrish to Lexington, down Lexington to Park, dropping pennies—and nickels even—right into Honor's hat.

And she was done with it. Done with the smell and sound and sun-baked rail. She divvied up her win to Mama and to Pride. And Honor swore never again, though anyone could see how pleased her mama was with all that commotion and green. Anyone could see how happy she was that she'd gotten her two babies all wrong, that Pride was Pride and Honor was Honor—and most importantly, that neither was either.

But everyone in downtown Baltimore could see Pride stumble-tumbling behind Honor stealing away to Pimlico, the one sighted sister running to lose the other around corner bakers and newsstands—telling her, Wait here, I'll go get us some lemon fizzies—then grabbing hold of every bead on her hat and sprinting fast as any horse ever won her a dollar. But Pride just let the hoofy rhythm take her there, wet her lips for the breeze of leather and manure. And soon enough, there was Pride gripping fistholds of Honor's skirt, behind her at the betting window. Honor turned around for her system, and bet on Pride's shoe leather and hair feather and where her finger fell on the program when Honor held it out.

But no matter if Honor takes Pride's hand, holds it all the way to Pimlico, or loses her for good in the fish stands at Lexington Market, Honor can't make her horses pay, can't make a win from Pride's anything and suspects her blind sister's changed her peculiar fashion of greens and pinks and reds, to blues and browns to spite her sister's penchant for the track. Now Honor's considering quinella bets, thinking that if she can just get the top two horses, no matter the order, she'll be back on top. But Pride and Honor come shimmy-shaking, *tap tap tapping* home each time not for the joy but for the coins in Honor's hat.

THE DAY THE SKY FELL

Dede Wilson

What comes down must go up. Something like that. Burma's got me pinned to the porch, my feet pushing, pushing, like they know I want to run, but all I can do is rock faster. And what's that awful pounding sound? Burma's not even hearing it, sitting there fat as a plum, sunk under her bulk, pumping with her feet, grit grit, on the porch floor. Waiting for me to say something. Silver polish drying on my fingers, making me shiver. I watch her flabby bosoms lap up and down under her blouse, up, down.

Burma. My neighbor next door. Whopping against my kitchen door like a pillow'd been tossed. There I am, polishing Freddie's baby cup. Shine. Shine. I liked to jumped out of my skin when she popped that screen! Now she's talking so fast and hard the rocker's like a metronome, clicking her off. No need for me to listen. Just say "um hmmm" or shake my head every now and then, and she never knows the difference. I can sit here and think about the accident. John all tangled up in that Chevy, the deer he hit dead on the hood. Freddie tight beside me, squeezing my hand so hard I don't think I'll ever be able to open it again. I let the scene play over and over, but I don't feel it anymore. All I feel is mad. Like I've been walked on. Like I still can't imagine this. Burma. And Joe. The Estradas. Buying my lot next door. My lot, the lot I was forced to sell when John died. My dream, of Freddie marrying and building a house there, of his children running under my skirts. At least he got the fruits of it, after all, paid his tuition to Columbia.

There goes that hammering again. I can't stand it. The way Burma and Joe got that bulldozer and shoved over all my gorgeous pines. How I just about died when I looked out my window and saw that WIDE LOAD, that half of a double-wide, then the other half, teetering and groaning right into the middle of my beautiful land. My land. It is mine. John bought it for me. And there sits that awful trailer. And those gourds. Gourds, gourds, gourds! Twisting and humping all over the ground. Sometimes I don't think I can stand it another minute. Then, to top it off, there's that THING hitched to Joe's pickup. JOE'S FUDGE TRICKLE painted in black and gold letters on each side. Joe pulls it around all over Texas, to fairs and grand openings and things, cooks fudge in it that he wraps up and sells.

There's that noise again. Oh no. I can feel it. That pressing in my chest. Doctor says it's nerves. No wonder.

"Miss Nellie," Burma's sighing her big sighs now, "you ain' been listening at all. I was saying how they..."

"You know I'm hearing you, Burma. It's just that nice breeze slipping through those camellias got me cooled off and I needed to shut my eyes. Go on. What?"

"...well, how they keep calling, day in and day out. Like we need security, like we got something somebody'd want to steal."

"They just run down the phone book."

"This last time, I know that man was right down the road, waiting to see if I said, 'Oh, yeah, I'm just loaded up with diamonds and PCB's,' so he could scoot right on over and dish 'em up."

"Hmmmm," I say.

"That's how come Joe got that big dish. Somebody called him up on the phone."

I'd almost forgotten the dish. Maybe I better ask her what that pounding is. Joe's up to something, I know.

"What! What was that?" Burma's shouting.

"Over there!" I hear myself hollering back. I'm pointing. "I saw it fall!"

We're down the steps before we know it. Something like a rock, brown, sits right there in the grass.

"It looks like a 'tater," Burma says.

She reaches down and pushes at it with her finger. It rolls over.

"It's got to be a 'tater. A old 'tater."

"Somebody's got to of thrown it," I offer.

We walk around the side of the house, see Joe bent over behind the trailer.

"Hey, Fudge!" Burma shouts at him. "You throw a 'tater over here?"

"A what?" he answers, slowly standing up.

"A po-ta-to!" Burma spells out.

"You crazy, woman?"

Burma looks at me and shrugs. We go around the back of the house, peek around the garage, look up in the sky. We're bumping into each other, looking all over. There's no one. Nothing. We go over to the potato. Burma picks it up by the tips of her fingers like it might bite. I'm still thinking of Joe. All those poles behind the double-wide. What's he doing back there, anyway?

"Maybe a bird dropped it," Burma's saying, trying on answers."I bet it fell outa airplane."

"You hear a plane?"

Burma shakes her head. "Beats me," she says.

We climb back up the porch steps. She lays the potato on the rail.

"Beats me," Burma says again, starting to chuckle. Hard as a try, I feel it, too. Burma drops to the rocker and bends over like she's in pain. I hear her snorting. Now I'm folded over.

"Oh, I hurt!" Burma is hugging her huge bosoms, throwing her head back, flinging it forward, bobby pins flying, giant curls as big as toilet paper rolls popping open one by one. I'm limp. I can't stop my right hand from patting the chair arm, the other one from fluttering like a broken bird on my chest.

"A po-tato!" Burma gasps.

The very word breaks us up. I'm laughing and rocking. I try to breathe.

"It," Burma says, nodding toward the potato, not daring to say its name, "fell outta the sky. Now, who'd believe that?"

"I've had a crazy thought," I say, trying to breathe. "Maybe these things...happen...all the time...and everybody's...afraid to tell. We all have...these spooky secrets."

I'm looking over at Burma to see what she thinks. Her hair's a shattered mess of unholy gold. The front of her blouse is so strained one button's flipped off. Her cheeks are pink and wet.

"It's not funny," she says, gulping at the air, suddenly sober.

"What?"

"Joe. What he's doing."

It feels like there's barely a squeak of space in the whole world. I know what she's going to say. I already know. If it had been the potato, it would of conked me on the head. I have to say it before she can.

"The gourds."

She nods. "He's doing it," she says.

I can't speak. The roof swoops down and pins me in my chair. The square posts around the porch buckle, one after the other. The arms of the rocker turn in and hold me.

So, he's doing it. Like he said he would. Taking all those gourds he's grown, all those gourds he's dried and cut and drilled and painted and stored all these years, and building the world's biggest martin house. So he, Joe Estrada, can get in that Guinness book. Like he said he'd do.

I can't move. Burma is still. Slowly, very slowly, the roof lifts up and the posts straighten and the chair lets go.

"I gotta get home," Burma says, her voice ragged. She's reaching up with one hand, trying to pin her curls back. The other's pinching her blouse together. She pulls up from the rocker, reaches over and pats the bannister.

"Goodbye, 'tater," she says.

We both start to choke. Try to breathe. I watch her walk down the steps and shuffle toward the trailer. Maybe she'll disappear. Maybe they'll both disappear.

I'm spent. I stare at the potato, silent and strange on the rail. I try to imagine gourds, hundreds of gourds, like whirligigs, up in the sky, poking up from the ground, from the trailer's roof. My poor husband. A good thing he can't know. I start to rock. I drift. I open one eye, peep out at the potato, half expecting it to be gone. Before I know it, I'm off, dreaming, dreaming I've stormed over to Burma's, I'm pounding on her door, shouting, and she runs out to see what's going on and I'm screaming at her, "It's not funny! It's not funny!" and she's saying, "Miss Nellie, I didn't take your stupid ol' 'tater, maybe it flew back to Kingdom Come!" and her rough old stone of a husband coming up behind her and wrapping his arms around and around her like his arms keep growing, and pulling her away from me and Burma standing there stout and firm, not moving, then I see all these gourds, it must be thousands of 'em, painted in oranges and pinks and yellows, and they have to be hollow, clattering in the wind, their round cut holes pulling into screams, thousands of dark birds entering their tortured mouths, soft bodies pummeling me, their wings clacking. I wake up with a start, disoriented, my mouth full of feathers.

I look around, ready for anything. Glance at the ledge. The potato's still there. I get up easy, sore from sleeping in the rocker, and plod back to the kitchen. The silver sits on the counter, dark and heavy, like a burden I can't bear. Maybe I'd better call Freddie, in New York. Lawyers know these things. Maybe there's a law. What if he laughs at me, plays with me, the way he does, acting too sympathetic. Worse than that, what if he doesn't want to hear about it, or deal with it. Doesn't want to come home. Ever.

What can I do, anyway? They live there.

There it goes again. That hammering. Joe Estrada, nailing crosses for his gourds, for me, maybe - I can't tell which. I feel like I'm staked to the floor. I've got to think. I've got to think.

Something glints in the sink. I look through the window. The sun is low and rosy now, and, way off, trees scribble a black line.

I pick up Freddie's baby cup. Press its silver coolness against my cheek. I think of the images it contains, how it has waited on the shelf all these years, reflected the laughter and the loss, stayed cold and unassuming, darkening again and again and needing to be stroked so it will shine. It's as though it is telling me something I don't want to hear. I put it back on the counter.

I head for the door, snatch it open, stride the length and turn of the porch straight to where the potato sits, waiting. In one smooth motion, never dreamed, never rehearsed, I scoop it up and heave it, like a stone, up and over. I watch as it soars into the gasp of space, my space, my yard, to their space, their yard, watch as it arcs and descends and plummets and pitches straight against the open mouth of Joe Estrada's biggest gaping gourd, sending potato and gourd and paint and clutter clattering to the earth.

And that, I beg myself to think, is that.

GET YOUR DEAD ASS UP

Sam Howie

The first time Tara tried to fake her death, I fell for it. And now here I am, her colleague in the telemarketing industry—jobs are not plentiful in our suburban Carolina region at the moment— sketching cartoon panels on my desk calendar while I'm supposed to be making dials. The manager comes by and I grab the phone. It's reflex. He'd have it easier if he bought headsets and the computer stuff that automatically makes the dials, so you have no choice about calling the people on the list. But I think he likes being the telemarketing slave driver.

He says, "Just practicing a little MBWA—that's Management By Walking Around."

When he's gone Tara's head pops up over the cubicle in front of mine. She smiles at me and we mouth to each other, "M—B—K—O—A," which is our acronym for the Management By Kissing Our Asses we will him to practice.

"Were you happy with the preparation of the body?" I hear the woman in the cubicle behind me say.

Seriously. This is a question we are supposed to ask. *Were you happy with the preparation of the body?* Maybe the poor widow or new orphan or whoever is on the other end of the line was *satisfied* with the mortician's art applied to his or her loved one's corpse, but who besides a necrophiliac could be *happy* with the cosmetic state of a stiff?

Tara and I believe it is our duty as human beings to identify the particular absurdities of telemarketing for funeral service consultants, as if the whole job is not absurd enough.

Tara's joke from last night:

Tara: What did the first necrophiliac say to the second.

Me: I don't know, Tara. What *did* the first necrophiliac say to the second?

Tara: Say, buddy, what say we stop in at the morgue for a cool one.

Guffaws were exchanged. Passively. Then we fucked. Quite actively. Tara fucks like nothing else makes any sense. Fucking Tara is like shooting the moon with a most highly powered slingshot.

Comic books used to advertise some really boss looking slingshots. You could nail Pluto with a pebble if those slingshots were as good as the pictures made them look. I have old "Archies" comic books I picked up at a flea market. I like the ads. They were the epitome of deception in the name of the almighty dollar. If there's anything less ethical than mine and Tara's jobs calling bereaved persons in the hopes of helping our company make some money, it's writing those ads for comic books. There is no truth in that advertising. There is verisimilitude, something *approaching* the truth, the way a number will approach zero or infinity or whatever in a mathematical limit, but it's not the real truth.

Tara nearly died in a car accident on I-85 two years ago. Ever since, she's been obsessed with death. She's the one who talked me into taking this oh so silly job. And I was well on my way to an exciting career in retail management.

A keyholder at just nineteen! I thought nothing could stop me. I dropped out of college, so sure of my fast track was I.

Really I flunked out.

Tara and I take out my comic books sometimes and look at them together. I have a couple of "Richie Rich" and a "Scooby Doo" or two, but mostly I just have the "Archies." I don't have any of that Marvel superhero shit, even though Tara likes it. She makes no secret about loving melodrama.

"Give me Good versus Evil, Life versus Death, Eros versus Thanatos," she said one night.

"Eros sounds okay to me," I replied, and we embraced Eros, which is to say we fucked, kicked Thanatos's grim ass all to melodramatic hell.

But I like it better when Tara pretends she is Veronica from the "Archies" and she calls me Archiekins. I call her Bettykins, just cause I know it will piss her off—she has dark hair like Veronica, not blonde like Betty — and then she starts talking dirty to me in her best Veronica voice, calling me Archiekins and kissing my ear. It drives me wild.

Tara and I like to eat butter pecan ice cream in the graveyard. Or, like last night, we'll do something like get loopy on Yagermiester and Old English 800 quarts and then write our own epitaphs.

Tara's epitaph: She fell from Grace and landed in the Roller Derby and never regretted it for a minute.

Mine: Though he had no workable plan thereof, he really REALLY wanted to make a lot of money.

Tara is always saying she's dying. When she has a headache she'll say her aneurysm is acting up again. "Old trick blood vessel, you know."

"Will you still love me when I'm dead?" she's fond of saying. I've never said I love her alive, but she's just being dramatic.

Once when she asked it I wanted to change the subject so I said, "I still love that little baby chick my sister got at Easter one year, and I don't even know what happened to it. What did happen to those cute little yellow fuzz balls? A lot of people had them, but nobody ever had grown chickens, so what happened?"

"My dog ate mine," she said, and then she laughed hysterically. I laughed too. It wasn't funny but we'd smoked a little doobie that night, so I thought it was funny at the time.

She still thought it was funny the next day.

Damn, but comic book characters are immortal. They don't even fucking age, much less die. And all anachronisms are forgiven in comic books. The "Archies" had a malt shop in the 1970s, but no one I know called bullshit, even though everyone who remembers the 70s knows that teens were smoking homegrown in Camaros—Jensen coaxials blaring AC/DC or Bachman Turner Overdrive—rather than sipping shakes around a jukebox.

She is lying on the floor with the unopened Advil bottle beside her. She must have been trying to get help for a headache when she dropped.

Yeah right. This is her most favorite of all her famously favorite jokes, faking the aneurysm death. The first time it threw me all out of sorts, because I was credulous, but now I know that she's not really dead but only trying to capture that oh so very similar to dead air about her. Very fucking similar. So very is her fucking similitude that she's scary. Tragic. Beautiful.

This time, of course, I'm hip to her shenanigans. I pick up an "Archies" comic book from Tara's kitchen table and

act like I'm zonkers with grief and all that shit, searching
for answers to help me oh-my-God cope with this *grief*. Oh
sweet ephemeral Tara!

"Why?" I mock. "Why did Tara have to die? Tell me
Jughead?" I hang my mouth open at the comic book.

Jughead is trying to get a sandwich from his mom, but
she won't give him one. I flip a couple of pages. Veronica is
still hot. The stupid dog still plays in their band. Moose is
still a goddamn oaf.

I flip through looking just for ads.

"I'll take a slinghot so I can shoot the moon," I yell,
noticing a smile pushing against Tara's lips while she tries
to suppress it, still lying on the floor. "I'll sell fucking Grit
newspapers," I say, "so I can buy a bike with a banana seat.
X-ray specs? I'll take some. I want to see through clothes
and skin, even through bones and marrow and DNA."
Tara keeps her eyes closed but laughs. I kneel beside her
and bury my head into the comic book. "I want those damn
specs to show me all the way to the inner chambers of the
human heart!" Ha ha.

I turn to the ad on the inside of the back page. Some
ninety-eight pound scarecrow is getting sand kicked in his
face. Charles Atlas wants me to gamble a dime so he can
give me some real muscles.

"Tara, get your dead ass up."

She stirs, laughs.

But it's a laugh too short lived, like all of her laughs,
which are becoming more rare.

Her infatuation with death is disturbing, too. At first
I thought it was cute, until it became so close to
obsession. Like now, *all* she wants to do is visit graveyards
and funeral homes. She likes to dress in black and crash
funerals. For a time I thought maybe it was a sexual fetish,
like she really and truly is into necrophilia, which is not my
cup of tea, but I would gladly play, as long as it gets me

inside her oh so sweet dreamscape of a pussy. But when I
suggest a roleplaying thing with her as the corpse and me
as the horny emblamer she just shoves me away from her on
the couch and says, "Guh-ross!"

No, death is obviously more idealized to her. Sacred.
Virginal. But that's bullshit. Death is no virgin; it has had
many lovers. Death is a slut. It's we the living who have yet
to have our morbid cherries popped. When Tara says she
wants to save some money and buy a coffin for her bedroom
I worry that she is ready to seduce the *real* Grim Reaper and
be deflowered.

I get her out of her dreary apartment one Saturday and
take her for a walk in the park, where shaggy-haired boys
ride skateboards and a young couple takes turns pushing a
stroller, and a teenage girl feeds pigeons, and a man in a Yale
t-shirt talks on a cell phone. Tara is wearing her wayfarers,
which went out, I believe with parachute pants. But she
wears them all the time these days.

When we see someone else talking on a cell phone
she stops me and says, as if bagging a major insight, "Cell
phones will soon render phone booths obsolete."

"Gadzooks," I say.

Then she screams it. "Cell phones will soon make phone
booths obsolete!"

I don't say anything.

Then she sounds really desperate when her voice cracks.
"What the hell will become of Superman?" It doesn't seem
appropriate to point out flaws in this theory, or to tell her
that this thought is not original, that I vaguely remember
hearing mention of the idea being in a Superman movie
or something. It doesn't seem appropriate to do or say
anything I can think of so I don't say or do anything. I just
stand there like a kid who is in shock because a parent has
yelled at him for no other reason than the parent had an
unusually bad day. She's never screamed around me like

this, or had such a desperate look on her face, as if she's terrified that Superman will really die and then the whole world will die with him. As if she's on his cape and the Reaper cometh bearing kryptonite and neither one of them is raging against the dying of light in Dylan Thomas fashion or laughing in dope smoking fashion or even accepting with grim relief in octogenarian-with-relentless-pain fashion, but rather shitting their pants in eighteen year-old in a foxhole fashion.

Then she runs away from me. I follow, but not for very long, because my skinny telemarketer's legs tote a beer belly further burdened by confusion and low blood sugar and she's flown with adrenaline and a head start.

Next thing I know she's up and gone to the malt shop, which is her euphemism for the loony bin. I visit her there but I don't feel like one of the malt shop gang. There's Ernie, Bossy Louise and McCoy, whose first name is Seth, but they call him McCoy. I don't think any of them are peachy keen. They're making time with my best girl and I want to pin her, cause nothing else makes any sense.

Still, I find myself talking to them sometimes. Actually, McCoy is not a bad guy, as whackos who live with the woman I wouldn't mind living with go. He's sad but his eyes haven't died, and if he's' cynical at all it's the lively cynical and not the hopeless kind of cynical, if that makes any sense. He's tall and thin but carries himself high and proud, the bearing of a soldier, but has a face as soft and sweet as a dolphin's. His ever so slight smile gives him the knowing look of a wise survivor, and the scar that begins at the corner of his mouth and extends about an inch up his face—as if the dolphin had once been gaffed—lends the imperfection needed for one to think he's earned such a sage countenance.

One evening I walk around the grounds with McCoy. It's late summer and there's a soft warm rain so that after a few minutes you're unable to tell how much of your body moisture is sweat and how much is rainwater. We see a lady playing with a Beagle. There are a few pets kept outside on the grounds, managed by staff but enjoyed by residents.

McCoy says, "Was it us or the Russians who sent animals up in space and just left them there? And was it dogs or monkeys?"

"I don't know," I say. "I think there's a John Prine song about that, but I don't really know the story. I know it was us who sent a teacher toward space and left her, kind of."

We walk past a man mumbling to himself.

"How did you end up in here?" I ask McCoy.

He draws a breath and pauses a moment, as if choosing a way to explain, but when he spits it out it's as if he has a scripted synopsis and just needed a minute to get it all straight in his head. "I was a computer programmer," he begins. "I had a good job and a bad boss, a good house and a sort of bad marriage, but I've learned now it really wasn't a terrible marriage. And it was as much my fault as hers."

He pauses and stops walking, looks intently at the ground for a moment, then begins walking and talking again, this time sounding a little more spontaneous and real in his speech. "I started lying in the street."

"Lying in the street?"

"Yeah. Right in the very middle of the road. At first it was just in our neighborhood, which really embarrassed my wife, and I have to say I took some satisfaction in that. Cars would see me and stop. Then they would usually ask if I were okay. I would say 'yes' and then get up and walk away. Of course, people started talking about it. My wife said I was going crazy and said she was going to have me committed, so I quit doing it for a week or so. Then I started up again, but this time several miles from home, where nobody would know me, and on a busier street. Not only would my wife be less likely to hear about it, but also it was more like playing chicken. Or at least that's how I felt about it. I was standing my ground—lying my ground, more accurately—and daring them to run over me. Of course, they would stop, and I construed that as some kind of twisted victory. It was like the only thing I could win. I wouldn't stand up to my wife or my boss, but those damn cars I could take on with the courage of a Green Beret."

"So your wife and boss, were they making life miserable for you?"

"Well, my wife wasn't bad, it's just that I relied on her so much that she naturally became the leader, and then I resented her for being the leader."

"What about your boss?"

"He really was bad, but I should have had more guts with him too. Anyway, things came to a head on Main Street. I lay there and this really loud monster pickup truck with tall wheels rode over me. I thought it would clear me with no problem but my lip grabbed a rusty hole in the muffler that was dangling by a thin strip of its last attached metal. I say my lip grabbed the muffler because I still like to think I was the aggressor, but maybe the muffler grabbed my lip—it's a semantic argument—but whichever way it was my face completely detached the muffler and I only got this scar, so I claimed victory on that one too at first. Then I realized that I had beaten only the muffler. The truck itself roared off like a lion. I heard it and heard it while a crowd gathered around me, all bloody-faced in the street. I still hear that damn truck roaring sometimes."

We sit down on a green park bench to talk some more. A pigeon on the lawn walks in a crooked line about ten yards away from us.

McCoy continues. "So now I've accepted that my acts were a convoluted courage and the doc wants me to work on something that's a little harder for me to swallow.

"What's that?" I ask.

"That embracing a good thing sometimes takes as much courage as confronting a bad thing. Doc says my resistance is because I can't be sure if something's a good thing, so there's risk involved."

I say, "Sounds like Dr. Phil pop psychology bullshit to me," and we watch another patient walk up and start feeding the pigeon something from a small brown paper sack.

My next visit Tara is sitting on a couch in her floor's lounge with Louise and Ernie, watching "Hogan's Heroes."

"Where's McCoy?" I say.

"He moved up," Tara says, rising to hug me.

"Up as in promoted to the world outside the malt shop?"

"No, up as in to the third floor. Where they supervise more carefully."

I wait for an explanation.

"A couple of nights ago," she continues, "Dr. Salvo was leaving and as he backed his SUV out of his parking place, he saw McCoy lying there, in the space. He'd apparently been resting there underneath the vehicle for who knows how long. Nobody had seen him since dinner, but we thought he was in his room. The staff caught hell about it."

"Is he okay?"

"Oh yeah. The Explorer passed right over him and he was lying there with his hands across his chest, calm as could be. At least that's the way I heard it."

"Have you seen him?"

"He waves to me from his window sometimes when I'm outside. He stands there looking out a lot."

We take a walk outside. Tara points out McCoy's window and I look up to see if I can see him, but I don't. We start walking again and when we reach the grass around the water fountain Tara asks me again if I would love her if she were dead.

Again I don't say that I've never said I love her alive, but apparently it goes without saying because she says, "I just thought... you know how your affection goes up for a sibling when one of you goes off to college and you're not around that sibling so much anymore? I thought that maybe by the same process, our being away from each other would send your magnitude of affection pointing skyward on the y axis, that maybe you would find something approaching adoration for me."

She breathes hard and says, "Look, Archiekins. You don't need your X-ray specs with me anymore. Here I am, to the bone. I wish you'd show me the same courtesy. I wish just one time you'd let me peek through your thick skin. I think I might like what I find there."

Zoiks, Bettykins, what have they done to you in this place? Zapped the part of the brain in charge of lightheartedness? I look at her for a few seconds not knowing how to arrange my face, let alone words. She throws her arms up and turns for the building. I try to say something witty but all that happens is my mouth twitches and I wonder if it's the beginning of a nervous tic I'll have for life.

I listen and watch the fountain spout off a moment and then walk closer, decide it was prettier from far away. Up close you see all this brown gunk caked around the pool, which catches the spouted water and (I guess) recycles it. Pennies, nickels, not even quarters tossed in from loonies and their loved ones can overshadow the gunk.

The next time I see her she is in her room at the Malt Shop, which she now calls Hotel Getwell. I'm glad she's retained a trace of her ironic, comical shtick, because I'd hate to think the only Tara I've ever really known was dead, but I can see that she's tinged with an optimism and a spooky sincerity that are foreign to me.

"I'm ready to live," she says with all the histrionics of a soap opera queen. "If all goes well I'll be getting out in about a week. Of course I'll be doing outpatient therapy and

I'll be on meds for a while, but I'm ready to reengage with the world."

Reengage with the world? She must sense my recoiling at this newfound seriousness of hers, because she gives me a small smile, just a baby of a smile crawling from one corner of her mouth to the other. "Besides," she whispers, "Bettykins is ready for some Archiekins dick." She stands on her tiptoes and without touching me anywhere else she plants a big wet one on my cheek. Then she smiles big, like nothing else makes any sense.

A couple of days later and I'm sitting at my cubicle. I think this will be the day I will be fired, because I'm not on the phone asking mourners if the funeral director they employed exhibited an appropriate level of sympathy. I'd rather ask my boss if he would take an appropriately long walk on an absurdly short pier.

And this is what I'm thinking while I'm not making my dials: my sister recently had a baby boy. He's six months now and I'm still scared to hold him. He can sort of hold his head up, but he still has that weird sort of bobble head thing going on, except he's not some stupid toy, and I'm afraid his body is too fragile to be trusted with my too fragile nerves, though Sissy and her hubby insist he's tougher than he looks and I won't hurt him. Still, I don't hold him.

But when I watch Sis and Hubby interact with this strange creature they call Little Man I have this bittersweet thought that most everybody was somebody's baby once. No matter how they grew to look or act, or what kind of situation they found themselves in, someone—typically a parent but at least an ephemeral social worker, foster parent, daycare provider, emergency room nurse or somebody—gave them that wide-eyed smile of my sister's. Probably someone held Ted Kazcinsky's head before his neck muscles were strong enough. Ernie at the Malt Shop probably once lay in a crib and smiled at parents smiling down on him while some silly twirly thing hanging from the side of the crib played "Twinkle, Twinkle Little Star" while it danced animals in a circle over him.

I feel a power I haven't felt in a long time. I want to go hold my nephew and try to get him to smile. I want Tara to ask not if I'll love her when she's dead but if I love her now. I want to say yes and I feel almost like I have the courage to do it.

I start drawing a comic strip on the back of a prospect contact sheet. At first I begin with Superman, with Clark K. getting a call on his cell phone informing him that a damsel needs his help so he ducks into an office where he finds and empty cubicle in which to morph into Supe.

But I scratch through this and start my own superhero on the back of another prospect contact sheet. My superhero is Neurotransmitter Man. He is from an organic planet which resembled a brain. Due to some mysterious interaction of serotonin, epiphinedrine, and dopamine, the planet spontaneously combusted and Neurotransmitter Man ended up on earth.

The boss comes over, evaluates my work for the day and promptly cans me. I'd meant to tell him off when this finally happened, but all I can do is laugh. I mean I fucking guffaw in his face until he starts calling building security from his cell phone. Then I still laugh, but head for the door. I take a moment to turn back and yell, "Hey, ex-bossman." But then I don't say anything else. I just walk off. I want to get to Tara as quickly as I can so we can talk about the here and now rather than the hereafter. Come on, Charles Atlas. I'm gambling a dime. Now give me some real goddamn muscles.

INSURRECTION

Rayne Ayers Debski

January 1, 1959, Camp Columbia, Cuba

Like the New Year's baby, General Fulgencio Batista emerges at the stroke of midnight. The upstairs living room of his house is thick with cigars, rum, and French perfume, and accented with fear. Castro's army is almost on the doorstep, but Batista insists on hosting his annual New Year's party. It is the one night when he is not the ruthless *el hombre*, the dictator who eliminates his enemies as casually as he lights a cigar. He and his wife, tall and chic in her black taffeta gown, move among their guests, kissing relatives, chatting with friends, patting the heads of children. His amethyst and diamond ring glints from his chubby finger as he discretely slips envelopes stuffed with cash into the moist waiting palms of his guests, a reward for services rendered, another of the general's New Year's traditions. It does not quell the anxiety that is building in waves around the room.

The musicians race through a samba. Waiters dressed in tuxedoes cannot circulate fast enough with trays of daiquiris. The local police chiefs gorge themselves on *Nata* cakes. Shots go off in the courtyard. The policemen freeze with the food half-way to their greedy mouths. Women scream and pull their children to them. But it is only Batista's son and his friends setting off fireworks.

Batista talks with Meyer Lansky. He tries not to show his disapproval of the gangster's companion, a woman with platinum hair, blazing red dress, and mocking brown eyes. When she reaches out her hand, he gallantly kisses it, excited by how silky it feels against his lips. She is known by most of his general staff for her skill and discreteness; still he has never availed himself of her favors.

The band lurches into a *merengue*. For a wild moment he looks as if he might sweep the woman in red onto the dance floor. His wife nudges him. He does not let go of the woman's hand but pulls her close to him, and says loudly enough for only his wife and the woman to hear, "If you ever set foot in this house again, I will slit your throat." He smiles and moves on.

After speaking to his guests, he calmly climbs the stairs to his study, holding onto the cold iron railing, refusing to suck in his stomach one minute longer. His gleaming military boots click along the marble hall as he makes his way around the nervous poodles and past the servants scurrying through the bedrooms stealthily packing the family's belongings. He enters his study and removes all the money from his safe. In a few minutes he will summon his military chiefs, and in less than two hours *el hombre*, his family, and close associates will swarm to the private airfield and depart the country forever. The end of tradition.

The woman in red slips away from her companion and returns to the city. At 9 AM she is listening to CMQ, the largest radio station in Cuba. When the announcer interrupts Beethoven's Ninth Symphony and says simply, "*Se fue Batista!*—Batista is gone!" she joins the thousands of people pouring into the streets of Havana to celebrate.

Miami, 1980

My mother leaned against the dresser in the bedroom we shared and read the essay I wrote for my family history assignment. "Fiction," she said and tossed it on her bed. Of course she recognized the woman in red. "Write about someone else. The nuns will expel you for this."

Okay, so maybe it didn't happen quite that way. Who could know? My mother wouldn't talk about it. She pretended her Aunt Elena didn't exist. She was *finuto* with that part of the family story.

I sat on my bed in my pajamas eating a chocolate chip cookie, one of those big ones with the gooey chips that stuck to my teeth, and watched my ninety-nine pound mother get ready for work. In her small dresser mirror, she surveyed her linen top and skirt, fixed a stray hair, and sprayed herself with perfume. With a steady hand she applied layers of gloss to her already darkened lips until they matched the crimson nail polish on her fingers and toes. As her finishing gesture, she stood pelican like first on one leg and then the other to slip her size five feet into a pair of stiletto heeled sandals. All this for a job at the deli counter at Publix, where her clothes would be covered with a smock, her hair encased in a net, and her shoes replaced with thick soled sneakers.

Giving her hair a final finger comb, she glanced at me in the mirror. "And *Madre de Dios*, stop eating. You're already thirty pounds overweight." On her way out, she picked up my essay and threw it into the wastebasket.

I held my tongue. If I answered back, we would argue until my school bus was at the door. Today I wanted her gone. Better to let my anger dry up and wither like the leaves on our gumbo-limbo tree. When I heard the front store close, I stood and let the breeze from the ceiling fan blow across my face. Our bedroom was divided into two zones. Hers had a dressing table that housed face creams and holy oils, a single bed with two lime green satin pillows, and a nightstand that held relief for her stomach upsets, migraines, and heartache. My half had a bed covered with library books, homework assignments, and stuffed animals my uncles continued to give me, The second hand chest of drawers, which housed my meager wardrobe, also served as a repository for snacks, music cassettes, and mementoes. If my mother's dresser, littered with cosmetics, held hope for a future, my dresser, topped with snapshots of my mother and my *abuela* at the beach, my uncles drinking beer in Key West, and faded pictures of relatives still in Cuba, was an altar to our past.

I brushed the cookie crumbs from my lips and stared at my chunky fourteen-year-old face in the mirror. To make my round chin thinner, I stretched my neck and tilted my head to the side. I tried to see Elena's features in mine, her mocking brown eyes, her sultry smile. "She was a *guajiritas*, a peasant girl," my grandmother told me. Elena was her half sister. My *abuela* knew how much my mother hated Elena stories, and after Sunday dinners, while my uncles relived their flight from the island, and my mother did the dishes, my grandmother whispered to me about the sister she refused to forget: how Elena ran off with a farm hand to Havana, how he left her when their money was gone; how she came under the protection of a *caballeroso Habanero;* how her father struck Elena's name from the family Bible.

I couldn't strike her from my memory. Sometimes when my mother got on my case about hanging with my "useless" friend Teresa, I retaliated by babbling about Elena, as if words could conjure up the black sheep she kept trying to bury.

I examined the bottles and plastic containers of cosmetics on my mother's dresser. Carefully, so she wouldn't notice, I opened a bottle of foundation and rubbed it onto my face, trying to reduce my fleshy cheeks. I moved closer to the mirror to inspect my work. My cheeks were undiminished. *You are not thirty pounds overweight,* I told the girl in the mirror. *You are Venus. A goddess.* That was what Rafael, Teresa's sixteen-year-old brother told me yesterday when he and I listened to music in his bedroom. Remembering how his tongue felt when traced his name on my stomach made me flush with guilt and anticipation.

With a small brush, I smeared peacock blue eye shadow across my lids. When my mother did this, her deep set brown eyes grew large. Mine remained buried inside my round face. I added another layer of color. Tilting my head just a bit to the side, I swore I could trace a resemblance to Elena. I laughed to myself. If my mother knew what I was doing, she would call a priest and have him sprinkle holy water throughout the room. I walked over to my dresser and chewed on another cookie.

The bedroom fan blew strands of wavy black hair across my face. I pictured Elena sitting in the *Hotel Nacional,* in a white dress and red stiletto heels, her blond hair pulled back, a few stray wisps fluttering in the breeze of the bamboo ceiling fans. Women looked at her with envy and disdain; men signaled her with their eyes. Few could afford her favors. None of them knew about the information she gathered from the generals and passed to the guerillas.

From a box in the corner of my closet, I resurrected an outfit I bought the last time Teresa and I went to Goodwill. The black and white halter top carried traces of someone else's perfume. I slid it on and felt the spandex tighten around my chest. The white jeans were snugger than my mother would ever allow, and the five-inch heels higher than any in her closet. I posed in the mirror lifting my hair off my neck and pursing my lips like the girls in the posters hanging over Rafael's bed. *Madre de Dios!*

Outside cars were starting up for the morning commute. Soon the school buses would be coming down the street. The uniform my mother pressed for me the night before hung on the closet door. On the next block Rafael, with his soft mahogany eyes and his musical laugh, would still be sleeping. It was Friday; I knew he was blowing off school and expecting me to come to his house. Me, the honor student who never cut a class. If I wasn't there by nine, he would hang at the beach with his friends and forget about me.

A spring breeze brought exhaust fumes from the school buses through the window. My school uniform, large and shapeless, dangled against the closet door. In the mirror as much as I tried to see her, the teen goddess morphed into an uncertain adolescent. I inhaled the scent of our house, my mother, myself. I refused to share her belief that heredity could be exorcized. I needed to make a choice. Venus or Fat Girl.

Hidden in my dresser drawer, beneath the cotton blouses my mother insisted I wear, was a picture of a woman sitting in a nightclub, surrounded by men in uniforms smoking cigars. She had platinum hair and a slinky red dress. She was thin and beautiful and smiling. Whenever I felt like I did that morning, I took out the picture and turned to her for assurance. Sometimes she looked sympathetic. But that day her mocking brown eyes saw right through me. I shoved the photo into the drawer. Then I picked up my mother's body lotion and went into the bathroom.

AT THE WORLD'S BIGGEST CRUCIFIX, INDIAN RIVER, MICHIGAN

Dick Bentley

We were going to Boyne to ski? Got lost around Indian River and the snow thickening on the road. Robbie says, "We're not going to make it up there tonight." He's tired from all the beers, plus we've been passing a little ganja around the car, the four of us. The smoke's quite thick? The car reeks?

Then, through the windshield, the headlights pick up this sign for the world's biggest crucifix? Robbie goes, "Shit! Let's check that sucker out.".

We follow the sign? We get to the parking lot and circle around? You can barely see the thing, just a big shaft sticking up through the snow and darkness. You can see some feet on the bottom though.

That's when Robbie dares me to climb it? There's this maintenance ladder that goes up it? With little rungs where you can stick your feet and hold on.

I go, "No way. No way I'm getting up that thing."

But here I am? Right at the top of the world's biggest crucifix. I can almost see the face, but it's dark and snowy. The thing is made of some kind of metal, bronze, maybe? Shit, not the first time I've done something stupid for Robbie.

I yell down, "Hey there's somebody already up here." Robbie and Max, I can hear them laughing way down below, laughing through the wind. Charlotte probably stayed in the car, the little pussy. Even though Charlotte's sort of a bitch? Still, she can be pretty funny. She says all the guys that like me are total jerks. That I'm like a magnet for them? Because I like to do crazy shit like this?

It's way cold up here. I'm not dressed warmly. Everything seems frozen. My nostrils are doing that thing where they stick together. Where they squinch up? My boots totally suck, and I'm freezing my little butt off.

I can almost see the Jesus face now? It's metallic and icy and the eyes are way blank, except when snow hisses across the metal and it almost changes the expression. It totally creeps me out.

It looks like Robbie at his creepiest. Me and Robbie have our creepy little dramas too. Pretty gloomy, I guess. Sometimes he scares me, sometimes I feel like throwing up practically or sometimes I'm just—I don't know...scared? I, like, don't know what to say? He has a bad temper. Ohmigod he goes like, totally mental sometimes? Or else he'll just hit me? Charlotte says, "Bad temper? Read my lips: how about *asshole*?" And she says the asshole thing long and loud, for effect. And to think I had my tits done for him. Had my lips collagenized. Now my lips are fake, my hair color's fake, and lots of my body parts are fake and Robbie says a lobotomy would've done me more good.

I look down through a swirl of snow and ohmigod—a cop car. I can see the flasher turning slowly, sweeping the snowy lot and making everything look blue. Robbie and Max are trying to hide the beer cans, but the inside of the car must reek of weed, plus they left all that shit in plain sight.

A cop gets out and he's talking to them. Another one is looking through the car? After awhile, they're all—even Charlotte—shoved into the back seat. The cop car drives off.

Thanks everybody! What am I doing? It's not like I even know. It's like I know where I am, but it's totally crazy, because I feel like I totally don't. Like I'm here, but I'm not here. That sounds so stupid, right? So totally dumb? Everybody forgot I was up here. That's how much they care. Leave me hanging up here on a ladder. And the wind blowing snow down the back of my neck and this creepy statue—this face.

Could I leer back at him? Could I make like a teenage vampire, and drink his blood? My curved fangs would make a wet, slick sound as they slid down from my gums. I'd work my tongue over the fangs, then I'd push out my bristled tongue and begin to lick the statue's neck, my rough tongue scraping over the smooth, bronze throat. I tell the statue, " I'm so hungry I need to feed."

Finally, I pretend it's real. I go like, "Now that we're alone, can I tell you some stuff?"

It stares back.

"First of all, I'm preggers. That's right. I think it was Robbie, but it could've been Max. How do you like that?"

No answer—the world's biggest crucifix has nothing to say.

"Next question. How come you get credit for all the good stuff that goes on, people giving thanks and all, but when things start to go bad, it's our sinful nature. That gets you off the hook, am I right?"

The world's biggest crucifix looks back at me blankly, the snow brushing its cheeks.

I'm like, "Shouldn't you stand up like a man and take the blame for some of the shit? Not just me being preggers, but earthquakes and floods and starving Africans?"

I'm starting to scare myself really good? Maybe I'll be left up here forever.

The snowflakes of the night continue to fall. I can't go down the ladder backwards. I'm numb with terror. Maybe I'll see another cop car down in the parking lot to rescue me?

Sometime-when? But going down is scarier than coming up.

Anyway, I'm stuck here. Whatever you say, here's a guy who doesn't go totally mental or hit you. He has no middle finger. Maybe he'll shake off the questions I asked him by claiming he doesn't exist, but that's a pretty lame excuse, a copout, a typical guy thing, I can see right through it.

Now, all of a sudden, I'm starting to feel nice, in a dizzy way? Ohmigod! What am I saying? This is like, what? I'm such a freak! Am I? Why am I telling you all this, like blabbing my head off? Right? Ohmigod! But I think about it. I try to think about stuff. I try to think about me as a person, like making my little shuffle through the world? And how am I doing? I'm hanging from a ladder on the world's biggest crucifix. Days could pass, and weeks, and maybe years. What more could a girl possibly want?

Dick Bentley

GINNY AND THE DEER

Cari Oleskewicz

Ginny slices cucumbers and babbles about her upcoming trip to the Badlands while I try to focus on the allocation schedule filling the spreadsheet in front of me. This morning, when I turned on the light in our office, I noticed a bowl of pasta sitting next to the keyboard on her desk, and a half-eaten orange had rolled into her scattered pile of paper clips. Sharing space with Ginny is not easy. Or antiseptic. Apparently, this is how the office became infested with ants last summer.

My boss has asked me to be patient. "It's only temporary," he told me two months ago, when I started. "This is the only desk we have for you until we move into the new building." He was apologetic, and clearly hoping I was not the confrontational type.

My corner of the office consists of my desk, a chair that squeaks, and a locked filing cabinet to which no one has the keys. The office manager keeps telling me we'll get a locksmith, but I'm not counting on that. This is an under-funded nonprofit organization, not a Fortune 500 company. Sacrifices have to be made.

Ginny's corner is a little different. It looks less like an office and more like the living room of a woman seriously obsessed with the American Indian. There are portraits of native men in full headdress and posters of roaming buffalo. Brightly colored feathers and other trinkets litter her desk and the top of her unlocked filing cabinet. There is a saddle on a stool near the door, which people always trip over, and woven blankets draped over every available surface. There are peace pipes and antelope horns on a shelf over her desk.

Every day, the receptionist delivers a new package. Sometimes, it's an item for her home, which she will open for me to see, expecting me to admire it, and sometimes it is an item for the office, and she'll ask where she should put it. She is a social worker, and from what other co-workers have told me, quite a good one. But she seems to spend most of her workday on eBay or the home shopping network, buying things for her collections.

She was especially excited on the day the turkey feathers arrived, and she brought them over to me.

"Look," she said, "you can still see some of the dried blood."

I nodded, and gave a cursory "ooh," even though I was slightly revolted. Sarcastically, I asked her when we could expect the tail.

"Hopefully in a day or two," she said. "I don't know why they shipped separately."

Ginny is short and heavy, with grey curly hair and crossed eyes. She walks with a cane and has multiple sclerosis. Most people in the office avoid her. I can't do that since we're officemates, so I am careful to be nice to her. She has taken my politeness for affection, and considers us very good friends.

When Victor walks into the office, I cannot help but to sit up straighter and suck in my stomach. He grabs an empty chair and uses it to roll over to me.

Hi," he says. That's all he says, but I feel myself want to giggle like a girl in high school with a crush on the most popular boy in school. Victor is beautiful. Blond and tall and studying for a master's degree in cultural and intellectual history, he is also involved in the local community theater and he cares for foster children. He knows he is beautiful and smart and he knows that women want him, even the married women, even the homely women, and even some men. He enjoys this, and is intensely flirtatious, even with the men. His wife must be a very secure person.

"Hello," I say, composed and turning away from him, trying to remember what I was doing.

"Hiya, Victor!" Ginny calls. "Are you hitting on my roommate again?"

"Oh, Ginny, you know you're the one and only woman for me," Victor says. "When are we going to run away together?"

"You're a charmer," Ginny says, chewing on a cucumber. "Watch out for him, Jessie."

"I certainly will," I say, smiling at Victor and squinting at my computer screen. Luckily, I am a happily married woman who would never be tempted by a Victor, at least not on the days that my husband and I are getting along. But I can feel my neck blotching, and that makes me self-conscious.

"What are you doing?" he whispers, looking over my shoulder. I try to ignore that he smells so good. My husband smells good too, when he remembers to use that woodsy cologne I bought him for Christmas.

"Preparing for an audit," I say, pushing his face away from mine, "and working on confidential financial statements."

"Can I see them?"

"Confidential means that no one can see them."

"Oh. Well, can you give me a raise, then?"

"No," I say with a sigh.

"I can beg."

"Then go beg the payroll clerk."

"Does anyone want some cucumber?" Ginny asks from across the office.

"No, thank you," I say, feeling slightly guilty because I know her feelings get hurt when I decline her offers of food. She brings in homemade hummus and Belgian waffles and ice cream and tomatoes and can never understand why I don't want any. I could never tell her that since observing her relationship with food in our office, I have strong doubts that I would approve of her methods of food storage and preparation. She once left a half-gallon of black raspberry ice cream in her backpack under her desk, not realizing she had forgotten to put it in the freezer until it was a puddle.

"Victor?"

"No, Ginny, I'm trying to cut back."

"On cucumbers?"

"On anything green. I'm not eating green this month." He winks at me.

"Well," she says, fixing her glasses and shoving a cucumber slice into her mouth. "You'd probably say no anyway, considering what I used this knife for last night." She chomps on the cucumber while talking. "I did wash it, though."

Last night, Ginny was driving home from work, late. It was almost 9:00 when she got on Route 83, heading north out of Baltimore and over the border into Pennsylvania, where she lives. Normal business hours at our agency are 8-5, but Ginny cannot ever make it into the office until around 11:00. Management allows her to work the hours that accommodate her illness. No one wants a lawsuit.

She sang along with Johnny Cash and followed a truck off the highway and onto a quieter, darker road, irritated that the driver in front of her hadn't used his blinker.

Ginny claims she sensed something bad would happen, even before she observed the hesitant deer up ahead, on the side of the highway.

The driver of the white F-250 in front of her did not notice the deer or try to avoid it, and collided with the unfortunate animal. His truck stumbled over it awkwardly, spun around, and then continued into the autumn night as if nothing happened.

On these rural roads straddling the Pennsylvania/ Maryland border, there is a lot of tractor trailer traffic and a lot of speeding vehicles. So, deer do not simply get hit and then limp into the woods to die. They get splattered and quartered all over the road. It is messy and ugly and obvious. Necks lay twisted, limbs get torn off, and internal organs ooze from ripped flesh into ruby pools. Such was the case with this deer, which was also still alive.

Ginny pulled over, skidding and screeching in such a reckless hurry that she fell out of her Saturn SUV.

After picking herself up and rubbing a sore hip, she flipped off the long-departed F-250. "Motherfucker!" she screamed after him. The deer lay bucking and bleeding in the middle of the road. It was not a busy road, just two lanes of country highway with travelers coming and going at irregular intervals. Ginny and the suffering animal were alone.

"Shit," she said out loud, approaching the deer.

She wished she had her shovel.

Ginny keeps a shovel in the car for dead animals. She cannot stand to see them plastered to the road and ground into the pavement. Her practice is to scoop up road kill with her trusty shovel and move the corpse to the side of the road, where she says an ancient Sioux prayer for its soul.

However, she had cleaned out her car to accommodate the three dogs she drove to Virginia last Sunday. They were homeless and abandoned, and the local shelter had found homes for them in Fredericksburg. Ginny was one of the shelter's best volunteers, and she had driven the dogs to their new home. She had forgotten to return the shovel to her car. It was in the garage, completely useless to her now.

She did not have any of her guns, either. Agonizing over what to do, Ginny grabbed the animal's legs and dragged. This was not good for her back. In a panic, the deer began to thrash violently, causing more blood to spurt from its multiple wounds. The deer emitted a terrible moan, low and earthy, making Ginny want to cry.

"Come on, work with me," she coaxed, ignoring the obscene way the neck was out of position. The grunting and groaning continued, and soon deer and human were in harmony, making deep, guttural noises together in a dark, bizarre symphony of distress and helplessness.

On the side of the road in the glow of her flashing hazard lights, Ginny wondered if she should try running the animal over again, to end its torment.

She looked at her vehicle, and back at the deer. That might only cause more pain, and who knew what her Saturn could do. What if she had to run over it multiple times?

Ginny remembered the pocketknife in her purse and hobbled back to her car, wincing as she went. It was hard to move out in the cold without her cane, and dragging heavy animals did not help. She fished around in her purple canvas bag, removing candy wrappers and crayons and an empty bottle of lotion used for her eczema, and finally felt it.

The deer looked at her and quivered, one large suspicious eye widening as she approached again.

Crying and shaking, Ginny touched its neck, trying to evaluate where the jugular would run. She whispered a prayer to herself and raised her knife, stabbing the animal. It continued to look at her with one wide, mad eye. The mouth opened, but no sound came out. Only blood. The front hoofs clicked against the grass and the gravel, and Ginny stabbed it again. The blood on her hands and her clothes was hot and sticky and the smell would have her vomiting outside of her car once this was over. She kept stabbing, not sure if she was stabbing the same place, or other places on the deer's neck, not sure if this was helping or hurting, not sure if this was even the right thing to do.

At last, the deer went still.

Ginny wipes tears from under glasses and shakes her head. "It was very intense."

I stare at the pocketknife next to the cucumber.

Victor looks at me with raised eyebrows and I shrug, waiting for him to say something witty or sarcastic, like he usually does.

Ginny stands and opens the door. "It gets so hot in here with that door closed." She is flushed and upset, and I wish I knew how to offer appropriate comfort or the right words. I am not good with words, though, that's why I'm an accountant. I prefer numbers and charts and order and exactness. She looks at me. "I just can't stand to see a creature suffer, Jessie."

"I know," I say, looking at the floor.

"Once," Victor says, walking over to her desk and picking up a cucumber slice, "I saw a guy hit a deer. I stopped to see if he was okay, because he was just driving a little Honda and his car was crushed. He was more concerned with calling his friend, who had a pickup, because he wanted to take the deer home and eat it." He puts the entire piece of cucumber into his mouth and salutes before he leaves the office.

We watch him go, and Ginny adjusts the large wooden crow that balances on the far corner of her desk. "Hey, Jessie, do you want a dream catcher for your wall? I have a friend in Montana who makes the most beautiful dream catchers. All of these over here are from his shop."

I thank her and say yes, I would love one.

"It can be an office warming present," she says. "When we move, and aren't roomies anymore."

I nod, somewhat comforted to hear that she plans for that day, too.

A HOUSE DIVIDED

Ray Morrison

My sister, Abigail, is in love with Abraham Lincoln. I don't mean a reverent fascination with his writings or accomplishments, but an honest-to-God, giggly schoolgirl crush. She thinks Abe's hot. Walking into her bedroom is like stepping into the souvenir shop at Ford's Theater. Photos of Abe plaster every wall, like he's some nineteenth-century rock star. Lincoln biographies and related knickknacks cover every surface in her room. Abby spent an entire Saturday going from junkyard to junkyard just to find an old Illinois license plate imprinted with "Land of Lincoln."

Don't get me wrong. I love Abby, but as an older sister who should be my role model, she leaves a little something to be desired. Heck, maybe a lot. And while I've accepted that she's harmlessly eccentric, if a bit annoying, and our mother has stopped wringing her hands and now just hopes that Abigail's crazy phase will soon pass, the biggest foe of my sister's unconventional romance has been our father.

Gerald Allan M^{C}Curdy is a man of routine. For as long as I can remember, my father has followed a single daily ritual. He rises at five o'clock in the morning to head downstairs to the coffeemaker, his heelless leather slippers flapping loudly as he walks past my bedroom. Once the coffee's going, it's back upstairs for a shower. After he's dressed, he pours his coffee into a double-sized mug and then he heads out for the ten-minute drive to his office.

My dad, like Abraham Lincoln, practices law. As best as I can tell, he sits in his office all day reading contracts, scratching out words here and there, scribbling notes in the margins, and flipping through law books. It all looks extremely boring to me, but Dad insists that what he does is quite important because if he does his job well, he can save people untold misery, not to mention thousands of dollars. I guess I'll just take his word on that.

At five-thirty each evening Dad comes home and swaps his suit for khaki pants and a polo shirt. He disappears into his den to sink into an overstuffed armchair where he reads mail and watches the evening news until Mom announces dinner.

In fact, it was at dinner one evening that Abby gave our family the first glimpse of the infatuation that soon consumed her. A new school year had just begun. Surprisingly, both Abby and I were excited about going back. I was beginning my first year of high school and it was the start of Abby's last. As it turned out, one of her first big school assignments was to research and write a biography of a randomly assigned figure from American history. I can only imagine how different the past six months would have been if Abby had been assigned Spiro Agnew or Clara Barton instead of Lincoln.

"Abigail! This is the last time I'm going to call you. If you don't get down here right now you'll get no dinner this evening."

That phrase, shouted by Dad, officially starts dinner each night. Gerald McCurdy insists that it is improper etiquette to begin eating before everyone is seated at the table. Yelling, however, is apparently just fine.

Abby has long blonde hair. She always wore it in one of two styles: straight down or in a ponytail, so when she came downstairs to dinner that night with her hair put up in a tight bun, Mom, Dad, and I stared at her.

"What's everyone looking at?" Abby asked.

"Well, gee, let's see," I said. "Do you think it might be your bizarre Susan B. Anthony hairdo?"

"Nicole, that's enough," Mom said. "But in all honesty, Abby, we've never seen you wear your hair like that. Is there a reason?"

"Jesus! Why is everyone acting like a new hairstyle is a crisis?"

"Watch your tongue, young lady." Dad didn't tolerate even a hint of foul language from his daughters. "And no one is acting like it's a crisis. But you can't expect to do something completely out of character and not have people notice."

"I want to wear it this way, that's all." Abby scooted her chair up to the table. In her hand she held a folded piece of paper, which she slid onto her lap. "Can't we just eat?"

"What's that paper you're hiding?" Dad asked.

Abby's eyes shifted quickly from Dad to Mom to me to the paper. Her wide eyes reminded me of a trapped rabbit.

"Just part of my homework. Dinner sure smells good, Mother."

My parents and I exchanged puzzled glances. Never had I heard my sister refer to Mom as "Mother." I sensed something odd in the air besides the aroma of my mother's tofu "meatloaf."

"Then why are you hiding the paper?" Dad asked.

"I'm not hiding it."

"May we see it, then?" Dad held out his hand.

Abby looked down at her lap, contemplating. "It's just a picture."

Mom's head and my own turned in concert toward Dad, waiting for the next volley in their verbal ping-pong match.

"A picture of what, may I ask?"

Abby sighed. I sensed the turning of the tide in Dad's favor.

"It's just a photograph of President Lincoln I copied from a book," Abby said. "Are you happy?"

"My happiness is not the issue here, young lady. Your disrespectful tone, however, is. Now, I'd very much like to see the photograph so that we can get on with dinner."

"Why do you need to see it? You certainly know what he looks like."

"Abigail!" Mom said. "If your father asks you to show him that picture, then show it to him!"

Red splotches appeared on Abby's cheeks and neck, a sure sign of anger I've witnessed many times.

"'Broken by it I too may be; bow to it I never will,'" Abby muttered.

"What the heck is that supposed to mean?" I asked.

"Tyranny, dear sister. It's a quote from one of Abraham's speeches."

An awkward silence enveloped our dinner table. My mother and father exchanged looks that went beyond confused.

"Abby, let's try to put this minor insurrection behind us. Show me the paper on your lap and we can eat our dinner in peace."

Abby glanced again at the paper, looked at Dad and then back down. She pulled the paper up, sat fully upright and held it out to Dad. "'Of course, you expected to gain something by this request; but you should remember that precisely so much as you should gain by it others would lose by it.'" She turned toward Mom. "May I have some meatloaf, Mother?"

Our father, who took the crumpled paper, was, for the first time I'd ever seen, speechless. After a minute, he let his eyes fall on the sheet and, had I not been looking right at him, I would have missed the flash of shock in his eyes. In typical Gerald McCurdy fashion, he was able to gain composure quickly—he was not a man who allowed himself to be out of control—and slowly folded the paper in half before sliding it across the table to Mom.

Mom studied the picture but said nothing. Her face and neck, on the other hand, developed the same blotchy appearance as Abby's. In fact, it was uncanny how much Abby resembled our mother. Both had the same blonde hair, blue eyes, and fiery temperament. When I looked at Mom, I knew I was looking at my sister some twenty-five years down the road. For my part, my parents' genetic stew had imparted to me my father's dark hair and complexion. Not to mention his lack of patience.

"Let me see!" I grabbed the paper from under Mom's hand. I unfolded it quickly, knowing I would be forced to return it right away. Abby shrieked, but I was determined to see what had shocked our parents. The paper contained a blurry reprinted photograph of a young Abraham Lincoln standing in front of a large white house. Across the face were lip prints in Abby's favorite shade of red lipstick. Drawn on the side of the picture was a heart containing initials, A.L. + A.M^{C}C.

Abby screamed, "Nikki! Give me that!"

"Nicole, give that paper to your sister this instant," Dad said.

Snickering, I handed the photograph to Abby, whose face had progressed from blotchiness to a uniform red.

"Wait until I tell everyone at school," I said, enjoying the special sense of power a younger sister gets when she possesses knowledge that can embarrass the hell out of an older sister.

"Well, Nicole, as Abe once said, 'I have endured a great deal of ridicule without much malice; and have received a great deal of kindness, not quite free from ridicule.' So do what you must, Sister."

Dad, about to sip his iced tea, froze with the glass tilted just short of his open mouth. His eyes shifted to Abby, then to me. I shrugged, holding my hands up. After a moment, the corners of his mouth raised and he nodded his head before taking a sip.

As it turned out, I didn't need to ignite gossip at school to embarrass my sister. Although Abby's antebellum style of dress and behavior soon became tolerated at home, there was no way she could maintain a façade of normalcy around a school full of teenagers. But to Abby's credit, she stuck with it. As Thanksgiving approached, so, too, did the deadline for presenting her biography project. And while our parents often voiced their hopes that Abby's history class presentation would mark the end of her "Lincoln thing," as they called it, it merely marked a new stage in my sister's strangeness.

The change started the day of her oral presentation. Abby went to school dressed in an ankle-length maroon dress, her hair done up in long, tight ringlets. She was quite stunning and, had the year been 1865, Abby would no doubt have caused a line of gentleman callers to form outside our house. Unfortunately, more than a century later, any would-be gentleman callers at West Forsyth High School laughed behind her back or made snide comments about her weirdness.

But that did not stop Abby from getting up an hour early each morning so she could fix her hair into long, tight curls and select just the right petticoat and dress for the day. She had scoured antique stores and vintage clothing shops until she had acquired what was certainly the largest private collection of nineteenth-century dresses and accessories anywhere in Lewisville, North Carolina. She was going to school everyday as though she was off to a new performance at Ford's Theater.

One evening the week before Thanksgiving, I was in my bedroom finishing my algebra homework when I heard the front door bang close. The digital clock on my desk confirmed it was five-thirty, the time our father arrived home. I listened for the creak of the wooden stairs from his customary heavy ascent up the uncarpeted steps. Reflexively, I counted the steps, knowing there would be eighteen. But at twelve the footsteps stopped abruptly. I was about to get up to check the hall when I heard the steps begin again, this time more quickly.

I heard a loud knocking on Abby's bedroom door. "Abby!"

I opened my door a crack, just enough to allow an unobstructed view down the hall. My father was holding a letter of some sort. He shook his head.

"Abigail, open up."

Her door opened slowly. Abby wore a long, high-necked flannel nightgown. Against her breast she clutched a book that I recognized as Carl Sandburg's biography of Lincoln. When she looked up at our father, her eyebrows arched primly.

"Yes, Father?"

"Abby. We need to talk. We just received a letter from school. Your teachers and counselors are beginning to worry about this obsession of yours. And to be quite honest, your mother and I are reaching our limit of tolerance for it as well."

"I'm not obsessed, Father. Anyone who doesn't conform to society's artificial standards of behavior is labeled a freak, or pigeonholed into some subcategory of mental illness."

"For God's sake, Abby, this is ridiculous. This is not about conforming to artificial standards. We are concerned that you don't lose touch with reality. You're an intelligent girl and surely know that how you've been dressing and acting is inappropriate."

"So, I suppose you'd prefer that I bare my midriff and get my navel pierced? Or maybe you think I should get a tattoo on my derriere, which is the 'normal' way to dress these days."

"There's no need to be sarcastic, young lady. Your behavior has apparently become disruptive at school. You must be aware that your actions affect others. Nicole has suffered barbs from fellow students because of you. Many of my clients have children who attend your school. I won't have my own reputation tarnished because of your silly fascination, so I'm forbidding you to continue to dress as you have been. As long as you live in my house and eat my food you'll do as I say. Do I make myself clear?"

"Oh, yes. Perfectly, Father. I am as beholden to you as a slave to its master. But remember what Abraham said: 'It is my pleasure that my children are free and happy, and unrestrained by parental tyranny. Love is the chain whereby to bind a child to its parents.'"

Dad placed his hands on his hips. "Yes, well, Abraham Lincoln didn't have *you* as his daughter!"

Dad turned away and Abby slammed her bedroom door. Dad stopped, raised his hand to knock on the door, but changed his mind. As he walked down the hall to his own bedroom, I ducked back so he wouldn't see me eavesdropping.

"Did you enjoy the show, Nikki?" my father asked as he walked past.

"No, Dad," I said. "Sorry."

However, neither that proclamation nor the conclusion of Abby's school project, marked the end of Abby's fixation with Lincoln. As Thanksgiving and Christmas came and went, our household settled into an uneasy peace punctuated only by sporadic skirmishes between Abby and Dad. Mom and I, for the most part, managed to avoid these battles, but I did get a lecture from Dad when I gave Abby her Christmas gift—a limited edition replica of an envelope with the words of the Gettysburg Address in Lincoln's handwriting, employing state-of-the-art computer-aided aging to give it the look and feel of actually having been written in 1863.

Like so many things that seem peculiar when you first observe them, Abby's aberrant behavior eventually became mundane at school. As the new year began, kids at school became bored by her oddness and she suffered fewer and fewer taunts. But, as we soon learned, the lack of overt insults did not mean no one gossiped about Abby behind her back.

Ironically, it was February 12, Lincoln's birthday, when a shift occurred in the course of life at the McCurdy household. The weather, which had been unseasonably mild for weeks, took a sudden turn as a cold front moved in and snow began to fall heavily. Again, it was during dinner that events changed. I was surprised that my father hadn't commented on the birthday cake sitting in the middle of the table. Abby had baked it that afternoon. It was square, with white icing and the words, "Happy Birthday, Abe" written with blue icing on the left side in Abby's handwriting. A small lopsided stovepipe hat was drawn next to the words. In fact, I noticed that my father was unusually silent. An undefined disquiet filled the room. He took furtive glances at the cake but said nothing.

"I wonder if school will be cancelled tomorrow." Mom said. She pushed a piece of squash back and forth across her plate with her fork.

"I hope so. I have a math test," I said.

Dad, who under normal circumstances would have berated me quickly for such a remark, continued to eat his dinner slowly.

"Would you girls like more casserole?" Mom scooped a large portion from the serving dish and held it up.

"No, thanks," I answered. I still had a plateful of zucchini and green beans.

"I've had sufficient supper, Mother. Thank you. May we cut the cake now?" Abby asked.

I looked quickly at Dad to see his reaction, but he just stared down at his plate. He scooped up the last bit of casserole with his fork, ate it, and wiped his mouth with his napkin.

"If you all will excuse me, I have some work to do in my study." Dad stood and walked out of the room.

After a brief silence, Abby began cutting the cake. Humming "Happy Birthday," she carved off one corner and passed it to me. She cut off the other and offered it to Mom, who folded her arms and glared at Abby with tight lips. Abby put the plate down and stopped humming. For her own piece, she carefully carved out the section saying "Abe." Abby and I ate our dessert in silence. Afterwards, she and I rinsed the dishes and loaded the dishwasher while Mom brought the last of the dishes in from the dining room.

"Will you girls finish the dishes, please?" Mom said. "I need to talk to your father." She handed me the leftover birthday cake and left the room.

"What do you think's going on with Mom and Dad?" Abby asked.

"Gee, I have no idea, Braniac. Do you think it might have to do with your little birthday party?"

"I mean, Dad's acting even stranger than usual, don't you think?" All traces of Abby's nineteenth-century persona were gone.

Abby was right, but I wasn't going to say that. "Stay here."

"Nikki, wait…"

I ignored her and crept down the hall leading to my father's den. The door was open and, as I approached, I could hear my parents' voices. I stopped at what I judged to be a safe distance for retreat should one or both of them suddenly emerge from the room.

"I just worry that there will be more," my father said.

"What do you think we should do, Gerald?"

"I don't know. Ed Brenner's firm is my second-largest account. Losing it would be a huge financial loss for us. And if what he says about Allan Myers also leaving is true, then that would be a significant blow to my firm."

"I find it hard to believe they'd be so childish and judgmental," Mom said.

"Reputation is everything in my business, honey. It may not seem right, but people like Ed and Allan don't want their own reputations sullied by association with anything or anyone they consider lacking in propriety. Abigail's behavior reflects on us. On me."

"Oh, like those little snobs Emily Brenner and Wendy Myers don't do enough on their own to embarrass their fathers. I'd like to get my hands on those petty, jealous little…"

"Calm down, Donna," Dad said. "You can't expect kids not to talk to their parents about something like this."

"I know. It just makes me so mad," Mom said. "Well, what do you plan to do?"

"I'm not sure. But I guess it's time to come to terms with this."

There was a long pause and I wondered what my parents were doing. I thought about trying to sneak a peek in the den but decided to hurry back to the kitchen. I kept expecting one or both of our parents to come into the kitchen, but they never did.

"What did you hear?"

I peeked out the kitchen door, but our parents were nowhere in sight. "Seems Wendy Myers and Emily Brenner have been talking to their parents about your Lincoln obsession—"

"I am *not* obsessed."

"Yeah, whatever. Anyway, it seems their dads are big clients of Dad's, and, well, because of you there's a chance they're going to stop doing business with his firm."

I noticed something shift in Abby's eyes. For the rest of the evening I sat in my room watching the snow fall outside my window, as I waited for Dad to approach Abby's room and lay down the law, once and for all. At last, I heard the slow, methodical sounds of my father's footsteps on the stairs. I braced myself and angled my chair so I could see. First, the top of his head, then, bit by bit, the rest of him appeared. He paused at top landing, sighed, and approached Abby's door, his head down. She must have been waiting, because before he could knock, the door opened.

"Hi, Dad," Abby said. No "Father" this time, I noticed.

"Abby, I just wanted to say goodnight. And I wanted to tell you something important."

"What is it, Dad?"

"I know I don't say it very often, but I wanted to make sure you know that I love you very much." Through the slit of my door I saw Dad put his arms around Abby and hug her long and tight. "Goodnight, sweetheart."

As he turned and walked toward his own bedroom, I whirled my chair around pretending to be studying.

"I love you, too, Nicole," he said, as he passed my door.

"Um, I love you, Dad."

The next morning we found that there hadn't been enough snow to cancel school. Abby came downstairs to breakfast dressed again like a teenage Mary Todd. She smoothed the front of her skirt, a prim mannerism I still found annoying, though she'd been doing it for months.

"Your food is probably ice cold," Mom said. "I called you down almost twenty minutes ago."

"I'm sorry, Mother. I had trouble with my hair."

"For God's sake, Abby, stop talking like that! Enough is enough. When are you going to grow up and think of someone besides yourself?"

Abby's mouth dropped open. Since the beginning of her Lincoln phase, both Mom and I had tried to remain neutral in the skirmishes that flared between my father and sister.

Mom scraped the remains of scrambled eggs into the sink and banged the pan loudly onto the counter. She put the milk and margarine back into the refrigerator, and slammed the door closed.

"You'd better hurry up or you'll miss your bus," Mom said, then left the kitchen.

"Listen, Abby..." I said.

"Shut up! No one asked your opinion." Abby stormed out of the room.

That night, Dad was unusually quiet at dinner. I kept expecting him to take Abby aside and explain how her actions were affecting his business. I actually found myself wishing for one of Dad's outbursts, finding the silence far more frightening. I picked at my food.

Mom had fixed a penne pasta dish that was Abby's favorite and the aroma of tomatoes and mozzarella cheese filled the dining room as she carried the steaming entree from the kitchen. She placed it on the trivet in the center of the table, then glanced around to make sure she hadn't forgotten anything before sitting down.

"Dinner looks and smells delicious, Mother," Abby said, extending her plate so that Mom could spoon some pasta onto it.

"Thank you. Nicole, may I have your plate, please?"

When she finished with my plate, she filled Dad's and then her own. We ate quietly for five minutes. Then it came.

"Abby," Mom said. "Do you attend any classes with Emily Brenner and Wendy Myers?"

I stopped in mid-chew and looked at my sister. Her voice was shaky and barely audible. "Well, they're in my history class."

"I see," Mom said.

I glanced at Dad, who only nodded slightly, and lifted a stringy forkful of pasta to his mouth.

Abby opened her mouth, but closed it. She stared at her food for several minutes but didn't eat any more.

"If anyone needs me, I will be in my room for the rest of the evening," Abby said. She was looking only at Dad, though.

Later, I sat in my room listening to music, peeking out the door, anticipating Dad coming up the stairs to knock on Abby's door and, once and for all, issue the final decree that would end her weird infatuation with Abraham Lincoln. When at last I heard the sound of his footsteps, I jumped up and clicked off my iPod. To my surprise, however, when he reached the top of the stairs, Dad turned and walked past Abby's room toward his own.

"Good night, Nicole," he said, poking his head in as he passed my room.

"Good night, Dad."

The next day at school, I was scraping my lunch tray into the cafeteria trash can, dreading Ms. Hunsucker's English class, when I heard a commotion in the hall. Ashley Wellington, a snobby sophomore, burst into the cafeteria, laughing.

"Hey, everybody, come check it out!"

In the hallway, a large group of students was gathered near one of the main entrances. I joined them, but even on tiptoe I was too short to see what the fuss was about.

"What's going on?" I asked a tall boy with bad acne who was standing next to me.

"There's some old dude dressed like a Confederate soldier."

"You're kidding?"

I squeezed my way through the group, and got knocked around. I was not prepared for what I saw when I reached the front. Standing before me, asking dreamy Chad Matthewson for directions to Mr. Carlson's classroom, was my own father, a cheesy fake beard glued crookedly on his face. He tipped a plumed hat to Chad, adjusted the sash that actually held a sword, and proceeded along the North wing.

As I stood there, I wasn't sure whether I should hurry after Dad, or, as my instincts were telling me, to turn and leave the building. Students pressed past me, following my father. I caught up with Dad when he was two doors away from Mr. Carlson's room. Embarassed, I ran up and grabbed his arm.

"Dad, what are you doing?"

He looked at me, smiled, then continued marching down the hall. "Pardon me, Miss, but ah'm on mah way to an important engagement, and mustn't tarry."

"Does Abby know about this?"

He didn't answer. Dad stopped to peek inside Mr. Carlson's room a second, before opening the door and striding in. I slipped in after him, closing the door on the curious crowd behind us. I tiptoed along the wall to stand at the back. Abby saw me, her eyes huge, and mouthed, "What the hell?" I held my hands up and shook my head.

Up front, our father stood at attention in his ridiculous get-up. He turned to Mr. Carlson.

"Ah beg your pardon at my intrusion, suh. I do not intend to take up much time, but I request a few moments to speak to your students."

Mr. Carlson rubbed his hand across his shiny, bald head, and bent forward to look over the top of his glasses. His eyes widened and then he smiled.

"Mr. McCurdy? What's this all about?"

Everyone in the room turned to look at Abby. Several students giggled. Abby, her face blotchy, sank in her seat. Wendy Myers actually rolled her eyes. She whispered something to Emily Brenner and they both pointed at Abby, shaking their heads. I felt my face flush.

"General Robert E. Lee, suh." Dad extended his hand toward Mr. Carlson, who hesitated before shaking it.

"Well...um...it's, uh, an honor to meet you, General."

"The pleasure is mine, suh. If it wouldn't be too much of an inconvenience, I request permission to briefly address your pupils."

Mr. Carlson nodded and gestured toward the class. Dad turned and bowed his head.

"Much, it seems, has been made about a certain student's eccentricities and the seriousness of their meaning. Some have even, I have found, been prone to spread petty gossip to their families, who in turn have, without renderin' benefit of doubt, cast aspersions on the entire family of said student. I, myself, have in fact been long engaged in a senseless and damaging civil war with this person. Indeed, I come before you today to publicly declare to her, Miss Abigail McCurdy, my unconditional surrender." Abby covered her face with her hands. "In a world where our children are easily caught up in painful and dangerous choices, I should never have made so much of such an innocuous oddness. I love you, Abigail. I am truly sorry."

Then Dad walked over to Abby's desk, leaned down and kissed her. "I nearly made a terrible mistake this week, but I have come to learn a simple truth, 'Never do a wrong thing to make a friend—or keep one.'"

Dad glanced over at Wendy Myers and Emily Brenner. Then he walked back up to the front of the room, bowed his head to Mr. Carlson.

"Ah thank you once again, Suh, for your kind indulgence of mah intrusion. With a grateful remembrance of your kind and generous consideration of myself, I bid you all an affectionate farewell."

Then Dad marched to the door. Before he left, he looked at me and winked. Nobody moved or said anything for what seemed like forever. Finally everyone started talking and laughing, and Mr. Carlson kept shouting for quiet. When I snuck back to the door, I looked over at Abby, but she didn't see me. She had her face buried in her hands, and I could tell she was crying.

"Abigail and Nicole. If you don't get down here right now you'll get no dinner this evening."

Mom and Dad were already seated when I walked in. On the table was a covered serving dish and a large bowl of steaming rice.

As I took my place, I looked at Dad, who was smoothing his napkin on his lap and acting like his performance that afternoon at school had never occurred. Abby walked in the room, fidgeting with the fitted cuffs of her calico dress.

"You look lovely tonight, Abby," Dad said.

I stared at the alien who was sitting in my father's place.

"Close your mouth, Nikki," Mom said. She lifted the cover from a serving dish, revealing meatballs swimming in a dark, red-brown sauce. "Pass your plate, if you'd like some dinner."

"I got an interesting new client today," Dad said. He then proceeded to tells us in great detail about a not-actually-interesting case involving stocks and tax shelters and other boring stuff.

Even though General Lee was the talk of West Forsyth High for weeks, he was never mentioned in our home.

It's been two months since Lee's second surrender and things have now returned to their normal weirdness around our house. I'm sure that when Abby graduates and heads off to college this whole love affair with Abraham Lincoln will fade into a funny memory, but this morning she's asked me to go with her to one of her favorite vintage clothing stores to look for a new dress. A black one.

You see, tomorrow is April 15th. The anniversary of Lincoln's death.

IN ANIMAL SUITS WHO GESTURE

Merry Speece

The same old political news world and local she wanted turned off. And as the television gave up the light of its ghost with the faint sound of crazing, the woman Fran wished for a miracle the last few days before Election.

Halloween, it was Halloween, and Halloween was a last chance, and she had hope enough left for at least one small world. But a question—she asked herself this in the dark, asked herself for the third straight night—was this Begging Night?

Every little place was different, and she hadn't seen in the paper any schedule, and for the first two nights of the weekend she'd waited for a knock. Tonight was Sunday and actually Halloween on the calendar and the last night possible. But would anyone come this far out, down the dirt road five miles and to her house in the dark woods, a strange little house, fanciful, folk victorian with spindlework?

Gingerbread, that was the word, the word for spindlework that came to mind (and it was as if her mind had gone for a turn on the lathe), and out of hunger she thought of biting into—soft wood (*dry rot*)—no, no, real gingerbread she baked herself. She should make herself a gingerbread man, bake him, chase him, nibble him, eat him up! Stop stop please!

"Franola Granola. Franana Banana," she said. Sighed. Franique!

She sat where she was and reached for the big bowl of candy and struggled with the first wrapper. This was candy she'd been looking at for days. Tonight, low, she felt deserving, and surely she was duty bound to consume the big bowl if not a soul showed.

It was late, and it was too late for little children. It was time for little children to sleep.

Only teenagers might still be about, and she didn't know if she would open the door to them. They were too old to ask for candy, and teens out on Halloween—wild.

She braced herself against the thought of teenagers, a hand on each arm of the chair, and *up straight!* out of the chair she came and began to unbutton. Be damned if she let another holiday pass with nothing different in her life to mark the day. She undressed and climbed into the suit that lay across the empty tv chair next to hers.

What a fine suit she had found herself—actually special ordered at some expense with money she didn't really have. She was enchanted by the suit, though she wasn't sure what she was supposed to be. It was very like the gorilla suits she'd studied in the catalogs of novelties and joke gifts but never mentioned to anyone. She had begun to admire the gorilla suits during that last long year of her husband's illness when he turned fiercer and fiercer as he zeroed in on heaven. She wanted to hide. He battered her with his soul, once threatened her with a rolled up newspaper. His final words were the call "Old Woman!" as if he were about to start in on her again, and Death caught him.

Him gone, she felt safe enough to possess this suit of a beast and do as she pleased at night. For her forty-fifth birthday the month before she had surprised herself.

To have in her possession this suit was a dream come true, for she had had since a child this desire to stop people in their tracks and make them laugh in spite of themselves. ("Were you afraid?" "No, you just startled me." Two people in the dark, and they would laugh.)

All set now, and she was eager to see herself and pattered to the big hall mirror under light. She had dark fur all over, and her face might have been a gorilla's, it was a face as kind as a gorilla's, as spiritual, but very terribly clever. Her face was naked, the forehead high and bare, the ridge brow not prominent. She was smaller than a gorilla and lean bodied. Bono bonobo! Woman walks erect.

All dressed up now she would go out. She said goodbye to an empty house and slipped a key under a rock—there— a complicated enough task certainly to prove herself a most intelligent animal. Did she know tricks.

She walked down the deserted road to the overlook, a point of stone on the bluff from which she could study the little town below her. She often sat here watching life go by, studying the march of civilization and along the way (the curve on the county road) wrecks; every time she hoped for something spectacular: a wrecked schoolbus would really show up (empty, the schoolbus empty, the children safe at home—to think otherwise—sick) and a big gleaming milk truck, the bus plowed into its side, and now a great flood of milk. The town was not so far away, as birdies fly, just below her in fact. But the road wound around the hill, spiraled down.

She hadn't lived here long, and in this town she was, as far as she could tell, the only stranger, and so far to everyone she had been invisible. She thought to descend tonight and change the course of a small town's evolution.

Once in town she could watch the cripples at the YMCA, the millionaire women arthritics (clinging to what they could of the old money left when their husbands, now deceased, had shut the town's glass industry down) trying to move in water to rock music. She had seen them many times but never gone into the pool with them, never wanted to interrupt their class. From the Y she would go on over to peer at the night shift at the last glass factory making Art Glass, molded likenesses of sad clowns and ewe sheep asleep and paperweights with a real mess inside. She wanted then to scatter out from behind closed doors the county commissioners, and she could scare up the mayor himself (already a nervous man who giggled whenever called upon to introduce a woman as Ms.). Such excitement, and next she would enter quietly a performance of the newly formed civic ballet and pray the young women could keep their balance and a leg up. God! Last stop she would go on over to the library to a meeting of the SOS Club, Search Out Sasquatch, look down upon the members with their maps and notes of sightings, tap on a basement window with her long toes, and watch as they stared up in amazement at those gorgeous hairy legs.

If they ran, oh, how she could run!

She laughed and laughed, beside herself, and began to cry behind her face and thought she might wet herself, and how her latex feet would slosh. She found the right clasp and slipped out the back and relieved herself with great purpose. Thus and so! On them! She trickled over the cliff, her well on the way to town.

The Sasquatch Club, sos, so, ho. Well if anybody could entice Sasquatch out of hiding it was her. Sasquatch'd take one look at her and come running, and they would grab up each other's hands and circle round in the blooming vetch in a girlie-girl dance of greeting—Sasquatch that lone female, not so unlike herself, sister, oh sister out in the woods all this time, know just how you feel.

Sasquatch so long out there on her own had had time to think and must by now have a message for the world; how with passion the beast would sign. A woman in an animal suit—*say*—her the perfect go between, oh missing link, oh media darling. A story like this she was sure to make front page. Be the early morning radio police report to which the whole town would wake up. Like a veteran of the campaign trail (see *Politicians, Political Tricks*: "How strange the power of silent people in animal suits who gesture, *Come here, come here*....") she'd stand on the top step of the combination county jail/courthouse and with the wave of a hand draw up the just awakened citizenry—her, yeah, a potential threat and now, everybody, for you at last a real treat, to life as we all know it, the end.

THE OPOSSUM

Charles Rammelkamp

Though she was only pulling into her own driveway, Meemo reflexively checked herself in the rearview mirror before switching off the headlights and opening the car door. A dim light still suffused the sky; the sun had only set within the half hour. She'd stopped at the gym for a run on the treadmill after work, where she'd flirted with Greg. In the soft glow of her neighbor's security light she noticed the long hairless tail of a rodent sticking out of the bottom of the garbage pail. Some sort of scavenging animal had evidently crawled in through the vent in the bottom of the barrel in search of refuse. Orange rinds and eggshells were scattered on the ground around the garbage can. The tail was large, over a foot long, a thick rope the color of dead human flesh. Meemo wondered fleetingly if it were an enormous rat and how she could kill it if it were.

Adrenaline rushing through her like a freight train, Meemo fumbled for her purse, stepped onto the pavement. The garbage can was by the fence leading to the back door. She touched the tail with the tip of her shoe — she couldn't just walk past it, any more than she could walk past a mirror without checking herself out — prepared to flee if there were a violent response, but it just twitched and stiffened. Meemo pried open the top and inside saw the frightened brown eye of an opossum. The animal almost looked like a domestic pet, a small cat with a pointy head, and she felt a twitch of compassion for it. She quickly put the top back on and went to the basement door.

"Brooks!" She'd never gotten used to her husband's name, even after ten years of marriage. It sounded pretentious, a last name turned into a first name. Not that it was his fault, but what had his parents been thinking?

"Yeah," came the dull distant voice, as if answering a roll call. Brooks was an engineer on a Defense Department contract. Originally he'd charmed her with his wit, but after they'd been married for several years he just became a know-it-all, the man with the answers, critical of her actions, telling her what to do. He'd get huffy about housework, as if it were all Meemo's responsibility, as if she were the only one making a mess.

"Brooks, there's a possum in the garbage can."

"You mean a raccoon?"

"A possum. Come see for yourself." But she was already climbing the stairs to the kitchen. The study, where she knew Brooks would be, was just through the kitchen door, off of the dining room.

"It's pronounced *an* opossum."

"Whatever," Meemo muttered. She had an urge to check the dictionary, sure he was wrong.

"Besides, I'm sure it was a raccoon. What? Did it tip the can over or something?"

"It's inside the garbage can. See for yourself. It crawled in through the vent at the bottom." Meemo pushed open the door to the study, which was already slightly ajar. Brooks was sitting at the computer, staring at the screen, his fingers clicking away at the keyboard like chickens pecking at feed. He did not turn around when she entered the room. The bald patch at the back of his head was an unseeing eye.

"Why'd you get one with vents in the first place? That was kind of dumb. I bet it's a rat. Probably a rat, come to think of it, yeah. They're always getting into the garbage. The city has a real problem with rats. It's like an epidemic."

"It's a possum—*an o*possum. I saw it. Trust me."

Brooks turned to look at her then. "What do you expect me to do about it?"

Meemo felt a violent rush of emotion. "Nothing." She turned to leave the room.

"Meemo," Brooks called after her a moment later. "What are we having for dinner?" When she did not answer him, he called her name again. "Meemo!" When she did not answer again, he called, "Miriam!"

"You spend a lot of time looking at yourself in the mirror," Brooks observed, surprising Meemo. They were sitting in the den after dinner watching a DVD, one of the *Lord of the Rings* movies, Meemo didn't know which. Was he suspicious? But no, Brooks was too arrogant to be jealous. It was just him being critical again, pouting because she didn't show any interest in his movie.

"No more than most women," she answered. But still she had the uncanny feeling her husband was reading her thoughts. Yes, she was curious about her attraction to other men since the guy at the gym, Gregory, had started paying attention to her, flirting with her, touching her bare arms. She wondered what it would be like to have an affair. Not necessarily with Gregory, but since he was available and practically wearing a sign proclaiming it—well, why *not* with Gregory? Because he was a slightly pompous English professor at one of the community colleges? Because he wasn't really a "challenge," too easy? Because he referred to himself as "Gregoire"? No doubt the man could become as tiresome as—well, as Brooks. Still, it thrilled her to flirt with him, actually made her wet to think about it. They were practically naked when they met—shorts, t-shirts, sports bra. Gregory was always adjusting his penis. She couldn't tell if he did it unconsciously, or if his jockstrap were too snug or something. His eyes always flitted from her face to her chest.

Meemo had been considering her reflection in the darkened window. "How do I look to you?" she asked, curious.

But Brooks had apparently already forgotten his comment. He was as transfixed by the movie as their eight-year old son Bret, who was stretched out on the floor in front of the television, his chin propped in his hands. Brooks only grunted. "Fucking Frodo," he muttered, shaking his head at the television screen.

"Gregoire!" Meemo smiled, liking that what he saw he obviously liked seeing. He'd just come from the weight room. Meemo had removed the Loyola sweatshirt she'd been wearing, and now she wore only her sports bra and bike shorts. She'd been on the treadmill nearly half an hour, paying scant attention to the talk show on the television overhead, scanning the room for her admirer. On the screen, a comedian famous for coming out as a lesbian during her previous television series was interviewing an actor promoting his latest blockbuster movie and also relating the joys and worries of being the first-time father of a newborn. Meemo stepped off the treadmill and took a slug of water from her bottle.

"Having a good workout?" Greg asked, smiling at the sweat trickling under her sports bra. His hand pulled at the front of his shorts.

"Great. How about you?"

"Just getting started."

Neither said anything then. It was as if something had been interrupted rather than initiated. The moment swelled to awkward self-consciousness. A mute appeal in Greg's eyes excited Meemo, but she didn't know how to respond. She took another slug from her water bottle.

"Well—see ya," Greg said to Meemo's sports bra. He reached over and patted her arm, a gratuitous gesture Meemo suspected he made for the sensual contact. She thrilled to it herself, the sensation of skin brushing skin. In a swoon, she forgot the treadmill was still running and almost stumbled.

"You okay?" he asked, exaggerating his concern, grabbing her arm to steady her, his hand lingering there. She nodded, a little flustered, embarrassed by her momentary inattention. Like a lovestruck schoolgirl.

"See ya," she said. It was always like this with Greg. She wondered if her voice sounded wistful.

The opossum surprised her. Again. Made her catch her breath. It straddled the chain link fence that separated their house from their neighbors, perched like a bird, its long pink tail stiff in the air behind it, its sharp pink nose at the end of the pointy death-white head aimed at the ground. The beady little eyes took Meemo in impassively, almost, it seemed to her, contemptuously. It did not seem alarmed by her presence. She noticed its paws, more like hands with its prehensile pink fingers, gripping the pole. Its dark fur was shot through with white, like the salt and pepper hair of a middleaged man, and Meemo thought she remembered reading that the hair turned color in winter, a protective camouflage, to blend in with its surroundings.

Meemo felt an urge to reach out and stroke it, to feel its fur under her hand, its spine in the center of her palm. She wanted to scratch the small, dark, shell-like ears. But she walked past it, within a yard of where it balanced on the fence, hunkered over as if for warmth. Still, even when she was less than a yard away from it, the top of its back even with her chest, it didn't twitch, unconcerned, unthreatened.

Meemo felt awkward walking past it, as if they should somehow acknowledge one another.

Inside, Meemo hung her coat up in the closet at the entrance to the kitchen, then walked over to the refrigerator to see about dinner, glancing at her reflection in the darkened kitchen windows.

"Meemo? That you? Miriam?"

She decided not to tell Brooks about the opossum.

In the locker room at the gym, Meemo looked at herself in the wall mirror beside the sinks. She liked what she saw. Slim, long legs, flat tummy. Her breasts weren't big, but they pushed out the sports bra attractively, with a hint of cleavage. Slender, muscular arms. She especially liked her face and the mop of short red hair that flamed up around it. It was a pretty face, an oval with even features, cheeks that narrowed to a small round chin, even white teeth. The face of a pretty woman, no longer a girl. The lines at the corners of her mouth and eyes did not distress her—they gave her character. Today she liked the mole on her left cheek, below her eye, a beauty mark in the retro Monroe style, though there were days she wished she could remove it, as if airbrushing a photograph.

The short red hair was her main vanity. She colored it, to preserve its natural shade, and she worked at fluffing it to look more "natural," more "unrehearsed." Her hair was thick, soft, unruly, and she preferred keeping it short, almost like a helmet over her ears, the nape of her neck visible.

Meemo liked the way her shorts hung down from her hips, limp as curtains, but with a roundness in the rear, suggesting a curvy shape. She turned briefly to look at her profile. Then, looking down at her white gym shoes one final time to check the laces, she emerged from the locker room into the exercise area, crammed with treadmills, stationary bikes, elliptical trainers, weight machines.

As if he'd been waiting to pounce, Gregory came up to her.

"I always wanted a sister," Gregory told her. He was standing next to the treadmill on which Meemo was running, his face at the same level as her chest. He spoke in a loud voice, over the noise of the machines, the other people, the television monitors. For a guy in his late forties Gregory was in pretty good shape—better shape than Brooks, for sure. He had less hair than Brooks, and it was mostly gray, but in his green gym shorts and gray Red Cross t-shirt—a freebie from a blood drive, Meemo guessed—he had a certain masculine appeal.

"I grew up in a household of boys. I had two other brothers, and I always wished I had a sister—you know, a close female I could open myself up to, without being lovers, someone I could have confidences with, share secrets, be intimate with." Greg reached his hand down to his crotch and shifted things around.

Feeling self-conscious about the other people in the gym around them, some of whom she worked with at the bank, Meemo tried to sound light, airy, almost impersonal. "I have a brother in Minnesota, but we've never been that close. He'd always tattle on me to my parents, try to get me into trouble, and he'd complain they loved me more than him." But Meemo mused to herself that what she always wanted was a hero, a daddy like her daddy never was. A Nobodaddy. All a husband turns out to be is a man who farts in bed next to you, not some magical lover-for-life.

"Soulmates without the—passion or sweat or something," Greg muttered, his voice lost in the whine and clack of machinery. He watched Meemo's chest as she inhaled and exhaled.

The Jerry Springer Show was on the monitor in front of the treadmill, and they both turned to look at it, buying time. Two fat women in bras and panties sat in chairs facing each other. Both had claims on the same man, a skinny white guy with a scraggly beard who looked like a junkie pimp. When he came out on stage, as if on cue the two fat women started swinging at each other, and a burly bodyguard stepped between them.

"What a strange show," Gregory said, looking from the monitor to Meemo's chest.

"Not my kind of entertainment," Meemo commented.

"Or therapy. Jesus. Talk about 'touchy-feely.' It's more like slammy-bangy. Look at those two going at each other. They're like sumo wrestlers."

The studio audience was hooting and whistling as the two fat girls pulled each other's hair and slapped one another. About as authentic as professional wrestling, Meemo thought.

"I believe in blood-knowledge," Gregory said. "D.H. Lawrence. I did my Ph.D. dissertation on the redemptive power of sex in Lawrence's novels, particularly *Lady Chatterley's Lover,* and with reference to the time he spent in Taos, New Mexico, with Frieda and their companions."

"Really," Meemo said. She wasn't sure about the transition. How did they get from Springer to Lawrence? Therapeutic options? Like the sister-shrink-confessor figure he'd been talking about? Was he saying he wanted *her* as a "sister"? Much as he made it sound special, exalted, it felt like an insult. She looked at their reflection in the television screen, which had gone suddenly to black, fading to commercial—she running on the treadmill, Gregory staring fixedly at her chest. She remembered the opossum and told him about discovering it in the garbage can. As much as anything, it was a way to change the subject.

"Did it scare you?"

"Until I saw what it was. But I *was* careful. I mean, he was so sweet-looking, so scared, I just wanted to pet him, especially when I saw him on the fence. But I don't know if they're vicious or not. He *was* a wild animal, after all."

"Opossums are marsupials."

"Like kangaroos and wombats, yeah, I know. They carry their young in a pouch. But what does it mean, to be a marsupial?"

"The word's Latin for 'pouch,' from the Greek for purse. The pouch contains mammary glands," Greg added, looking at her chest.

"They're mammals, Gregoire," Meemo clarified, putting a sarcastic spin on his name. "Like squirrels or raccoons."

Gregory shrugged. He didn't get where she was going. "So did your husband do anything about it?"

"My husband has abdicated all responsibility for the opossum and the garbage can. It's up to me."

"He sounds like a jerk."

"Not really," Meemo defended Brooks. "It's just one of those divisions of labor sort of things between a husband and wife. He mows the lawn and does the dishes. I cook and deal with the wildlife. Aren't you married?"

"I tried it for a while, but like I said, I'm looking for a sister," he told her tits, and Meemo knew she would never have an affair with him.

Meemo remembered meeting Brooks at her sister's, a surprise birthday party for somebody-or-other Patricia knew. Patricia had a wide acquaintance. Meemo had met Brooks in the intimacy of the loud party. He'd come as the friend of somebody who knew Patricia from college. He'd been trying his personality out on her, like an audition, but she'd found him amusing in spite of it.

"You look just like your sister," he'd said, "only prettier."

She'd laughed. Did he know she and Pat were rivals as only sisters can be? No, it wasn't a coup de foudre, but he'd enchanted her nevertheless, and when they'd finally had sex after a few dates, she was wet and ready for him. They were comfortable together, tidy as knives and spoons at a dinner table setting.

It was dark again by the time Meemo got home from work. The opossum had already raided the garbage can. An egg carton and some used paper towels were scattered around the ground, along with some potato peels, clear plastic wrapping paper and a grapefruit rind. She collected all the refuse in a plastic bag and put it back into the pail. That's all the opossum meant, she decided, something that made a mess.

Meemo went into her house through the basement door and climbed the steps to the kitchen. Bret was having dinner at a friend's house. Brooks was in the study, seated at the computer. She grabbed his shoulder.

"Brooks, I want you to come upstairs and fuck me."

Smiling, surprised, Brooks got up from his chair, stumbling over a leg of the desk. He looked so pleased. So grateful.

HALF IN JEST

Pat Lynch

"I think that little Flash chick might be...you know," Hoffmann said. He put down his archery magazine and watched from the faculty lounge window while Flash headed to her van. Curly, dark head bent, she aimed her walk from her shoulders, and seemed centered there, not at the hips like most women, and her stride was definitive and unafraid. She was five feet tall. Hoffman's deep set eyes followed her. "Look at her. Brother."

"You think she might be what?" I said.

"Well, I think she likes girls. You know?"

Flash reached her van, a clunky, lavender colored thing. Two entwined women's equality symbols were painted on its sliding door, a somewhat clarion political declaration in my view, but Hoffmann didn't get it. I thought this a tad remarkable, but fortunate, because if he'd known he'd have gone into who knows what kind of polemic. He didn't approve of things, especially causes. It had been a bad season for him: Nixon, whom he admired, resigned in disgrace, the country careening down a slope of acceptance, younger colleagues like me gleeful about it.

I joined him at the window. "She had her van painted. She's got style."

"Her hippie van," he said with a small sneer. "And right across from my parking space." So that irked him too. When I first met him, last year when I came on board as a long term substitute, I thought him almost handsome: he was tall, trim, probably late thirties, had a nice head of brown hair and a careful mustache. But his looks didn't improve upon acquaintance and now I found him generally pale and sour. "Keys hanging off her belt," he said. "Like a janitor. Like a guy."

Our principal, Brenda Chavez, got the A Victoria flu and would be out for almost three weeks. Two Vice Principals also got it. That put Hoffmann in charge of the next faculty meeting, and to my mind, awakened the Reich. On meeting day he pulled the never used podium to the front of the conference room and placed his notebook on it. When I saw the notebook, with its pastel tabs alternating along the sides, I reached into my purse for my paperback. It wasn't there and I swear I felt stomach sinking despair. People filed in, Flash and Dave Costner, the boys coach, coming last. Both of them perched on the heater near the back.

"You'll need to take a seat, Dave," Hoffmann said from his podium. "Both of you," he added coolly.

The coach shrugged and slid off the heater and went to a chair in the last row but Flash said, "I'm fine here, Mr.–I'm sorry, I forgot."

Now heads turned and we livened up. This was an unexpected bright spot. An untenured newcomer giving lip to Hoffmann.

"I'm Bill Hoffmann. I'm acting principal." Hoffmann kept his voice steady but his eyes narrowed on her. "You'll need to sit because you'll need to take notes."

Flash's eyes flashed and maybe that was why they called her Flash. The eyes were dark and for an instant looked dangerous. But she grinned at Hoffmann and said, "Okey-doke," and went to a chair next to the coach. So that was that.

The meeting commenced and fell quickly into the torpor zone. Hoffmann slowly turned tab after tab and delivered staff announcements as if they were proclamations of national and alarming moment. And of course there were the others, the pent up drones who launched ten minute narratives each time he said, any comments? We had descended an hour into this misery when Hoffmann, reading monitoring assignments for next week's testing, looked up, stopped, scowled. "Miss Arden. I think I mentioned. You'll need to take notes."

I roused myself to turn and look again at Flash. Flash Arden. Now there's a name for you.

A bird like alertness crossed her face and she sat up straight. "I remember my assignments," she said.

"Let me explain again. We take notes at meetings." Hoffmann took a breath here. "This isn't your call. It's what we do."

Todd Graham stirred from his doze and turned to look at Flash and this signaled another palpable group awareness, no murmuring, no nodding off.

Flash Arden folded her arms and said, "Monday, Room 12 with Mr. Gibbons, Wednesday afternoon–from one till three–Room 4, Thursday morning till ten–general fill-in and then from ten till two Room 12 again with Miss Franks."

The coach said to Flash, "Hey. Remember mine too, will you?" and a rippling chuckle made its way along the back rows.

Hoffmann ignored the laugh and looked stonily at the coach, "Everything's a joke, isn't it, Dave?" Then he returned his gaze to Flash. "We take notes to keep everybody current. You'll need to comply. Period."

Flash met his look and held it, then made a curt nod and took a pen from her pocket. She didn't carry a purse. The coach tore a paper from his loose-leaf notebook and handed it to her. She took it and nodded at him but didn't look up again at Hoffmann.

This pretty well squelched the uprising. Hoffmann was a punisher and last year persecuted this goofy college kid who worked as a math tutor, criticized and complained until the kid quit. And yeah, the kid was long haired and tie-dyed and wasn't the sharpest knife in the drawer, but he'd needed the job. Hoffmann drove him out. If we'd had Brenda Chavez last year that wouldn't have happened. But we didn't and it did.

The meeting went on. Tense, pale Elena North with the bad perm, under the pretext of asking a question, delivered a querulous report about rude and noisy beer drinkers on bingo night. One day, if Hoffmann ascended, Elena would be his Minister of Extermination. I snuck a look at Flash. She watched Elena, then bent over her paper and scribbled dramatically, looked up again, shook her head in mock dismay and scribbled anew. It made me laugh out loud. After that I was beset with giggles. Hoffmann glanced sharply down at me and Elena paused and frowned, then resumed her lament. But I couldn't stop laughing. Adult giggling fits were not appreciated by some of the big shots here but I was shielded by a relationship with the absent boss. I am the lifelong and dear friend of Brenda Chavez, the first Latina principal of this school, the youngest principal ever, and a woman who will one day be Mayor or better. So I was safe to laugh.

After the meeting I went to the back of the room to introduce myself to Flash and warn her about Hoffmann but she and the coach had disappeared. I didn't see her again and avoided Hoffman and the weekend came quickly.

The next Wednesday I had a conference with my golden girl–that student who makes you hope that what you do might have some shaping influence on a life. She was Donna Jackson, she was black, her widowed mother played the organ for the Baptist church, and Donna was more than smart–she was intellectually alive and I was helping her apply for scholarships to Berkeley, Princeton, UCLA, several of the great schools. But today she had a problem. Miss Arden, the new P.E. teacher, had accused her of lolling during gym warm-up.

"Lolling?" I said.

"Yeah. She blew her whistle and yelled and said I was lolling and gabbing."

"I'll talk to her. What's she like, overall?"

"Well," said Donna Jackson, my genius, my five foot eight inch child looking down upon me, "she's kind of a martinet."

Hoffmann stopped me in the hall after third period and said he was calling an emergency faculty meeting tomorrow morning to implement plans for flu containment. The District had sent down a memo. "This is mandated," he said, holding aloft a blue paper. "The District." He seemed to shine from within.

So good. I could see Flash Arden tomorrow and tell her Donna needed A's. Then I took the blue paper and gave Hoffmann a somber nod. "I'll be there," I said. I try not to be unkind.

The damned toady–he called the meeting for seven a. m. and we bumbled in on a chill, drizzly morning. At least he had the industrial coffee pot going and I huddled in the front row to be close to refills. On the podium lay a new folder with new tabs. Christ almighty hell.

Hoffmann came in from the side door like a visiting guest speaker and gripped the podium. "Good morning," he said loudly. "This is serious so let's get to it." But he stopped and his eyes shot to the back of the room. I turned with everybody else. In a chair against the back wall sat Flash Arden. She wore a green velvet court jester's costume, complete with cap and bells. She looked up and the bells jingled. But that wasn't the thing that shocked the laugh out of me. It was the four foot tall pencil she held against her shoulder like a rifle. A stage tablet, probably five feet by five feet, perched against the back of the folding chair she had placed in front of her.

"Ready to take notes, sire," she said loudly.

The coach laughed and I laughed. From the rest came nervous tittering, some clucking, and Elena North said with a near hiss, "Well, how childish is *this*?"

Hoffmann said to Flash, "I guess you're supposed to be funny. Children are sick but you're the big comedian."

With both hands Flash lifted the enormous pencil, aimed it at the tablet, began laboriously to scratch.

I have a stupid, cackling laugh which I try perpetually to subdue. This time I leaned over to pretend I was coughing. It was the pencil that did it, that yellow huge log of a pencil.

Hoffmann straightened himself at the podium "There's the door, Miss Arden. This prank is over. You can see me in my office later."

Flash got up and hoisted the pencil to her shoulder. "*Your* office?" she said with cheery false confusion. "You're not a teacher?" She shook her head and the bells rattled.

"I'm acting principal." Hoffmann pointed to the door and opened his notebook to tab one. "We'll need a sub coordinating team," he said, looking hard into the center rows and compelling those people, mostly the English Department, to look back at him.

So Flash Arden left the room at a largely unwitnessed military step, like a tin soldier, pencil on her shoulder, while the usual hands went up to volunteer for Hoffmann's needless sub coordinating committee.

I waited almost till the end, then went to the gym. I found her in the coaches' little anteroom near the lockers. Now she wore dark pants, a dark sweater and a bright periwinkle rain slicker. I introduced myself and said I taught History. We shook hands. "Where did you get the pencil?" I said.

"I have a costume shop. I live on top of it. "She presented a wide and appreciative grin "I know you. You're one of the in group."

I said that I was not, was only the personal friend of the principal and that's why people had to be nice to me. "So you own a store?"

"Yeah. After I work the year I can afford to open. Pucks. That's the name. I've got quality merchandise." The grin took over her face. "I can wear any outfit I like whenever I want."

So dressing from the stockroom was apparently not an uncommon practice. "Be careful with Hoffman," I said. "You've made an enemy."

She unsnapped her slicker and revealed a silver dollar sized purple Dyke Power button pinned to the inside flap. "He hates me because I'm gay. He's an idiot." And this time I saw again the glint of something deeper than mischief in her eyes—if it wasn't anger it was something near, a dark thrill. "He's against me. From the first day. He's got a pole up his butt."

The bell rang, saving me from having to say, Don't get caught with that dyke button. But I did say as I turned, "Listen, Donna Jackson. Senior. She's brilliant. She needs an A."

"Miss Yackety-yack? Gotcha." Flash Arden snapped and zipped her periwinkle jacket, and I felt her eyes on me as I went out the door. "Don't tell her we talked though," she said. "These brainy girls need to sweat like the rest of them."

Hoffmann had a lunch meeting with Elena North and a couple of other duds and I knew they were contriving to visit some revenge on Flash.

After school I paid my third visit to sick Brenda who wore flannel pajamas and lay on her sofa. I made tea for her, sat on the wicker chair at a good remove from the A

Victoria Flu, and told her about Hoffmann and Flash Arden and Flash Arden's Dyke pin.

"Well, it matches her van," Brenda said with a weak laugh. But then she pulled up wearily against the cushion and said that Hoffman had been waiting to launch a coup. "I'll have to fight him. She's as good a reason as any, I guess."

I said that Flash seemed brazen and likable. "And that pencil. You should have seen that thing."

Brenda returned to work and Hoffmann was forced to go back to teaching, unlucky for his students and the sub who'd been filling in for him, but better for the general civic life of Muir High School. But Brenda was right. The coup came at the end of the next faculty meeting. When Brenda asked calmly, "Anything else?" Hoffmann stood up. This made him the only person standing because the podium wasn't used in Brenda's meetings. "I've got a petition here," he said, and started to read. It was a confusing thing. It actually began with, We, the undersigned, and went on to call for increased security personnel and parent volunteers to patrol the gym, the playing fields, the locker rooms and showers.

"I don't get this," the coach interrupted. "We're fine. No problems. No fights."

Hoffmann pivoted slowly so he could address the whole group. "Kids changing clothes, kids undressed. Who's to say they can't come under the wrong influence?"

Brenda went to the front of the room. "Please explain what you mean," she said calmly, but I saw her shoulders tense.

Then the shout from the back row. "How the hell dare you?" Flash got to her feet, which wasn't saying much because she was too short to loom like Hoffmann, but she pushed down to the center aisle, eyes locked on him.

Hoffmann ignored her, raised the petition, and said to Brenda, "I've got signatures here."

But Flash bulled up the aisle, came to a halt near the piano, and shouted across three rows of heads to Hoffmann: "You'll bring your signatures to court, asshole." Her face flushed fiery red.

I was up now, like maybe six others, and I said to Hoffmann, "You should be ashamed," and Todd Graham from Art said, "You're way out of line, guy"

I don't know how Brenda got Hoffmann and Flash into her private office but she did. The rest of us left our seats and waited in high excitement. I tried to get into a fight with Elena North, Hoffman's lieutenant, but she opined prissily about filthy movies to three of her cohorts, none of whom would meet my eyes. I went to the coach and his group. "What *is* this?"

The coach had a round, sweet face and an old fashioned crew cut. "Hoffmann's been hanging around the gym, taking notes, talking to the kids. You can see where he's going with this." Five or six others drifted over and we had a pretty good time excoriating Hoffmann.

But everyone stopped talking when we heard Flash's voice from Brenda's office. "You jackass bigot son of a bitch. You think I'm a *threat*? To *kids*? I'll sue you. You prick, you bastard prick. You'll sit your fat ass in jail. I'll sue your ass. I'll sue this school. Get your lawyer, prick, because I've got mine." The door opened and she came out, head down, shoulders hunched. Looking at no one, she pushed down the aisle, crossed into the foyer and out the main entrance. We watched through the windows as she ran to her lavender van.

Brenda and Hoffmann remained in the office.

The next afternoon Hoffman's written apology appeared in the daily bulletin. It was right under Brenda's declaration that unsubstantiated insinuations like those heard yesterday were repugnant and in the future would be forwarded to

District representatives. Then Hoffmann's barely cringing sentences: "I regret it if my remarks about improving school security gave the impression that I thought Miss Arden's performance was in any way questionable. I am willing to put this misunderstanding behind us so we can carry on with giving our students the best education possible." Hoffmann stayed in his classroom all day and Flash didn't come to school. But Brenda said Flash would return tomorrow and told me in luxurious detail how pale and silent Hoffman got when Flash let loose on him.

My golden girl Donna Jackson, the only student I ever knew who read faculty bulletins, asked me what I thought of Mr. Hoffmann's apology. "Weak, sorry piffle," I said, making her laugh.

"I like Miss Arden now," she said. "Everyone does. You should see what she's got on the wall."

So I strolled over to the P.E. foyer after school. The first thing that struck me was the big, framed portrait of Shakespeare. Next to it, a sprawl of butcher paper covered an entire six foot by six foot slab of wall, and a felt pen, cap in place, hung by a long string on the side. The paper was filled with printed and scrawled quotations, all from Shakespeare. A chunky boy carrying a stack of towels came by and I asked him about the paper and he answered tonelessly. "If you git docked by Miz Arden you kin git yer demerits off if you stick on a quote. It's gotta be outta Shakespeare. You gotta write neat and say what play an' sign yer name."

I uncapped the felt pen and wrote–
"O! When she's angry she is keen and shrewd.
She was a vixen when she went to school;
And though she be but little, she is fierce."
Midsummer Night's Dream

Flash returned to school but I didn't see her until the end of the week when she walked into the staff Christmas party dressed in a Santa suit. Accompanying her was a young blond woman with pixie haircut who wore a fairy costume with glitter sewn somehow deep into the wings. Flash headed straight for Brenda, Laura Hines, Paul Baker and me. "This is Teri," she said to us. "My lover."

There occurred an instant's pause. The words, my lover, seemed kind of, well, blatant. But almost immediately Brenda smiled and put out her hand to Teri. "I'm Brenda," she said, and that corrected the pause and established the vibe. Within two minutes a half dozen others gathered, most enthusing over the fairy costume which even to my uneducated eye showed unusually detailed craftsmanship. Across the room Hoffmann and his coterie tightened their semi-circle and determinedly did not to look our way.

Flash looked up at me with sparkling eyes. "I saw your quote on the wall. Excellent."

Cute blond Teri with the pixie cut said, "Oh, are you the one? It was perfect. Though she be but little she is fierce. It's why they call her Flash. She turns fierce. Like that. " She snapped her fingers. "Like a flash flood."

They explained the wall of Shakespeare. They liked his comedies, and had staged parodies of them with an amateur troupe.

"Shakespeare parodies?" Brenda said.

"With a lesbian theme."

This brought another tiny silence.

"She likes Midsummer Night's Dream," Teri said, glancing with a smile at Flash. "She likes Puck. She likes mischief."

Flash pulled a couple of small gold paper bags from her Santa sack. "Confetti for New Year's Eve. Take a pack," she said and we all reached in. Then she walked with big steps to the coach and his pals. "Ho ho ho, merry Christmas," she boomed. "Take some New Year's confetti," and they reached in like us. She went to every group except Hoffmann's, and everybody smiled and took the gold bags. Hoffmann and Elena North walked away, heads bent in discourse.

At the exact moment the Rudolph song ended on Brenda's portable stereo the bell rang and Brenda flung her confetti and said, "Merry Christmas, everybody. Happy New Year."

"Happy three weeks off," I said, and threw my confetti, and so did everyone else, and tiny flakes of sprayed gold paper swirled to the floor.

Flash got up on a chair and people paused on their way out as she shouted, "Citizens. Hear ye this. This confetti? It's from our last newsletter. You're walking all over a phony apology. Merry Christmas." She jumped down while Teri clapped and Hoffmann shook his head and walked out the door. I heard somebody say that this was no way to start the holidays but I thought it was fine to start a public announcement by getting up on a chair and shouting, Hear ye this.

I invited Flash and Teri to my New Year's Eve party and they came, Flash dressed as Robin Hood and Teri as Aphrodite, goddess of love. My parties were exuberant affairs in those days, and 1976 was particularly lively because my brother Danny came. Danny was a charmer, possessed a subversive fearlessness and had a history of what I liked to call escapades. He had longish gold-red hair and was on the hunt for women. "Who's the little blond with the wreath?" he asked, and I told him to forget about Teri, the lesbian lover of Flash, the lesbian gym teacher who wore a Dyke pin and whose van was actually painted lesbian. Later Brenda pointed to the corner where Danny bent with laughter while Flash gestured broadly as she talked to him. "That is the birth of danger," Brenda said.

Danny called the next afternoon and said groggily that the party was great and he was glad to have met Flash and Teri. He said we should cultivate them. They had spirit. They had a theater troupe and a costume shop. And Flash, he said, had marrow of steel down her spine. I told him not to try to romance Teri, and he said, "Do you think I'm off my rocker? Besides, Flash is my buddy."

I returned to school in January, resolved to quit in June. I was too young for this work—was frequently mistaken for a student, and I didn't like teaching enough to earn a credential and age on the job. If it hadn't been for Brenda taking over as principal I'd have fled in September. But now I could cruise through the winter helping Donna get some juicy scholarships and in spring we'd both be sprung. On the other hand, Brenda, ten years older than I, was eager to return; she was establishing herself as a good administrator, and liking it. "You've brought order and harmony," I told her toward the end of the month. "There is peace in the valley."

But of course I was oblivious and wrong. The next day Hoffman alerted Brenda that he was circulating another petition, this one calling for the institution of an adult code of conduct and dress. Why? Flash, again. She was an example, he said, of lax standards. She dressed up for all the games. Kids brought cameras now to take pictures of the spectacular outfits she wore as she ran nimbly up and down the bleachers talking in whatever accent or dialect her costume authorized. And her attire was historically accurate—she was a Renaissance scholar, a frontiersman with coonskin cap, an Irish paddy cop, a Roman Centurion, an elf, an Elizabethan courtier, sword perched jauntily at her hip. When we played the girls volleyball game that we were certain to lose she came in whiteface and black cloak as the Grim Reaper, and leaned on her staff staring weirdly from under her hood at our adversaries, the somewhat startled girls from Belmont High, and when the final whistle blew she pointed the staff at our own defeated players and held it there for a long still moment.

That was the last straw Hoffman told Brenda. "Are we teachers or clowns?" he said.

Flash waited for me in the parking lot after school. "Can you believe this?" she said. She held up a Xeroxed copy of Hoffmann's petition with its thirteen signatures. "I should have sued that prick. I let him off. Now this."

"Nobody worth anything will sign it," I said. "Don't waste your energy." Something like disappointment cut across her face as I spoke, and I understood. It was a stupid thing to say. Rage has to be spent; it can't be saved, and allocated, and called energy.

She put the petition in her gym bag. "Am I the only one who gets this guy?"

"He has to have an enemy. It's how he …places himself. I get him. I don't go roaring down the street is all." I felt her relent under my excitement and added for a finish, "He's a Nazi. He's despicable."

It won her back. "Yeah," she said. She turned to go to her van. "People like him, they love their mean streak, but they're gutless."

Hoffmann put a flyer in everyone's box the next morning. The headline in red caps from his new electric typewriter read, ARE WE TEACHERS OR CLOWNS? He called for a meeting in his classroom at 3:30, and I could imagine the god-awful pills who would show up for that one. I was off campus by 3:15.

Flash came to work in a clown costume the next morning. She padded down the walkway to me, giant, wrong-way feet flapping, nose blinking. "How do you like it?" Two early-bird Asian girls watched her and put their hands to their mouths and giggled.

"You might be insane," I said. But I had to hand it to her. She brought the place to political life; she gave the drear something to cluck about and bored folk like me a chance to be stouthearted and tolerant. "This would be a sleepy country village without you," I said.

"Lemme tell you. I went to breakfast and this guy who always eats there said, are you in commercials or something? and I said nope, this is just what I'm wearing. And he got mad. He said, you dress in costumes for *no reason?* and I said, the reason is, I like it. You wouldn't believe how pissed he got. There's a lot of people like that." She paused to wave her fat, polka-dot glove at a grinning custodian. "But Hoffmann doesn't hate me for the costumes. He hates me because I stand up to him and I'm queer."

At lunch teachers hovered in groups around the petition posted in the faculty lounge. Irene Fielding from Home Ec studied it and said, "It's not that she's gay. But she goes too far with those outfits." But she didn't sign.

Todd Graham from Art sat near the petition and watched people read it, and said that anyone who signed was sneakily using the costume issue to justify a bias against gay people. Nobody signed it in his presence but by 2 p.m. five more names had been added. I did my part by going into the lounge whenever new groups were sure to be there, pretending to read the thing for the first time, then turning away in a grand show of disgust. "This is putrid," I said at one point. And, "How contemptible," at another.

That afternoon Brenda privately suggested to Hoffmann that he abandon his petition. But he said he was protecting the reputation of the faculty and commenced a deadly harangue about dignity. She couldn't stop his crusade but asked him to tone it down. I was with her when she next sought out Flash and asked her to tone it down also. "How can you say that?" Flash said, scowling. "That prick is the devil. I should have sued him. You should fire him." The scowl made her features pointy and her painted clown tear looked suddenly jagged, like a tool. Brenda only sighed and let her go. Some things you can't control, Brenda said, and since everybody had gotten in on this thing it had to run its course. She was right about everybody being in on it; even cafeteria workers now journeyed to the lounge to read the petition.

It would never get a majority of signatures, of course, because Brenda wouldn't sign it, and without her signature none of the department heads, the V.P.'s, and the people who always showed up on steering committees would sign it. Still, it helped rehabilitate Hoffmann's image as a significant personage. He ostentatiously conferred with his supporters in the hallways, not a trace of the old Christmas humiliation in his voice or posture.

After school I passed kids straggling to his classroom. Hoffmann sponsored the archery club which was called On Target and was composed entirely of male students who were failing in his classes. The kids joined, listened to Hoffmann's stories about his adult archery competitions, watched him demonstrate pulling the big bow he kept on the back wall, and thereby earned passing C's in his Chemistry class. "They jus' listen to him say about his memories and then he don't flunk 'em," Donna's simple but pretty boyfriend, Jay, told me once. As I walked by his room Hoffmann came around the corner, petition in hand. "Gonna have to cancel the club today," he said when he saw me. He lifted the cover sheet of the petition to show that signatures extended to the second page. "Don't see your name here. Your little clown pal wouldn't like it." His smile came slyly, nastily.

"You should deep-six that thing, like your little Nixon pal should have deep-sixed his tapes." Pleased to have reminded him of Nixon, I walked away.

Hoffmann's voice followed me. "She won't last. She's going."

In the morning during first period prep I saw him, Elena North and two other teachers I didn't know by name–a middle-aged man, a middle-aged woman–whispering in the lounge by the refrigerator, the four of them bent over a large, floppy manual. The petition hung on the wall. I found Brenda under an umbrella in the rain outside, going to her car. She said the manual was a copy of the District Code and they were pouring over it to find some specific regulation that Flash violated. "Hoffmann got a sub today, so he could 'work on this,' she said, dryly. "He's escalating. I've been too easy." Now she was leaving for a scheduled District meeting downtown, and intended to add dress regulations to her list of policy matters. "It's so frigging petty," she said. "It's an embarrassment."

When the bell rang I headed to the gym to tell Flash that Hoffmann was reading the District Code in the lounge. But something was happening. Kids poured from the gym doors and from the nearby classrooms and headed en masse toward a small but blinding white light in the rainy quad. I followed. Two men in suits and dress coats stood under umbrellas with Flash, while a third man in a leather jacket aimed a TV camera at her. Today Flash wore the traditional P.E. running suit, tags and whistles around her neck, keys clumped at her waist, and tilted a lavender umbrella over her head. One of the men held a microphone to her face. "I won't be persecuted," Flash said loudly. "There's a Nazi mentality on this campus. But they can't crush me." Some of the kids yelled, Yeah, and others clapped, and the reporter turned his head my way and smiled. Danny. It was Danny, his red hair clipped.

I pushed through the crowd. The other man was Danny's friend, Nick, a fairly dissolute person who chain-smoked marijuana day and night. I'd never seen him in a suit before, never seen him clean shaven or even cleaned up. But he looked spiffy today and peered through round John Lennon glasses. He spoke into the microphone. "Miss Arden has no choice but to seek legal redress. Life style prejudice has no place on a school campus." So Nick was the lawyer, hence the spectacles. The cameraman in the leather jacket was someone I hadn't seen before.

Danny turned to Donna Jackson and her boyfriend, Jay, who watched eagerly from the front of a group of kids. "Do you think there is a Nazi element on this campus?" Danny said, and the white light shone on them. Jay nudged Donna to talk and she said, "Yes. There's racial prejudice. There's lifestyle prejudice. We have to put a stop to this." She blinked under the light and smiled prettily.

I saw Elena North squinting nervously from the crowd. Flash saw her too and said something to Danny and Danny smiled his thanks to Donna and walked over to Elena North. "Would you care to comment, Ma'am?" he said.

Elena North made a small, delicate swallow. "What station are you?" she said weakly.

"KMLB, out of Connerville," Danny said promptly.

Elena North nodded as though familiar with KMLB. "I'm not clear about all the facts," she said quietly. "I couldn't say anything at the moment."

"I can say something," Flash boomed, and the bright light and Danny turned back to her. "My father fought the Nazis in World War Two. And I'll fight today. And my attorney has advised me."

Nick leaned his head under Flash's lavender umbrella and said, "Miss Arden will file a writ of advancement and summary notice." And then, perfectly, the bell–it came with three deafening, long beeps. Danny and Nick made a big show of shaking hands with Flash and the camera guy turned off the light and the three men walked to the parking lot. I couldn't run after them because Donna and Jay were by my side now, Jay telling Donna, "You were good. You were real good." Flash left, engulfed by kids, and all I could see of her was the lavender umbrella, bouncing along over a bunch of bent, dark heads. Elena North walked hurriedly ahead of Donna, Jay and me, and in ten seconds we broke into runs because the sky cracked and let loose a new and ferocious downpour.

During class the kids buzzed about the TV people and Donna said the reporter said her interview would be on the news at 11 p.m. either tonight or tomorrow at 6 p.m. "My interview," she repeated.

At lunch I went to the gym where I knew Flash and the P.E. crowd usually had pizzas delivered on Thursdays. But only the coach and Flash were there, Flash perched on a small ladder, dropping the triangle tip of a pepperoni slice into her mouth. "Hey," Flash said when she saw me. "Celebrate. Have some pizza."

But I made her step into the hall. "How could you tell Donna she was going to be on TV? That girl's mother is a widow. How did you scare up that equipment? Everything looked so authentic. Why didn't you tell me about this? You're all insane. This is just so potentially–I don't know. It has terrible potential."

Grinning, Flash said, "I'm basking in your admiration."

"This is not admiration." But in part it was.

"Your brother's a genius," she began, and the only other time I'd seen such joy in a grin was when it occurred on Danny's face. Flash liked telling the story. She said Danny procured the cameraman, one of his drinking buddies who worked for the cable access channel, and the only difficulty they had was keeping Danny's other friend, Nick, straight enough for the assignment. Flash authored the persecution theme, inspired in part by my calling Hoffman a Nazi, and Danny assured her that everyone would believe in channel KMLB. Same thing with Connerville, the town he made up. "He was right about everything," Flash said, and now she chortled. "You saw Elena North, you saw how she got."

"What about Donna? She's so proud about her interview."

Flash folded her arms, put her head back, closed her eyes, and the joyful grin returned. "Donna was part of it. She's my girl. She's a plotter."

So you think you know fundamentally what's afoot in your universe but there's a subterranean hive of scheming and industry about which you remain obtuse. This is what I told Brenda when she returned and said she'd heard TV reporters were all over the campus, and this is what I repeated when she said, "It was *completely* fake? Everyone believes it."

Everyone did. One student, Alonzo Gomez, maintained that he saw part of the interview on morning TV the next day, Channel 3, he thought, (an actual channel) and his report spread widely. Another boy said he saw Miss Arden's lawyer guy talking 'real mad' on Channel 10 (also a legitimate channel) and this spread as well. The petition disappeared from the faculty lounge bulletin board. Elena North disappeared too, out for a week. "Bronchitis, she says," Brenda said with a wink.

Hoffmann remained on campus but all day Friday stayed in his classroom or the Chemistry lab, emerging from the latter only to walk quickly to and from the supply room with boxes labeled, Sci. Equip. I nailed him on one of his trips. "The petition's gone," I said.

"I've got to get this lab renovated. The stuff in there is dinosaur era." He delivered a small, forced laugh.

"I wonder if Brenda's going on TV too. And I know they'll want to talk to you."

He looked down at his armload of boxes. "There's no time. We need new lenses. We need new wiring." He gave one of those weary teacher shrugs.

I walked off. I did not over gloat. I was somewhat seemly. I also decided to wait until Donna Jackson was safely graduated to confront her with her role in the false TV interview.

On Monday morning a freshly painted, psychedelic golf cart sat in Hoffmann's designated parking space. Multicolored streamers and tassels hung from it, and in its front seat sat a huge, tilted, stuffed donkey, maybe eight feet tall, and around the donkey's neck a sign painted in thick, shiny black letters said, ASS.

I rode into work with Brenda that morning and when we passed the donkey in the golf cart Brenda said, "Crap.

Can't she just win?" But she laughed at the tassels and a whirling pinwheel protruding from the donkeys' behind.

I watched from the lounge window when Hoffmann arrived. He drove slowly by the cart, now being examined by three boys who stared with open-mouthed interest as he neared. Hoffmann kept his eyes down, fiddled with something on his dashboard and continued on to the Visitor's Parking lot. Flash did not come to school that day. And Hoffmann did not complain to Brenda about the ass cart. It took Brenda nearly the whole school day to get it removed and finally at 1:45 a truck came from the District and towed it away.

Brenda couldn't reach Flash but I called my brother. "You might tell your cohort that her vehicle has been towed," I said.

"I filmed it going," he said. "It was a beauty." He'd been across the street in Win's Chinese restaurant with his Super 8 with the new zoom.

"Where's Flash?" I said.

And he said it was better for me, and for my job, to know as little as possible. "Just trust that she is the champion of the people."

After that things calmed down. Flash came back to school, usually in her regular gym outfit, though she continued to dress splendidly, often royally, for the games. Hoffmann sank into teaching, rebuilt the Chemistry lab and began sending Brenda polite requests, then pleasant memos about his progress. He worked quietly and met no more in public with his supporters.

In mid March Flash called me. "Don't tell anyone I'm leaving in June. I don't want them to think Hoffmann drove me out."

"All right. But he has no more power." I imagined this had to be the worst time in his teaching career, having to do nothing but teach.

"He'll wait. Like a snake. He'll try a comeback."

This was disconcerting because comeback made me think of Nixon. But Flash protected her triumph. Every other week or so she appeared on campus with Nick in his lawyer suit, and they walked around conferring importantly. "Let the asshole sweat," she told me." Let all the asses sweat their asses off."

I liked this because Hoffmann was owed some disquiet and he got it. Every time Flash and Nick showed up he stayed in his room and ate lunch at his desk.

The real media arrived in April, summoned by Brenda. A reporter from the Sacramento Bee came with a photographer and interviewed Flash and the next day a picture of the Shakespeare wall, Flash standing next to it with Donna Jackson, appeared on the front page of the Metro section. The accompanying article quoted Brenda's observation that Flash brought a lively spirit to education. Brenda told me later that the reporter omitted some of Flash's perkier comments, particularly her reply to his question about how other teachers felt about her methods. "Those who like me, fine," Flash declared. "Those who don't, screw them."

Flash called the night the article came out. "You didn't call me. I always call you."

"I was going to. The story was great. You're famous."

"You're always just going to call. You don't initiate. You and Brenda, you're...dainty."

This was too much. "I'm not *dainty*. And Brenda got you in the papers. Jeeze."

"Well, I'm having a celebration. The ascendance of Puck over foulness and treachery. Your brother Danny will be there. I'm inviting you."

She invited Brenda too and we went, and I still have faded Polaroid's of that night in the costume shop, Danny dressed as some kind of satanic warlock, Brenda in an artichoke suit that matched the green beer bottle she raised to the camera, Teri as a nymph in white gossamer and me in a gold turban and shimmering gold robe, laughing, waving a big feather at somebody. It was quite a night. There were a lot of sprites, and toasts, and Nick, stoned out of his mind and dressed in a loincloth, chugged peach brandy and threw up in Flash's old fashioned wash tub outside. "Nice lawyer," I said to Flash as we propped him up.

"Good thing he's not the real one."

I didn't pay much attention at the time. I was glad to be partying in a costume shop and glad to be with theater people because they can attain the finite limit of merriment.

Back at work Donna Jackson came to me and said, "You're my number one teacher in case you worried I changed to Miss Arden." Her boyfriend Jay took our picture and gave me a copy the next week, and I still have that too–and Donna and I look like a couple of buoyant, smiling girls,–friends, not student and teacher.

Donna started early on her valedictorian speech, brought me every draft, and I was excited because she was going to talk about big stuff–women's rights, racism, and, in a bow to Flash, intended to include a variation on the sentiment: 'It doesn't matter who you love, or how you love, but that you love.' So that was good and it would be a worthy, worthy speech for a struggling school on the edge of a ghetto.

Hoffmann told Brenda the week before graduation that he had accepted a position at Hiram Johnson High School for next year.

I called Flash, and after asking her to note that I was initiating the call, told her that she'd won, Hoffmann was leaving.

"Do you see?" Glee in her voice. "Do you see? Never back down. Fight till they drop."

"Most people say, fight till *you* drop."

"That's why they don't win."

On graduation night we put on our robes and filed down the aisle and I ended up next to Hoffmann who sat calmly enough, ignored me after a nod and murmured occasionally with Alice Freligh on his right. Then Pomp and Circumstance and then the Seniors, Donna the tallest of the lot. Brenda made her welcoming speech and then Donna went to the microphone. When she came to the part about vowing to battle sexism and racism, Hoffman muttered, "Oh brother, here we go," and bent over his program which he began to fold into narrow strips. But when Donna said that it wasn't our place to judge one another's lifestyles he sat erect, and when she said it didn't matter who or how you loved, Hoffmann said clearly, "Can you believe this? This is the limit," and stood up. He wedged his way down the row and walked with a frown down the center aisle and out of the auditorium. Donna didn't lose her rhythm, probably because she was reading and couldn't take her eyes from the page, but she said later that she was aware of the rustle of interest that attended his departure.

After, on my way to talk with Donna and her mother Flash stopped me, grabbed my wrist and pressed hard. "That prick," she whispered.

"You got that right."

We had one more week of school, a quiet week with no Seniors. On Monday Hoffmann's students began moving his books and papers to the trunk of his car. On Tuesday morning he unlocked his classroom door, then ran for Brenda who had to call the police. One of Hoffmann's big arrows had been shot through the chair behind his desk; another arrow was embedded in the desk itself. Across the board, spray-painted in tall red letters: *Prick*. It really was a shocker. These were real arrows, not props, and I was surprised to see how deeply they penetrated the wood.

The police, a fiftyish guy in a suit and a younger uniformed officer, hung around, providing fascination for the kids. But they wouldn't arrest Flash. "There's no evidence, sir," the uniformed cop told Hoffmann. They agreed to talk to Flash but the coach told them that she had taken her volley-ball girls out for an end of the year feast at the Hauf Brau, and that was that. After talking casually with the chief custodian the police left.

Hoffmann said to Brenda, "That does it. Get a sub," and wrenched his arrows from the wood, took his bow and walked to his car without looking back.

"How did she do it?" I said to Brenda.

"My question is, how did she get in the room?" Brenda said.

But I thought I knew the answer to that one. I thought I might be related to him.

Flash's van pulled in after lunch and the volley-ball team poured out, then Flash herself, wearing her Robin hood costume. I went out to meet her. "You're mentally ill," I said with a fake smile to keep the kids from listening.

"His car's gone," Flash said. "I wanted him to see my outfit."

"He left forever. Forever."

"I'm not done." That's when she told me a lawyer, a real one, would contact Hoffmann to inform him he was being sued. She seemed unsure when she used the words, harassment and defamation, but her eyes burned when she said, "He tried to lie about me and he insulted me. And he insulted Donna during her big speech. He needs to pay."

The lawsuit went on for almost four years and many of us were called on to present affidavits: me, Brenda, the coach, even Donna Jackson, who, I add proudly, went to Berkeley and then to law school and eventually became a civil rights attorney. Somewhere near that fourth year

Hoffmann surrendered, but part of the settlement required that Flash be quiet about the terms. Thereafter she merely smirked when the topic rose but my brother told me that Hoffmann was bitter and justice and liberality carried the day.

Brenda continued to run the school. I asked if it was nicer for her with Hoffmann and Flash not working there, and she said at the beginning it was, but before long other disturbed individuals surfaced, and she came to realize that you always, always have nut cases in education. She got married in 1980 to a genial guy from the Franchise Tax Department, and he, Gregory, was surprised when Flash showed up at the wedding in a magician's outfit with a black satin cape. He said he was glad to meet the famous person who owned the costume shop and Flash told him she didn't want to wear anything white because it might take away from the bride.

Toward the end of the reception Flash danced with Brenda and I watched Flash's black cape swirling. She was agile and light in motion, almost graceful, and on the dance floor I saw how truly slight she was. I thought about Hoffmann's arrows plunged deep into the desk and chair. I really didn't think a woman could pull that off, especially a little woman. But she could, and she did.

BAG HEAD

Kerry Langan

Whoever coined the expression, "Easy as pie," never met my Aunt Martha. She served cherry pie, the pits still in the fruit, at a church picnic and was stunned when the minister cracked his front tooth and had to be rushed off for emergency dental surgery.

"*Cherries have pits?*" she marveled. "Well, the rest of you just eat around them."

That was how our family functioned, we did things *around* Aunt Martha. Although a single woman with lots of spare time, none of the relatives asked her to baby-sit. Mother instructed Martha to gather pinecones for the Thanksgiving centerpiece rather than cook anything. She was encouraged to give gift certificates at Christmas after the year she gave us all economy size versions of Mr. Clean. "Sniff it, Clare," she told me, "that's *real* cleaning power."

Mother was mystified as to how Martha managed to keep her job as a personal assistant to Marvin Genkins, an eccentric crime novelist who churned out a new potboiler every year. And Daddy, well Daddy was just relieved that Aunt Martha had a job, period. I speculated Aunt Martha was the reason I was an only child. Daddy had spent the better part of his life bailing Aunt Martha out of self-concocted situations. When she was in first grade, she pulled the fire alarm in the school hallway because she thought the little red and white plaque was so pretty. While the fire trucks were at the school, the local diner caught on fire and burnt to the ground. Once Martha climbed up a tree to rescue a cat, but Daddy ended up having to rescue both of them, breaking his collar bone in the process. Aunt Martha hit the same tree with a car some years later when Daddy was teaching her to drive.

We gathered that her duties for Marvin Genkins consisted of typing up his manuscripts, which he wrote in pencil, emptying ashtrays, and serving him coffee before three PM and bourbon after. We knew little else. When Aunt Martha visited us after work, she smelled of cigarettes and eraser shavings. On one of these occasions, when I was about eleven, she was jubilant, announcing, "A new record! I typed nineteen pages today!"

Handing her a glass of sugary iced tea, Mother remarked, as she had so often, "That secretarial class you took has really paid off." Actually, we didn't know how much money Aunt Martha made. We only knew that since working for Mr. Genkins, going on five years now, Daddy had never had to pay her rent as he often did before when she worked as a waitress, a shoe store clerk and, finally, a perfume woman at a department store where she managed to squirt a customer in the eyes.

When she first went to work for Mr. Genkins, Mother suggested having him to dinner, but Aunt Martha said, "Oh, no! Marvin is a very private person. He never leaves the house. He even has his groceries delivered."

Daddy referred to him as a "reclusive agoraphobic" and Mother was simply fascinated by this man who was not a famous author, but seemed to have something of a cult following. The two drug stores in our town always had his latest book on display in the window. Peering through the glass, Mother would shake her head and say, "And to think Martha knows him."

When I turned 12, I got my period, grew four inches and lost my equilibrium. I became clumsy, bumping into furniture and tripping on the stairs. At school, my mind wandered and my grades fell from B's to D's in a few months.

"Clare is turning into Martha!" Mother wailed to Daddy one afternoon when they thought I was out of earshot.

"No, no," Daddy assured her. "Martha was always ditsy, from the day she was born. Clare was a normal child."

"Was! Was!" Mother shrieked. "What's happened to her!"

I sensed them watching me. Nervous under scrutiny, I became even clumsier. I failed an eye exam and had to get glasses. Mother couldn't keep from blurting, "Now you even look like Martha!"

I lost friends. In seventh grade, who you hung around with could make or break you, and I was an asset to no one. I stayed home and read a lot. When I'd exhausted the young adult section of our library, I asked Aunt Martha to bring me some of Marvin Genkins books.

"He's so *pleased*!" she gushed, the first time she brought an armload over. "He thought the books might be too advanced for you, but I told him you started reading at three, just like me."

This approval, from a man I'd never met, meant too much to me. I stayed up late reading his books until the words danced on the page. My eyesight worsened and I had to get new glasses that magnified my eyes to an alarming degree.

Mr. Genkins books were formulaic, to say the least, and I took comfort in the predictability. The main character was Detective Hal Hittman, a gruff, burly detective in his forties, who "knew every dead end street in Milwaukee."

With seemingly few clues, he found dead bodies, pointed his finger at the most unlikely, therefore the most likely, suspect, and concluded the case by sitting at his desk in the dark and musing about the "dame who seems to know a little too much about me." Although there was a different dame in every book, they were all shapely blondes with a pair of "baby blues" who needed rescuing of some kind. They were married to brute husbands or being blackmailed by former boyfriends. Hal Hittman never had a physical relationship with any of these women, but he gave every one of them "a long look that said it all."

Reading in my bed, my heavy glasses slipping down my nose, I squirmed at what I thought was an intimate statement. But why? I wasn't a shapely blonde; Hal Hittman would never give me a second glance. My baby blues moved like sluggish fish through a looking glass bowl.

But I wanted to meet Marvin Genkins, tell him in person how much I loved his books.

"Clare, honey," Aunt Martha stammered, "it takes Marvin a while to warm up to an idea. It took me more than a year to convince him to let me sharpen his pencils each morning."

"Huh?"

"Sharpen his pencils. He used to throw them out when the point wore down. Well, he threw them on the floor and left them there. What a mess. Pencils everywhere." She took a breath, erasing the ugly sight from her mind, "But I convinced him my system was better. And now there are no pencils on the floor," she finished proudly.

I didn't ask to meet him again.

Mother was desperate to improve my poor social standing. She enrolled me in charm school and urged me to walk around the house with a book on my head.

"Stand up straight! Throw your shoulders back, for heaven's sake."

I tried to comply but was shocked at how far my new breasts stood out. A group of boys at school had started calling me "Bag Head." It started when Ronnie Lambert looked me up and down in the cafeteria one day and pronounced, "You wouldn't be half-bad if you wore a bag over your head." Horrified, I watched him slap his crotch as he growled, "Any time. Any place."

As humiliating as this was, the backlash from the junior high girls was worse. Jealous that my breasts were eliciting male attention, they started a rumor that I stuffed my bra, a whole box of tissues in each cup. Then my face erupted with acne and I really did want to put a bag over my head.

To avoid school, I feigned illness as often as I could get away with it, re-reading Marvin Genkins books until I knew entire chapters by heart. When Aunt Martha visited, we sat side by side on the couch and quoted favorite passages aloud:

"The sky was a furious purple when Hal Hittman reached the ocean. The waves crashed ferociously upon the calm sand. He listened to the roaring surf, knowing it had something to tell him. Be patient, he reminded himself, listen carefully. Then, with a brief nod of his head, he turned and walked to his car. He knew who the murderer was and he knew what he had to do make the bastard hang himself with his own noose."

Aunt Martha and I giggled over "bastard." Such daring language! I asked her how Hal Hittman could drive to the ocean when he lived in Milwaukee and Aunt Martha just blinked and said, "Why, I never thought of that."

"Maybe he drives to Lake Michigan?"

She nodded thoughtfully. "Maybe, maybe"

I asked her if she'd point this out to Marvin and tell him that it was me who noticed the error.

"No." She shook her head widely. "I never make suggestions. I tried once and Marvin didn't write for three whole weeks. Now I just type."

Mother went to visit her sister in Joliet for a week in late spring. On a Friday morning, after Daddy left for work, I dialed my school's number and affected my mother's breathy, girlish voice, saying, "My daughter, Clare Burnham, has strep throat and won't be at school today." The principal's secretary wished a speedy recovery and hung up.

Our whole family knew where Marvin Genkins lived, just a couple of miles from our house on a quiet, residential street. Sometimes Mother drove by his house, a small bungalow with an overgrown lawn. She'd make a small sucking noise with her tongue and say, "You'd think he'd hire a gardener. He certainly can afford one."

On the bike ride over, I shivered with excitement although it was an unusually warm day. I parked my bike against the enormous tree on the curb lawn and hid behind the trunk. Peering out, I noticed that Marvin Genkin's lawn was as yellow as it was green because hundreds of dandelions dotted the grass. Aunt Martha's old Buick was parked crookedly in the driveway.

I took a deep breath and started to sprint toward the back of the house. Rounding the corner, I crouched low under a window and dared a peek. I found myself gazing at Marvin Genkin's kitchen. Through a narrow part in the curtains I could see a tall stack of pizza boxes on the table and a carafe of coffee simmering on the stove. But no sign of Marvin or Aunt Martha.

Bent over, I moved around the house until I was on one side, a large picture window over my head. There were no curtains, but the window was too high to look in. I heard music, a familiar melody. Frank Sinatra? Yes, that song he sang with his daughter about strangers in the night. Daddy had the album.

I ran to the garage and found the door locked, but then I noticed a small entrance on the side. I pushed the door open and stepped inside the garage. There was no car, but I found at least twenty cardboard boxes filled with Girl Scout cookies. There were a few other boxes filled with the Hal Hittman books. Against the back wall were a few cans of unopened paint. I picked up two, surprised at how heavy they were, and carried them out of the garage and back to the window on the side of the house. I heard Frank Sinatra's voice again, this time a song I didn't know.

With a foot on each paint can, I stood carefully and slowly raised my head until just my eyes reached the bottom of the window. I was peering into a dark living room filled with books and papers stacked everywhere. Ghostly white cigarette smoke coiled up to the ceiling from at least three ash trays.

And there he was, Marvin Genkins. He seemed to be one size, extra large, from his neck to his ankles. His body was like some huge rectangle under that a dark blue or black bathrobe. He was mostly bald with gray hair striping either side of his head. He had a mustache beneath a dinky nose. He was wearing glasses with big black frames, but his eyes appeared to be closed.

More startling than his appearance, however, was that he was dancing with Marilyn Monroe or someone who looked just like her. An incarnation of one of Hal Hittman's dames. With big, broad steps, Marvin ushered this shapely platinum blonde in a black and pink polka dot dress around the room. Singing along with Sinatra, they bumped into furniture, knocked over a stack of books, and stepped on a cat's tail, the animal wailing as it fled the room. They never stopped dancing, Finally, they moved close enough to the window so I could see the woman's face. So beautiful and so strangely familiar. Too familiar, even with the blonde wig. I should have looked away.

Instead I watched their every move, this odd twosome clumsily dancing around the room together out of step with the music. At the end of the song, Marvin opened his enormous robe and extended it to cover Aunt Martha, the two of them now one enormous terry cloth creature with two heads. Clouds moved overhead and the sunlight died. Marvin and Aunt Martha became shadow silhouettes. Then Aunt Martha's head disappeared beneath the robe, her body traveling down until she was kneeling on the floor. Instantly, Marvin threw his head back and opened his mouth, his large body swaying slowly at first and then faster with broad side to side movements. He started to moan, then holler loud enough so I could hear him through the glass, "Oh, Oh, OH, OH, ATTA GIRL, MARTHA! YES, OH, OOHHHHHH!!"

I leaped off the paint cans and landed flat on my back in the soft overgrown grass. The clouds opened up and the light dropped onto my face. Slowly I turned myself over and then, on my hands and knees, I crawled around to the front of the house and got on my bike. My legs barely had the strength to turn the pedals but somehow the bicycle's wheels rotated over and over until I was home.

Our basement was big and drafty with damp spots in the corners. My old baby doll stroller was down here along with a box of tap shoes in various sizes that I wore when Mother was convinced I could be the next Shirley Temple. Old lamps, rusted patio furniture, a broken television, all of this was down here.

I put the stacks of Marvin Jenkin's books under the stairwell. Climbing the stairs, I inhaled the dank basement air, the musty blanket covering our family's relics. I emerged blinking in the bright light of the kitchen where Mother sat sipping her creamy coffee. There was hope in her eyes these days. My growth spurts were over and the clumsiness subsided. I saw a dermatologist regularly and my skin was greatly improved. My bathroom was now stocked with an arsenal of Bonnie Bell cosmetics. The changes that could be wrought with concealer, blush, mascara and lip gloss were astonishing.

The biggest change was the contact lenses. They irritated my eyes and I dreaded putting them in and taking them out. Still, when I looked in the mirror, shyly at first but then with mounting eagerness, I saw someone who shocked me with her beauty. The deep blue of my irises was startling, and mother bought me a whole wardrobe of blouses and sweaters to play up the color.

A couple of girls in my class began sitting with me at lunch. Misfits who giggled at stupid jokes and stole glances at the boys on the basketball team. Then one morning when I was called up to the blackboard to solve a math problem, popular Ken Whitman whistled at me and some other boy said, "You ain't kidding." I dropped the chalk.

At lunch that day I stopped at the cheerleaders' table and said in a besieged little whine, "Can I *pleeze* sit here? Cheryl and Judy are *sooo* strange." I glanced towards my usual table.

Susan Trimmer, prettiest of the bunch, stared at me as if she were appraising me. My heart stopped until she slid her tray down the table to make room for me and said, "Tell me about it. This morning Judy started crying in gym because she couldn't climb the rope."

That was all it took. I ate with the cheerleaders every day and in eighth grade I was on the squad. I stood in the back row, but still, I got to wear the uniform. Mother took pictures of me with my pom poms and proudly included it with her annual Christmas letter.

Aunt Martha was disappointed that I stopped reading Marvin's books. "You won't learn anything from those *Seventeen* magazines," she admonished me. "Those models aren't real people, you know."

When Marvin Genkins died two years later of a massive heart attack, Aunt Martha inherited almost half a million dollars from his estate. But she was lost without the job, without him. She sat in a trance at family dinners or asked for a glass of bourbon which she only sniffed, never drank.

For some reason her fingers were always smeared with typewriter ink. When someone at the zoo called us and asked us to come get the hysterical woman weeping in front of the gorilla cage, Daddy grudgingly insisted that she move in with us.

Aunt Martha tried to help Mother with the housework, but after smashing a crystal vase, Mother urged her to plant tulips in our backyard. For several days, Aunt Martha was enthusiastic about the project. She pulled weeds and constantly watered the yard. She bought at least thirty pairs of gardening gloves in bright floral prints. Martha got frustrated when she had difficulty digging six inch holes for the tulip bulbs, but later thought herself ingenious for getting out my old pogo stick and jumping through the back yard.

I was mortified one day when my friends witnessed Aunt Martha on one of her garden rampages, but I hid my embarrassment by rolling my eyes and shaking my head. "Daddy says every family has an odd ball and Aunt Martha's ours."

As she toppled off the pogo stick onto the lawn, I knew I should run over and help her up. But I was scared, scared of my friends seeing the two of us side by side. I averted my eyes as Aunt Martha stood. I knew she would jump back on the pogo stick and continue hopping until the yard was filled with holes. And for an all too brief period next spring, we would have the most beautiful yard in the neighborhood.

POSH WOMAN AND THE DEAD BIRD

Lisa Zerkle

After the Broadway play, my family walks long blocks to the dark streets of midtown, returning to our hotel. The busy bustle of commerce gone with the taxis and the white collar workers in long, dark coats. Even the Starbucks are closed. We stop to admire the steam rising up from the subway grating and a clear voice calls out, "That's a quail, isn't it? I mean, it's too large to be a pigeon." We look up to see a high-heeled woman in a black fur-lined cape. At her stilettoed foot lies a small, brown carcass. The children bustle over, crouch down around the dead bird. My husband and I follow. The woman admonishes, "Don't touch it, it might have germs." She turns to me. "It IS a quail. The reason I know," she confides, "is that my ex-boyfriend took me to an event for the opera. I had to have a hat for the occasion and I had one made with quail feathers. It was one of those, what do you call it? Like Jackie Kennedy used to wear? Pillbox!" she answers herself, and places the memory of the hat at an angle on her head with black-satin-gloved hands. Her hair is dark and swept up in an elaborate do. The diamonds on her ears flash in the street light. "But where did it come from?" I ask, looking at the steep cliffs of buildings rise up around us. There are no parks nearby, no blade of grass, not even a sad caged tree.

A breeze ruffles the small bird's black- and tan-stippled feathers. "It could be sleeping," my youngest says. The bird looks as if it scratched for insects in a meadow that very day. "Maybe it fell out of a catering truck?" I suggest. The woman shrugs, "I don't know, but it IS a quail. My boyfriend, he used to hunt them." She turns and her cape flares out from her shoulders. The children stand and we watch her click down the sidewalk alone. I want to say something to her. Thanks? But for what, exactly? She seems invincible somehow, like an arch villain. Walking back to the hotel, we decide she needs her own graphic novel. One that explains her powers, how she lures small gamebirds to the metropolis, only to cause their demise.

MY WIFE, THE PORN STAR

Steve Cushman

y wife, Carissa, is a porn star. That was my first thought as I stood in the adult section of Cheap-O-Video staring at her picture on the cover of *Young Lust #17*, naked with black stars covering her various private parts. For a second, I felt dizzy and told myself it couldn't be her. But it was, about ten years younger, sandwiched between *Dirty Debutantes #103* and *Up-N-Cummers #34*: the same long straight black hair, dark Italian skin, and the birthmark shaped like the state of Texas above her belly button. I closed my eyes and opened them, hoping that might be enough to remove her picture from the movie's display box. Of course, it was not.

I'll admit that at the first moment I spotted Carissa, I was a bit thrilled. But this quickly faded as I realized just what might be on the tape. I grabbed it and walked to the front of the store. The girl at the counter, a redheaded high schooler wearing a Monty Python T-shirt, smiled at me as she placed the video in a plastic bag. I didn't bother smiling back.

Driving home, I considered stopping at the hospital where Carissa was working a rare Saturday shift and confronting her. Of walking into the Ultrasound department, throwing the video into one of the VCR's they use for recording prenatal scans and asking her what in the hell this was all about.

I had tried to get Carissa to watch a porno once. It was in the first year of our marriage. She squirmed and only watched one scene before hugging me and saying, "Joe, we don't need this stuff." And, to be honest, we didn't. After six years together, the sight of her naked still excited me. I knew she liked sex as much, if not, more than I did. At least I thought she liked it, but maybe she didn't. We hadn't been together in almost three weeks now.

I pulled into the driveway of our house, a fixer-upper we'd bought two years ago. Spanish moss hung from the oak tree in the center of the yard like an unruly gray wig. I had spent the morning cutting down a dead orange tree in the backyard and replacing it with a new Sago Palm. I took a break for lunch with the intention of driving to the store to buy some beer and bologna. On the way home, I passed the video store.

Suzi, our black lab, barked and scratched at the door as I walked up the front steps. "Stop it," I said, but she didn't. When I opened the door, Suzi ran past me toward a squirrel skirting up the Oak tree, then stood at the base of the tree like a Pointer, a breed she wasn't.

I left the door open and set the video on the kitchen table next to some walnut brownies Carissa had made last night. I opened one of the beers before putting the rest of the six pack in the fridge. Suzi came back in and sat on her black and white striped doggie bed, which was nothing more than a large overpriced pillow. Shutting the door, I slid the tape in the VCR and hit PLAY. As ads for 1-900 numbers rolled by, I finished the beer in quick mouthfuls. My stomach felt light and empty, like that moment at the top of a roller coaster when you feel the rush of excitement but know you're about to go down. I wanted to take the tape back to the store and forget about the whole thing, but it was too late for that.

How could I pretend it didn't exist when I'd held it in my hand?

I felt certain that the first scene would be Carissa with some well-hung guy, Mr. Super Sex or whatever the hell his name might be. Then I tried to convince myself that maybe she'd just done some modeling, and they'd used her photo for the cover. I didn't know if they did that or not, but it was the only bit of hope I had.

A young couple, and not my wife, appeared on the screen. That was a relief. The woman was cute with long straight red hair. He was tall and thin with a tattoo of a duck on his right shoulder. They started taking their clothes off. He called her Tammy. She called him Baby. I leaned back into the couch as he climbed on top of her. She moaned, smiled playfully at the camera. The movie was middle of the road, not the shaky tripod of amateur video nor the silly plot and soft lighting of high-budget porn, but somewhere in between.

After fast-forwarding through the rest of the scene, the screen went black. I tensed again, actually stopped breathing for a moment or two. But the next scene didn't include Carissa either. It had the same guy, Ducky, with two slim brunettes.

I couldn't help but wonder why Carissa would do something like this. Was it about money? I didn't think so. This was years before we met, but her father, out in Colorado, still sent her monthly checks for $300, something she told me he'd been doing since she went away to college. Was it a rebellious act? I doubted it as she was one of the few people I knew who got along with both of their parents. Maybe it was a youthful experiment one of her college roommates talked her into. Regardless of the reason, I didn't like the idea of watching my wife have sex with some other guy. Sure, I knew she was no virgin when we met. But it's one thing to be aware of your spouse's past intimate behavior and quite another to see it in on a color TV in your own living room.

There was a knock at my door. Suzi jumped up and started barking. Through the peephole, I saw a blonde girl in her early twenties. I'd seen her jogging in the neighborhood before. She was cute, had on cut-off jeans shorts and a white T-shirt. She was moving her lips up and down like someone trying to spread lip-gloss evenly.

"Just a minute," I said, glancing back at the TV. Ducky was shaking his head, and slapping his hands on the white throw rug he was laying on, as if he couldn't quite believe his good fortune. I stopped the VCR and un-tucked my T-shirt, letting it fall past my waist. Suzi stood beside me, still barking. "Suzi, go lay down." When I stepped outside, the sun's glare shocked me.

"Hi," the girl said. She smiled and put her hands behind her back in what I'm sure she meant as an innocent pose, but all I could see was the way this made her breasts stick out toward me. I hadn't noticed it at first, but now standing closer saw that her eyes were different colors—blue on the right, green on the left. I'd never seen anybody with different color eyes before. I wondered if this girl had ever been in a porno, if the girl at the video store or the mailman had. It seemed possible that everyone I came into contact with could have starred in one.

"I'm Lisa. I live down the street."

"Joe," I said.

"I was wondering if you could help me."

I was in no mood to help anyone. "Sure," I said, hoping she didn't look down at my shorts. She looked right, left, and then back at me, as if trying to gather the courage for her question.

"I feel so stupid. You're the fifth door I've knocked on."

"What is it?"

"I grabbed the wrong set of keys and locked myself out. There's an unlocked window at my house, but it's too heavy for me to lift by myself."

"Sure." I walked back in the house. Suzi looked up at me with disappointed eyes. "Shut up," I said. Grabbing my keys, I remembered a porno I'd seen where a woman asked a neighbor to help her with a window and afterwards rewarded him with a trip to her bedroom. Jeez, Joe, I thought, she just needs a little help.

As we walked on the sidewalk toward her house, she told me she was home from college, working as a hostess at Outback Steakhouse for the summer, said she was getting a degree in Business Administration. "Good for you," I said. I hoped none of my neighbors saw us walking together. But what should I care? They had probably all seen my wife having sex on big-screen TV's.

Lisa's parent's house was one of the nicer ones in the neighborhood. A tall, yellow faux-Victorian with red-trimmed windows and a wrap-around porch. Last week, on our nightly walks with Suzi, Carissa and I had passed the house and she'd squeezed my hand, smiled at me, and said, "Some day."

Lisa led me through a gate on the side of the house, past a kidney-shaped pool, and toward a chest-high window on the far side. Standing in the rust-colored mulch that bordered the house, she tried to push the window upward, as if to say this is all on the up and up pervert guy from down the block whose wife is a porn star so don't get any funny ideas. She stepped aside and I gave the window a good push. It didn't budge. I bent my knees and pushed again harder and this time it opened.

While she climbed in the window, I walked over to the pool and ran my hands through the luke-warm water. It felt inviting and open. "You wanna go in?"

Lisa was standing a few feet behind me now. She was barefoot now. Her toenails were clean and unpolished. A white puff of cotton stuck to the outside of her right big toe.

"No, I should get back," I said, trying not to stare at her breasts as I stood up, but I couldn't help myself. She'd replaced her shirt with a pink bikini top.

"You can use one of my father's suits."

"No, that's okay." Why not, I thought, just a quick swim to cool off? But I knew why not. Without the shirt, I could see her pierced belly button and the thin line of blond peach fuzz below it. I wondered how Carissa would like it if I went for a swim with a college girl. Maybe I wouldn't tell her. How would she like that?

Lisa stuck her hand out to shake. I took her hand in mine and squeezed it. Leaning forward, I looked into her eyes, and it was like looking at two different women, neither of them my wife. I imagined taking her in my arms and kissing her, the two of us falling into the pool, but then her cell phone started ringing, pulling me back to reality. As she answered it, I waved and walked away.

Carissa and I met eight years ago. I was in the darkroom developing a set of tibia and femur X-rays on a trauma patient when she walked in. She didn't see me and turned the overhead light on, exposing all of my films. "Fuck," I said.

"What?" she said, before realizing what she'd done. "I'm sorry."

"You ruined my films." I stormed out of the darkroom.

An hour later, I was standing by a view-box, looking at the X-rays I'd re-shot, when she walked over to me and said, "Nice work." I'd noticed her before, but most of the ultrasound girls seemed uppity, as if they were doing something more important than those of us who shot X-rays.

For the next two weeks, we courted over broken bones and cancerous growths. If I shot an X-ray with a fracture, I'd show it to her. If she scanned someone with cancer, a cyst, or an extra kidney she'd show it to me. Then, one day, as we stared at a femur shattered into four pieces, I asked her out to dinner.

I had kissed one other woman beside Carissa since that first date. A respiratory therapist named Shan cornered me at a Halloween party, a month or so after Carissa and I started dating, and said, "I've never kissed a man with glasses before." She had been flirting with me the whole night and I had been drinking and was flattered. Although our relationship wasn't that serious yet, and it was only a kiss, it still felt like cheating to me. I never told Carissa about it. At the time, I didn't think she needed to know; it was an error in judgement; I'd fucked up. Period. Now, I wished I'd told her.

When I got home, I checked the answering machine but Carissa hadn't called. I took a bite out of one of the brownies and hated to admit that they tasted good. For the first time, it occurred to me that she might not even be at work. Maybe she was making another video. While I knew that was ridiculous, I called her work number anyway.

She picked up on the second ring. "Hello, Ultrasound."

"Carissa."

"Hey, honey." She sounded tired.

"How are you?" I walked around the living room, trying to take it easy and not blurt out what I'd discovered.

"Beat," she said. "It's been a busy day."

"When you coming home?"

"Couple hours. Did you get that tree planted?"

"Carissa, we have to talk."

"About what?"

"It's about your video."

She didn't say anything for a moment. I heard a printer spitting out paper in the background, probably an order requisition, which meant she'd have more work to do. "It was a day late."

"That's not what I mean."

"Don't you dare call me about some video that's two days late when I'm working."

"That's not what I'm talking about."

"It was two days, Joe. Four dollars. Don't be an ass."

"Two days. I thought you said one."

"I don't know. A day or two. What differences does it make?"

"You lied," I said.

"Grow up, Joe," she said, then hung up.

I slammed the phone down and walked into our bedroom. Two days, one day. What else was she lying about, what other secret is she hiding? I opened her top drawer and lifted a yellow silk bra I'd bought her last Valentine's Day to my nose and smelled detergent. Underneath the clothes, I found a manila envelope and thought it might be the contract from her movie, maybe a review or two, or some other memento from her good old days. I undid the clasp and looked inside. There were twenty or so post-it notes, each one stuck to a 3 x 5 index card. I read one, *I miss you, Wes.* Another, *I love you xoxoxo, Joe.* I turned the envelope over and there was a hand-drawn heart with my name in the center of it. Sliding the two notes back inside, I clasped the envelope and placed it back where I'd found it.

I sat back on the couch again and pressed PLAY on the remote. The next scene was a girl-girl scene, both blonde and undeniably attractive. A framed poster of Cupid holding a bow and arrow decorated the white wall behind them. An inch-long surgical scar was visible under one of the girl's left breasts.

While usually a fan of girl-girl scenes, I fast-forwarded through this one, feeling the need to get to Carissa's. Enough was enough; I couldn't wait anymore. The screen went black; I tensed; there she was, laying on a bed in a pair of white lacy panties. She looked beautiful and nervous, kept turning to someone off-camera as if asking for direction. I pushed STOP and got up and grabbed another beer.

I walked out onto the back porch, stopped at the railing and set my beer on the gas grill. The new palm tree looked good but there were weeds I should be pulling, grass to be mowed, a fence that needed to be painted. I considered not watching the scene, of taking the video out of the VCR, maybe throwing it away. But I knew I'd always wonder just how much my wife was willing to do and not tell me about.

Sitting back down, I pushed PLAY. Carissa began to run her hands along her perfect little breasts, squeezing the nipples until they hardened. She closed her eyes. Was she thinking about Doug, the guy she had dated through college? Maybe Wayne, the guy she lost her virginity to at sixteen. Hell, I had no clue what she was thinking.

Slowly, she took the panties off and started to rub herself down there. Her pubic hair was dark and bushy, more so than she kept it now. I spotted that mole on her right shoulder I'd kissed so many times over the years. There was a knock at her door. Carissa feigned surprise, covering her body with both hands. She was not a very good actress.

Tammy and Ducky walked into the room. The two girls hugged and Ducky rubbed his hands together as he turned to the camera and winked. Christ, not Ducky, I thought.

Tammy climbed on the bed and the girls started kissing as Ducky got undressed. Tammy went down on Carissa as Ducky entered her from behind. It was strange seeing my wife with another woman, something I had always imagined would be great, pure male fantasy. The woman on the screen was my wife, but at the same time she wasn't; she was some younger version of her, someone I had never known, someone I tried to convince myself who didn't owe me an explanation of her life before me.

After a couple minutes, the girls traded positions. Carissa seemed to be enjoying herself with Ducky—though thankfully not too much—and I listened for sounds that were familiar to me, things I had heard in our bed, but still

I was not able to match up what I was seeing and hearing with what I knew and had experienced with Carissa. When the scene ended, I wasn't excited or angry but numb. Maybe I was too tired by then, felt as if I'd been thrown against a wall all afternoon, beaten senseless, and left for dead.

I picked the remote up, pushed STOP and then EJECT. I closed my eyes and tried some deep breathing exercises, something, anything to help me not think of what I'd just seen. But Suzi started to bark and a moment later there was a knock at the door. For a second or two, I didn't know where I was. Although it was only three in the afternoon, the room had darkened. The only light came from the lines of white across the gray screen.

It was Lisa. She still had on that pink bikini top and a pair of jean shorts. I could invite her in—something told me she would be willing—and take her into our bedroom and screw her on our bed. I could set up our camera, record it all and leave it for Carissa to find. I reached for the handle of the door, felt the cold knob, turned it an inch and then stopped myself. There were things I could do and others I could not. And it was clear to me that I could not do that.

After knocking again, Lisa slid a white envelope into the mailbox and walked away. I waited a couple minutes before opening the door. Inside the envelope were a couple $20 gift cards for Outback. I pulled the tape out of the VCR and dropped it on the kitchen table on my way out back to mow the yard.

Pushing the mower back and forth, occasionally a wave of anger would come over me, but the mindlessness of the work and the sun beating down on me helped me forget, for a little while, about the tape and what I would have to do or say when Carissa got home.

Carrying a bag of leaves to the garbage cans on the side of the house, I heard a car door shut. Shit, I thought, the tape; I'd left it on the kitchen table. I made it into the house as Carissa was unlocking the front door. I grabbed the tape from the table and ran back outside, considered throwing it over our neighbor's fence, maybe tossing it under the porch. When I heard the front door shut, I opened the top of the grill and threw it in there. Behind me, I could hear Carissa dropping her keys onto the kitchen table.

She opened the screen door and said, "Hey, handsome." She was wearing her blue hospital scrubs, her dark hair pulled up by a hair band. She smiled at me. I forced a smile back. She walked over and hugged me. "Joe, I'm sorry about the tape," she said. "I should have told you. I forgot about it."

"You should have told me," I said.

"I know. I will next time. You want a beer?" she asked.

"Yeah," I said. She kissed me and walked back inside.

I sat down in one of the white plastic chairs on the deck and looked out at the work I'd done that day. The new palm tree and grass looked good. The grill, her tape, her past, was less than a foot away. I still hadn't decided what I was going to say to her about it.

She handed me a beer and sat across from me. "What's up with those Outback gift cards?"

"I helped a girl down the street break into her house and she gave them to me."

She shook her head as if she didn't believe me.

"Do you have anything you want to confess?" I asked.

She took a mouthful of beer and said, "I don't think so."

"Nothing?"

She smiled, drank again. "I did take forty dollars from the ATM last week. I might not have written it in the checkbook."

This was going nowhere. "Have you ever been with another woman?"

"Haven't we talked about this before?"

We had, in our first year together, talked to some degree about our past sexual experience, but I didn't remember her mentioning anything about a brief career in pornography, or a threesome for that matter. "How about a man and a woman at the same time?"

She winked. "I'm not going to let you bring Heather home."

Heather was the second shift X-ray supervisor and we'd both commented on how good looking she was. "Have you?" I asked.

"What does it matter what I did before I met you?"

"It does."

"It shouldn't." She walked over and sat on my lap. "Are you frisky? Do you need me to take care of you? Is that what this is all about?" She turned and kissed me playfully on the forehead three or four times, bit the edge of my nose.

"No," I said. But my arousal was obvious to both of us.

"Your loss." She stood and walked into the house. In the kitchen, she stripped naked, then blew me a kiss and disappeared down the hallway. For a couple minutes, I was alone on the porch. It was surprisingly quiet, one of those deafening late afternoon silences. The freshly mowed grass smelled sweet. I could walk in the house, show her what I'd discovered, demand she tell me why she'd done it. But if I did that it would always be there between us. If I kept it to myself, then she could continue to believe her secret was still a secret. And maybe the reason she hadn't told me was that she didn't think it had anything to do with me, with us; it was simply something from her past she wanted to forget about.

From down the street, the sound of a dog barking drifted over the fence. I knew that sitting out here was doing neither me nor Carissa any good. With a couple inches of beer left, I stood up and pulled the tape out of the grill. I walked in the house and dropped *Young Lust #17* into the garbage can on my way back to our bedroom where my wife, Carissa, was waiting for me.

AGAINST THE WALL

Dorene O'Brien

Sammy noticed it first in her fingernails, the skin overtaking them, the edges growing closer together, the cuticles crawling upward. There was no doubt about it: She was shrinking. She called her best friend at the office.

"I'm shrinking," she said.

"I should have such problems," said Wanda.

"I'm serious."

"You mean as in losing weight?"

"I wish."

"When did it start?" asked Wanda, who had very recently begun to believe in the impossible.

"Just after David left. I felt smaller, so I started taking height measurements."

"How'd you do that?"

"All you need is a wall and a pencil, Wanda."

"You can't take an accurate measurement of yourself."

"Why not?"

"Because of the whole angle thing with your arm."

Sammy sighed. "Can you come over and measure me?"

"Sure," said Wanda. "Just feed me."

Wanda stood next to the television and eyed the scribbles on the wall of her best friend's bedroom with suspicion. "You're all over the place," she said.

"Yeah, but see how they're getting lower?"

"Not really."

"That's because you haven't witnessed the progression."

"Tell ya what, let's erase this and start over."

Sammy stared at her friend in disbelief and tapped her fingernail hard against the wall. "*This* is evidence," she said.

"Okay, okay," said Wanda, "we'll use a new wall. But don't ask me to come over and paint when we're done."

"I'll be living in a Barbie Dream House," said Sammy. "One bottle of nail polish will cover it."

Sammy insisted they use a wall perpendicular to the one inscribed with the hieroglyphs of her height's demise so she could compare the second phase of the project to her initial work with a tape measure. But each time Wanda flattened her friend's auburn hair with a cardboard pantyhose insert, her pencil landed smack dab in the middle of a flower or on a bird's eye.

"This ain't gonna work," said Wanda. "This wallpaper's screwin' me up. You know that no one wallpapers three walls anymore," she griped, irritated that a long-defunct fashion trend has swept in from the past to thwart her efforts.

"I'm standing here shrinking and you're complaining about my interior decorating?"

"There's only one thing to do," said Wanda. "We gotta move the TV."

The women struggled with the 27-inch console television, wrestling it over the thick carpet until they felt it cleared a place for Sammy to stand far enough from the initial evidence to avoid confusion. Sally gave the TV a hard kick in its side, cracking the wood.

"What the hell are you doing?" asked Wanda.

"David's coming to get it next week."

"Oh," said Wanda, scraping the sharp end of the pencil across the top before ordering Sammy into position.

"Okay, get in the square."

Sammy stepped into the carpet indentation left by the TV and leaned back.

"Did you always lean your head against the wall?" asked Wanda.

"Yeah."

"Well, that's not accurate."

"It is if you do it the same way every time."

"Did you?"

"I don't know now."

"Okay," said Wanda, "stand up straight."

Wanda placed the cardboard on Sammy's head and pressed her thick hair down firmly before drawing a line across the beige wall.

"Hey," she said, "was your hair ever wet when you took a measurement? That can make a difference. You got hair with a vengeance."

"I always measured right before bed, and I never go to bed with wet hair."

"Yeah, you'd catch your death. Hey," she added, "your hair shrinking?"

"Gee, I don't know. Now I guess I'll have to measure that too."

"Let's just work on the height for now."

Wanda ate leftover lasagna as Sammy talked about the symptoms of her crisis: the capacity to eat only half a Happy Meal, how her locket now hung between rather than above her breasts, the difficulty she had hearing because her ears had shrunk.

"David called the other day to say he'd pick up his stuff next week and I could barely hear him."

"Maybe you had bad reception."

"My mother called later and I heard her just fine, telling me David is a lazy will-o-the-wisp and that *I* should have dumped *him*. I heard *that*."

"She actually said 'will-o-the-wisp'?"

"I think so," said Sammy while absently tracing a small arc around her right ear with her index finger.

When Wanda left, Sammy made herself a cup of gingerroot tea and crawled into bed. Life held strange surprises, and Sammy was well aware of this. So aware, in fact, that she had bought a six-month supply of coffee when prices plummeted, posted a fire evacuation plan on the refrigerator, created a living will commanding doctors to unplug her in the event of a debilitating accident. Sammy blamed herself for shrinking. She was prepared for anything and was, as a result, stricken with the impossible. What would David say? Would he even see her by this time next week, or would she be nothing more than a munchkin voice screaming from between the carpet fibers? She felt suddenly grateful that they didn't have any pets, unlike the poor guy in *The Incredible Shrinking Man* who was terrorized by the family dog each time he ventured outside the confines of his daughter's dollhouse.

Sammy slurped her tea, something David hated, and noticed how heavy the stoneware cup felt in her tiny hand, how her finger looked like a child's looped awkwardly around its handle. She placed the cup onto the nightstand and stared at her hands, remembering how her wedding ring had just slipped off her finger as she scrubbed the toilet, floated down gracefully through the blue water before tapping the porcelain and sliding into the hole. *I'll flush once,* she thought. *If it's gone, it's gone. If it bubbles back up...well, I'll deal with that then.* She did this a week after David left. She flushed once, then gazed into the empty bowl as if it were a crystal ball.

Why had he left? she wondered. He had told her, she felt certain, yet the telling felt like a distant, hazy memory.

Something about stockpiling coffee, and then her mind drifting to a place where coffee prices had risen to $55 a pound, David's grateful, satiated smile at her over the morning paper. Clearly he would not stay around long enough to understand.

As if fulfilling an unconscious desire to make her misery complete, she called her mother.

"Hi, Ma."

"What, you're calling me from work? Is it my birthday or something?"

"I didn't go to work, Ma. I don't feel well."

"I suppose you have a money tree growing out back?"

"I have to tell you something."

"You're not getting back together with that schmuck?"

"No, Ma. I'm shrinking."

"Thank God."

"I'm shrinking, Ma. Getting smaller."

"You're bound to lose a little weight, sweetheart. When that deadbeat is out of your life you'll fatten up like a pig. You'll see."

"I'm not losing weight, Ma, I'm shrinking. Getting smaller all over. Disappearing."

"Oh," she said, "you're watching too much *X-Files*."

Sammy pulled shoeboxes from her closet shelves, canisters from kitchen cupboards and books she thought she'd need from the upper reaches of her bookcases so she wouldn't have to bother anyone in the later stages of her condition. She scolded herself during these bouts of preparation, realizing it was this compulsive mentality that had gotten her into this mess, but she couldn't stop. "And why should I?" she asked herself. "What else can happen?"

She stretched her fingers toward the line Wanda had drawn across her bedroom wall but pulled them back after considering the line's temporality, how the oil on her skin could blur its boundaries, taint the results. Sammy spent much time staring at the wall, forsaking thoughts that normally held her attention for hours: exactly when will the Middle Ages no longer be middle ages? Did ancient linguists deliberately place the word "ear" within the word "hear"? What's the difference between paradox and irony? She finally called Wanda at work.

"I'm obsessing," she said.

"Any why not?" said Wanda. "You're shrinking, for chrissake."

"I'm coming back to work tomorrow while I can still reach the top drawer of the file cabinet. The bills won't disappear just because I am."

"I don't think anyone will notice. Not at first, anyway. I can reach the high stuff for you."

"Maybe I can sit on a phone book," Sammy laughed, "or carry around my nephew's bunk bed ladder to close the blinds. Later I'll be able to clean the inside corners of the microwave in the lunchroom."

"We can get one of those remote control cars to shuttle you around the office," said Wanda.

There was a long pause before Sammy said, "That's not funny."

Wanda stood beside her desk, bit down on her thumb and index finger and let out a shrill whistle. "Listen up," she announced to the office staff, "Sammy's comin' back tomorrow. She's goin' through a rough patch and I don't want anyone givin' her any grief. About anything." She sat back down and resumed typing. Everyone at the office would be kind to Sammy if for no other reason than that they all liked Wanda, who entertained them during lunch with dirty jokes and stories about her near death experience, the conversion event that had made her a believer in the unbelievable. She had been eating taco chips when she keeled over onto a snack table, snapping its spindly aluminum legs. When her sixteen-year old son found her he yelled "Mom!" as if she were deaf and not undergoing a near death experience. After being out for several minutes, she popped into a seated position and yelled, "Jesus Christ, I was dead!" Her son wanted to call her ex-husband, to which Wanda responded, "What, you're trying to kill me again?" Wanda's colleagues loved this story and they loved her. They would, by extension, love Sammy too.

Although no one at work said as much, Sammy could tell by their comments they'd noticed her shrinkage. "Nice dress," they'd say or "New haircut? You look great." They were undoubtedly overcompensating for their shock, reeling from the blow to their expectations of a Sammy who would displace just as much air as the one they knew before her husband had left her. Sammy held her head high and stumbled through the day in what felt like oversized shoes. When she reached for her coffee cup, which had been pushed to the back of the lunchroom cupboard in her absence, a voice from behind said, "Let me get that for you." It was Ned, the payroll clerk, a tall, shy man who had grown accustomed to being summoned from his cubicle by the secretaries to sweep spiders from walls into tissues or to water the ferns that loomed well above their reach. Sammy spun around and looked up at him.

"*Don't* feel sorry for me," she said.

Ned stepped back, flustered. "I was only trying—"

"To help me because I'm short?"

"To help you because I'm *tall*."

"Ah," she said, "you are a cruel man."

"Ma, do you still have my clothes from high school?"

"What, no 'hello, Ma'? No 'How are you, Ma, after forty-nine hours of labor and then a C-section for all my trouble'?"

"I'm sorry. How are you, Ma?"

"Don't ask."

"So do you have my clothes?"

"Of course I do, princess. I pull them from the boxes every night and clutch them to my chest before falling asleep. What am I, a storage unit over here? I gave them to the Salvation Army ages ago." Then panic entered her voice. "The schmuck didn't take your clothes?"

"No, Ma. I told you I'm shrinking. Pretty soon you won't be able to see me."

"Nonsense."

"Cousin Leo walked right past me at Hagelstein's yesterday."

"Leo's a moron."

"You said he was the family genius."

"There's a thin line between genius and insanity, and Leo's got one leg on each side of it. Depends which way the wind is blowing."

"He didn't see me, Ma."

"Good," she said, "then we don't have to invite him to Passover."

Sammy was leaning against the kitchen wall, balanced precariously on her new spike-heeled pumps when David breezed through the front door.

"Hi," she said, her fingers wrapped tightly around the refrigerator handle.

David stared at her so long she grew anxious. "Wow," he said, "you look different."

He then turned toward the bedroom, a suitcase in each hand, and Sammy's fingers slid down the length of the handle until they could barely touch the chrome molding at the bottom. She sat on the floor, removed the stiletto heels and then scampered down the hall toward the bedroom, where she noticed David running his finger along the scratches on the top of the television set.

"You know I still love you," he said without turning, "but I just don't understand you."

Sammy, who was staring at the lines on the bedroom wall, barely heard him. She was wondering if the square root of 9,999 was a whole number or a fraction.

"What?" said a tiny voice she didn't recognize as hers. "What did you say?"

David continued to pack, folding his former life with her into two oversized cases before sweeping past her, almost grazing her with his luggage.

"You didn't even see me, did you?" she yelled.

He continued down the hall, long-strided, silent, and as Sammy heard the front door close with a thud she turned back toward the dresser, on which sat the white rectangle of cardboard. As she ran it through her fingers and tested its heft, she suddenly realized that it was thinner than the cardboard she'd first used to measure herself. This meant that she would have to start over, she knew. But for now she placed the cardboard on her head, snatched the pencil from on top of the TV and leaned firmly against the wall.

RHODA

Steve Fayer

Rhoda, pigtailed, in boy's body and with boy's stride, goes before me, leaning her weight on a branch found at the bottom of the black widow tree, an oak of many limbs on which my grandfather has nailed rungs for climbing.

At age ten, her orange hair deepens to red in the shadows, but when the sun is caught in it, I see that it is really gold extruded by the same alchemistry that has made her female, incomplete of body but with a mind that makes my own brain ache, reasoning that marches leagues ahead of me, imagination that opens windows I have never dreamed onto expanses of wood and grass and meadows and acts of love I would never in a lifetime have experienced. Bubbles float from my brain, like thoughts drawn in comic strips, toward places that only Rhoda can see.

How can things not end and not begin?

Rhoda knows.

If God watches us, what is the quality of his vision?

Rhoda knows.

If he sees us all, how vast is he? Rhoda draws for me his exact dimensions. Until I feel myself surrounded by the sea of his skin.

I am eight years old. And three inches the lesser. She is my cousin. And I pray in the long summer nights that I can watch her and breathe her always, see the daylight touch her in the mystery of her bed, dance naked for her on the bare wood floor, watch her thin-legged embrace of the stool in my grandfather's water closet, and study always her lack of intrusion into the world.

She holds me in her hand and kisses me, and neither of us giggle.

"It is a secret," Rhoda says. And I nod solemnly.

I have two birthdays. The city birthday, celebrated with my mother and father, is three days before Christmas and is drowned in it. Each gift is suspect. For me, or for Jesus, I ask.

My summer birthday is August 2. My grandfather picked it for me, separated with a purpose from the Fourth of July and from Labor Day. It is celebrated with corn on the cob and charcoal-broiled frankfurters.

My mother and father are in the city, and never experience it.

On my eleventh birthday, my grandfather who until then has always loved me and kept me close in to the farm, gives me a baseball and a Ted Williams fielder's glove, and tells me I should play more with the boys in the village.

Rhoda is then thirteen.

I am nine.

"Listen to the naked people," she says.

I dutifully press my ear to the earth.

"They live in the ground," she says. "And are colored blue, and talk in strange languages."

I ache to hear them.

"How did you find them?"

"In the winter," she says, knowing how I envy her the time I am stuck in the city and she runs free on the farm. "A blue man was peeing in the snow."

"What color was it?" I ask.

"Like ink," she says.

I nod, satisfied.

"Look in the hole," she says, pointing with a twig.

I see nothing, only blackness that could be blue.

"See them touching each other?"

"Yes," I say, gasping.

Rhoda lies next to me. Breathes chocolate on my nose. Her long red hair tickles my ears, my forehead, the back of my neck.

"I can hear them," she says. And begins to whisper in my ears words scribbled on city sidewalks.

When I am eleven and she is thirteen, I press my ear to the ground and she giggles above me.

"You're still a baby," she says, and wriggles out of her shirt, and ties it to her waist, and whirls around me in the sun. I reach for her, and she begins to run, longer-legged than me, through the high grass and over rocks, laughing and swinging her loose red hair.

I follow the flash of her pale back through dark, tree-hung trails. Where the ground is fern-covered and dangerous with imagined snakes, she springs at me from behind a tree, arms and legs wide, hands up and all fingers spread, screaming, "Yaaaaaaaaaaaagh," and my boy's heart almost stops.

I trace the beginnings of one thin, gold hair which curls around a flat nipple. It raises like a tiny pink thumb.

"It's a miracle," she says, laughing.

Then she begins chewing on a strand of her long red hair. "You, boy," she says, kicking me hard in the knee. "You mind your manners."

We have a conspiracy of words.

"I see your epidermis," she screams in the front yard.

"I see yours," I giggle.

My grandfather, ignorant, immigrant, ruined by age, limps heavily onto the front porch.

"To hell with such rotten talk," he shouts. *"Shame!"*

Rhoda runs to him shaking tears into her orange hair. "But it's only a word from school," she says.

She leans against my grandfather's chest, weeping.

"You must be good," he whispers. "You must be like a flower," patting her.

At me, he glares man to man, seeing me as he thinks he was, understanding in me all the evil I have not yet imagined.

"Make us proud," she says, as we stand on the porch with my aunt and uncle, all of us waiting for the country taxi to take me back to the station.

Her red hair is cut close to her long, narrow skull. She smokes cigarettes and her teeth are a pale yellow.

"If only the old man could see you," my aunt says. "So proud he would be, of the uniform." The porch creaks under the weight of my grandfather's ghost.

It is late March, there is still snow in the mountains behind the farm, and I have almost seen the winter for the first time, and still long for it although I do not know what good it would do.

The red clay drive is deep with mud, and impassable, and when the car arrives, it waits out on the highway. I kiss my aunt and shake hands with my uncle, and strike out along the dead grass in the middle of the driveway, Rhoda balancing with me.

"Remember what I said," she whispers. "Sleep with a lot of women, and tell me what you learn."

I slide across the leather seat. She leans through the door and with her back to my aunt and uncle kisses me on the lips, the tip of her tongue against my teeth.

"I don't know why I came here," I say. "After all this time."

Rhoda laughs, and leers.

It is the most fearful moment of my life. I am less than two. Rhoda is a freckled, red blur.

"But it's only your shadow," she says.

I suck desperately on the suspender of my sunsuit. I know that she is in league with it.

"Move your arm," Rhoda says.

The thing rears to attack.

"See," she says. "It's *you*."

I begin to cry, blind with despair, liking the warm sting of it. My body shakes. I feel myself making water.

Rhoda deposits in my mouth her own chewed gum, and I discover also the sandy taste of her finger. I stop crying and lift my hand to be led away.

Rhoda always knows. And conditions me to acceptance.

"It's only your shadow," she says again, and as she takes my hand I ponder the whispering music of the word.

"There's something missing in this house," Rhoda says, leaning forward, her breasts suddenly heavy against her sweater. "A joy. A tension."

"Wrong," I say.

"You know what I'm talking about," Rhoda says. "You've given up on everything."

She sprawls in the living room, chain-smoking, smiling yellow-toothed at me, drinking her third whiskey, and I wonder as I have for hours why she felt it necessary to pay this visit.

"I wish I were a child again," she says loudly. "I should be the envy of all women. It was a wonderful childhood."

I am astounded by her. She makes no judgments, is removed from all knowledge of sin. I see her in my grandfather's meadows, an orphan running with wolves, suckling at foxes.

"You saw no evil in it?" I ask.

"The only evil," she says, "is that children become old."

I pull myself up from the chair.

"I'll bet," she says behind me. "That you often imagine it's my body, not Susan's."

"Wrong," I whisper.

In the morning, my four-year-old son takes his cousin Rhoda by the hand and walks with her down our winding suburban street, the two of them scattering the dry, fresh snow. I watch them through the window and wonder what they are waving their arms about, what stories she is telling.

Behind me in the guest bedroom the whine of the vacuum cleaner stops, and my wife complains through the open door that Rhoda's orange hair is everywhere, caught in the vacuum brushes, clinging to wool blankets.

"It's red. You notice it more," I say stupidly, and walk into the first floor bathroom and there lock myself in. In the tub, I find two short curls of orange wire and lift them to the light to see them turn color. Should I save them? I still believe in her, and feel all at once, in the scented humidity of the bathroom, the god sea whose vastness she had once described and, looking down from a giant limb into a red scar, shiver. My grandfather is old and fuddled, with snow-white hair. I am twelve, and she is fourteen, and, at her invitation, am perched in the black widow tree, frozen above them, watching.

U.F.O.

Claude Clayton Smith

lso, whenever we made love—right after her shivering liquid climax—she would roll off of me and say, "Thank you, and goodnight from all of us here at WPDQ News."

Then, within seconds, she was fast asleep ("Isn't that supposed to be the *guy's* role?" I asked her once. "Wham, bam, thank you, m'am?") and snoring. She had been born with a condition known as *unilateral choanal atresia*. Quite simply, she couldn't breathe through one nostril, and so she had a tendency to snore, mouth agape, whenever her good nostril was closed off by the pressure of the pillow. (She confessed to this abnormality on our last night together because, as she put it, I "would understand." She told me many things that night, much as we tell our life stories to perfect strangers in airports and train stations. But I wasn't a perfect stranger and I didn't understand.) Ursula Ford Owens. *Fordie*.

Her name was linked, according to one of her "former fellows," to Henry Ford himself. But the connection was never proved. There *was* money, however, or seemed to be— her Corvette, her summer home on a vast lake in northern Michigan, her semesters in Europe (a bout at the Sorbonne). But any claim to a large inheritance—the "dowry," as she called it—was based, finally (according to another of her "former fellows"), on rumor. Rumors attributable to Fordie herself.

She liked to sail on that big lake in Michigan in a little sailboat, a Sunfish—a triangular sail (her initials monogrammed in red above a faded Greenpeace symbol) attached to a kind of surfboard, and she is said to have made love once out there, right in the middle of the lake, to a lifeguard from the yacht club who had the perseverance to swim the distance. (Word had it that she simply pointed him back to shore, the lifeguard, after the long swim, too tuckered to perform.) They had drifted behind a small island, out of the range of the binoculars of the old biddies back on the sundeck...

And don't feel sorry for her because of her nose. It was a perfectly lovely nose (the defective nostril an *internal* aberration), a freckle-tipped nose that turned up of its own accord as well as at the bidding of its mistress.

We had met (that last time) in Iowa, on a bitter cold and snowy January night. Fordie was en route to New York from California for a reunion of her sorority (she belonged to three—one at each of the schools she'd attended). I was en route to California from New York. We had agreed to spend the night together somewhere in between, mid-way across the country, but I came up short, initially slowed by a blizzard in Illinois. Fortunately, we had drawn up contingency plans, rubbing noses finally ("like little Eskimos," Fordie said) in the outskirts of Iowa City (a little motel, the name of which escapes me, on Route 6—a bleak stretch of gas stations, Laundromats, and fast food places not too far from the Interstate—still ablaze in Christmas lights).

Fordie's forte (according to *this* "former fellow") was her uncanny ability to make the guy on her arm feel certain that he alone was her destiny. There was no guile in this, no art. I am convinced that it was unintentional. She had a natural charm and warmth that flew out to those about her, disarmed them, and reeled them right in.

Once, as I called at her apartment to pick her up for a Broadway show, the door was opened by some handsome, strapping lad who was "just leaving." I remember the way he smiled—as if he felt sorry for me because, although Fordie was mine for the evening (and perhaps the night), he had had her all afternoon. His smile said he was sure she'd soon get over me, leaving her all for himself. But my smile, too, was condescending. Poor fellow. Didn't he know that Fordie was a "night person"? How good of her to entertain the brute of an afternoon.

So I felt as I checked in at that Iowa motel, drawing a wide grin from the hunk of a desk clerk. So I felt as I carried my suitcase to the room where Fordie waited. So I felt the next morning when I woke and she was gone. And so I feel now, regardless.

"The 'Vette is definitely not engineered for winter, *mon petit*," Fordie said, as I ducked inside and closed the door against the snow and wind.

"Nor is the Nova, " I assured her. "Nor is the Nova."

Then we hopped into the sack. The sheets were icy. My feet went numb.

Fordie was silent.

"How was your New Year's?" I said finally.

"My parents are getting a divorce."

"I thought your parents were dead."

"Same difference, *mon petit*. Same difference."

She had had a tubal ligation over Christmas, having convinced herself that "this is no world to bring a child into." All that poverty and everything. And now she was depressed because she had suddenly decided that having a baby was the only real act of hope against the future. So she was going to have the operation reversed in New York, right after her reunion.

"Look," I said, surprised at my own boldness. "Let's go to your place in Michigan. Open up the summerhouse for the winter. Chop wood, go fishing through the ice."

But no, she could "smell a rat" in that scheme. She was positive that I was going to be a great lawyer one day ("You *are* in law school, aren't you?" she asked, interrupting herself. I wasn't, but it didn't seem to matter.) She didn't want to obstruct my "straight and narrow path to fame and fortune."

One of the earliest photos I have of Fordie (a Polaroid, taken on the sundeck of that yacht club in Michigan, *circa* her college graduation) shows her to be much shorter than I ever realized. She couldn't have been, in reality, more than five-two or five-three, and yet she always struck me as much taller than that, so long and willowy, her yellow hair (she was a bottle blonde) always cut opposite the fashion—short, when long straight hair was "in," long and straight when others were almost bald. (The photo is not a very attractive one, Fordie squinting into the glare off the lake. She was not, in fact, photogenic. "I'm much better," she insisted, "live and in person." Rather in the sort of way that Zelda Fitzgerald drove men crazy.)

She was small-breasted, her body lean and firm, the most delicious part the small of her back, which seemed made for my spread hand. I was irked once to learn, from Fordie herself, that someone else had loved that very spot. *"The small of your back,"* she recited to me one night, *"is a deep, still pool beneath the waterfall of your spine."* She was standing above me naked on the bed, one hand on her ass, as if doing an ad for Sealy Posturepedic. "That's from a poem by a former fellow, *mon petit*. What bullshit! I couldn't face him after that."

Any display of sentiment made her uncomfortable. She preferred the world in a hard-ass, wise-ass way. And yet I recall her bursting into tears, watching television one afternoon, over a schmaltzy rerun of "Little House on the Prairie." Those ads for Kodak moments killed her too.

She was basically a hardliner, playing hardball when she had to, uncompromising on certain issues. The quickest way to become one of her "former fellows" was to offer her a toke of marijuana or a snort of cocaine. Her only real vice was drinking (rum & Coke, always rum & Coke: "The caffeine picks me up," she explained to me one day, "and the alcohol brings me down, so I wind up, you see, right where I started.") The habit began in high school, according to a girlfriend who had been a cheerleader with Fordie, when word got around that she had "gone down" on the captain of the football team. Soon after, she quit cheerleading and took up rum & Coke.

And to the "former fellow" who claimed that Fordie, finally, was "dumb as shit," her high school cheerleader girlfriend pointed out that Fordie had made the National Honor Society. *As a junior.* But that was more years ago than I care to remember.

Once, at the *second* college she attended, one of those all-girl eastern finishing schools ("It certainly finished *me*," Fordie was fond of saying), Fordie was made chairperson of the annual Bloodmobile drive, setting a record that stands to this day—thirty-nine percent participation among the undergraduates. Yet she herself did not donate a single pint, and when the Dean of Students called attention to the obvious hypocrisy, Fordie became indignant. "I give blood," she snapped, *"every day!"* Then she quit the campaign, failed to return in the fall, and the participation fell to thirteen percent.

"Don't we get any *heat* with this room," I said, shuddering beneath the sheets in icy Iowa. The temperature felt about forty degrees.

"I've got my love to keep me warm," Fordie said.

Now how the hell does one respond to *that*?

I put my hands on her breasts—as soft and white as marshmallows (and to my tongue they tasted just as sweet). But Fordie never liked them. Her breasts, that is. She was the first to admit that she wished she were buxom. ("Big tits!" she was fond of saying. "I want big tits!) I walked in on her once in her apartment (I had a key in those days) rolling a set of barbells under the bed. She had been, she admitted, "pumping iron" into her "cleavage." True love, she admitted too, made her feel stacked.

"How do you feel now?" I asked in Iowa.

"Flat-chested. Absolutely flat."

The bed in her apartment was actually a bunk bed. Sometimes she slept on top, sometimes below. Sometimes, after we made love, she would request that I sleep "upstairs," sometimes *vice versa*. And sometimes we slept together (Fordie conking out and snoring), but the bed was uncomfortable for two. She said that the bunk bed had been left by her former roommate, a Dallas debutante who had married a chain of pharmacies, but a neighbor across the hall swore that she had seen it being delivered the week after Fordie's roommate moved out.

"I'm going to ask you something now," Fordie said in Iowa, "and I want you to answer me truthfully. OK?"

"Of course, Fordie. You can trust me. I mean—"

"Are my roots showing?"

"Your *what*?"

"My roots!"

She bent her chin to her chest, stabbing a finger madly at the severe part in her tangled hair. The yellow along the part *was*, in fact, dark in several spots. Orange and brown elsewhere.

"A bit," I said.

"I knew it!"

She got up and flipped on the TV. The only channel with any clear reception had a test pattern. "Bulls-eye!" Fordie said, leaving it on. "Testing—one, two three, four." She hopped quickly back into bed (she *was* cold—I could tell). "This is a test. I repeat. *This is a test.*"

She wrapped her chilly fingers around my dick, and what was left of a semi-erection turned as limp as a wad of uncooked bacon.

Fordie had been assaulted once—molested, actually—in the elevator of her apartment building. She put up a fight, screaming wildly (forgetting all the Karate moves she had once tried so hard to perfect: "Out the window they went," she later chirped, "like startled birds!"). Fortunately, the elevator had stopped at the very next floor and an old woman came on board with a Mexican Chihuahua that, excited by the fracas, started nipping at the heels of the attacker, who promptly fled. The next day Fordie got herself a Doberman pinscher, whom she called "Bear," a ferocious animal that was killed by a bus several weeks later. But she didn't mind. In the brief time they had spent together, the dog had proved "a pain-in-the-ass to care for."

What struck me about all this—and what is to Fordie's everlasting credit—is that the attack left no scars. It didn't mess up her mind. She took it in stride, without any psychological problems. And our lovemaking—for a while after the fact, at least—was fantastic.

Towards midnight (I had arrived in Iowa around eight p.m.) Fordie got thirsty.

"There's a Coke machine in the parking lot, *mon petit*" (its red plastic front, I had noticed on my way to the room, cracked by the cold). Would I be so kind?

I would. (Fool that I was.)

"And get some ice," Fordie added. (That was cruel.) "There's an ice machine right beside it. I've got a bottle of rum in my suitcase. I'm thirsty. Let's tie one on."

I broke out some plastic cups from the bathroom, their sanitary wrappers striking me (frozen beyond belief from my jaunt outside) as more than sterile.

"Would you do the honors?" Fordie said, knees up, bedspread to her chin. She nodded at her open suitcase in the far corner—one of those cardboard jobs you see in Broadway musicals, plastered with stickers from her European travels. Its tarnished snaps stood at attention like upright thumbs. The bottle of rum (dark green, with a black label whose name I forget) was tucked between several bulky sweaters (hand-knitted in Norway) and half a dozen jars of Oil of Olay (one without its lid, perfuming the air).

I broke the seal. We drank heartily, the initial shock of the icy liquid replaced, eventually, by a warm glow in the belly. We laughed. I got up to turn off the test pattern ("Don't you dare!" Fordie warned), then left it on.

I frowned and shook my head. Fordie, Fordie.

Later, quite drunk, I mentioned that I would like for her to meet my parents. When I got back from California. When she was done with all her business in New York.

She sobered instantly, the look on her face a mixture of disappointment, disbelief, and chagrin. If our "relationship" ever had a turning point, that was it. I didn't know then (spilling more rum into my plastic cup in a hasty attempt to appear nonchalant) that that would be our last time together.

"Just kidding," I said finally when Fordie didn't speak. Then she curled up like a cat and feigned sleep.

I listened to her feigning sleep all night long (she didn't once snore), succumbing at last to enormous fatigue just before sunrise, when—by some miracle—the heat came on and the room turned quite balmy.

When I woke she was gone, of course. Suitcase and Corvette. And no note. But on my Nova (which wouldn't start until I called the Triple-A, using my father's card number which I had jotted down and tucked into my wallet once for an emergency such as this) I found remnants of a parking ticket (the offended yellow hydrant concealed beneath a mound of frozen slush), torn like confetti and frozen to the windshield, the tiny pieces—as I touched them to my lips—smelling faintly of Oil of Olay.

HISTORY

Marilyn Harris Kriegel

Virginia knew that getting a sexually transmitted disease at 62 signified more than a moment's bad judgment. Yet no matter how she ran the information through her tortured mind it left her dumb. More unfamiliar than the HIV virus replicating its way through her body was her sudden inability to categorize, or fix the situation.

Distracted, she sat at her desk trying to assemble an agenda for the History Department's annual budget meeting. This time of year was fraught with fear: The younger staff afraid of being fired; the tenured terrified that prized classes would be reassigned to the more published and popular; the petty politics of possession, greed, position and power all of which had been a source of amusement and challenge to her, today seemed trivial.

At the top of the page she wrote AGENDA. Under Roman numeral I she wrote Death. When she wondered, in a year? Longer? Should she resign? Wait out the disease? Wait out the predatory professors already competing to step into her place of supremacy and power when she retired.

Virginia had worked long, hard and carefully to secure the leadership of the department. In every way possible she had made sure her position was unassailable. Yet, she had not covered her flank. She could not complete one thought without her mind drifting away to the diagnosis.

Year after year she cautioned her undergraduates that one small digression from an otherwise circumspectly lived life could radically change the course of history but had never applied it to herself. Christ, she thought, and then ran into a dead end, a pile up of clichés: it wasn't fair, it wasn't worth it, and it wasn't what she had planned for her last years at the University. She would have asked why me, but the banality of the question was too humiliating to pursue.

Mortified, she told no one. Her colleagues noted her distraction with disinterest assuming she once again was immersed in research. Her closed door along the corridor of offices indicated work in progress. There was no need of a sign, a closed-door read do not disturb.

Virginia had read Gideon's letter, written on Marriott Hotel stationary, in disbelief. Then, accepting his advice, she drove herself South of Market Street to the clinic where she exchanged her blood for a number. They were kind when she returned to receive what she thought of as "the death sentence". They tried to explain that HIV generally could be managed with some relatively insignificant changes in her daily routines. They were full of pamphlets and suggestions, but she could not wait to leave and be alone.

She drove immediately across the city to the Great Highway to walk the long empty beach in solitude. She embraced the comfort of the infinite horizon while she sorted through what might be left for her of life.

What is left in anyone's life? What does any older woman have to look forward to? Perhaps this is simply a gift, she thought, a foreshortening of the inevitable, the other shoe finally dropping. Perhaps, she should be grateful instead of frightened, humiliated, and alone. Nothing she could think of had ever left her feeling as abandoned as this.

Virginia continued to return to the beach for solace and to contemplate her alternatives. Regret was not one of them, history was made by moving in the only direction possible, forward. Nothing could be undone. The fact of HIV was incontrovertible. Her work had always been the study of that which could not be changed, but which with luck and persistence, could possibly be understood. She would think about her own life as history, look for undiscovered patterns and then she would write the last chapter. There was research to be done. And, there was swimming.

Years before Virginia had taken to swimming laps regularly at the university natatorium, loving the rhythmic repetition and profound isolation. Now she bought a wetsuit and began to swim in the ocean, sometimes at Stinson Beach, occasionally just beyond the Gate at Kirby's Cove. Friends thought of it as a fitness craze born of vanity, a last ditch effort to defeat the ravages of gravity. She thought of the vast ocean as the beginning and end of history, as her escape.

Every afternoon she swam out as far as her breath allowed, and then after resting on the swell, turned back, riding the waves to shore. It was a new way of life for her, one in which chance became a dominant player. At any moment the weather could change, or the wind or the swells. She could over-estimate her strength, or underestimate the undertow. She began teaching herself to live on the edge of the danger she had for so long carefully tried to avoid.

Virginia thought of a swim to the Farralon Islands as an elegant final solution. She rehearsed for it, leaving her car keys and clothes in a neat pile on the shore. Of course, she knew she could never make it but if she became strong perhaps she would be able to swim out far enough to become dinner for one of the Great Whites that cruised the north coast for seal. She could become a part of a shark's history, or simply sink to the bottom, an anonymous woman from the end of the millennium.

At the same time she rehearsed for her death she researched life. In spite of having in the past frowned on what she called the web's plethora of misinformation, she found her way into the intricacies of HIV protocols. She had chided her students for having little respect for history because, at some limbic level, they believed that it could be rewritten in blogs, cut and pasted into posterity. Nevertheless she read everything she could find, grateful for the volumes of material she digested in the privacy of her den.

She sat at her desk staring at the piece of paper. Perhaps, she thought, running the end of her freshly sharpened pencil back and forth under the word *Death*, nothing would happen until after she retired. Perhaps she would get away with… she laughed. Murder.

Up until the phone call from Gideon, Virginia had lived a scholar's life, studying, writing and teaching, her area of expertise, the role of women, in particular widows, during the Civil War. From the sanctuary of her position at the university she investigated another century's debacles, other women's tragedies, terrible times rich in pathos, replete in dramatic values. The boundaries she had drawn so precisely around her own life, until that night, had provided the security that is found in consistency. Predictability. Only twice in twenty-five years had she invited a student to visit her home.

She pushed her old, comfortable chair away from the desk to pace, searching for a clue as to how Gideon had so easily penetrated her defense.

He had phoned, a voice from the past, deeper than she had recalled. Sweeter. Yes, sweet. She paused recollecting his soft appealing drawl. Damn she said circling back to her desk only to stare at the one word she had written under the heading, Agenda. She turned away to the window. Outside were all the signs of a West Coast spring: tulips, daffodils, acacia and broom. Inside, her office felt airless and small.

Yes, she had told him, she remembered him–his exquisite paper about the singing soldiers, the ballads of the Civil War.

What have you been doing? Music? Where? Yes, of course, let's have coffee.

Let's have coffee. Let's have coffee? What had she been thinking? What had his call awakened? Why hadn't she met him in any one of the myriad coffee shops surrounding campus? What had she wanted enough to invite the enemy behind the lines?

Invasion. Loss: the inevitable consequence of an incursion. Virginia leaned her forehead against the windowpane, the cool glass against her brow providing a brief respite as she parsed each moment of the formidable late afternoon.

Within the hour Gideon had been standing at her door. Taller than she'd expected (or was she shrinking with the years?) More commanding than the undergraduates who deferred to her, he had walked in tossed his well-worn leather bomber jacket over a chair and sat down as if it was his living room and she, still standing, his student. "Well," he had said in bit of a hum, "It's been too long."

Virginia thought about the agenda that needed her attention. She was familiar with the pull to her desk, the urgency to attend to the task at hand. She had relied for years on her ability to focus, to put aside any distraction. Not now, she cautioned herself. Not now. Now, she would stand at the window and watch the sunlight ebb across the campus, casting shadows. Now, she would remember.

Gideon had followed her, leaned over her at her desk where she went to search for the lyrics of a tune she thought he would like. She had wanted to give him something. He had only touched her shoulder, breathed against her neck, but when she turned to face him, to make space for herself, he had seemed to envelope her.

I was off balance, Virginia thought. I must have held on to him for balance. She could not understand her complete absence of resistance when he held her. I must have wanted... what? She thought she had turned to Gideon the way poor Sergeant Absalom Peters had led his rag-tag Tennessee brigade north to certain death, writing in his diary that to retreat would have been the greater loss.

Virginia smiled, embarrassed at the memory of having desired Gideon. She had made no protest, allowed him each step. After years without touch she wondered if her body had simply rebelled. Eddie had always made the point that revolution was natural. Why hadn't she known? Why was it such a surprise?

The incomparable couple: Eddie and Virginia. College sweethearts they had found each other as freshman at one of the great state universities. By the end of the first week of school they discovered they shared not only exact schedules, but also were living on the same floor of the freshman dorm. Their meeting and then meeting again and again catapulted them into a mystery of coincidence and the excitement of waiting to see what would happen next. They seemed destined for each other and were happy to cooperate with circumstance and become inseparable. For four years they studied together, slept together, and enjoyed friends and food together. They swore they were not competitive; they complemented and goaded each other on to the top of their class graduating with identical grade point averages and applying to the same graduate schools as a married couple.

History scholars, they came to the crossroads of their young married lives in the sixties, in the community of small cottages on Leland and Stanford streets named for the founder of the prestigious private University they thought they'd take by storm.

Nothing had prepared them for the possibility of paths more divergent than the particular aspects of American history each chose to investigate. Virginia immersed herself in the study of the Civil War because a country divided against itself was something she intuitively understood.

Eddie identified with revolution and the philosophers of the Enlightenment.

He teased that America would have remained a British colony if it had been up to Virginia and she'd countered with the accusation that had he lived in the mid 1800's he would have been a Northern Copperhead, taking, the repugnant to her, moral position that the South should secede and the country split in two. Hey man, no problem. You do it your way—we'll do it ours.

Their differences deepened. Eddie discovered lysergic acid diethylamide and though he tried to convince her that he was participating in a major paradigm shift, his interest in the exploration of consciousness raising drugs frightened her.

"God woman," he cried, "You want to study history, I want to make it."

It was inevitable that they would part she to the academy, research, authorship and tenure, he to the ecstatic possibilities of pure Sandoz acid and a quest to find within himself Rousseau's noble savage, uncorrupted by society.

When Eddie died ten years later of a heroin overdose in Mexico, she had mourned not her loss but his choice. Now It amazed her that in one unpremeditated evening almost thirty years later she'd accomplished what she had spent her life avoiding. Oh Eddie, she thought, you would have appreciated the irony.

Then Gideon phoned. He would be back in San Francisco the next day. Could he come? Would she see him? She listened to the green gray depths of his voice the way she had been learning to read the ocean. "Yes," she said. "After four." Tomorrow was an intensely busy day she told him, starting off with the most difficult faculty meeting of the year. Then she would need a few hours—a few errands to run, some exercise. "Exercise? Oh, I swim", she told him. "I'm an endurance swimmer." Virginia smiled, shifted her weight on to one hip and lowered her eyes like a young girl. "Gideon," she whispered, "come with me. I'd like that, just the two of us, I'll pick up a wet suit and goggles for you. It's exhilarating, you'll love it and then," . . . her eyes focused inward to the vastness of the sea and reaching for a word and finding it in the vernacular of her young students, she grinned, "and then, whatever."

SMALL DEAD MONKEY

Josh Woods

October 26, 1956
Broadmoor, California

Small dead monkey discovered in tomato garden at home of Mrs. Faye Swanson. Clothesline, 4x4 inch, splintered, presumably struck by the animal when falling from the sky. Airport spokesman reported no planes in the area had been carrying monkeys that night.

—The Broadmoor Dispatch

She was enthralled at how his little paws curled, frozen in a grasp as if for some lost toy, some absent parental finger. Infants hold this way: their little hands clamp, taut cord muscles under pudding soft skin. As if their need for a mother—desperate—to never leave them channels strength into their small bodies, channels down strength like bolts of lightning, those sudden columns of God. Channels down strength in direct plummets from the strange halls of Heaven.

"Faye?"
"Kitchen."

"Hello to you, too. What's all this?"

"Leftovers in the oven."

"What's all this? Out there."

"They're taking photos of my monkey."

"In the garden? They're taking photos?"

"I think it was only a baby."

"Did they talk to you?"

"It was a boy."

"Did they talk to you?"

"Yes."

"I'm going to go talk to them. What's all this about a monkey?"

"If I held three tomatoes in my hands, I could have been holding him. He's that small."

Their Chevy was a steam engine, the radiator sucking two gallons of water at a time in Evansville, then St. Louis, then Kansas City, then north of Topeka, then so on and so on into the west. Faye wanted to wear her big sunglasses the entire way, even at night, and Tim said that he could always tell the difference between when she rested her eyes and when she slept. Her bottom lip pouts when she sleeps.

Faye finger-tapped AM tunes onto her belly and propped her bare feet out of the passenger window and wiggled her piggies through hundreds and hundreds of miles of wind. Angels run this way.

Tim said that the first big bug to splatter into her foot would make her scream bloody murder. A sharp one hit like yellow yolk, and she screamed bloody murder. He laughed. She laughed. He needed to stop making her laugh because she had to pee—the baby was making her have to pee a lot more.

San Francisco. Breathe in through the mouth. Lick the air. Ah, San Francisco. A fresh place at the end of the earth before the globe turns on itself and begins again. She and

Tim would begin again. They would start a new calendar, just a few unmentioned months off from nine, and in a year or two the family back home would never be able to tell the difference, and the air back in Kentucky, inside her father's house, would taste far less bitter. Here, the air had been salted by the great cosmic Cook from His golden kitchen — salted by the Master of ingredients who, unlike Faye, never drops a thing.

> *For my own part I would as soon be descended from that heroic little monkey... as from a savage who delights to torture his enemies, offers up bloody sacrifices, practices infanticide without remorse, treats his wives like slaves, knows no decency, and is haunted by the grossest superstitions.*

> —Charles Darwin, *The Descent of Man*

Tim seemed the most decent of men. Sure he wanted to drive her out to the hill overlooking his campus, cut the headlights, and descend onto her just like the high school boys wanted to. But she allowed Tim because he talked rationally at her. She surrendered the sonnets of her someday, shining knight — off to the clouds with them. *Tim* told her why her father succumbed to the ever-present lure of ancient irrationality. Worshipped it, required it like a junkie. Opiate of the masses. She learned that although her father was a savage of sorts, he was surely not an evil man because evil, again, was a fabrication of his system. A system of superstitions.

After meeting Tim — being with Tim — little things changed. Dinners with her father changed:

"More."

"More of what?"

"Girl, I said more."

"Yes, sir, but more what?"

"Faye. Do I need to teach you again about your Eve tongue? Your forked woman tongue?"

"I can't know for certain what your needs are, so I can't truthfully answer that question, and it is wrong for me to speak untruthfully. Shouldn't we all say just what we mean?"

"Potatoes."

"Yes, sir. They are. Baked in orange juice, wrapped in tin foil, just as you prefer." She felt like Tim's Socrates. Forcing her father to be obvious. To unveil.

"I mean, *pass* the potatoes."

"Yes, sir." She won.

And she won, and she won again. Small pebbles of a mountain victory. Tim spoke through her, and the balance of control slid grain by grain to her side of the house. Surely a father of such great faith could appreciate the movement of a mountain at the scale of a mustard seed.

Or perhaps he simply appreciated the patience of mountains.

How else could he have known if he had not been waiting for it—suspecting, but biding his time? How did he know she had been crying in the bathroom that day? How did he know she had tossed the calendar and the pen to the tile floor and held, trembling, the unblemished pad of cotton? So small in her hands. How did he know exactly when—exactly when—to strike at her?

Tim, I think I have to keep him. I have to. Go back out there and tell them they can't take him."

"It really is a monkey. Can you believe that? Actual "monkey."

"Tell them they can't."

"Did you see what it did to the clothesline? The little thing must have been frozen like a rock. Or frozen inside a chunk of ice; now that might make sense. Of course. From an airplane."

"Tell those men that I am keeping him."

"What? Surely we should leave it to them. The officials, honey. You don't have any idea if it's diseased or not. You have to think about your health first."

"Tim, you let them take my baby. They will not take *him* too."

Faye knelt in the dry dirt. The nape of her neck could feel Tim, back there at a distance, whispering and exchanging bewildered, excusing looks with the photographers from *The Broadmoor Dispatch*. Most likely exchanging cash as well since their engines started back up and began pulling away. A splinter from that broken cross of a clothesline was stabbing into the skin of Faye's knee, but it didn't matter if she bled just a little into the earth. It would only help the tomatoes grow more red and robust.

But her poor, small monkey was as wan as sand—his fur nearly the same color as the rubbery skin around his little mouth. And he was so very fetal. The rounded, fluffed end of his tail almost touched his brow, as if he had tried to turn in on himself to begin again. The soil beneath him had darkened with his melted ice, and Faye knew that his ice, his water, was meant to sink into the ground of her garden and no one else's. He could easily have fallen 20 feet over in the onion and chive rows of her neighbor who still remained on her porch, on the phone, breaking the privacy of this moment. But he didn't fall into the neighbor's garden. No, he was meant for Faye's garden, his water meant for her soil, and under the earthy surface, the trickles of his water wove around roots and over mole tunnels to meet with the trickles of her own blood. And together the trickles formed a stream. His water remembering a distant Heaven, her blood remembering a dead son, and together their stream would drive straight down toward the center of the earth as if it had gushed from the ribs of Christ himself. And no one would ever know this except for Faye and her small, dead monkey.

Her father stood motionless in the doorframe of the kitchen—the most logical place to stand in the event of an earthquake according to Tim. And the earth still seemed to shake beneath her, even here outside of the bathroom, in the kitchen, in front of that radiating, expectant oven. Her hands still trembled, even though she now held a wooden spoon and cradled an old mixing bowl.

She planned on baking a German chocolate cake for dessert in hopes that he would both delight in the taste and distract himself by railing against Germany and all the atheists of Europe. As if she could find shelter at the center of a storm. A fragile plan, but a plan nonetheless.

Her father watched her. Watched her. He said, in almost a whisper, "Don't drop that bowl."

All of Faye's words were stuck at the wet base of her lungs. Uttering a single sentence would make her burst again into tears. She couldn't reveal anything, not in front of him, so she balanced her brittle silence like a lump on the back of her tongue.

"Your hands don't look steady. That was my grandmother's bowl. She was a forthright woman. Hard worker. No secrets." Now he did actually whisper, his voice creaking like a slow rocking chair. "Don't drop it, Faye. Don't drop it, Faye. Don't drop it, Faye."

For a moment, she had clarity and calmness enough to allow rational thought into her mind: Just how did he know how to break her? How did he know exactly when?

"Don't drop it, Faye."

Then everything broke.

And behold a great red dragon, having seven heads and ten horns, and seven crowns upon his heads. And his tail drew the third part of the stars of heaven, and did cast them down to the earth: and the dragon stood before the woman which was ready to deliver, for to devour her child as soon as it was born.

—The Revelation, 12:3-4

The doctors and Tim talked about her condition as if she were not lying on the bed in front of them. Tim tussled and twisted the top of his own hair; the doctors kept nodding, then shaking, their heads, the white room lights dancing weirdly off their metal headpieces and shiny framed glasses. They seemed to hover over only one of the choices as if it were an inescapable revelation, and they took turns repeating: We don't have a choice. We have no choice. We don't have a choice.

She called, "Tim?"

"Shush. Shhhhh." Tim swooped down to her, scooped her arm in his, and petted her hair away from her eyes. "Quiet now, baby. Shhhh."

"Tim, I know what y'all are talking about. Do *not don't* let them."

"Baby, honey, any other option would require a miracle. A *miracle*, Faye. There is no other option."

"He's my baby."

"What we're talking about is your life. It's your life we're talking about. And it's not a *he*, baby; at least no one knows, anyway. I know things are fuzzy to you right now, but trust me. It's your life against impossible odds. We're talking about smack down out of the clear blue, falling star, impossible odds, honey. You have to let me do what's best."

"But I believe in miracles."

"You're on morphine."

She set an unused round hatbox beside her monkey's little body, and she removed the lid evenly, carefully. Then she laid a hand towel over him and softly shoveled her arm under to lift him. She swaddled him tightly then propped him in the crook of her elbow.

With her fingertip she petted his hair away from his closed, nutshell eyes. But the hair returned to its own pattern of near-swirls.

She lowered him onto his side in the hatbox, and grains of dirt fell from her forearm and scattered in dry taps across the bottom of the box.

As she carried her monkey in his hatbox inside the house, Tim stood back and talked rationally at her. She remained silent, and the farther she walked from Tim, the more his questions sprouted into sharp warnings. The more "Shouldn't you reconsider this" turned into "Stop. Come here, right now."

Without saying so, she wished, then, that some shining knight would descend from the clouds too, and that it would slay Tim.

The voice came out of a heaven-white cloud that smelled cold like rubbing alcohol.

"You made it through everything just fine."

"My baby?"

"*You* made it through just fine, Mrs. Swanson. The procedure went as planned, and we're very pleased with the results."

She said, "Dead."

"You made it through just fine."

"He's hitting me in the stomach."

"No one is hitting you. You are under some pain, and you need to rest."

"It was my father. All because he hit me in the stomach. I dropped it and he hit me and hit me in the stomach. Isn't it?"

"No, no. Only natural complications, like we discussed. It wasn't from any trauma, I promise you. It's just a thing that happens, naturally. It's biology."

"That's Tim."

There is grandeur in this view of life, with its several powers, having been originally breathed by the Creator into a few forms or into one; and that, whilst this planet has gone cycling on according to the fixed law of gravity, from so simple a beginning endless forms most beautiful and most wonderful have been, and are being evolved.

—Charles Darwin, *The Origin of Species*

What species of monkey is he? It seemed rude not to know—un-motherly in fact. She had locked the bedroom door and now knelt beside the bed, elbows propped on the mattress beside her monkey in his hatbox, and she leafed through the pages of Tim's book for the answer. For all the brimstone she had heard about this book growing up, and for all the praise she had heard since Tim, she figured there would have been more to it. Surely it would have exhaustive charts of all possible species; instead she found one underlined sentence at its very end, and instead of answering her question, the passage changed it.

What species of monkey am I?

She had been fixed to this planet in accordance with gravity her entire life. She had cycled around the gravity of her father, whose weight bent the air around him, whose soul was so dense that it seemed to pull the very blood out of her. She had cycled around the gravity of Tim, whose brain sent her into orbit through space, leaving her unable to touch any anchored body. And every gravity that moved her had only accumulated. It solidified in layers over her, could have been counted in years like the rings of a tree except the layers that weighed her down were as transparent as ice. Blurred, indistinct, cold. And within her block of gravity, she knew she was not his species of monkey. She could never have been any wonderful form of life from the sky.

But there is a grandeur in the way a womb wraps every living creature into the same curve. A common form.

The Creator's great nostrils had inflated the atmosphere, had filled her stomach with breath not unlike the way her monkey was filled—filled with enough breath to keep him floating in the air until October 26th. Until he was pulled down to the planet by Faye's gravity alone. A primordial, common breath had remained in both of them until they could converge again, here. Now.

The door hammered the room with noise.

"Faye. Open this thing."

The door quaked.

"Faye, I want to think this over with you. We can bury it if you want. I'll even make a little cross for it if I have to, but it is not staying in this house. Faye? Faye! You are being completely irrational. Faye!"

She took the hatbox with her into the closet, wedged the door shut, and burrowed deep into the cave of gowns and raincoats. Blackness. With her entire body, she encircled his round box. She lowered her head near him and breathed his soil odor deep into her nostrils. The voice from the bedroom door was now only a distant muffle. The dark was absolute.

Her father stood over her. She could hear the fumes pouring from his mouth.

He said, "It's over now, girl."

He was right. Even though the pain lingered, kept her curled tightly on the kitchen floor, it was over. She had ridden his violence out until its end.

The rumbles in the distance could have been the bedroom door. It could have been Tim. It could have been that his foot followed the tossed door, and he caught himself. Hunched over in still tension like a hungry savage. Standing in the doorframe in the middle of his earthquake. An earthquake that could force the upheaval of every piece of ground and turn it all on itself again.

Her father said, "I shouldn't even have to bring the rod to you like this. You shouldn't even have secrets in the first place so sinful that you'd take a beating to keep them.

Not any daughter of mine. It don't make any sense that you should be under my roof any more."

The kitchen tile squeaked against her face as she nodded. He made perfect sense.

The closet door opened and the splash of light broke her eyes. On the closet floor, she curled tighter around her monkey's box and said, "You can't take him. Goddamn you, Tim, you can't take him."

"Jesus, Faye. Look at you." Tim knelt and crawled closer to her.

She flinched.

"What are you doing? Faye, look at me in the eyes. Look at us. What the hell are we doing?"

"If you hadn't opened that door to let the air in, he would have started to move. He would have touched my nose with his little cold palm. Would have wiggled his fingers."

"What?"

"He was a miracle."

"We need to get you to a hospital. This is not how you are. This is not how we are."

"Maybe, but everything's changed now. The evolution is dead and gone."

"That's not what evolution means, Faye. That doesn't make any sense. Nothing has changed at all except that you have a dead animal in a box. Listen, I want to give you a minute and calm down. I know everything must seem fuzzy to you right now, but I'm not going to drag you out of here or take that monkey out of your hands or anything because you need to show me that you can do this right now, all right? You need to decide how this is going to end."

"It's already ended, and everything's changed."

A LONG WAY FROM DERBYSHIRE

Jane Bradley

He hadn't touched her yet, but she knew he wanted to. She could tell by the way he had kept his eyes on her back in the restaurant, watched as she dipped her fork in the *fungi crostini*, spread the mixture of mushroom, garlic and cream on the toasted bread tip. He had leaned forward, just a little, when she raised the bite to her mouth. As she swallowed, his gaze followed the movement of muscle down her throat. He took a swig of his beer and asked if it was good. She had said yes, even though the sauce was too thick, almost gelatinous in the way it held the mushrooms in a clump on her fork. He had laughed, said, no it isn't. I can tell by the way you eat. She couldn't lie. So she shrugged and said it was normally a dish she liked. Minutes later he grabbed her plate and talked her into eating his steak. She had resisted a little, but ate it, a lovely rare filet topped with gorgonzola cheese. He nodded and smiled while she ate his steak, and she'd had this little rush of a feeling that between bites a deal had been made.

Now she was considering what else he had seen about her while watching her eat. She was wondering how she would respond when he touched her, when the red neon sign of the Belladonna restaurant behind them flickered, went out. Once again she had closed down a place, sipped the dregs of her wine as the busboy vacuumed carpet and the bartender handed off the night's profits to the manager who had given them that look—*get on with it you two, it's time to go.* Now she stood silently under the awning and wished the man she barely knew would say something, because after all the usual middle-age first dinner date conversation of marriage and divorce, and children or not, and moving for job options and retirement plans, she had run out of words. The parking lot stretched out before them under a dull night sky, and a fog sat like wet gauze over the lights of the sporadic traffic going by. The fast food signs down the street signs grew blurrier, seemed to move farther away as the fog thickened to a mist.

She could hear him breathing. She glanced around, saw that all the shops of the strip mall were closed. "I didn't know it was so late," she said, the stock phrase hanging in the air like a burp, barely noticed, politely overlooked. She wished she could summon up some witty banter as Lizzy Bennet certainly would have done while verbally sparring with Mr. Darcy in *Pride and Prejudice.* But Longbourne and and Netherfield were just fanciful places where the protagonist walked purposely through muddy fields to sort her troubles out, where she possessed the patience and wit, and integrity required to get the happy ending. But that was another world.

Twice divorced and resigned to a new job in the industrial wasteland of Northwest Ohio, Hope was long past what most considered a marriageable age. Here I am, she thought, a new city, a new job, and new potential man for my bed, but all she could manage to feel was smudged once again from too much talk, too much listening, and too much wine. She looked out at her Camry and his SUV, like pets waiting in the dark for their masters to claim them, take them home. They looked alone, forlorn somehow in the otherwise empty parking lot. She gave a hard little sigh.

It would be a long walk in the high-heels that were already burning her toes.

"You all right?" he said.

"Sorry," she said. I was just thinking."

The mist turned to rain with a whooshing sound.

"What were you thinking?"

She could smell his cologne that reminded her of streams, and trees, and cold clear air. "I was thinking how I'd get to my car in the rain."

"No, you weren't thinking that." He nodded toward a wrought iron bench behind them. "We can sit back there until the rain passes."

She followed him. "I was really wondering if this night were a story, how would it end."

"If it were my story, the main character, he'd end up getting laid."

The rain made a steady thrumming sound. She breathed the smell of rain on pavement, the mildly acrid scent of asphalt. After awhile, if rain kept coming the air would turn sweeter, clean. "But it's my story," she said.

"Really." He tugged at her arm, pulled her further back under the awning. She liked the way he wiped the bench first with his handkerchief. She sat, relieved.

He pulled a cigar from his pocket. "Do you mind?"

"Go ahead," she said.

He clipped the cigar, lit, inhaled and looked out at the lot as if it were his own yard and he could just sit back and watch it rain all night.

His name was Mike. A mechanic's name, she thought, like Joe or Frank, a name for a man who took things apart with his hands. She had watched him at parties, in restaurants, at her gym. She knew he was somewhat dangerous with his way of quietly possessing a room when he entered, pausing to let his thick muscled presence sink into position, lifting his head slightly like a lion sniffing the wind for prey. But she liked that animal kind of thing in a man. There was a time when she was hungry too, going through men like meals, carefully chosen, savored, swallowed, then gone to the realm of memories: *remember that night when we had… oh yes…it was good.*

He blew his smoke above them, looked at her, grinned. "Did you like my steak?"

"You know I did. I ate all of it."

"I liked watching you eat," he said. "You eat like a kitten, such fierce and hungry little bites."

She felt herself blushing. "Nice metaphor," she said. "Where'd a contractor learn to talk like that?"

"Where'd a professor learn to eat like that?"

"It's a primal thing." She liked the word primal, the way it upped the ante in any conversation with a man.

"Mm, hmm." He grinned, gave a quick little nod as if he'd checked off a point. She heard his cell phone vibrate in her pocket and watched as he checked the caller. "My son," he said. He listened then went on to view the other calls missed.

He was a handsome man, big and broad with thick graying hair and a well-trimmed beard, and blue, blue eyes that sparked like a lit fuse ready to explode. In spite of all his talk, she didn't really know him, just she knew of him: a man who bought properties and with a little dry wall and plumbing and paint turned ruin into gold. They said he had the Midas touch. Yes, she thought, he looked like a man who could have been a greedy troubled king, who wielded thick swords, bedded pretty women, and fed freshly killed deer to his dogs. He snapped his phone shut, shoved it in his pocket and gave her a smile. She had heard he collected women like those distressed properties he bought and sold, and now his appraising eye had settled on her.

She looked out at a parking lot dimly lit by a security light far away where the pavement gave way to scrubby grass and a line of trees. And there at the far corner of the lot by the street was a boat, a luxury boat all white and chrome and sitting there like something marooned. She hadn't noticed it when she pulled in, her mind preoccupied with how she looked, with whether he'd be waiting for her at the bar. She nudged his arm. "Why is a boat sitting out there in a parking lot? We're nowhere near a marina."

"It's the Commander," Mike said. He looked out at the boat as if any moment it could rev to life and take off. "It's got an inboard V8. Goes up to fifty miles an hour, can take rapids and streams only four inches deep. Got a power to weight ratio you wouldn't believe."

"Why is it sitting in a parking lot?"

"Promotional," he said. He nodded toward the plate glass window of the tobacco shop behind them. "They sell high end fishing gear along with those cigars."

She stood up and peered in through the dark glass of the storefront. In the dull electric glow of the display cases she could see leather wing back chairs, some chess boards, taxidermy fish placed on shelves, a deer head on the wall and something like a fox, she thought, in the corner. "Pretty pretentious."

"It's just good cigars and good gear." He put his hand on her shoulder, turned her back toward the parking lot. "Come summer they give fly fishing lessons out there."

"On pavement?" she said. "People stand out there and cast in a parking lot."

"It's one way to learn." He stood with his arms crossed over his chest and studied the boat with that way men have of looking at a job to be done.

"Desperate people in desolate places," she said.

He shook his head, walked away from her. "I grew up here. It's not a bad place to live."

"I'm sorry. I didn't mean that."

"Anybody anywhere can be desperate."

"Yeah," she said. "I know that." She looked out at the boat. "It's just back home it'd be strange to learn to fish on pavement. We've got all these lakes and rivers, and streams."

"Learning how to fly fish on pavement seems pretty resourceful to me."

"Yes, it is." She sat back on the bench, hoped he would join her, but he just stood a little ways behind her, smoking.

"Wouldn't it be nice," she said, "if we could jump in that boat and crank it up and fly away."

"Boats don't fly."

"I was being metaphorical."

He sat next to her, leaned close. She could feel the soft heat of his beard on her face. "We can fly in that Range Rover of mine out there. I've got a way with engineering things."

"Not tonight," she laughed. She shifted away from his touch and stood as if to go. She thought he'd stand to stop her, but he just sat there enjoying his cigar. "People at work told me that the Belladonna is where all you upscale local types go to." She stopped. "You know."

"You upscale local types?" he said studying the glowing tip of his cigar.

"You know what I mean," she said.

"Yeah, I know what you mean."

She sat beside him. "I'm just saying if I were making a movie of a yuppie pick up bar I'd show that. All the beautiful ones. Tanned and toned and groomed. The dark-haired men fondle cell phones while botoxed blondes nod and smile. Hooking up, networking, hanging out, whatever word we use, it's just another form of sniffing, marking turf, moving in to gauge which way the power goes."

"I thought you taught literature," he said. "Is this a political science class?"

"I'm just saying," she said. She wasn't sure what she was saying.

He blew smoke above her head and smiled. "Sounds to me like you're saying you had too much to drink."

"No. Well yeah," she said. "But I'm saying it's like dogs. These rituals. When they meet at the park, their eyes lock, ears perk. Little sniffs, steps forward, back, and then off they go nipping, yapping, running circles in the grass." She sighed, wished she'd just quit talking. But she couldn't. "It's just that we like to think we're so evolved."

"You don't ever want to get laid?" Mike said.

"What?" she said.

"Laid," he said. "Don't you ever want that, professor? Instead of all this talk."

"Well of course I do."

"Good," he said.

"So," she said.

"So."

"Well," she said when she saw the pulsing yellow light of the security guard's truck turn into the parking lot. He was heading their way. "Guess he's making the final rounds. Must be time to go."

The guard slowed in front of them, gave Mike a smile and a thumbs up sign. Then he turned away

"He knows me," Mike said. "This place, it's like my neighborhood bar."

The guard flicked off the flashing light on top of his truck, sped up and headed for the exit. He darted across the street and pulled quick and sharp into the Taco Bell.

"I thought cops preferred diners and doughnuts."

"He's not a cop, just a guard they hire to make the place look watched over."

"I see he's really good at his job."

Mike shrugged. "He's got a girlfriend at the Taco Bell. She's married; he's married. So they meet there, have a quickie on her breaks and when she gets off."

"In that little truck."

"In that little truck." Mike grinned. "He says she's very flexible."

Mike threw his cigar to the ground and moved closer to her.

"How delightfully sordid," she said. She was tired but wouldn't dare say it. Claiming tired before two was a sure sign of getting old. "The rain's let up." She stepped toward the lot. "Thanks for the steak and the wine, Mike. We'll have to do this again sometime."

"You good to drive?"

"Sure." But as she walked out, her high heels slipped a bit on the wet pavement. She felt him beside her, yet just behind her as if he'd catch her if she fell. She couldn't decide if the gesture were rude or chivalrous. It was so difficult to know what was what these days.

At her car, she felt in her purse for her keys, and looked up at him studying her as if he were measuring something. She stood still, wondered what kind of kiss a man who knocks down walls for a living would give. A jack hammer? A wrecking ball? Or would it be a slow and steady, tearing thin walls down board by board. Her mathematician husband had been tentative, as if calculating just where and how long lips and tongue should move. Her geologist had gone at her full-force, but precise and intense the way a rock climber guesses the danger as he gauges each grip for purchase, but he was always too in a hurry to get to the peak. She couldn't remember why she'd left him exactly. She couldn't remember why she was so quick to find love and then so eager to bolt, leave anything like love behind. Her last one had said, you're going to be a lonely old woman, Hope. No kids, no family, no man. Just a lonely old woman. She'd hit him in the face for that.

Mike stroked the back of her head, said, "Sweetie, you're too buzzed to go."

"I was just thinking," she said.

"You were dreaming on your feet, professor." He held her hand, squeezed it. She liked the strength of his palm.

Ok, she thought, he's going to kiss me now. He lifted her hand to his mouth and gave a light brush with his lips.

She liked the feel of his beard on her skin, the moist pressure of his lips.

He moved beside her, leaned against her car, not seeming to mind the wetness there. He lifted his face up, closed his eyes, breathed. Then he looked at her as if this were just the beginning of the evening and not the end. "Smell it," he said. "I love that smell of rain on pavement."

She breathed the acrid scent still in the air. "It should smell cleaner by now with all that rain. But it still smells like a parking lot."

"That's 'cause it is a parking lot."

"Back home," she said. "When it rains you smell the dirt and the water and the trees. It's like you know you're an animal when you're out in it. You smell.... " She searched for the word.

He leaned, whispered, breath warm on her neck. "Fecundity of earth."

She laughed. "Where'd you learn to talk like that?"

He shrugged. "I watch PBS sometimes. I know a lot more than you think I know, professor. I know one way to get in a woman's pants is to get her laughing."

"Oh," she said. "Is that what you're after?"

"That's what I'm after." He put his hands in his pockets, and looked up as if something might happen in that sodden sky.

She looked down, saw her red pedicured nails and strappy black sandals. Her legs were still lean, long under the short skirt. She'd dressed for a man to pick her up, throw her down and screw her. She figured she had about a decade left to dress like this. Still, she was grateful for the soft light of the restaurant, and now the darkness. If she were to sleep with him, in the light of morning he would see the lines at her eyes and lips, the age creeping across the back of her hands, sags slipping at her throat. And those

tiny spider-web creases growing between her breasts. But
then, he'd said he liked all kinds of woman: heavy, skinny,
young, not so young. He'd named every kind of woman as
something he'd be after. He just loved the chase, he'd said.
But he'd never mentioned the pleasure of chasing someone
old. No one, not even he, wanted old.

He gave her a glance. "You all right?"

"Yeah, I was just thinking."

"You do too much thinking.

"I was thinking you're something of a swashbuckler
when it comes to things like…" She was thinking of sex, but
said, "Romance."

He laughed. "Swashbuckler. I like that. So pirate, wild,
and bad. But Johnny Depp never got laid in that movie,
wasn't even interested. I'm no pirate. But I am the kind of
man should be wearing a sign: Beware all you ladies. This
is the devil here."

"Don't flatter yourself. You're not a devil, you're just a
dog." She had the urge to yawn, swallowed it back, and felt
the little surge of moisture in her eyes. "It's time to get on
home." She beeped the car unlocked and reached for the
door.

"No," he said. He grabbed her, his mouth covering hers.
One hand squeezed at the back of her neck, his other hand
squeezed her ass. I'm too old for this, she thought, but she
let him at her. It had been months, almost a year since she'd
been touched by a man. He pressed her against the cold
dampness of her car and pulled her into him. His hand was
warm under her shirt, squeezing her back, fingers running
along her bra strap, then reaching to find the clasp in front,
unhooking it. His hand was warm, soft and firm on her
breast as if he really, really appreciated what he was holding
there. The other hand squeezed between her legs, not poking
past the panties like some eager boy, just a gentle pressure, a
slight stroking and releasing as if coaxing a stunned animal

                                    A Long Way from Derbyshire

to move. He pulled her skirt up around her hips, lifted her to the hood of her car.

She thought, stop, but couldn't say it.

"Look at you," he whispered. She looked down, saw her thighs spread taut and smooth and this man moving between them. This is like one of those steamy scenes, she thought, animal man tearing at French lingerie, a perfect moment in soft core porn. But such a cliché. He lifted her quick and yanked her panties to her thighs, his fingers pushed in. She grabbed his wrist. "Stop. You have to stop now."

He straightened. "Why?"

"I'm not ready," she said.

He pulled back, rubbed his fingers together, grinned. "Yes, you are."

"People get arrested for things like this."

"Not me," he said. "Keith, the guard, he'd just laugh." She looked toward the Taco Bell where Keith was busy with his flexible girlfriend in a truck.

"I know this place," he said. We might as well be on the dark side of the moon."

She looked out at the parking lot spreading dark and wet around them.

"Keith won't come back until he sees my truck is gone. Anybody driving by, all they gonna see is that goddamned boat at the edge of the lot, because that's the only bit of light around."

I'm a professor, she thought, half naked with a man in a parking lot. She looked at him, his shirt open, his thick muscled chest. She wanted it. He stood there, cool, patient, just waiting for her to give in. She smiled, shook her head and said, "We're a long way from Derbyshire."

"What?'

"It's a place. In a book. A place where people don't do things like this."

"Well sweetie, this is the world where people do things exactly like this." He grazed his palm across her breast, a gentle movement, just enough to make her nipple rise.

"This is ridiculous," she said. She looked down at herself, white breasts, flat belly, long thighs. "If this were a movie, it'd be pretty hot."

"It *is* pretty hot." He took her nipple with his mouth and sucked while her body grew small under the weight of him, and she gave and gave until all she felt was a fluttering whir. She could feel him pulling at her panties, felt them snag at the back of her knee. He pulled until she felt the silk slip off her ankles. He tossed them and went for his zipper.

She slid off the hood pulled down her skirt. "No," she said. "Not here. Not like this." She tried to see in the darkness around her, wondered where her panties went. She stood, buttoning her shirt. "We can't do this yet. You don't even know who I am."

He stepped back and studied her, as if she were a blurry thing on the horizon just coming into focus. "Yes I do. You are a woman named Hope in the dark." He grinned. "How's that for a metaphor?"

"Too obvious," she said. She crouched and looked around on the pavement. "Where are my panties?"

"Maybe I ate them," he said.

"It's good stuff. French silk."

"Okay, Miss French Silk. I guess you're not a first-date-do-it-kind of gal," he said.

"I'm not," she said. And she wasn't, not really, just sometimes.

"We'll find your panties," he said. "Just so you know I can be a gentleman when I have to." He opened his truck, fumbled in the glove-box. He pulled out a flashlight, clicked it, re-clicked, no light. "Dead," he said. Sometimes my son plays with it."

He tossed it back inside. "We'll use my lighter." He flicked on the flame and they bent to search the pavement. "Here's your purse," he said.

She took it, held it to her chest, didn't want to admit she'd forgotten all about her purse.

"And your keys," he said. "Now on to the panties." He gave her a grin. "It's like a treasure hunt." They crouched together and looked.

"Jesus," she said. "I knew you tossed them, but how far can a pair of panties go?'

"All the way to heaven if they're French."

She laughed, and then the rain came pounding down. They stood up, laughing, drenched. "My poor panties," she said.

"Your poor hair." He pushed the mess of it back from her face. "Let's wait in my truck 'til it stops." She let him open the door, climbed in, watched him walk around the front and get in his side. He handed her a roll of paper towels from the back seat, and she mopped at her face knowing her mascara had run, her foundation had smeared to reveal the blotchy, ageing, every-day woman she was. She wished for lipstick, a mirror, a light, for two minutes alone to repair the damage of being smudged, smeared and rained on. She had wanted to think that when she walked away tonight, it would be with some kind of grace. She could smell his cologne still, the scent of cigar in his shirt, but more than anything she smelled the wet sweat smell of her hair. "Do I smell like a dog?" she said.

"A dog?"

"A black friend of mine has once said when a white woman's hair got wet, it smelled like a dog. She had said there was nothing worse than getting stuck in an elevator with a bunch of white women who'd just been caught out in the rain."

"You smell like a woman," he said. "I wish you'd let me fuck you. We both could use the stress relief."

"Yeah," she said. "We could."

"But I'm not the kind to fight you for it."

"So the prince of darkness *is* a gentleman."

"Yeah," he said. "I am." He wiped his face dry and looked out at the boat glimmering in the flickering light and rain. "God, I love that boat."

"You thinking of buying it?"

"I have a boat. We had some great times on that boat. My wife, she'd sunbathe naked out in the middle of the lake. I taught my son to fish. Good times. Until I started screwing around. But that's another story."

"There's always another story," she said. God she hoped he wasn't going into how his marriage went wrong. "Let's have no sad stories. It's too late for sad stories." She reached in her purse for her compact, dabbed some powder on.

"Yeah," he said. "But you should see my boat. It's a 1967 Owens. Twin engines. Turns on a dime. Got two bedrooms, two baths, perfect wood, all mahogany and teak. Old brass fixtures. A true beauty, and I got it for change. Some guy's wife died of breast cancer, then he kinda went nuts on coke and booze and women. Lost his job. Was selling off everything he had. Living the life, I guess to make up for the grief. Two days after I bought that boat he died. Crashed in the brand new red Mercedes, he'd bought with her insurance money. Wasn't much left for their kid."

While he talked she'd managed to quick fix some lipstick on and give some kind of shape to her hair. "That's awful," she said.

"Damn good timing on my part. Got a hell of a boat." His gaze remained on the boat out there in the dark. He glanced at her, looked away. "It's not like anything was my fault."

"No," she said. "He did it himself."

"We all do it ourselves."

"I dated a guy once, he said with a hundred bucks and a boat you could get just about any woman you want."

Mike made a huffing sound, something like a laugh, but not. "For a night." He poked her in the arm as if they were old buddies. "How long did he have you?"

"Two or three times I think. I never even got the boat ride. It was winter. Guess I lost interest by spring."

"You lost interest by two or three times." He sighed, leaned back in his seat. "Guess I'm shit out of luck, 'cause my boat's in storage now, has been for years. And to tell you the truth I'm in debt to my ass, and don't have the cash to pay the storage fees, so it sits in dry dock, the fees just rising. I know I'm gonna have to face it, let it go. Some things float and some things, you gotta let 'em sink."

She nodded, thinking about sex, thinking about whether they'd have another go at trying to do it or if they'd already decided to let it go. She remembered the hundred-bucks-and-a-boat man. He moved fast. Just went at her the way Mike did. She remembered he had a little penis, but was really good with his hands. She knew Mike didn't have a little penis. She'd felt enough of him to know he'd feel good inside. She knew he'd feel even better holding her afterward, rubbing on her back, burying her in the thick weight of his arms. No matter how the sex went she always loved the feeling of being held when it was over, that sense of comfort, ease, even when the guys were pretty much strangers, there was this little moment of peace after the surge of blood and sweat and saliva and cum had done what it does in the end. But this man had just had his fingers inside her, had grinned rubbing his fingers together, and said, *You're ready.*

And she had said no. And now she was waiting for the rain to ease so she could climb in her car, all damp and chilled to go home, where there was nothing but a stack of papers to grade and books, so many books piled, half read by her bed.

"But there's always more boats," he said. He looked at her. "The rain's eased up. You want to have another look for those panties?"

She looked at his face, the mouth that made her feel like a thing sweetly swallowed, consumed. "Nope," she said. "I want you." She climbed to his side of the truck and straddled him.

"There you go," he said squeezing her hip with one hand and reaching beneath the seat with the other. She heard the hum of the machinery as the seat moved back, giving room. She rose up, unbuttoned her blouse, unhooking her bra, hoping he'd put his mouth on her again.

He unzipped his pants, bucked up a little to yank them past his knees. She could smell this sex, a scent like simmering onions and meat. He took her face with one hand, grinned at her. "Look out, you're running with the dogs, now."

She wished she could say something smart, something witty, something he might remember. But he pulled her to him, shoved his tongue in her mouth and squeezed at her nipple until it hurt. She held his wrist, pulled back.

He grabbed her hips, lifted her a little, then settled her onto him the way he might have set a beam in place. He closed his eyes, and she smiled at the little gasp he gave, the sound men make when a woman opens, lets a man push in. He held her there. "Not too fast," he whispered.

Then they went at it, without a word. She remembered her panties out there on the pavement, remembered a line of soft porn she'd read as a teenager. At her boarding school, there were no greater pleasures than good chocolate sent from mothers and soft porn stolen from big sisters. They'd read it together, savoring the good parts and laughing at the blur of soft breasts heaving, and quivering members thrusting, and all the usual things that made sex on a page. But the line she precisely remembered was about a girl being pressed against a tree by the boy she wanted, and how she "stamped her steaming panties to the ground." At fourteen and a virgin, she knew she wanted one day to be that girl, being pushed by some guy who wanted it and she'd give it stamping her steaming panties to the ground.

He gave a thrust, and she pushed back. Eyes shut, rain pounding all around, they humped faster, nothing elaborate, just a hanging on and going at it. She came hard and fast, heard his little laugh."Damn what was that? Ten seconds?"

She nodded, kept moving, her eyes closed. "Come on," she said, hoping he'd come soon, that he wouldn't soften and they'd have to get started all over. Men his age, could come quick or rise and soften and take all night long to get off. He grabbed her hips, pulled her up and down, going hard, whispering, "Shit, shit, shit this is good." Then silence. Then the air shuddered with his deep groaning that rose to something like a scream between them. She'd forgotten the sound a big man can make when he comes, like a roar of a mountain falling down.

She leaned into him, nuzzled her face against his neck, felt his heart against her chest. He patted her back the way teammates do, kissed the top of her head, then lifted her off him. She climbed over to her side, pulled her skirt down and wondered how rude it would be to just grab her purse, get out and go home. But he took her hand then, squeezed with a gesture that would be something like affection, but she knew it was just his way of being polite. So she settled back into the plush sheep skin cover of the seat, closed her eyes and listened to the rain pounding harder now. The truck seemed to rock with the storm. She opened her eyes, ran her fingers through the sheepskin seat cover and gripped it as if she needed to hang on. "Listen to that rain."

"It's coming down." He yanked up his pants, zipping then leaning back in his seat. He closed his eyes. "I needed that." He sighed and settled deeper in his seat. He rubbed his palm up and down her forearm, patted the back of her hand, then leaned back in his seat and closed his eyes. "This is nice," he said.

"Yeah," she said. She sat there wondering how long she should wait. His breath was already deepening in the sound men make when committed to sleep. Five breaths and he'd be out. She counted. Yep, he was gone. She wondered how long she should wait for the rain to let up, while his wetness grew sticky between her legs. Soon she would need to pee. She rubbed a clear space in the window, looked out to the darkness, the empty lot, the boat out there rocking in the gusting wind as if it could break free from its moorings, drift off.

He made a little snoring sound, jerked. She hoped he was awake, but he settled back to sleep as if he were safe, secure, stretched out at home. She wished she could let go like that, go unconscious by simply closing her eyes, flicking a switch. "You are a good animal," she said. He didn't seem to hear her. Animals didn't need bottles of wine, aroma therapy, Ambien, to go to sleep. They just got comfortable, sank down, closed their eyes, clicked off, then with another click could spring awake fully aware of what comfort or a threat was around.

His breath stayed deep and steady. She sighed, hooked her bra, buttoned her shirt and wondered again about her panties. They were lost. She looked out at the parking lot shimmering like a shallow lake on the rise. She imagined her silk panties swirling in some puddle, lifting with the flow of pools forming, eddying down toward the drain in the dark. By morning they're be somewhere in the sewage drain in the mix of Taco Bell bags and cigarette butts, the remains of things enjoyed, and dropped, tossed, let go. That was the way of things of this world. Except love, she thought. But no, love like anything else wore out, expired in time, got tossed.

He made a grumbling sound, shifted a bit in his seat toward his window like a man who was accustomed to sleeping in cars. She wished he had held her a little longer, just a little. So went the disadvantage of screwing in cars or trucks or even upscale SUV's with aftermarket ultra-plush seats.

She lay back, listened to the rhythm of his breath. It was late, but it would be a long, long while until the grey light of morning. She looked at the Commander out there, brave, as if ready for any ride the storm could offer. She didn't know anyone who could afford a boat like that. She leaned back, looked at it through half-closed eyes. It seemed to rock on water, a gentle rhythmic movement. "It's like it's moving," she said, but she knew the illusion of moving was just the effect of her breath rising, falling. Nothing was really going anywhere.

Mike made a little grunting sound, stirred, then as if by choice sank back to the deep breath of sleep. She reached and took his hand, wanting to feel something of the man who'd just been inside her. She squeezed his hand, got no response. He was gone. She let go, sat back in her seat, and closed her eyes. She remembered a poem, the first she'd ever remembered by rote. She spoke it softly with the cadence it needed, something like a song, but not. "Oh western wind where wilt thou blow, the small rain down can rain."

He stirred up, gave her a wide awake and friendly look. "I like that," he said. "The small rain down can rain."

"How long have you been awake?"

"In and out," he said. "Then I heard that. It was like you were telling me something."

"It's just a poem that came to mind. Want to hear the rest?"

He cleared his throat, reached under his seat for a bottle of water. "Not really, but I bet I'm gonna hear it." He took a swig and offered it to her. "I'm not sure how fresh it is, but you want a sip?"

She shook her head. "It's only one more line to it. You can handle that."

"Shoot," he said and took another hit of water.

She looked straight ahead, spoke to the Commander as if it were her audience. "Oh Christ, if my love were in my arms and I in my bed again."

He looked at her. "You a Christian?"

"No, I'm not a Christian."

"Good," he said. "I'd feel weird about that."

"It's just a poem," she said.

He held the bottle toward her. "You sure you don't want some of this before I finish it. Screwing makes me thirsty."

She shook her head and watched him gulp down the water. "It's a poem about love, well, about longing I guess. It's anonymous," she said.

"I can't believe you're not thirsty after all that wine. Must be a hundred poems about wine, right."

"Yeah," she said. Oh god. She'd just screwed an idiot.

He was looking at her. "Know any poems about wine?"

"I'm not like a jukebox, plug a quarter in, pick a poem."

"Yeah, I get it. You always so serious?"

"No," she said, thinking yes, wondering when she started believing things were supposed to mean things and got pissed when they didn't.

He reached between the seats, found his keys, and turned on the engine. "We could use a little defrost in here."

She watched as the air hit the windshield, the clarity spreading slowly, steadily from the bottom, rising up to give a clear view of the lot. The rain had stopped and now the boat shimmered as if newly made. All clean.

"Time to get home," she said. She felt around the floorboards for her shoes.

He nodded, stared ahead, hands on the steering wheel, like a taxi driver done with his fare. "Nice time," he said.

Shoes, purse, keys in hand, she opened the door and stepped out. She liked the feeling of her bare feet spread cool and solid on the pavement.

He buzzed the passenger window down, called, "I'll make sure you get started all right."

"I'll be fine." She opened her door, tossed her things inside, but just stood there, looked up at the dark. "It's nice out here," she said. "Cool and fresh, but it still smells like a parking lot."

"That's because—"

"I know," she said. "I know where I am. Go on." She waved him away and made a move to get into her car.

He shrugged, gave a little lift of his hand off the steering wheel, then took off. His truck moved across the lot, thick wheels making a whooshing sound that faded as he neared the exit. She watched until she saw him pull out onto the street, disappear into the dark. If this were a story, she thought, that would mean something. She got in her car and started the engine. She liked the feel of her bare feet on the pedals, remembered the way she liked to drive barefoot in high school. She shifted the car into drive, but kept her foot on the brake, tried to make some sense of what she'd just done. But it wasn't a story. No plot, no protagonist, no resolution. It was just another man gone, and a woman going. No meaning at all. But it had to mean something surely. Things had to mean something. Tomorrow, she thought, maybe tomorrow she'd figure it out. She lifted her foot off the brake and let the car rev forward a little on its own. She saw the guard truck heading her way, just the way Mike said he would. She stomped the gas and moved on.

HANNIBAL'S VICTORY

Daniel Pearlman

Erica's "See ya later, Hel!" thundered through the door. Helga could now set down her paintbrush, peek out of her bedroom, and scan the living room for signs of disturbance that she knew she would find in her housemate's wake. The television stood like a toothless mouth retracted against the wall, silent now after disgorging its bellyful of morning news that garnished Erica's habitual breakfast of eggs and fried onions. The smell took time to go away, but go away it would, and Helga could then count on several hours of olfactory freedom till Erica's return from work at 5:30—not to mention day-long deliverance from the TV, a birthday gift, kindly intended, from Erica. Its ostensible purpose was to provide Helga with a "window on the world" to supplement her stock of visual vocabulary with a store of contemporary idioms. Last week it had intruded with that obituary clip of shriveled old Maurice, a writer she'd slept with eons ago. Yesterday it had dumped images of dead pigeons into her living room. They were being smitten by some contagious new disease whose ghostly threat now hovered about within her very apartment, flapping its batwings somewhere over her head.

Helga took a step forward into her living room—*their* living room for a month now since she'd invited her young admirer to move in with her. She was under no illusion about the modest size of the room—indeed, of the whole two-bedroom apartment—but it was strange how the presence of that TV, unlike a "window," seemed to shrink the room even further. Some things took getting used to.

Hannibal, meanwhile, his eyes narrowing above a set of frayed white whiskers, glared at her from the cushion of one of the four high-backed chairs that belonged to the glass-topped, circular living-room table. That antique table—Third-Empire French, originally with marble top, upper legs still graced with bronze griffins—had been with Helga time out of mind, for many more years than old Hannibal bore on his scruffy black back, accompanying her, like Hannibal, in a Manhattan odyssey from one successively smaller apartment to another. If Hannibal looked put out, the reason was immediately clear. Erica had piled books on his favorite chair, the one flattened with his grungy, indelible imprint.

"Don't look at me like that, Hannibal. She's young, in a constant dither, and occasionally forgetful." She had been such an assiduous student, Helga remembered, respectably above-average in talent. And she had such *lovely* white teeth.

Helga crossed the room into the narrow kitchen to the left. Sunlight filtered through the metal bars and ageless grit that covered the single window. "Look," she said to the cat, who followed at the hem of her housedress, "Erica cleaned the frying pan and also her plate and fork. She's learning. She means well."

"You certainly are quick to defend her," said Hannibal, looking up as he rubbed his chin against the refrigerator.

"She needs no defense," countered Helga, planting her fist on her bony hip and eying Hannibal askance. "She is a young person with her own needs and habits and we all have to learn to adjust to one another."

"Yes, accommodate, learn to compromise. How often do I have to listen to this bullshit, Helga?"

"You're cross because you haven't eaten. Why don't you let her feed you?"

"I told her once what I wanted to eat. A slab of liver and nothing more. But she has the gall to tell me it's no good for me!"

"But maybe she knows better than I do, and that you ought to have more variety in your—"

"Ha! We'll see how *you* feel when she starts cooking in for the two of you and decides what *you* should eat."

"A highly unlikely scenario," said Helga.

"Oh, really?"

"Really." Helga opened the refrigerator to retrieve a plastic container of cow's liver.

"Open the meat and vegetable bins. You'll see what I'm talking about," said Hannibal.

Helga was surprised to see tomatoes and green peppers and sausages and ground beef from D'Agostino's. Apart from the expected onions and eggs. "I don't know what in the world she intends to do with all this," she said. "Make herself lunches to take to work?"

"Dinner, more likely," said Hannibal, following the trajectory of a juicy slice of liver as Helga forked it out of the plastic and into his bowl.

"That's absurd!" said Helga. "We agreed to eat dinner out. It's my one meal a day and my chance to see people and enjoy the city a bit."

Hannibal mounted a stool from which he was able to jump to the countertop. He chewed savagely at his liver, in utter self-absorption, and Helga watched and listened with a deep, visceral satisfaction.

"Let's face it, you don't need her companionship," said Hannibal, stopping for a bloody-jawed break. "Did you take her in because she slobbers all over you? Young as I was, even I didn't fawn all over you when we met—or at any time after."

"I took her in because she needs a place to live. When she can fully support herself—"

"Thousands of people need a place to live. Why her?"

"She is the best of my former students."

"And she worships you, yes. But I still can not believe that for such a petty reason you are willing to share what precious little space we have with this … this clackety young woman."

"What do you mean, 'clackety'?"

"She makes a racket wherever she goes. Clack, clack."

"I am too quiet. I've spoiled you, Hannibal. Young people tend to be doing, moving, flitting around a good deal. I remember, back in Paris, when *I* was twenty-three—"

"You're all generosity, aren't you? No 'What's in it for Helga?' in all this, is there?"

"Just what do you mean?" said Helga, her hand retreating limply to her chin.

"You don't mind living alone," said Hannibal, licking his lips. "But you're afraid of being *left* all alone, to die all alone. Frankly, I don't see why you need company to die. Dying takes a minute or so, and for that you would give up months, maybe years, of precious privacy?"

"Hannibal, I assure you…" His whiplike words drew tears to Helga's eyes. "I assure you that my personal demise is the farthest thing from my mind."

"Sure, like yesterday, when you combed me, and another big clump of hair came out—and what did you say? You said, 'Hannibal, what if one day I have a stroke and I can't get out of bed? Or what if I'm mugged in the hallway picking up the mail? Who will take care of my darling?'"

"Is that so odd? I was expressing my concern for you."

"You were expressing your concern for yourself. I'm not that stupid, Helga. I've been sniffing for quite some time now—in you, of all people—embarrassing whiffs of weakness, of abject fear."

Hand thrust to hip and head held high, Helga marched out of the kitchen. "You refuse to grant me even one generous thought," she shot back.

The click of the deadbolt sent a shudder through Helga's shoulders as she bent over the glass-top table, now puffing at an elegantly poised Gauloise, now gluing sequins to the tiara of a cold-eyed Minerva that she had painted on a plywood panel.

"My God, it's so warm in here, how can you stand it?" shouted Erica, depositing her attaché case on the chair next to Hannibal's, from which those trespassing books had been removed. Her flower-pattern dress exposed the sweaty upper slopes of her small, firm breasts—breasts on which Helga had modeled her Minerva's.

Helga never paid much heed to fluctuations of temperature and humidity—at least not when she was working, not when absorbed in the pain and pleasure of making esthetic decisions—like whether or not she should paint in eyeballs or leave the divine orbs stone-blank. She could have continued for several hours more—work obliterated the dimension of time—but now she was party to a Social Contract. Reluctantly, she capped her tube of glue.

"Warm, Erica? It's the middle of August. Wasn't it warm in Ohio in August?"

"You never turn on the air conditioner. Like I said, all you have to do is open my bedroom door and it's strong enough to cool the whole apartment."

Helga did not want to admit how much she disdained air conditioning. She had got through life without such a disease-causing "convenience" and could only deplore the fact that young people had come to regard such a groaning, hissing beast as indispensable. "I'm better off without it," she said. "It causes my paints to dry too fast."

"I *love* her!" said a wide-eyed Erica, staring at the wooden panel. "Her brow is so cold, but that sly mouth of hers contradicts it, doesn't it?"

"Really? I didn't intend that. Perhaps I ought to—"

"Please, please don't change it, Hel. It's so much richer that way. This is one of the best of your mythological pieces."

"Wait till it's finished before pronouncing judgment," snipped Helga. "Right now you can get me a glass of white wine. The Riesling will do."

"With pleasure!" said Erica, disappearing into the kitchen.

"And please, bolt the door. I know you're from the Midwest, but this is New York, darling. Besides, the door swings inward just enough for Hannibal to pry it open with his paw. We wouldn't want you running out, would we, Hannibal?"

"Why in hell would I want to?" said the cushion-sprawled Hannibal, jerking his tail and opening one lazy eye.

"Did you find those books on classical statuary helpful?" yelled Erica.

"Quite inspiring, particularly the one on Egypt, *ma chère*. I thank you for running to the library again, but I would not have discovered these newest treasures if Hannibal hadn't knocked them off his chair."

"Oh, shit! Sorry, Hannibal," Erica shouted. She emerged rolling a chilled beer-bottle over her breast.

"I propose to begin getting drunk *chez nous*," said Helga, accepting the wine-glass from Erica's long, slim fingers, "and then to complete the process when we go out. What do you think, Erica? Chez Jacqueline for dinner?"

"This evening? No, Helga. Actually—"

"La Ripaille, then?"

"I'd really like us to eat in tonight, Helga." Erica squeezed her Bud with both hands.

"Eat in? But sweetheart, you know I never eat in."

"I'm not saying to make a habit of it, Helga. Just occasionally. You'll love my sausage and peppers."

"I hardly think so, *ma petite*." Helga folded her arms across her chest and cast a stare at her young friend as cool as the look on her Minerva. "My last lover, Alberto, was chef at the Tea Room, but I never let him cook for me at home. He adored me. After a while, as I recall … he became unable to perform."

"You should have let him cook."

"Sweetheart, I think that during the time we cohabited we were both undergoing a spiritual transition beyond bodily desire."

Erica knitted her brows. "I know I'm nowhere spiritually, Hel, but—"

"There you go again," said Helga, shaking her head, "taking what I say personally."

"—but if you really think of it, Helga, cooking at home can be a far more spiritual experience than impersonal dining at restaurants."

"Sweet baby, you and I have an agreement. You pay no rent, only the utilities, and we go out to dinner together. We split the bill. It isn't as if I ask you to pay for me."

Erica sat down across the table and took a swig of beer. "Helga, in the beginning I thought that would be fine. But we linger in those restaurants for hours, and the more we drink, the more the waiters fawn over you, and then we drink even more—and the bills we rack up…"

"You resent the few social pleasures that I have?"

"No, no! That's not it. But if I ever expect to save enough to stand on my own two feet, well, a beginning programmer's salary for a city agency doesn't leave me much room for continuous high living."

Helga made a face, dreading the prospect of yet more cooking odors than those of egg and onion. She exchanged a glance with Hannibal. "And how often, darling, are you proposing to—"

"Helga, if we could eat in just once or twice a week ... Honestly, I'm not such a bad cook, but of course, compared to Alberto ..."

"I don't understand," sighed Helga. "Here I am, sparing you from having to share the rent."

Erica stared at the floor. ""I know, Hel, and I'm truly grateful, but our month of dining out has wound up costing me the same as paying a *full month* of your rent."

"Oh, dear!" said Helga. "I just never think of toting things up."

"I know," said Erica. "And that's one of the things I love about you. If I didn't have to earn a living, I'd paint all day too and think about nothing else."

"I never meant to squeeze you," said Helga, feeling her face turning red. "You should have told me earlier."

"And if you don't like my food, I'll be serving all your favorite wines to compensate."

"Well," said Helga, wringing her hands, touching her face and neck with her fingers, "what can I say?..."

"Say no!"

"Mind your business, Hannibal," scolded Helga.

"He's stubborn as hell," said Erica. "He won't touch dry food. All he wants is liver. He needs a more balanced diet."

"Cooking smells upset him."

"You smoke all day. Doesn't that bother him?"

"Smoking enhances creativity. Hannibal adores my smoking."

"Okay. How about I'll put a fan in the kitchen and blow the odors out through the window?"

"I didn't invite you to live with me in order to use you as a cook. I wanted a social and intellectual companion. You haven't read a book since you've been here."

Daniel Pearlman   219

"I do. I read computer manuals. And I learn from you—I learn a lot about painting just living with you. Sort of by osmosis. After you left Ohio State, I painted for the next two years getting nowhere. The woman I lived with never encouraged me. I knew that if I was ever to get back on the right track—"

"And so you came to me, and you've hardly lifted a brush since! That computer art you do … that is *not art*."

"I won't argue with you, Helga. But what else do I have time for? If we didn't go out and get sloshed every night—"

"Are you blaming me for turning you into an alcoholic?"

"I didn't say that."

"Young women are not deflowered without at least their passive consent," said Helga.

"I'd *encourage* a challenge to my virtue—if it came from the right person," said Erica with a steady stare into Helga's rapidly blinking eyes.

"Enough!" said Helga, uncomfortable with Erica's innuendoes. "I'm sure you will eventually find appropriate companionship. Meanwhile, as to easing your financial situation … I see I've been insensitive. A mutual living arrangement does require compromise."

"Thank you, Hel. I really need you to understand…" Erica reached out and clasped Helga's hands. Helga allowed her hands to be clasped.

"Hannibal dines with us, of course."

"Of course."

"I mean right here, between us. He shall have his own place setting."

"Helga! An animal? At table?"

"Oh dear! You've hurt his feelings." Hannibal dropped to the floor and swaggered off to the kitchen. "Erica, I've always treated Hannibal as if he were a male avatar of the Egyptian cat-goddess Bast. If Hannibal is an 'animal,' then what, pray, are we?"

"Helga, on my parents' farm we never let cats indoors much less at table."

"I'd like to assume you've come a long way from the farm, baby."

"I'm sorry, Helga. I love Hannibal, you know that. And you know how much I want to please you, how that painting class of yours so completely changed my life—"

"Hannibal hated Ohio, poor fellow."

"It was all those students dropping in all the time," said Hannibal, his head poking out from the kitchen. "The racket they made!"

"He's not so young that compromise comes to him easily, you know." Helga shifted nervously in her chair.

"Okay, Hel. Okay, he eats at the table." Erica dropped to her knees next to Helga and embraced her, pressing a tear-stained cheek to her breast.. "Sometimes it's just so hard … adjusting."

"I know, *ma choute*," said Helga, running gnarled fingers with long purple nails through Erica's silky brown hair. The rich, heady odor of Erica's hair filled her lungs, like a drag on a joint. Fearful of vertigo, she closed off the passage of air through her nose and breathed only through her mouth.

She wouldn't take the hint," said Hannibal, looking up from his chair through the glass tabletop as he spoke and breathed through the gauze face-mask that Helga had "modified to fit him. "And *you* wouldn't believe me for a hell of a long time either."

"But we've solved that problem now, haven't we, dear? After today, no more mask, my sweet."

"Did you have to wait an entire month? She damn near killed me, you know."

"You've been grouchy and uncommunicative. You ceased eating at table with us—to my chagrin and to her evident delight."

"My withdrawal from your dinner table was intended as a polite hint, Helga. Her cooking—two and even three times a week, it turns out—is not a result of my grouchiness. It is a consequence of your indulgence."

"My indulgence?"

"Absolutely. You've been too timid to object, so what does she do—strong-minded as she is, self-involved as she is? She thinks you actually *like* her cooking, so now I've put up with those fumes and stinks almost every other day for a month now. And that's not counting her daily eggs and onions! The house smells like a dumpster in back of a greasy spoon."

"That's not fair, Hannibal. How many times did I suggest to her, with you as witness, that her cooking methods were affecting your health?"

"Well, your young idiot of a housemate assumed that it was her choice of oils and spices, so you encouraged her—"

"But that's what I assumed too, dear."

"—so you encouraged her to cook at home even more, to try various permutations and combinations, to perform a series of culinary experiments that have resulted, for me, in a horrible case of asthma."

"You could have more openly voiced your objections yourself," said Helga.

"Me? Do I have the power around here?"

"Instead, what do you do? Throw hairballs up on her blanket, pee on her bedroom rug!"

"Really? I don't remember *any* such things."

"You've been semi-delirious. How could you remember? Anyway, it was I who finally deduced that the cause of your worsening condition was cooking odors in general."

"I've never in all my years been subjected to such an assault," said Hannibal, slapping the chair with his tail.

"Erica will be delighted that I've found such a simple solution," said Helga with an elegant flick of her paintbrush.

"I'm not so sure—but we'll find out soon enough," said Hannibal, cocking his ears toward the door.

Seconds later Helga heard the deadbolt click.

"I smell a stranger," said Hannibal, crouching on his cushion, his ears laid back.

"Hi, guys!" said Erica, shutting the door behind her—but neglecting to bolt it, as Helga was quick to notice. How tiring to have to constantly utter reminders! she thought. Jaunty in beige suit and matching heels, Erica strode up to the table.

"Erica, darling, yesterday I was shocked to see our next-door neighbor staring at me from the hallway. You had forgotten to lock the door."

"Shit! I'm so awful. I apologize."

"He was worried that something might be wrong. But it could have been someone with entirely different motives."

"I'm such an asshole. I'll learn. I promise," said Erica.

"Darling, I'm sure you will."

"Hannibal," said Erica, "you still look so unhappy in that muzzle."

"After this evening," said Helga, "he will not have to wear one."

"I hope not. And how's Actaeon today? Sprouting antlers, I see."

"Hannibal disapproves. He would prefer me to paint the final scene where Actaeon reaps the Peeping Tom's reward."

"And is slaughtered by his own hounds? Yuk!" said Erica, making a face. Pink blooms sprouted from her smooth young cheeks. "In my opinion, when he discovers he's got antlers—that's the true climax."

"The psychological one," murmured Helga.

"Exactly. The moment the poor slob realizes he must be punished for his blasphemous desires."

"You look flushed," said Helga. "Is it still so hot out there?"

223

"No, Hel, it's just that I have a surprise."

"For me?"

"For you *and* Hannibal." Erica planted a kiss on Helga's brow.

"You hear that, Hannibal? Erica has a surprise for you."

"I'm old but not deaf," said Hannibal, his ears aquiver, his forepaws covering his eyes.

"*We* have a surprise for *you, too*," said Helga.

"It was not my idea," said Hannibal. "You can take all the credit."

"You thought of a… surprise for me?" said Erica, smiling, her lips beginning to tremble.

"I have deduced what has been ailing Hannibal and have done something to benefit the three of us."

"And that would be …?"

"Uh-uh. First tell us your surprise," Helga insisted.

"Well, I'm walking home, as usual, past Tompkins Square Park, when all of a sudden I hear this pitiful voice. I look around and see a young guy leashing a kitty to the fence. He asks me if I want her. He's a Hispanic cook and he tells me she's lived in their restaurant kitchen all her life. But the boss found out she was there and they had to get rid of her."

"And so?" said Helga, stiffening.

"She told me her name. Caterina. She's a skinny orange tabby."

"You *didn't.*"

"What would *you* do, Helga?"

"You should not have struck up a conversation—"

"Well, she wouldn't survive in the street. And would you rather someone took her to a shelter? Strays get put to sleep there in forty-eight hours."

"Don't even mention those disgusting shelters!" Helga clapped her hand to her face.

"Didn't you rescue Hannibal from the ASPCA?"

Helga sighed, slouching back in her chair. "So where is this Caterina?"

Erica lanced a smile so bright it made Helga blink. Scurrying back to the door, she slowly pulled it open. A leash was attached to the outer knob, and attached to the leash was Caterina, who hopped over the threshold and took in the scene with a couple of swift glances and several exploratory sniffs at the hardwood floor. As much as Helga wished to resist, the puss overran her defenses.

Dragging her leash, the tabby turned to the right and, with increasing speed and confidence, sniffed her way along the edge of the floor, encountering the base of a bookcase, then slinked past closed bedroom doors, examined the legs of a sofa, nosed along toward the kitchen—then stopped and stared back into the center of the room. Helga had been taking note of Hannibal's behavior as well. Maintaining a low crouch, he shifted around in his seat, following Caterina as a compass needle follows a magnet. As soon as their eyes met, the newcomer bounded to the foot of Hannibal's perch. Stretching herself up a chairleg, she extended the nose of friendship by bumping his gauze-covered snout with her naked little pink one. Hannibal hissed, and the stranger dropped back to the floor. But not for long. They stared at each other for several seconds. Then she raised herself to cushion-level again—as though caution were not in her vocabulary. Hannibal's tail flapped madly as their noses advanced and retreated.

"It's a big download for the two of them," said Erica. "But fear not. They'll be pals in no time." Caterina made a sudden leap but failed to land on the cushion. Startled, Hannibal dove to the floor and dashed under the sofa, extruding his head through its skirts.

"My, she does take liberties," said Helga.

"Hannibal will civilize her. Just give them a little time. And now," said Erica, "I'll introduce Caterina to the splendors of our kitchen."

"Wait a bit!" Helga reached for Erica's arm, but Erica was already making the turn into the kitchen.

"Holy shit!" she exclaimed. "What happened to the goddamn refrigerator?"

Helga drew up behind her. They both stared down at the miniature fridge that now stood in place of the big one that had been there for ages.

"You gave us no time to tell you," said Helga. "About your surprise, I mean."

"Surprise?"

"Yes, I decided that the time had come to do what would be best for the three of us."

"But there was nothing *wrong* with the old one!"

"There was plenty wrong with it, darling. It enabled—and in fact incited—you to do all this cooking of yours. Believe me, dear, while I myself have adored your culinary prowess, the apartment has been reeking with odors that are the cause of Hannibal's symptoms."

"You don't know that."

"I'm sure of it."

"So this is a … surprise?"

"My dear, it isn't as if we can't *afford* to dine out. You did, after all, receive a promotion recently."

"Not all that big of a one."

"Darling, you are becoming a successful New Yorker. New Yorkers don't stint. They live beautifully, in the confidence that their income will eventually exceed their expenses."

"But Helga—"

"Really, sweetheart, I don't see why I ever kept such a big, old, inefficient refrigerator. Your utility bill alone will be significantly reduced."

"Wow," said Erica. "I can't imagine what I'll do with all those savings."

"We now have all the refrigerator we need—for wine, beer, and food for Hannibal.… And for Caterina, of course."

"Yes, of course. But you forgot one thing, Helga. My friends from work are coming over for dinner tomorrow."

"Oh yes. That couple again. The ones who could talk only computers."

"Bob and Ann are really quite cultivated. You have to give them a chance. They were nervous about meeting you. They were familiar with your work from the early eighties, when you made a big splash."

"And they were familiar with nothing since. Apparently, nothing but splashes attract their ..."

"I had planned a great dinner." Erica turned her face away. Her shoulders heaved.

Helga reached out to her with shaking fingers, then pulled her hand back and held it in front of her mouth. "They shall *have* a great dinner! Entirely at my expense. We shall dine out at that exquisite little place in the Village—oh, now, what's it called?—that serves that marvelous *crème brulée.*"

"She is rude, uncultivated!" Hannibal complained. On his haunches at the edge of the bed, he stared across at Helga. She looked back at him in the mirror above her bureau, where she huddled at night to read. She had only a desk-lamp on. She'd been browsing through the new batch of library books that Erica had checked out for her. Hannibal looked like a shadow with golden eyes—very narrow golden eyes. And a little golden necklace as well. He looked like a mortuary statue. His stillness made her shudder.

"But Caterina can sometimes be amusing, don't you think?"

"It doesn't matter. I've tried to be friendly to the little twit, but you extend a paw, and she grabs the whole leg."

"But she genuinely likes you, Hannibal. If she's overzealous in courting your attention, it's perhaps because she senses your ambivalence."

"I have no difficulty forming friendships," said Hannibal, "but I simply demand a little more distance than she is capable of respecting."

"Have you voiced your complaints to Erica?"

"What do you expect Erica to do? She's not usually home during the day, when most of the mischief takes place. And you, you're lost in your painting. You know I never disturb you when you're working."

"But something must be done, dear!" Helga glanced at her bedroom door. A blue light of changing intensity illuminated the cracks around the frame.

"We are stuck in here like jailbirds," said Hannibal. "This is *your* apartment. We never used to spend time in here until you were ready for bed!"

Helga clapped her hands over her ears. "It's the sound of that television. The more she turns it down to accommodate me, the louder it seems."

"Well I say go out there and reclaim your ground. Tell her you've decided to work again in the evenings. Or that you'd prefer conversation when you got home from dinner. But, of course, if you preferred conversation you wouldn't let her turn on that box every night."

"She doesn't want conversation. She seems to just want to sit with me and … I don't know what she wants."

"Well, you can damn well get rid of that box! You had no trouble ditching the other one."

"For you I would do almost anything, my love."

"So do it! I can't stand being cooped up in here either."

"Hannibal, I do not believe in countering inconsiderateness with violent behavior of my own."

"Gandhi can go to hell," said Hannibal. "Passive resistance does not apply to the sphere of personal relations."

"There you are entirely wrong, *mon amour*."

"Really? And what if some mugger threatened you with a knife?"

"I should bare both throat and purse to him," said Helga, lifting her chin and stroking the gold-plated necklace she wore, an exact twin to Hannibal's. "I'd rather he sinned against me than if I, in defending myself, sinned against him."

"Sounds to me like a cowardly bunch of crap," snorted Hannibal.

"You are interrupting my reading, sir."

"Bullshit! I've watched you for almost an hour. You haven't turned two pages since she took over that room."

As Helga considered a foray into the noise- and cathode-irradiated living room, the issue was decided *for* her. "Helga," shouted Erica, "you have to see this special! It's on Egyptian myths and mummies and shit—like the stuff you've been working on lately."

Helga turned to Hannibal and shrugged her shoulders. Hannibal jumped down and bounded to the door, looking back at Helga, who decided to tarry a while and examine herself in the mirror. The necklace, she thought, highlighted patches of wrinkles that might look even ghastlier in the light of the TV. The solution, perhaps, would be that same company's inch-and-a-half-wide "dog-collar" version. Holding herself erect, she finally teased the creaky door open and made a wordless entrance. The sofa crouched against the opposite wall. The TV sat on a cart rolled out on an angle to the right of the sofa, nearly blocking the path to the kitchen. The TV squealed and burped and bleated and lit up Erica's eyes like a pair of blue torches.

"It starts right after the commercials," said Erica. "Sit down. I figured you could use some refreshment." Downing a slug of beer, she pointed to the wine-glass on the fold-up coffee-table. It stood beside a freshly opened bottle of wine and three empty beer bottles that lay on their sides.

"My, aren't you prescient!" said Helga.

"A good servant anticipates her mistress's needs."

"Oh?" Helga raised an eyebrow, then padded up to the sofa. Her glass had an animated window in it. She wondered if the wine had been absorbing all those rays.

"Make room, Caterina!" said Erica, giving the tabby a shove. The cat landed on the floor, then dashed toward Hannibal's favorite chair. She arrived an instant too late. To Helga's delight, Hannibal beat her to it. Caterina contented herself instead with Helga's seat, a default behavior that Helga did not tolerate during regular working hours. The felines glared at each other.

Helga settled into the cushion to Erica's right and raised her wine-glass, which Erica clicked with her bottle. "I must deposit all these empties in the trash," said Helga. The bottles made her uncomfortably aware of how heavily Erica had been drinking—sometimes late into the night, when she would find her sprawled on the sofa asleep with the TV on and Caterina curled up in her lap.

"Leave them," said Erica. "I like them there. I play spin-the-bottle with them, three games at once—to increase my odds of winning. TV too loud for you?"

"Oh, I pay no mind to it at all."

"Helga, that necklace is beautiful! A gold-link chain. Wow! And look at those matching bracelets! I thought you despised jewelry."

"For myself I consider it vanity. As one transcends the level of ego, one finds such trinkets increasingly inappropriate."

"The Egyptians didn't think so. Anyway, what made you go out and buy—I'll be damned! You got one around Hannibal's neck too."

"It's not exactly jewelry, Erica. Its decorative function is secondary."

"Really!"

"These are magnets. Each 'bracelet,' for example, consists of six evenly spaced magnets."

"I'm attracted to you without magnets, Helga."

"I'm glad that you are, *ma petite* cabbage." Helga pursed her lips. "But these magnets do not have an attractive purpose. They are worn to ward things off. To rid the body of injurious processes and to protect against negative influences."

"Negative influences like what?"

"Like the harmful radiation from this television set."

"Helga, these modern sets have absolutely minimal leakage of radiation."

"So they tell you. But do you really know?"

"And you're protecting Hannibal as well?"

"Being much smaller than we are, he is disproportionately vulnerable."

"It gives him a rakish, drug-dealer look," said Erica.

"That computer of yours is another source of household concern."

"Damn it, Helga, it sits in my room!"

"Baleful radiation penetrates everything but lead."

"Does my CD player bother everybody too?"

"Don't be ridiculous, sweetheart. You've usually been mindful of the noise-level, and anyway, it stays in your room."

Erica shoved her bottle between her legs and stared at it. "Helga, is everything I bring into this apartment a source of contamination?"

"Nonsense. I'm not at all worried about myself. If I were, would I be sitting here beside you?"

"Aren't those mummy images great?" said Erica, her mood suddenly changing. The narrator was explaining the process of embalming. The Egyptians removed the brains and internal organs, soaked the body in carbonate of soda, injected balsams into the drained blood vessels, and filled body cavities with salt and other spices.

"As I was saying," Helga began again, clearing her throat, "I'm not so much worried about myself. What really worries me is Caterina's treatment of Hannibal."

"Really? They seem to get along pretty well. She fascinates him. I've never heard him complain."

"Hannibal," said Helga, refilling her glass, "come over here, will you?"

"I don't wish to."

"Don't be such a curmudgeon, my pet."

"I have no interest in images of dead human beings."

"He is too much of a gentleman to air his concerns in public, my dear, but when his pain is excessive, he spills his soul out to me."

"Pain? I can't believe... Caterina, come here!" shouted Erica. Caterina's eyes gleamed back at her. Reluctantly, she stretched and yawned and then hopped down from her chair. Seating herself on the floor at Erica's feet, she looked up and twitched her ears.

"Caterina, have you been annoying Hannibal?"

"*Límpiame la vajilla, maricón!*" replied Caterina.

"What is that supposed to mean?" asked Helga.

"Her English isn't so good yet. She speaks Spanish," said Erica. "She's repeating one of the phrases she learned in that kitchen. It's not very polite. It means 'Wash the dishes for me, faggot!'"

"And what is that supposed to mean?"

"I think she uses it when she doesn't want me to bother her."

And at that, without another word, Caterina loped back under the table and leaped back onto Helga's chair.

"Perhaps Caterina will admit it to you in private," said Helga. "I'm afraid that some of her behavior can be quite rude. For example, she'll occasionally run up and bite Hannibal's tail. I've seen her do that myself."

"She's being affectionate."

"Tell it to Hannibal."

"Is that all?"

"Well... she can be absolutely raucous during the day. Even when Hannibal does want to play with her, she dances around him making such a medley of noises that he eventually flees. I've seen him cover his ears with his paws."

"Little cats are frisky, Helga. It's natural behavior."

"When he's sleeping, she'll come over and yowl and even slap him. It makes him quite nervous."

"She only wants to play."

"Perhaps."

"Look at that, Helga. That's very interesting." An archeologist, admiring the Egyptians' great skill at embalming, mentioned that the soles of mummies' feet, even thousands of years after entombment, are often still soft and supple.

"Amazing!" said Helga. "But you know … there's something else."

"What else?"

"About Caterina. She eats his food. I've seen her. Not content with the dry food you feed her, she'll snatch away Hannibal's liver. I think the poor chap is getting thin."

"Can't he defend his own food?"

"He's asked me on occasion to allow him—quote—'to teach the little upstart a lesson.' I caution him always to eschew violence. I remind him that *noblesse oblige*."

"I'm really sorry, Helga. If Caterina's busting his balls—"

"*Ma chère*, he lost those pointless accessories shortly after I met him," said Helga. The wine relaxed her, and she was surprised that she had ventured such a joke. Erica smiled, showing her beautiful white teeth. "But sometimes," Helga persisted, "she displaces Hannibal from his chair. She'll pursue him so relentlessly that he'll jump off and hide under my bed. Upon occupying his chair, to add insult to injury, she'll make all kinds of yammering noises to try to draw him out again."

"She doesn't know any better, Helga." Erica's mood suddenly darkened, and she covered her face with her hands. "She just wants a little attention."

"I suppose," said Helga, now wishing she had not decided to act as Hannibal's spokesman.

"I'm sorry," said Erica, bursting into sobs. "I'm sorry, I really am sorry," she kept repeating.

Helga, too, felt her nose get stuffy with tears. Reaching out to Erica, she cradled her in her arms, rocking her to and fro. Erica cried herself out on her bosom. Her jaw felt so sharp it seemed to cut into Helga's sternum. Unlike Erica, Helga wore a bra—out of habit, since for many years it had served no practical purpose. "Don't cry, my pumpkin, my sweetheart," Helga murmured, using words she had often showered upon Alberto, who liked to seek comfort with his much heavier head against the same bony spot on her chest. She breathed deeply of the heavy, seductive perfume from Erica's hair, and when Erica faced upward, she inadvertently tasted the girl's smooth, tear-soaked cheek.

"I love you," whispered Erica. "I need you so much," she said, placing her warm, salty lips on Helga's. Helga was unsure of how to react. She felt invaded and yet utterly immobilized. While enduring the gentle pressure on her mouth, and the probing tip of a tongue that wormed its way through her wine-slick lips to her barricading teeth, she glimpsed the golden slits of Hannibal's eyes. He looked at her in disgust. Helga yanked her face to a side. Erica, however, seemed not to take offense. She turned around and rested the back of her head against Helga's thin shoulder.

While Helga worried that the weight of Erica's head might snap her collarbone, they continued to drink and watch TV. The narrator estimated that the Egyptians had made over seven hundred million expertly embalmed and securely wrapped mummies. The ka, the spiritual twin of the body, depended on the body's continued existence. Without it, the ka could not live on, could not assume its place in the kingdom of the dead.

"So what did you solve?" said Hannibal, nestled on Helga's pillow as she tried to go to sleep. "The one who should have listened to you paid no attention. She hasn't a freaking clue how much she crowds me!"

"But she only wants to play." The nightlight showed, along the opposite wall, her frieze of black cats all in a row, their golden eyes aglow as they sat in identical pairs, tails joined between them in caduceus-like twists. "It's her way of saying she loves you, you silly."

"First of all, Helga, you smell from wine. Second, at my age I have no interest in being 'loved' if it means losing my favorite seat and wearing a ridiculous necklace."

"Hannibal, I saw what you did the other day."

"What did I do?"

"Out of anger, you pulled open the door to the hall."

"Your bedmate left it open."

Helga's cheeks stung. "If Caterina hadn't been sleeping, she could have gotten out."

"Can't say I didn't think of it."

"Luckily, I saw it before she awoke."

"It's her or me, Helga!"

"Don't be so apocalyptic, Hannibal. Give her another chance. Remember that people's motives are what count."

"Motives, my ass! You wonder why I hole up in this room most of the day? I'm literally afraid to go out. She'll jump out at me. Or she'll sneak around me and claw at my tail. I *am* losing weight. I am close to a nervous collapse."

"You aren't letting me sleep, dear."

"Nonsense, Helga! It is your conscience that is preventing you from sleeping."

"Stuff and nonsense! Hannibal, promise me you'll try to be more flexible."

"Damn!" said Hannibal, dropping to the floor with a thump.

"Where are you going, dear?"

"Under the bed, where I shall curl up and die."

"Hannibal!"

There was silence, then a tap at the bedroom door. Helga didn't stir. The door creaked open and a slender, robed shadow slid in. Erica dropped to her knees at Helga's bedside. She laid her warm, soft cheek on the thin blanket that covered Helga's thigh.

"I'm frightened," she whispered. "I need to be near you. I'm afraid to sleep by myself tonight. May I?" She waited, and as Helga couldn't find the will either to invite her or send her away, Erica stood up and shrugged out of her robe. In the nightlight her skin glowed as smooth and creamy as ivory. Her small breasts formed perfect cones. Helga watched her move around to the right side of the bed as if Erica were an image on TV. When she slipped beneath the coverlet, Helga did not move a limb. She pictured Hannibal jumping between them, but Hannibal stayed out of sight.

"You're cold, even with your nightie on," said Erica, leaning over her.

"I'm always cold," said Helga. "Aren't you too... like that?"

"I'm always warm. I never sleep in nightclothes. Yes, you *are* a bit cold," said Erica. She sat up, shaking free of the blanket, and passed her right hand over Helga's right leg, slowly, from thigh to toe. Wordlessly, she leaned forward and massaged Helga's feet. The hands felt good on her perpetually cold feet. "The soles of your feet are nice and soft and supple," said Erica. The warmth of Erica's hands seemed to steal up Helga's legs. Suddenly, Erica's face hovered smotheringly near. "Your cheeks need warming too," she said, laying long, languorous kisses all over Helga's face. Helga wanted to speak, to ward her off in some kindly, gentle way, but the words wouldn't come. Her tongue seemed to cleave to the roof of her mouth. A crazy-quilt of odors settled thickly around her—sweet from Erica's hair, pungent from Erica's armpits, and musky from the whole length of the electrifying body that snuggled up against hers.

"It's time to go to sleep, dear," Helga chided, turning away. "Really, my sweet—"

"Your legs are still cold," replied Erica, reaching down to massage Helga's calves, tugging at Helga's silky chemise till it slid up over her crotch.

"We *really* must go to sleep, Erica," Helga heard herself inanely repeat. The naked Diana had beauty to hide from an understandably moon-struck Actaeon. But she? What was it that *she* so dreaded to expose? She caught Erica's hand as it lightly, caressingly cruised to the top of her thigh. What she felt in her belly, produced by Erica's hand, was a powerful, frightening tremor.

"I love you," said Erica.

"Stop, dear," Helga replied in a cracking, pleading voice, a voice that had lost all authority.

"I will not stop loving you," said Erica, bending down over Helga's body, nuzzling her unwrapped stomach. "You're shivering," said Erica. "You need me to make you warm."

Memories of past lovers flashed through Helga's mind. Maurice, the novelist so recently deceased. Chef Alberto, of course. Sandor, the gentle playwright. Wesley, her guru for five years... All had once been beautiful, and so had she, once. They whirled through her brain and sneered! A *woman* in your bed! So this is what you've come to? She tried to beat them back. The past was dead, deserved to be dead, should stay dead. She too was dead—a drunken fool who had momentarily forgotten the shadow she had become. Corpses are of indeterminate sex! she shouted back at them. Love was a charred spot at the base of her belly. Ghosts hovered above her: laughing, knee-slapping specters who regaled each other with the hilarious tale of a bunch of old bones that attempted to ignite but splintered and cracked in the unaccustomed heat of a living flame. The pain in Helga's belly, and now between those sticks of jerky that once had been her legs, threatened to tear her to shreds.

"Stop!" she shouted, pushing against Erica's head. Her parted knees kicked back at the limpet-like body that had fastened itself between them. She felt Erica slide away. She heard Erica crumple to the floor, then lie there quietly weeping.

The first thing she felt when she awoke in the morning was Hannibal sprawled on her chest. "About time," he said.

"I'm sorry, Hannibal. Are you hungry?"

"Who the hell knows? I'm too pissed to care."

"You're angry at me."

"At you? Only very indirectly. It's that bitch of a Caterina."

"Hannibal!"

"Don't 'Hannibal' me when I'm trying to tell you something!"

"You haven't seen her all night. What makes you so cross?"

"You mean you didn't *hear* her—all damn night? She sat hollering and moaning right by the door, pleading with me—in that horrible foreign accent of hers—to come out and play."

"I didn't hear a thing, dear."

"Oh, no? Well, after your girl friend left, the little siren kept me up all night. As soon as I'd doze off, she'd be at it again. I'm absolutely exhausted. Lucky for her the door *was* closed between us.... I'm announcing it to you right here and now," said Hannibal, tapping Helga twice on the chin, "I've had it with her—and that's that." He yawned, showing yellow teeth and gaps in dentition, then rolled off Helga's chest and groggily slumped to the floor.

"We cranky old people have been short on patience, haven't we?" said Helga, hearing Erica still bustling about in the apartment. Sitting up in bed a mite too fast, she felt dizzy, then waited until the blood flowed back to her brain.

"This apartment is much too small for two incompatible felines," said Hannibal, warily approaching the door.

"Learn to forbear, sweetheart. And try to be a gentleman." Helga draped her purple bathrobe around her and swung the door open. The sun-filled living room promised a pleasant working day. Erica, in a dark brown suit, was just coming out of the kitchen.

"Hi, Helga. I left you some coffee."

"Erica, dear, I wanted to see you before you left for work."

"What for?"

"To apologize."

"For what?"

"For last night."

"No need to. I shouldn't have come on so strong."

"It was entirely my fault, my dear."

"You don't really believe that, Helga."

"Oh, but I do. I'm a stick."

"I promise to be patient with you next time," said Erica, reaching down to scratch Caterina, who stared at Helga with bright, mocking eyes from her perch on Hannibal's cushion.

"Next time?" said Helga.

"Isn't there always a next time?" said Erica.

"Not necessarily," said Helga, placing her hand against her sternum, over the part which still felt bruised.

"Of course there is, my love." Erica smiled and grabbed her handbag from the table.

"Have a good day," said Helga. What she wanted to say was, Haven't I made it abundantly clear ... that there can *be* no next time? Why hadn't *Erica* seen how absolutely clear she had made it?

"I'm giving you fair warning," said Erica with a wink as she marched to the door.

Helga shuddered as though she'd been issued a threat.

"See you later, sweetie." Erica unlocked the door and slipped out into the hall.

"Lock up, sweetheart," Helga whispered after her. But Erica did not lock up. Helga heard the squeal of the front door, then the clack of Erica's heels down the four steps leading to the street.

It was time for Hannibal's liver. She stood guard until he finished it.

"I'm starting to work now," she announced. "And I don't want to be interrupted." Hannibal scrambled to take possession of his cushion. Caterina, on her best behavior, took the seat next to him—but Helga knew what the little vixen was thinking. Putting the pair out of mind, she began to sketch the idea for a new painting. The door to a tomb accidentally left open. The goddess Bast seen through the door, seated on a lofty pedestal.

A series of cries coming from the street distracted Helga from her sketch-pad. She glanced at the clock over the sofa. Past five-thirty already! What was the hullabaloo all about? Hannibal jumped from his cushion, scrambled up onto the arm of the sofa, and peered through the curtains behind it.

"Can't see a damn thing!" he said.

"We must clean some windows," said Helga. "Sometimes one does want to peek outside."

"You do know who that is, don't you?" said Hannibal.

The cries grew sharper, and Helga did indeed know the voice. It was Erica's. Reluctantly, she closed her sketch-pad. She threw on a sweater, since it was nippy out there, as she knew from stepping out about an hour before. Or was it five hours ago? she wondered. Objective time and the world of 'reality' meant nothing when you were working. Unable to stop thinking of her unfinished sketch, Helga shuffled in slippers through the still-unbolted door, out into the hallway, then out through two sets of doors and onto the front steps.

Erica knelt at the curb in front of the hydrant some yards to the right. Neighbors that Helga neither knew nor wanted to know were already gathering near.

"Whatever is the matter, Erica?" said Helga, almost *sotto-voce*, as though speaking to herself. She tried again, speaking aloud, but how could she compete with all that commotion? So she climbed down the steps and made her way over to Erica, who saw her and uttered her most agonizing scream yet—blood-curdling, Helga thought.

It did not come as a complete surprise when Helga saw, stretched below the curb, the squashed little body, its bloody mouth open in a silent scream of gleaming-white teeth. Someone had at least had the decency to scrape the poor thing out of the middle of the street, where a stain—overrun with tire-tread marks—showed where the accident had occurred.

"*You* killed her!" shrieked Erica as Helga grew near.

"Whatever do you mean, dear?"

"You killed her!" Erica repeated, then bent again over the broken body, her torso rising and falling in grief. All these strangers, these carrion-sniffing buzzards, began to stare at Helga, then at Erica, and back at Helga.

Helga raised her hand to her throat in dismay. "How many times have I warned you to bolt the door?" she said—but Erica wasn't listening.

"Hannibal did it," Helga explained to her grim-faced neighbors. Among them she recognized the man who had stood in her doorway. "I can't keep tabs on him all day, you know. He loves getting into the hall, if you give him a chance."

The man she recognized stared at her and slowly shook his head. Erica wept. A woman, meanwhile, spoke softly to her and held her to her breast.

"Caterina obviously sprang out after him," Helga continued, rounding out the scenario to be sure that they all understood. "People come and go through the front doors all the time. It could have been one of you let her out."

How dreadful to feel that no one was even listening!

"Who would have bothered to keep her in?" said Helga. Erica, convulsed with sobs, clung to the bosom of the stranger who tried to console her. "I ask you, now, Would any of you have thought to keep her in?"

SUSTAINING FALLS

Kathleen Gerard

The minute Coolidge pulled into the driveway and cut the engine on the pickup, Amarilla burst out the front door and came running down the porch like the house was on fire. There she was, my kid sister. She was as slender as a Q-tip, and her frosted hair was all swept up like a tidal wave. As she ran toward us, I spied her braless chest springing up and down inside one of those cheap, brazen, little hussy sundresses. It was better suited for a Clearasil-using teenager, not a spider-veined woman creeping toward the far side of her forties.

Amarilla stuck her Barbie-Doll pink face through the passenger's side window. "Oh, Marjery," she said. "I'm so happy to see you…"

Well, at least that makes one of us, I thought.

"…But I feel so bad about the way you've been suffering with your leg and hip since you took that fall. I thought by now you'd be back up—dancing."

"Well, these days, I'd merely aspire to walking across the hall to the bathroom."

Amarilla frowned and swung her head. "Marjery, I'm gonna do all I can to make you comfy. I promise."

I turned and leered at Coolidge. "Well, I would've been plenty *comfy* staying right where I was - if *somebody* would've just left me be."

Coolidge tugged on the brim of his John Deere cap. "Darlin', you know I'd like nothing better than for you to be home, but I just can't be there to help you. It's just a couple of double shifts. It's not forever." Coolidge looked past me, over to my sister. "Her leg and hip are so bad." He said this to Amarilla as if I weren't even there. "She can't even stand long enough to measure out a teaspoon of instant coffee and stir herself up a cup. And the thing is, the bills are piling up."

"No need to fret," Amarilla assured. "That's what family's for."

When my kid sister reached in and rested her red-painted fingernails upon the age spots on my arm, I swung out the door and forced her to take a step back.

That left my man to quickly jump out of the pickup and rush to my side. He held out his hand to help me step down, but I disdained his offer - latching onto the steel frame of the truck for support instead.

"Well, then, ladies…" Coolidge set down my walker in front of me. "Maybe we ought to go inside and get ourselves settled."

"Great idea," said Amarilla. "I've made us a nice, tall pitcher of iced tea—"

"—Without the hooch, *I hope.*" I firmed my grasp around my walker and hobbled a step.

"You'll be pleased to know that I've been on the wagon for five whole years now." Amarilla held up her right palm and wiggled her long fingers in my direction.

I looked at Coolidge. "Yeah, I guess wrapping a car around a tree and losing your driver's license can work miracles on some people."

My man scowled at me while Amarilla heaved my suitcase from the back of the truck. It dropped upon the gravel driveway so hard a cloud of dirt kicked up all around it.

"Marjery, please," Coolie whispered. "This is only for a couple of weeks. You'll be home before Christmas—"

"—But you know how I hate taking from my sister." My voice was as taut as a banjo string. "It only means I've gotta work that much harder at keeping the peace."

"Darlin', you are sixty-two years-old. When are you finally gonna bury the hatchet?" Coolidge didn't say another word. He darted away from me, chasing after Amarilla. She was lugging my suitcase up the front porch as if it were her cross to bear.

I couldn't believe how the two of them were showing more concern for a battered, old piece of luggage than for poor, old me. By the time I heard the screen door close with a single clap, I stood there outside—left to my own disabled devices—going nowhere. But alone, I wasn't. I saw a large, shadowy image framed in the window of the house next door. Why, it was Lace Curtain Lorena—Lorena Dixon, the eyes and ears of Tallulah Falls. I spied the outline of her egg-shaped head gawking at me from behind her kitchen window. As I put up my hand to let her know that I had spotted her, her image suddenly disappeared. Oh, how I wished I could, too.

I kept my leg propped up on pillows day after day. I wasn't getting much better even though I'd stayed put in my old bedroom in Mama and Daddy's house. I still called it Mama and Daddy's house, 'cos I'd never get over the fact that in her will, Mama left the place solely to my kid sister. Amarilla had moved around the furniture, and she'd tried to make it her own by redecorating the rooms in perky shades of sherbet. The parlor was painted cotton candy pink; the kitchen, lemon yellow; the powder room, lime green; and my old bedroom, ripe raspberry. But none of that changed the way I felt. Some days I swore that if Amarilla would've tacked up some letters of the alphabet, it would've seemed like I were convalescing in a preschool. Yet, even with all my kid sister's bright cheerfulness surrounding me—and her responding to the bell I rang so she could cater to my every whim—I couldn't help but keep revisiting the past and feeling as dark as a cave on the inside.

It was Mama who used to say that there ain't no such thing as a saint without a past or a sinner without a future. And it wasn't until after Mama died that my kid sister went in search of forgiveness and redemption and found Jesus once-a-week. Yet I was probably the only person this side of heaven who knew the truth as to why Amarilla sat in the first pew at church on Sunday mornings and volunteered two days a week down at the Old Folks Home. For the better part of her years, Amarilla was a hot number who had a long litany of men pass through her life the way eighteen wheelers haul through a truck stop.

It was a few years before Daddy died—and Mama passed on—that Amarilla fell so hard that the earth shook for everybody around Tallulah Falls. My sister's first mistake, but certainly not her last, was falling for Baltimore Butterworth, the Fire Marshall. Mama always said that any decent Southern lady ought never get involved with a married man - especially not a colored one named for a city north of the Mason-Dixon Line. But at the time, Amarilla was so high-minded that she didn't heed Mama's wisdom. All along, Baltimore kept promising my kid sister that he was gonna leave his wife, but I always knew that Baltimore Butterworth was a man as married as red beans are to rice. After my kid sister told him that he'd laid his claim inside her, he pleaded with her to get rid of his seed. But I knew better. Baltimore was never gonna leave his wife and kids for her—ever.

When Amarilla finally learned this painful truth the hard way, she started to plain, old unravel. She went all around town, mouthing off about Baltimore and their love child. In the end, my sister's carrying on drove Baltimore straight to the bottom of a bottle. He lost his job. His wife threw him out. And on Christmas Eve of that same year, Baltimore drank himself into a stupor. He must've slipped, hit his head, and then collapsed on the concrete steps in front of the church because folks found him frozen to death on Christmas morning. Nobody around Tallulah Falls could figure what Baltimore was doing down at that church. He'd never set foot in a holy place a day in his life - except if there was a fire.

It was after he died, that Amarilla started drinking to drown away her own sorrow - but I guess Amarilla's sorrow knew how to swim. She shamed herself and our good family name. And folks started calling her *The Limb of Satan*, 'cos she not only destroyed a man's life and reputation, but now she was five months pregnant, liquoring up, and getting behind-the-wheel.

It was a few months after Baltimore's casket was still mounded with a pile of dirt that Amarilla got so stinking looped, she wrapped her car around the oldest Angel Oak tree in town. It was a miracle she survived, and to this day, everyone in Tallulah Falls believes my kid sister lost the baby that night. But as I stood over her stretcher at the hospital after the accident and took one look at her washboard flat stomach, I knew there was never anything but a made-up ghost story living inside Amarilla's womb from the very beginning.

"You awake, sleepyhead? I brought you a cup of tea," Amarilla said, carrying a tray, steady, through the shadows of my raspberry-pie colored bedroom. "The doctor's office called. They want to see you at the hospital tomorrow."

"Tomorrow? But Hanging Dog's forty-five miles from here. Coolie's never gonna be able to get off work on such short notice. And you? You can't legally drive no more, can you?"

She swung her head. "I can't go with you anyway, Marjery. I'm working downtown at the thrift shop t'moro."

"But I can't afford cab fare. And there's no way I'm gonna be able to hoist myself up into a bus or a train."

Amarilla calmly handed me that cup of tea. "Marjery, don't worry. It's all taken care of. A nice lady I know through church is going to take you to your appointment."

"You mean I gotta drive forty-five miles with a stranger?"

"She's a nice lady," my sister said. "She's even offered that she'd treat you to lunch — if you're feeling up to it."

"Well, I'm not some sort of a charity case." The spoon on my saucer clanked as I set down my tea upon the nightstand. "I don't make it habit to put folks out—"

"—Marjery, I don't see what other choice you have. You really need to get that leg tended to…"

In the end, I figured that if some Bible Blazer was trying to arrange for her eternal salvation by offering a forty-five mile ride and a free lunch to a perfect stranger, then the polite thing to do was simply just enjoy the trip and eat to your heart's content. At least that's how I reckoned all this in my mind until ten-thirty the next morning, when I heard a car kicking up the gravel in the driveway. Whoever was driving was leaning on the horn like it was doorbell announcing her arrival to the whole neighborhood. I pulled back the curtain in the parlor and took a gander. There was one of those little Japanese automobiles idling outside like it had been gassed up with MSG or something. But that was only the beginning. By the time I hobbled outside with my walker, I saw these great, big, flashy stickers that read, *Honk! if you love the Lord* sprawled across the bumpers of that car. The minute I spotted them, I spied Lace Curtain Lorena's egg-shaped head pressed up against the glass window of her kitchen door. I couldn't believe that I was gonna have to pile into this church-on-wheels.

"Marjery Pettigrew? Is that you?" A familiar zealous voice preened. I cringed as I shot my sights from that image of Lorena's head in the window over to a teased, stiff bouffant that poked out from the driver's side window of that car like a small, brunette shrub.

That pile of hair leapt from the car and rushed toward me. It was Georgette Whittamaker. She had so much spray plastered on her head that not one single hair moved in the breeze she was creating.

"What a glorious surprise," Georgette squalled. She barreled against my walker and smothered me with her long gangly arms. "I didn't know Amarilla was your sister?"

"It's times like these that I'd sell my soul to be an only child," I mumbled, using my walker like a barrier to keep her at bay. "When did *you* move back to Tallulah Falls?"

"I'm only visiting—came in early for the holidays—and I'm so glad I did. I think our meeting like this has got the Lord's fingerprints all over it." Georgette flung out her long nails so that tiny rhinestones glistened on each tip.

"Yeah, it looks like the Lord's putting his grubby hands on just about *everything* these days." I thrust out my chin toward those *Honk! if you love the Lord* bumper stickers slapped on her car.

"Oh, don't you just love them? Aren't they great? Now I get to pay homage to my Personal Savior even while I'm in transit."

I shook my head. "What is it with you, Georgette? Why can't you ever just go quietly about your faith?"

"Why should I?"

"Because you just scare folks away plastering the Lord over everything—that's why." I waved my hands above those stickers like a wizard trying to make them magically disappear.

"Don't be silly. I've lived long enough to know that what other people think of me ain't none of my business. And, besides, if somebody's talking about me, at least they're leaving somebody else alone."

Georgette lifted the cuff of her jacket and eyed her watch, and I could feel my hands seizing into hot fists around the cool, aluminum handle of my walker.

"C'mon. We better get a move on, Marjery—or else we won't have time for lunch before your appointment."

I didn't like this arrangement one bit, but I had no other choice, so we both plopped into that church-on-wheels and set off for Hanging Dog.

While Georgette kept her hands firmly around the wheel and her eyes steady on the road like billboards of concentration, I started to tell her about the complications I'd been having since I fell on the ice and how those doctors from upstate had put my hip and pelvis and femur bone back together again. But I didn't get very far into the details. I swore that if I were only watching Georgette and not the speedometer, I would've thought she was driving in a race at a hundred miles per hour. Her eyes were unblinking and her knuckles were white around the steering wheel. That poor needle on the dash was straining to keep steady at a measly twenty-five—and there we were, driving in a sixty-five mile per hour zone. Other vehicles tooted their horns in a fury, trying to find a way to whiz by us on that road.

At one point, I got so fed up trying to compete with all those horns honking, that I finally just burst into a fit. "Georgette, where the hell did you learn to drive—and are you even listening to me?"

"Oh, I'm listening, all right, Marjery." A smile beamed across Georgette's face. "Do you hear what's going on all around us? I mean, can you believe how many folks just love the Lord?"

I grit my teeth so hard I thought they might crack.

I didn't know it at the time, but that free lunch courtesy of Georgette Whittamaker would be the last decent meal I'd have for a week. It didn't take the doctors up in Hanging Dog long to look at my leg and admit me to the hospital so they could run some tests. I was pleased that I was finally going to get my aching body tended to and even more tickled that I could send Georgette on her holier-than-thou way.

A blood clot—that's what I had in my leg. They started pumping all kinds of thinners into my veins and with the bed rails raised all around me like I was a baby in a crib, I started feeling real sorry for myself. That was until the phone rang a few days later, and I heard Georgette Whittamaker's voice blathering on the other end.

"I think the blood clotting in your veins is God's way of showing you that you've stopped letting joy into your life," she said. "Why, you've got to open your heart to joy and let it in, no matter what the circumstance."

"If you're so smart that you think you know the mind of God then you tell me, where's the joy in being a cripple?"

"Marjery, every creature on God's green earth is crippled in one form or another. I don't know why some folks are forced into using walkers and wheelchairs - maybe it's just to remind us *all* of that—"

"– How dare you preach to me!" I lashed out at her. "You're not in this bed. You're not in my body. You don't know nothing about the life I'm living, the pain I'm feeling–"

"—All I'm saying, is that I think He's just waiting for you to come around and make peace with Him. And if I were you," she told me. "I'd do it now before it's too late."

"Well, that's just the thing - you're *not* me," I scolded, hanging up the phone on her.

A week later, I rolled out of the hospital in a rented wheelchair and glided onto a bus that hauled me back to Tallulah Falls. My dander was still up about the way Georgette had spoken to me. I figured if there was a God,

I didn't reckon His favor - not anymore. Why, it's so unfair the way He gets you to believe in Him. Here you spend your good years filling up your life, making all kinds of plans. And all the while, you keep pulling yourself up by your bootstraps—you honor Him and keep raising your hopes—'til one day you take a fall and everything just starts spilling out, and you're forced to spend the rest of your time idling by, watching, as He keeps on taking a little bit more out of your life every day.

I kept thinking about all that the morning of Christmas Eve day. There I was, still put out of my own house, with my legs once again elevated above my heart. I was missing Coolidge, who'd decided to work overtime for holiday wages down at the railroad straight through the New Year. And I was so tired of listening to my kid sister bicker with her latest beau down in the parlor of my Mama and Daddy's house. You see, ever since the Baltimore scandal rocked the town, Amarilla kept doing for other people, getting nothing in return, and acting like she was satisfied with that. I reckoned she thought it was her penance or something. She was another Georgette, except for the fact that she wasn't always praising God for fixing the clothes dryer or finding her a close parking spot down at the *Piggly Wiggly*. Amarilla wasn't always a holy roller like Georgette, though. I imagine Georgette was spat out of her Mama's womb, and the umbilical cord was like a string of rosary beads, pumping religion through that child's being right from the start. No, it was living and life that made my sister fit for finding her redemption. But even sitting with Jesus once-a-week couldn't really change her. It was like she was helpless. And in all the time we'd spent together—living back under the same roof—I knew the only real difference between Amarilla past and Amarilla present was that she now wore a cross on a chain around her neck and dragged Jesus through the mud of her still-wretched life.

Hatcher Daye, her latest beau—from out of town, this time—was another married fella who fell hard for my sister. He promised he was gonna leave his wife before Amarilla's forty-eighth birthday. But by the time my kid sister blew out forty-nine candles on her birthday cake, his promise held about as much clout as Amarilla's make-believe pregnancy. It looked like Hatcher Daye was gonna prove to be like all the rest.

It has been years since all that Baltimore stuff wreaked havoc everywhere. Yet, for me, the whole thing seems like it happened only yesterday. First Daddy died and then Mama had a series of heart attacks. And I swore that for as long as I lived, I'd never forgive my kid sister for all the trouble and heartache she caused. I vowed to stay far away from her, but somehow, I never could. Amarilla lived under the same roof with Mama, and because Mama got so sick after Daddy died, she needed my kid sister. And every time I went over to sit alongside Mama's sickbed and hold her hand, I kept saving up my feelings to tell Amarilla a thing or two after Mama crossed to the other side. But Amarilla, she just kept doting on Mama and taking such good care of her, that Mama lived another seven years - long enough to clamp a lid on all my resentment.

It wasn't until after I heard the front door slam closed and Hatcher Daye's pickup peel out of the driveway that Amarilla finally responded to the cry of my bell.

"Jesus Christmas, Marjery. What the hell do you want?" The tone of my sister's words sounded like unplanned fireworks in an empty sky. I gathered that whatever she had been arguing about with old Hatcher was even worse than I'd imagined.

"W-Well," I stuttered, "I was just gonna say that a cup of tea would suit me fine about now."

After the kettle stopped whistling, I listened to Amarilla's heavy footsteps march up the center hall staircase. She paraded into my room, carrying a small tray with my tea cup.

"Where'd Hatcher go?" I asked.

"I sent him home - *for good.*" She steeped my tea bag up and down in the cup like a yo-yo.

"Now why'd you go and do a thing like that?"

Amarilla attached her gaze to mine. She glowered at me. "God, I should think you'd be in your glory," she brayed. "Go on, don't you wanna say *I told you so*? Don't you wanna say I told you all married men who cheat are bunch of rotten, lying, no-good, sonofabitch bastards?"

My mouth unhinged.

"Go on, say it, Marjery. I give you my blessing. I know how you've been dying for this day all these years…"

I noticed Amarilla's shiny mascara-smudged eyes. Her slim body was beginning to tremble.

"A-Amarilla?" I peered at her sideways. "Are-Are you all right?"

"Damn you, Marjery! Damn you!" she yelled, her face now flaming red. A close, cloying odor of alcohol suddenly filled the room. "Holding a grudge against me all these years—passing judgment and giving me your lip… Well, I'm sick and tired of it!"

In all my life, I don't think I'd ever heard the sound of such wretchedness welling up from the bottom of another human soul.

"Amarilla, honey," I purred, narrowing my eyes on her. "Have you fallen off the wagon?"

"Why don't you just mind your own damned business and shut up!" Amarilla's words tore through her throat. She flung that tray with my tea across the room. "Just shut up for once in your dog-gone life!" I flinched as the cup crashed against the wall above my bed and shards of china flew everywhere. As droplets of hot tea started to burn my skin, the doorbell suddenly rang.

My kid sister and I, we both froze.

"Who are *you* expecting?" Amarilla asked through clenched teeth.

"Nobody," I told her. "Maybe it's Hatcher?"

When the doorbell rang again, Amarilla tiptoed over to the window. "Jesus Christmas," she sighed. "Doesn't that Lorena Dixon ever miss a thing?"

Amarilla scrambled to fix her face and press the wrinkles from her denim skirt. Then she hurried down the staircase toward the front door. I propped myself up in bed and tried to listen close.

"Merry Christmas!" Lace Curtain Lorena greeted Amarilla.

"You shouldn't have—"

"—Oh, it's just a couple cookies the kids and I whipped up. Tell me, how are things, Amarilla?"

I heard the hesitation in my sister's voice. "Well, being you're the eyes and ears of this town, maybe you ought to *tell me*."

I could hear Lorena clear her throat. "That fella who's been calling for you—you gonna marry this one, Amarilla?"

"Marry?" my sister roared with laughter. "Why I ain't never getting married. I'm having myself too much fun being single."

"Oh, you're wrong. I think it'd be the best thing after all these years—"

"—Why, if I got married," Amarilla told her. "Then what would you do with all your free time? C'mon, you wouldn't really want me to stop performing my service to you and the whole community, now would you?"

A beat of silence hung amid their conversation. I could just picture the eat-crow look on Lorena Dixon's face as my usually sweet, honey-tongued sister floored that nosey, old goat speechless. In spite of the way Amarilla had just spoken to me, I was so damned proud of my sister for finally sticking up for herself that my heart was swelling with joy. Why, I was rooting her on. And as if to underscore the thrill of my sister's stunning victory, the telephone started to ring.

"I ought get that," I heard Amarilla tell Lorena Dixon before bidding her goodbye.

After she closed the front door, I heard Amarilla's fired-up footsteps as they started to rush upon the stairs. But mid-way, I heard a terrible *thud!*

"Amarilla?" I called out to her from my bed, straining my voice above the bright, persistent sound of the telephone. "Amarilla - you okay, honey?"

When I heard sobs followed by moaning sounds coming from the staircase, I hoisted myself out of bed, grabbed my walker and hobbled into the hallway.

I gasped at the sight of my sister. She was sprawled out on the stairs with Lorena Dixon's tray of cookies splayed all around her.

"Here, let me help you up," I told her.

"No," she insisted. "Just leave me be and get the damn phone!"

Relying on my walker, I limped over and lifted the telephone receiver. "Marjery, have you come to your senses yet?" Before I even had the chance to say *hello*, the sound of Georgette Whittamaker's voice was buzzing like a bumblebee in my eardrum. "The Lord ain't gonna set you free 'til you make your way back to Him... You know, life's too short and eternity—it's just way too long..."

I let Georgette babble on and looked down at my sister. With her head resting near the top step, Amarilla's body shivered like she'd been left outside in the cold too long. I wasn't quite sure why she was sobbing this river of tears. It could've been because of her falling up the stairs? Or maybe it was 'cos of Hatcher and her falling off the wagon? Or maybe it was the words she put between us or the way she lit up on Lorena Dixon? Whatever it was, I didn't know. The only thing I knew was that while my kid sister was blind with weeping, this churning feeling was growing inside me. It was linking the past, the present and the future all into one, and then clearing it away in one fell-swoop like a bulldozer barreling right on through me. Suddenly none of it mattered. All that had kept me from my sister suddenly seemed like a foreign land where I just didn't speak the language no more.

"... So what'd you say, Marjery? How about you dust yourself off, oil up your wheelchair, and I'll pick you and Amarilla up for midnight services tonight?" Georgette asked. "Wouldn't that be the best present you could give yourself and the good Lord this year?"

I eyed my sister. I thought she'd never stop crying. "I don't know, Georgette," I moaned into the phone. "I reckon I just don't know—"

"—Well, I ain't taking *no* for an answer this year, you stubborn old mule. I'm gonna keep hounding you until the stroke of midnight ..."

" ... I bet you will, Georgette. I'd bet my last dime you will."

Numbly, I hung up the phone. Then I hobbled over to the top of the stairs and stretched out a hand to my sister. She wiped away her tears and struggled to catch her breath. I swallowed a lump growing in my throat.

Holding one hand tight on my walker, I felt my sister's cold fingers firmly grab hold of mine. She used all her strength to get herself back up on two feet. And then, there we were—Amarilla and I—standing a step apart, braving our pain. Through veils of tears, we both stared down at all those cookie crumbs that covered the stairs.

I said, "I think the trash might've been an easier way for us to dispose of Lorena Dixon's cookies."

Together, Amarilla and I, we both just burst out howling at the same time—laughing like we ain't never laughed before.

IN PRAISE OF BIG WOMEN

Steve Taylor

I wish I had resisted your American enthusiasm this morning. I retreated to the kitchen, but you stood outside calling like a prophet, "Come to the desert, Fritha McClean," and, of course, your students joined the chorus.

I came out to try my puny wit. *Miss McClean thanks you all very much indeed, but regrets to say she has a previous engagement at the dishwater.* But, of course, you rallied them, spread your arms and turned to face them. *Who will clean with me?* you bellowed, and all twelve of them arose, a host of merry workers. Ten minutes of happy clatter. They even sang *Hi Ho. Fri-tha,* you called, *it's all mc-clean now.* And so, of course, I really had no choice, swept up in your tide of laughter and deposited in the Dry Lake Mojave to search for flaked edges and Pinto points.

I have been doing my best for the last two hours, wearing the ridiculous hat you gave me. With my height, I must look like a human cabana. You could walk under my shade. Even so, I didn't mind, until you paired me up with one of the bright, ambitious ones to map what we find. He insists I do some of the searching, although I clearly slow him down.

His voice congratulates itself for being patient with me. *No, that's just natural erosion, but put it back carefully anyway.*

Still, I keep my pluck as I was trained to do. *One must always try to maintain good humour and modesty.* Even in primary school when slides of a preying mantis remind a classmate of one's long, spindly body, causing one to be dubbed "Mantie." Even more so later when one's body fills out and a boy invents one's permanent school name, "Fritha McLean the Amazon Queen." But I am irritable by the time you call us back together, and I'm not sure if it's with him or you.

You call us to a little hill near the highway where there is a pile of huge boulders.

"Wanted to show you a petroglyph while we were here. It's right below this other important cultural artifact." You turn and point to a rock behind you where "Chuy 87" is spray painted and get the laughter you wanted. "Other one's a little older, by about two thousand years. You don't see many petroglyphs around this area. The ones you do aren't too elaborate. Neither's this one, but I like it."

You indicate a hollow place, and we queue up to lean in and look. It is the image of a human hand, a delicate little hand, the fingers rounded and neat. It would have taken days to finish, scraping rock against rock, and it is a small space, too cramped and awkward to reach in and work. It must have been made by a child, I think, or a very slight adult. I have the vague picture of a girl kneeling there, her black hair almost covering her bare behind.

You turn to my tutor, who has dutifully stood next to me, and ask, "So, Mike, whatta ya make of that?" He licks his lips as he squats and tilts his head to look at it again, stalling for time. I know how his voice will sound. It makes me cringe even before I hear it. He goes on about how the same kind of figure has been found in caves in South Africa and other sites etc. etc. and how it may indicate the presence of mystical belief etc. etc. and how they are often accompanied by dots which indicate psychotropic etc. etc. I'm being unfair to him. He's telling us important facts, but his voice keeps them from penetrating. You don't seem to notice it, or, rather, you're wearing your pleasant checkers face, the one that disguises the traps you set. It didn't change the single time I beat you, but maybe *that* was a trap to get me to play more games. You maintain it for the whole ten or twelve hours Mike goes on and nod decisively when he is done. "Well those are some interesting connections," you say.

But suddenly you pivot and face *me*. "So Fritha, whatta *you* think?" My cabana wobbles as I flinch.

"I... I don't know. This wasn't my subject at..." I start to burble, but you cut me off.

"Yeah, I know. You're the only one here who hasn't *studied*," you say as if your education irritates you. "That's why I'm asking."

I bend to look again, then stand up straight, although I feel exposed. *To slouch suggests discomfort with oneself.* You tilt your Aussie side hat to look up at me.

"Well, I don't think very much really. I just suppose they both had the same feelings."

"Who?"

"Chuy and the girl who did the hand."

You nod. A grin creeps into your checkers face. I hear a snicker somewhere behind me.

"What feeling?" you ask.

Now, of course, my thoughts embarrass me. "I don't know," I mumble. "I'm here. Think about me. Something like that."

"See that?" you exclaim and show me all your good American dental work, the results of fluoridation. "See that?" you repeat and look at Mike. "Sometimes maybe it's better not to know too much. What will I notice if I approach this like I'm looking at it for the first time and don't know anything about it?"

You pat Mike's shoulder and he smiles, but it looks like a mortician sewed it there. What are you doing? Did you select him to humiliate on purpose? I admit it feels exhilarating to be praised by you. The others smile at me. You turn to me again and ask, "Why do you think it was a girl?"

I've had enough of your questions, thank you very much. "Oh, I don't know," I tell you.

"Well don't stop now," you nearly bellow. "You must've had some reason."

I glance at Mike. He's clearly blushing now, embarrassed by his learning.

"Not really," I answer. "I just pictured her."

"See that?" you ask again in the voice of your American enthusiasm. "I hope every one of you pictures *somebody.* Objectivity's fine, but it's easy to forget we're looking at people too. It's good to remind yourself of that from time to time."

You actually tip your hat to me and say, "Thank you, Fritha."

So this is why you brought me out here, needing my ignorance to make your point. But how did you know I would? I wonder what Mike is picturing as you send us back to our observations. Not that he broods exactly, but now he steps away from me as he finds his true flaked edges and makes sure I write the notes correctly. I am worn out by the time you shout, "Everybody ready for our mid-day feast?" It's a relief to be the serving girl again, to be handing out the sacks of bologna sandwiches and boxed juice.

But of course you won't allow it. You must ham it up again, telling them that "Fritha has prepared the feast," asking them to applaud me. And then, an instant before they do, you bellow, "Our Zyzzyx Maiden has provided."

Just good-natured merriment to give me the same name as the wrecked boat in the concrete pond, the one you always use to break the ice. You used it to break the ice with me when I first arrived in answer to your advert, extracted myself from my Honda Civic, the average size of a car back home, and extended to full height. You had the good grace not to ask me if I played basketball. Instead you focused on my name, parsing the syllables, savoring each one.

Fri-tha Mc-Clean. Saxon wed to Scot. Delightful.

Mum wed to Dad, I mildly joked, but of course you trumped me shaking hands.

Joe Malone. They said there was a wedding, but who knows?

Then you stowed my duffle bag, gave me the cabana hat, and took me to the pond to charm me with the story of the little cabin cruiser. You stood with your back to it, addressing me in your merry lecture voice.

This place used to be a resort during the forties. The guy who owned it bussed out retired people for a couple weeks at a time. Built this pond too and called it a lake. You'd think they'd be mad as hell when they saw it, but apparently most of them weren't because he made a bundle. Guess they liked drifting around. Didn't get too seasick anyway. Can't you just picture them?

And, of course, I could. There was enough left of the boat to see them. A little group in full regalia—starched white trousers with blade-sharp creases, blue blazers with anchor insignias, captains hats with gold cloverleaf. Desert sunset and happy hour cocktails. I glanced at you from the corner of my eye and saw you picturing them too.

But do you grasp the implications of the name? What makes you think I am a maiden? Well I am not, thank you very much. There were *two* different men at university. Nothing very permanent you understand. They were both insecure brooders, what some women call *sensitive*, but they do count. "Thank you, Maiden," some of your students say as I hand them their sacks, and I must share the joke or be thought prissy. "Eat well, my child," I answer. I almost think I could dislike you.

A girl to my left is addressing me. She has the sort of looks I've always coveted—lean and vigorous and compact, but pretty too— green eyes, her blond hair in a French braid, the sort of girl who could model, say, rock climbing equipment.

"I'm sorry," I tell her, "I was in a daze."

"Yeah," she says, "I noticed."

I've been watching you play checkers with the students, setting your traps to dispatch them one after another, all with your pleasant face unchanged. Now I see by the girl's face that she's gotten the wrong idea. It flusters me, of course.

She grins, her teeth so white they almost look transparent. I pass my tongue across my own involuntarily. "Carrie Brooke," she says, extends her hand, and gives my bigger paw a forthright squeeze and shake. "Fritha McLean," I answer as if she's never heard the name. She nods.

"Don't worry," she says, "I totally understand." She leans toward me, lowering her voice. "He's not what you'd call *hot* even for an older guy, but I still got a pretty big crush on him."

"You have?" I say with a little too much surprise.

She leans closer, whispering now. "Yeah, dumb isn't it? Think I'd even do him if he wanted. Pretty sick, huh?"

Her figure of speech leaves me blank for a second. When it dawns on me what she means by "do him," I giggle with her. "No," I say, "I don't think it's sick." Then her face changes, loses its mirth. Her eyes widen and blink.

"Oh god," she whispers, "I'm sorry. I didn't mean I was going to. I mean I wouldn't, you know, try to get in the way or anything." What has dawned on her now dawns on me. How could it not? How thick could I be? Of course she thinks I'm already doing you. I don't know what to say. I should object, but something in me wants her to think it, although I've never actually pictured us doing *that*. For an instant, I start to, and it isn't a pretty sight, the awkward forms of mismatched animals. Before I can say a word, Mike steps over the bench and slides in next to her.

"You two look engrossed," he says. "What's up?"

Carrie shuts and opens her eyes to me before she half turns to include him.

"Hello, Mike," I say.

"So, still high about what the old man said?"

"I didn't take it seriously. I think he was just being nice," I tell him.

"No he wasn't," Carrie says. "He was making a point."

Mike scoffs soundlessly. "Yeah, he's always got a point, doesn't he?"

Carries turns her head to him. "Yeah," she says, "he does."

Mike scoffs again, but he swallows before he does, blinks and swallows again. Now I see what's happening. This isn't the effect he hoped to have on Carrie. He wanted to look cynical and smart so she would want to do him. Now he's trapped himself with sarcasm and doesn't have the strength to stop. He smirks and looks away from her.

"Yeah," he says, "the man straightened us all out. We gotta cut all this *scientific* crap. What we gotta do is, like, sit around and, like, you know, *imagine* stuff."

Carrie instructs him to go and do himself. She swings back toward me, the thick cord of her French braid almost whipping him in the face. Of course, he scoffs again. "Well," he says, smirking venom directly at me, "I'll leave you ladies to imagine something."

"Yeah,"" Carrie says without looking up, "we'll imagine you don't exist."

All I can do is wince as he tries to saunter across the dining hall and out the door, awkward with knowing he's being watched. It reminds me of when I was forced to be in a play in primary school. *Julius Caesar.* I was only a soldier and didn't even have a line. I merely had to walk across the stage with another soldier who delivered a message, but in rehearsal I had to repeat the scene half a dozen times with new instructions until the teacher said, "Oh for pity sake, just stand there then."

Carrie begins to praise me, going on about my "powers of observation." I suppose it's a kind of apology for saying she'd like to do you, but I'm not listening anyway. I'm picturing Mike pacing about in the dark, trying to reassure himself he's right. I wish I had her ability to erase him. I really do. Clean and efficient. Never suffer fools or let them trouble you. Label and erase. After a few minutes, I can't stand it. "Um, listen," I tell her, "I had better go talk to him."

Carrie's face exaggerates itself. "Huh? Him? What for?"

"Oh, I just think I ought to make peace," I tell her. To my surprise, she nods.

"Oh yeah, I get what you mean," she says, and I see what she's thinking—that I'm keeping *your* path smooth. The Zyzzyx Mistress serving her man. I like that she thinks it, though it makes my exit even more self-conscious than trying to walk across the stage.

Mike is not pacing about. When I step beyond the ring of light from the dining hall and my eyes adjust, I see him by the pond. He is sitting in the cattails at the edge, turned toward the boat with his knees tucked up, his arms around them. He's probably relating its wreckage to the wreckage of his life in all sorts of painful ways. That's what I would be doing. I sit down next to him and wait.

"So," he says without turning his head, "what's up?"

"Um, oh, nothing. Just thought we had better talk."

He turns his head still cradled on his arm. "What for? This *his* idea?" he asks, and I see he has the same assumption as Carrie. Maybe everybody does. It feels like it's getting out of hand.

"Whose idea? You mean Professor Malone? Why would he want me to talk to you? No, no, I wanted to talk you. You know, clear the air."

"Don't bother," he says. "I'm the asshole in the group. I accept it."

He's so transparent, baiting me to deny it. If his head was turned away, I'd roll my eyes. But it makes me feel more sorry for him too—having to be that obvious. Brooding has never appealed to me though. Not in the long run. Not even the artistic kind, and I studied art. I think I even liked his smugness better. Not that it matters. I'll give him what he needs because it's easier. Somehow brooders seem to know this.

"You are not," I insist. "In fact, you're quite the opposite."

"Oh yeah I am. I'm the guy in class who puts his hand up too much. You know, the answer boy? I get on *everybody's* nerves. I know it."

"You don't get on my nerves," I lie.

"Yeah, right, sure I don't," he says, but I can hear that he just wants me to be more emphatic. I try.

"Cut that out right now," I tell him. "I do not think you are an asshole, and you do not get on my nerves. In fact, I wish I had your learning, and I think you have a perfect right to be annoyed with *me*. I don't know the first thing about any of this, and I don't think people ought to be given the impression that I do."

It works. He stops hugging his knees, straightens up, swivels around to look at my face for a long moment before he says, "Actually, I gotta admit, what you said *was* sorta interesting."

"It was nonsense," I say with a last burst of emphasis.

Mike releases a mirthless laugh and shakes his head. "Well, we're sure a hell of a pair." I match his laugh and nod. "The asshole and...." he starts to add but then doesn't know what to call me.

"And the know-nothing," I say.

"Now *you* cut it out," he tells me. He pats my back. Then his hand rests on my shoulder. We stay that way, gaze at the ruined boat resting on a gash in its bow as if it ran onto a sea wall in a storm. But then Mike slides his fingers to the back of my neck. Oh my god. He's going to try to.... And yes he does all right, half turning, pulling me down to him. I don't know what to do, so I do nothing. In fact, I hunch a little to make it less awkward for him. His tongue worms against my teeth, flicks all over my unfluoridated dental work. He certainly seems passionate, but perhaps he is only grateful and it will all be over soon. Then, god save us, I feel his hand. It's only a vague touch through my work shirt and my practical brassiere, but it's there all right, and I don't know what I'll do if he starts to move it elsewhere. I feel as if I'm letting a twelve-year-old have his first grope.

He squeezes a little and kisses harder. Then his lips slide to my neck. My eyes are open and I see him out of focus—a creepy sensation—like he's a remora stuck to my whale body. I can't help pushing him away. He tries to persist, raising himself to graze my ear with his tongue, as if I am merely afraid of losing control in my passion. I take him by the shoulders, move him to arm's length. He looks at my hands. My strength surprises him. I can tell he doesn't want to test it. I loosen my grip to make it less obvious.

"I'm sorry," I say, "I just can't."

"Why?" he starts to ask, then shakes his head and sighs, "Oh, I get it. I shoulda known."

"Known what?" I say though my voice pitches a note too high.

"You and *him*," he says.

"That is *not* the reason," I tell him too emphatically. "*Nothing* has happened between myself and Professor Malone."

"Oh yeah? So what's the matter?"

You're a presumptuous little boy, I ought to answer, but I know I won't.

"It's...well, I hardly know you."

I'm irritated with myself, of course. He looks up at me, but at least I don't slouch to his eye level.

"Oh," he says, "I'm sorry. I apologize."

So my accent protects me more than my size. Like most Americans, he assumes it comes with inhibitions. The truth is we probably all do each other at about the same rate these days. I did the two artistic brooders without much courtship, all of us mismatched animals. I'm glad I sound like I didn't though, glad to play the big maiden with bigger inhibitions.

"I really *would* like to get to know you better," Mike says respectfully.

His eyes look earnest, almost innocent. That's all I need, another *sensitive* little boy. I doubt he means it anyway, although it's clear he'd do me if he had the chance. Probably for the challenge more than anything. And then he'd want to be reassured.

"Well, that would be..nice," I mutter in return, wishing I could erase him.

You cannot be this clueless. Even I think there's something going on, making me the center of attention so often. Is this your way of trying to seduce me? With public displays because you cannot manage an approach in private? *That* would be a truly American sort of inhibition. The entire fortnight before they came, you weren't the least aggressive, a perfect gentleman, my mum would have said. At some point, though, you'll have to make your intentions clear and close the deal alone, unless, of course, you plan to do me publicly as one of your object lessons. Maybe you'll make me their love goddess.

As usual, the students carry on your joke, competing to lay their trinkets at my feet, singing incantations to my goodness. *Protect us in the hunt, oh goddess of life and death.*

I'll play along, but I do not enjoy the fantasy. They, however, love it as they stalk the dining hall in their hunting bands, wielding the throwing shafts and darts you shaped from wooden spoons. They look around with real desperation every time the lights go on, as if the ancient predators they must hit before your timer dings will really savage them. Only Mike looks half-hearted, as if he doesn't want to play your game but hasn't the strength to refuse. He essentially commits suicide, throwing last, not even trying to beat your bell, his spoon dart falling short. I have no choice but to erase him, and his band looks glad to see him gone. He sits on a table in the corner, watching like one of the predators. Why don't you work on *his* self-esteem? Carrie competes most ferociously, throwing fast and cursing when she hits your stand-up human by mistake. I'm glad to declare her eaten by the short-faced bear. She bows to me and says, "Your will be done."

But no one else slays both predators and kills the bison. "Well, guess this means your species went extinct," you bellow, click your tongue, shake your head, crinkle your eyes, and sigh. Honestly, Malone, do you practice in the mirror? I know what's coming before your impressive eyebrows arch above your widened eyes and you exclaim, "Unless the goddess wishes to resurrect you." You do not even look at me as you say it, as if my presence is invisible. I hold my hands up like a pope and tell the bones to live, so now there is even greater tumult, more elaborate offerings and incantations. Why not simply tell them to pray that I'll drop my knickers for you?

This time Mike's band begs him to concentrate, says things to build his self-esteem, so he is forced to try. I know exactly how he feels, have had experience with it. It's worse than being mocked, gaining a moment of their mock acceptance on the chance he might somehow exceed their expectations. So when the miracle happens, when he hits the saber-tooth and topples it as the timer dings, I know his little rush of joy. His fellow hunters cheer and clap his back, but the others shout it was too late, so everyone turns to me. "Kill shot," I declare. A few of them moan loudly at my decision. "Ah ah, careful not to insult the goddess," you say as if I might kill them randomly. At the moment, maybe I would.

Now, of course, I root for Mike, who needs to prolong the feeling, wish I really had the power to grant him another miracle. He still doesn't look like he's having fun, though he tries hard not to show his desperation. I think it would have been kinder to kill him off. Now when he misses his next shot and I must, he slumps back to his corner as Carrie hoots and dances.

She's a wily one, applying her own little strategy. I can't hear what she's saying, but I can tell she's been flirting with the two boys in her band, leaning subtly closer to them, letting her shoulders slouch a little to make herself seem weaker and more do-able. One of them looks ripe to sacrifice himself. I hate it when her band kills off the predators. She misses the first shot at the bison, but the last boy gallantly hands her his atlatl. Now she kneels before me. *Goddess, I ask you for your help*, tries to ham it up like you, but, of course, she lacks your imagination.

I preferred Mike's brooding to his getting to know me better. His interrogation is more tiresome than all the job interviews I've had since leaving school. Yours, of course, wasn't tiresome at all. In fact, it could hardly be considered an interview. Then again, who else would have answered your advert, promising as it did, "mediocre pay, primitive conditions, endless opportunity for sunstroke." It's weirdness was irresistible. Back home, I'd pictured America as a place of complete audacity, as huge and brash. Crude too, of course, but unapologetic, and I was weary of apologies. I imagined even my size would be a small thing in a land of no proportion. Before you, though, only the cars seemed truly oversized. The rest just seemed a noisier sort of blandness. Even worse, a good many Yanks sounded apologetic, as if my accent made them feel inadequate.

"I bet you're a whole lot better than you think," Mike whispers because I have told him my paintings were nothing special, reasonably competent but too conventional, just good enough for a degree. His voice sounds too intense as he works on my self-esteem, even rails against modern art and what he calls its "bias against realistic form." It would actually be rather insulting, if I cared, as if he imagines me painting pretty landscapes like some Victorian hack. Actually I painted all sorts of ways, and all of it expressed the way I felt—indifferent. I could never convince Mike of this, of course. He's much too busy looking for insecurities. "I envy your imagination," he says.

"Matter of fact," he says, "that's why I want to show you something."

He looks toward the dining hall, then swivels his head slowly from one side to the other, squinting to pick up any movement in the dark. He reaches into a rucksack behind him in the cattails, squints and looks around again.

"Hold out your hand," he says and sets a smooth white stone on my palm.

"It's a mano," he says, "a grinding stone. This is a special one though. You can't see it very well, but feel the top."

I run my fingers over the surface and feel swirls of tiny stitches, delicate and even, as if the stone were needlework.

"I found it on the site this morning. None of the manos around here ever have decoration. Soon as I saw it, I knew you'd appreciate it. I wanted to give you a chance to see it, you know, without some big lecture. Figured that'd ruin it for you. So I sneaked it into my pack. Here, take my pen light and have a look. But only for a couple seconds, ok? I'm not really, you know, supposed to do this."

I can well understand the anxiety in his voice. I feel it too immediately. You must have warned them twenty times not to disturb the site, even read them the law against it. It was the only time I can remember you sounding completely serious.

"Jesus, Mary, and Joseph," I whisper, "you shouldn't have done this," but he puts his little flashlight in my hand.

"No, it's ok, just look quick," he says. "Don't worry, I'll put it back. I have it's exact location on my site map."

I feel so tense I don't even want to look, but it sounds so important to him—not that I look really, but that he has been a brave little boy—that I do flick on the light for two seconds. So it's like a flash picture in my head, but long enough to see it *is* special, the swirls so tiny.

"Yes, it's lovely," I tell him, and his voice sounds pleased.

"Yeah, you can see her working on it, can't you?" he asks, and the question is so transparent I do not imagine her. Instead, I think of him wanting to do me again, wonder if he'd go to such lengths for it. But maybe I'm being too cynical. Maybe he's just awkward at being sensitive.

"Yes," I answer, "I can." And I try to picture her, but I'm still too tense and conscious of it. And Mike keeps quiet for what seems a long time to let me think of her, though I can hear him fidget in the cattails. Then I try to give it back to him, but he stops my hand, puts his over mine and leans to kiss me. For a second, it is something like a sensitive kiss, a sharing-the-moment sort of kiss. I even close my eyes. Then, of course, he presses harder, and here comes the tongue again. So I open them and wait for the hand to follow. And it does. But still I don't slap it away, mostly I think because it feels so pathetic, the brave boy groping for his reward. Like some children's story, except that he has to deflower the giant. Mike and the Amazon Queen. But he doesn't go further, at least not yet. "Let's go to my room," he says.

"I don't think that's a very good idea," I say and wish I'd put more firmness in my voice.

"Come on, it'll be ok," he breathes close to my ear and tries to turn my chin for more tongue work. I pull away.

"No, um, no, I'm not going to, sorry."

For a moment he says nothing, pouting I imagine. I can hear him breathe. But when he talks again, his voice sounds reassuring.

"It's all right, I understand. Well, will you take a walk with me then? Don't worry, it'll be safe. I have a bigger flashlight in the pack."

I'm surprised at his lack of whining, at how quickly he's given up.

"A walk? All right, sure," I answer.

"Great," he says. "I'll be back in a sec. I gotta get a couple things."

I try to give him the mano again, but he has already turned to jog to his room, and suddenly it dawns on me what he has gone to get. My god, I think, he plans to do me on the ground somewhere, out on the dirt road or maybe even the shore of the dry lake. He'll probably bring a blanket. It's such a pathetic scheme that now I'm angry, *pissed* you Yanks would say. Back home that would mean I was drunk. Now, though, I'm distinctly sober. I sit with the mano in my lap, working myself up to tell him off. That's why I don't see you coming, don't hear the sound of your boots until you're almost to me. I gasp and tuck the mano under the tail of my work shirt, petrified that you've seen me do it.

"Hello, goddess," you say, so I feel relieved.

"Hello."

"Meditating?" you ask.

"Just sitting."

"Well, listen, the hunters are demanding another round and they're calling for their goddess."

"I'm just enjoying the quiet right now. Please just ask someone else to..."

But, of course, you could never allow yourself to be dissuaded from your mirth. For the first time ever, you lunge to seize my hands. I try to pull away, but you have me firmly.

"No, no, now, you can't make'em settle for just any old goddess," you declare and start to pull me up, look down still holding both my hands as the mano tumbles from my lap.

"What's that?" you say, an instant before you recognize it.

I cannot sleep, of course. Not because I'm tense. In fact, it's weird how calm I feel. *Where'd you get this?* you demanded, already assuming I couldn't possibly be responsible. But then you didn't make me answer the question, somehow knew I wouldn't in any case. Mike must have seen us, hiding in the dark. He, I'm sure, is very tense, getting to know himself better than he ever could have wanted. He surprised even me, reappearing in the dining hall to join his hunting band. Of course, he committed suicide even faster than before, didn't look at me even when I erased him. I'm thinking of the way you held the mano and reached for my hand again, squeezed it once to chide me without speaking, not enough to hurt, and how your firm grip softened just before you said it was all right. You didn't let it go when one of them came to see where you had gone. *Just give me five minutes, ok?* you told him and didn't even turn your head. But after that, you couldn't think of what else to say to me. My god that was endearing. You had to use a quieter lecture voice to reassure me. The sweet absurdity of giving me background about the mano. Of course it wouldn't have escaped your notice. You mapped it long ago, already intending to show it to me.

Ya gotta understand what was going on in this period. The lake was dry by then. All the big animals were gone. Oh yeah, there's evidence men still practiced their hunting rituals, but that was just wishful thinking. The women actually fed the tribe most of the time by gathering. So a mano wasn't for some side dish. Even lizards and insects got ground up for the protein. But this is the only one I've ever seen like this. She took her time with it. It was hers. See what I mean?

And of course, I did see, an instant before you said it. She knew her worth.

Now I think I know my worth to you, though I don't know why. For once I don't intend to analyze it, talk myself out of it. I like how the night air chills me through my work shirt, shiver at the feeling. I haven't even laced my boots. I don't know what I'll say to you, can't imagine what you'll say to me. Maybe you'll start another lecture so I'll have to stop it with a kiss. Our bodies will be mismatched, of course, but I can see you smile at the awkwardness, hear you whisper endearing jokes. There is still a lamp on in your room. I can see its vague glow as I shuffle around the corner in my unlaced boots. So you're still awake. Maybe you're thinking of me. Even expecting me. I wouldn't be surprised.

For a moment I hear the whispering in my mind. Then I freeze as I hear it because the glow leaks out at your doorway. I stand stock still to listen. But why am I so calm when I should be shocked? I think I could laugh aloud at myself. And at you, together in one great laugh. I do not, of course. One does not when one has been taught so constantly to be discreet. I almost do though, hobbling backwards in my flapping boots, trying to be quiet. I duck behind a Joshua tree and cover my mouth with my hand to hold it in. And really I bear you no malice, neither of you. I understand completely. She wanted some of your power and couldn't think of any other way to get it. And you are always glad to exercise it, need to remember that you have it. I know you would still do me if I asked. I hope she isn't disappointed. Your two bodies are nearly as mismatched as ours, but maybe your enthusiasm was enough.

It's all so funny I quiver at it as she passes. So serious. Stepping carefully, her French braid barely moving, as furtive as if she's still in her hunting band, as if the lights will suddenly go on and she will have to take me down with her atlatl.

In the porch light and waning moon, I see the wriggling of tiny legs. They curl their tails but scurry as I walk. I step gently—not to spare them but simply to be quiet. I am afraid you will hear me and come to make me forget myself. What is it like to have such power?

I can make out the wreckage of the little pleasure boat and pause for one last look. Without your buoyant voice to keep it afloat, I begin to wonder how it wrecked like that, start picturing the disaster. A false move and the motor jams. They jolt and splash each other with their cocktails. Before they can even get their footing to look up in horror at what is happening, the Zyzzyx Maiden completes the hundred feet of pond and runs against the concrete. Retirees are airborne, their brittle arms and legs splayed outward, still holding their glasses. But, of course, I know that's not the way it really happened. The truth is it just swamped eventually, collapsed into its own decay. In any case, I'm done with metaphors. In yours, I am linked to the mano forever and to the guilty weight of your forgiveness. That is how you will erase me.

I set the gear in neutral and begin to push the little car across the clearing toward the dirt road. I will turn in one direction or another at the highway. America is large and open and half empty, and I am a double curiosity, the very sort of aberration Americans fear and can't resist. Not like the woman whose grinding stone you will put back, who had no choice except to celebrate herself so small men who posed as big could still be fed.

276   *In Praise of Big Women*

SOON WILL BE THE BREATH OF DAY

Christopher Bundy

Whoever Mary Kay Keegan first saw the announcement on the entertainment news program she paid it little attention, her mind and body slumped on the sofa in a mist of Gallo and Paxil. She had only caught the tail end of the segment, really no words at all, just a photograph and a familiar song. Beneath the photograph were the dates 1943—2001. The meaning of those dates, birth and death, did not become clear until Mary Kay woke in the early morning with a whimper of understanding. George was dead.

Please don't be long, she sang to herself, then called her daughter, Sadie, in Boston.

"Mom, it's 4:00 in the morning."

"George is dead. I need to see you."

"George?"

"Harrison. You know."

"Right, I'm sorry." Mary Kay heard exhaustion in Sadie's response and knew she had to wait for her daughter to continue. "Can we talk about this tomorrow? I've got work."

"I know you think I'm crazy. I can accept that. But I want you to at least hear what I've got to say. Can you do that?"

"I don't know, Mom," Sadie said, her voice fading. Mary Kay waited again for her daughter to reply. She unconsciously scratched the word OK into a notepad with the tip of her aluminum nail file.

With a sigh, Sadie finally agreed. "Fine. So, when are you coming?"

Mary Kay would arrive at Logan the next Friday. And while she was taking the first step by going to Boston, Mary Kay hoped her daughter would recognize her efforts in return. *You came all this way. Why don't you just stay for Christmas?* Mary Kay imagined Sadie asking. Still her only wish was that she might convince Sadie of the truth: that her mother was not some ridiculous stereotype. That she had done something special once. And Mary Kay wanted her daughter to finally accept the truth behind her own remarkable entry into this world: that George Harrison, former Beatle, Krishna devotee, and wondrous spirit, was her father.

WHEN MARY KAY WOULDN'T WAKE UP

For the flight, Mary Kay felt justified taking the extra Paxil, the gentle buzz swaddling her in an eagerness to find better things ahead. She reasoned every little bit would help, even the wine to wash down her repose. Mary Kay knew it was difficult for Sadie to accept the truth she had been telling her since she was old enough to understand her mother's words. She knew Sadie told others her mother had lived *no kind of life*, chanted nonsense—*Ohmm pati pati… whatever.* Mary Kay had made peace with her life even if she was not always peaceful. But with George's death, she decided it was time to make peace with Sadie too, to recover her bluesky baby, the gift of that long ago holy union she had always treasured. Even when things went wrong and there was nothing but the noise of her daughter's dissatisfaction, the only thing Mary Kay wanted from her simple life, other than recognition from George, was Sadie's trust. Mary Kay had always been honest with Sadie about her father, as much as she felt she could, but now, with George dead, it was time to tell Sadie the whole story of what happened in Rishikesh, of how she was conceived under a blessed February moon on a warm night in 1968.

Mary Kay fingered the prayer beads she wore around her neck. One bead at a time she rolled her way to serenity, an unconscious habit she had never dropped. Baba had given her the simple sandalwood beads upon her arrival in Rishikesh, her only keepsake, save for a few bent photographs of daily life at the ashram. The composite scent of red and yellow sandalwood, cedar, cardamom, jasmine, and nutmeg had never faded and served as a constant reminder of her devotion to Baba.

When she was feeling blue, Mary Kay wondered if she romanticized something that wasn't as wonderful as she remembered. Maybe she was living in the past, she thought when she was weary of considerations and couldn't seem to find balance in her life. The doubt, Sadie's doubt, crept in then. From the first moment she had set eyes on Baba's gentle soul in Rishikesh, Mary Kay knew, feeling corporeal warmth inside her, she had come across someone extraordinary. Mary Kay looked into his eyes, alive with so much light, dancing with giddiness, and wanted to know what he knew there in such a beautiful place on a hill above the Ganges, jungle surrounding them on all sides. Some complained of the food, the flies, and the heat, the absence of drugs and alcohol, but Mary Kay hardly noticed, so happy was she to be where for once in her life she felt a kinship.

Life was simple in India, she a girl of twenty with fewer worries to stir her up and keep her mind from clearing, her body in a state of rest she could hardly remember anymore. Baba showed her a path to freedom from anxiety, and while there were times when she lost her point of reference, her light dimmed by years in Myrtle Beach and the sun-burnt and assailing tourists that swept through the Myrtle Beach National Wax Museum where she worked each day, Mary Kay never lost her treasured talent for meditation completely. When life disappointed or troubled her, especially when Sadie, such a stormy child, filled up their small trailer with so much noise, whether as a toddler or a teenager, the sheer vibration of her child making it nearly impossible to focus on her point of light, Mary Kay recalled Baba's words. *I am full. I am empty just the same,* Mary Kay would chant and chase a Paxil with a glass of Gallo, a rerun of Kung-Fu and an orgasm in the green chair thinking of David Carradine.

Still, there was a tear in Mary Kay's life story she had spent more than thirty years trying to stitch together with letters and travels. But the more letters she wrote to George and the farther she traveled, the less of her past life she had been able to restore. In its place, there was a terrible knot she could never untangle. Mary Kay recognized her mistakes too. Her daughter's name had been meant to serve as tribute to Baba, when a backpacker had told her about a Beatles song that alluded to the Maharishi. What the traveler hadn't told her was that the song was written as a lampoon of her beloved teacher. Mary Kay had meant well. In India, Baba had revealed to her such a pure discipline, one in which her life was meant to roll out like a ball of yarn, pushed by the inescapable hand of providence, its single thread tethered to birth and death, knots in between to untangle and pursue. George's death felt like another tangle of her life undone, this one returning her again to Sadie, and to that long ago in an ashram in the high mountain jungle of Rishikesh that her daughter so often accused her mother of *overremembering*.

Mary Kay's last thought before she fell asleep was how quiet the airplane seemed save for the hum of its jet engines, not a whisper in the entire rear of the cabin on the evening flight, the dark outside an infinite softness. Then a flight attendant shook her by the shoulders, the young woman's voice polite but firm in her ear, and Mary Kay opened her eyes to find airport medical staff and a security team hovering over her. Smelling salts had roused her from her stupor. Airport staff wheeled her to a first aid station, where she waited for Sadie. When Sadie arrived, Mary Kay tried to respond to the anger and shame blossoming on her daughter's face, but her tongue refused to move.

"Mom? What happened?"

There was no need for the hospital, but you shouldn't mix alcohol and pills, the nurse scolded Mary Kay, who wanted only to go back to sleep and to the forgiving darkness she had seen through the airplane window.

THERE IS NOTHING OF ME

The only quality of her daughter's home Mary Kay recognized was its difference from her own, something plainly urban about the blonde wood and the stainless steel, the red and green of apples covering the simple straight lines of two sitting chairs. Compact discs lined the wall, labeled with not a single recognizable name. A laptop in platinum sat atop a utilitarian corner table. More than anything she realized there was nothing of herself in Sadie's apartment. Nothing of Sadie's family. No photo album or 4 x 6 on a bookshelf. No pictures of Sadie, either, except for a photo on the refrigerator of Sadie laughing with a drink in her hand beside a dark man in sunglasses.

"I'm sorry about what happened at the airport." Mary Kay reflexively counted beads with her fingers.

"You really scared me, Mom. What were you thinking?" Sadie looked ready to pounce.

"I guess I wasn't. I was nervous about seeing you again." She found it difficult to meet her daughter's eyes, the heat of her critical gaze overwhelming. Mary Kay wished that she could step back and start over on the airplane where everything felt more promising.

"I thought you gave up the wine? Don't you know how dangerous it is to mix that stuff?"

"I know. And I did—I hadn't had a drink in, I don't know, awhile. It takes time. I was nervous." Mary Kay knew how her words sounded, but she wanted Sadie to believe her mother was trying.

"Yeah? You said that last time I saw you."

Mary Kay's chest heaved—tears were nearby—a quick stab of heartache that wouldn't lie still for long. It *hurts...* Mary Kay wanted to tell Sadie. This was not a part of her plan. She suspected Sadie was trying to distract her. Mary Kay would have to ease her daughter into the discussion she wanted. The last time Sadie was home, Mary Kay tried to talk with her about George. But Sadie raged like she had never seen before, destroying much of Mary Kay's prized record collection.

I am so sick of this! Sadie threw Bob Dylan at the wall. *I have had it, you understand.* Ravi Shankar at the television. *I can't be a part of your fantasy anymore.* Badfinger flew from her hands. *It's embarrassing, Mom. Honestly, if you could hear yourself. Aunt Jane thinks I should have you institutionalized.*

I know it's difficult for you to understand.

No, it's easy, Mom. What's hard is listening to the same story every time I see you.

I'm sorry, Sadie. I don't know what else to tell you.

Ever since I was a kid it's been Baba this, Beatles that, George Harrison all my life. I can't take it anymore.

Baba always said my life would be difficult for others to understand. But you were the new branch. You, Sadie Louise Keegan, were the blessing of a holy union, a gift from God.

Stop it, Mom, please.

It's the truth.

Aunt Jane is right: you just make it up as you go along. Doesn't matter if facts don't exactly fit. Mary Kay Keegan knows a better way. But you couldn't even get my name right.

Why are you so mean to me?

Listen, I didn't come home to fight with you. We both know where this conversation goes. For a minute I thought you might actually have something serious to say. Do you even know who my dad was? My guess is you had sex with some hippie asshole, who split when he found out you were pregnant. And if George Harrison is my dad, then where has he been all my life?

Sadie, don't be this way. I've tried. He's so famous, sweetheart. I'm sure there's just some misunderstanding. Give it time.

Don't play dumb with me.

You know what I mean.

You know what—I just don't.

Mary Kay had pushed the bad feelings away as *mothers and daughters*. Maybe one day Sadie would know different of her mother. Not that day though; you couldn't move inside the trailer on Lot #9 without crushing some broken piece of Mary Kay's records underfoot. She went through much of Dylan, pieces of Taj Mahal, Otis Redding, The Byrds, Santana, Free, Phil Ochs and Tim Buckley, Donovan, and much of the years 1971-1974, including Van Morrison, Cat Stevens, James Taylor, Stevie Wonder, and Carole King. And of course, her Beatles and solo Beatles, which Sadie destroyed with a special slowness. She smashed *The White Album* against the kitchen wall, crunched *Abbey Road* underfoot, and karate-chopped Paul McCartney's *Ram*. *Imagine this*, she said as a John Lennon's record sailed out the door and into their dirt yard.

That was two years ago; Sadie returned to Boston and hadn't been back since, though she did write a note of apology: *I'm sorry I broke your records,* on lovely blue stationary. She called once or twice a year, the last time in September after the attacks in New York, a phone message on Mary Kay's answering machine, *Hey, Mom, guess you're not home. It's Sadie. I was just calling 'cause, well, everything's so screwed-up with what happened and I just wanted to say hello. No biggie.* Sadie didn't call again, and Mary Kay never returned her call, always stuck with what to say. When Mary Kay felt at odds with her daughter, already defensive and weak with the frustration that came out of her as anger, she felt she was burning her life up in pure exasperation, what Baba would say was a waste of life's vitality. She could not, *would not*, she vowed, wind up at the end of her life feeling as if she had wasted it. She tried to steady herself.

"Let's not fight." The words came out rushed, her fear that if she didn't get them out then she would lose again. And she wouldn't even know why.

"Who's fighting?"

"It's just that, I'm sorry for putting you out at such short notice. And for embarrassing you at the airport. It's not the way I wanted things to start. So, what are your plans today? Want to show me Boston. I've heard it's nice."

"I don't know. It's no big deal, really, and by the time we walk back to the station and all that it could take like an hour and it's really cold out. Besides, I'm going in to town tonight. I have a date. Do you mind if we don't?"

"A date?"

"I'm sorry, Mom, but you didn't give me much notice. I can't just drop everything because George Harrison died. Life moves on, you know. Isn't that something Baba said? Anyway, I'll be back. We can talk then. Or tomorrow."

"Sure, I understand."

"Come on, Mom, don't pout. Listen, we'll do something tomorrow, alright? I promise."

For a heartbeat Sadie appeared calm, her dark eyes friendly behind jet-black bangs, a touch of color in her olive-skinned cheeks. Mary Kay wondered what her daughter saw when she looked at her. Myrtle Beach had not done much for Mary Kay physically or materially for that matter. She had always been thin, a ragged young girl awash in plain clothes, her hair in a single long braid, her knees and elbows, ears and chin reaching out from her body in caricature. And her light auburn hair had turned a color she could not name with one word. Grey was one of them, but its dry wavy roots suggested chemical damage that wasn't there. Mary Kay had vowed to stay away from dyes. She would not run from aging. But nature punished her early for her conviction—her hair brittle and gray, not white or some silvery (and grandmotherly) sheen, but the dullest non-color. If she started with hair dyes like a gateway drug it might not stop there.

"Yes, tomorrow then."

THINGS TO SAY

When Sadie left, Mary Kay tried to watch television but couldn't concentrate. She thought music might settle her down but again she hardly recognized any of the names and put on something from a band called Soundgarden because she liked the idea of a garden of sound, but got awful plodding guitars and downright screaming. She had no taste for it and gave up. When she found a small bag of pot on the shelf behind the CDs, she wasn't surprised and rolled a thin joint from the pungent weed, thinking it might relax her and still the pacing while she waited for Sadie to come home. But the marijuana was strong, and she had not smoked in years; again she found herself at the mercy of her drugs. She was much too high and this made her nervous. What if Sadie found out? Would she be angry? The smell of the strong dope would certainly linger in the tiny apartment. When she rushed to open the balcony doors to let in the cold New England air and let out the strong smell of pot, she worried that the neighbors might call the police. Back home, she knew what to expect from her fellow tenants, most of them no friends of the police anyway; but here she was in the dark. She went to replace the baggie on the shelf behind the CDs, but couldn't remember which one. A pretty name, but what was it? Had she forgotten something else? Had an ash fallen to the carpet? She flushed the still-smoking joint down the toilet so she didn't forget that too, afraid she might burn the house down, every object in the small apartment an obstacle to her peacefulness, something of her daughter's that she might ruin. Was that a knock at the door? A voice from next door? In the bathroom she caught herself in the mirror and recognized guilt masking every other emotion from her face. She was a dead giveaway. She needed to lie down and relax before her daughter returned. She needed to be still. What time was it? She was certain that Sadie would return at any moment, and when she tried to close her eyes, the cold winter air across her chest, she was again rehearsing what she would tell Sadie, if and when her daughter let her, about that night in Rishikesh—the most wonderful time of her life.

Mary Kay woke with such a start that she thought she was falling and put her arms out in front to brace herself. Sadie slammed the deck doors closed. The apartment was icy cold, and Sadie's weed baggie was open on the coffee table

"Sadie...oh, what time is it?" Mary Kay didn't know what else to say.

"It's about time for you to wise up, Mom, that's what *time* it is."

"I must have fallen asleep."

"Yeah? You know heat isn't free around here. And neither is that premium herb."

"I'm sorry. I was nervous. I wanted to relax. I guess I was looking for some music and found it behind... I didn't mean to."

"When did you get so careless, Mom? You're scaring me."

"I don't know what's wrong with me. I just want things to be OK between us. I'm tired of living the way we do. You're my daughter and I'm your mother—I want us to act like it again."

Sadie sat down on the couch next to Mary Kay, put her arm across her mother's shoulder. "I know. But you know why things are like this. Don't you?"

"I guess I do. And that's why I'm here. That's what I want to talk about. When George died, I realized there were things I still hadn't told you about Rishikesh."

"But that's what I'm talking about. That's the problem. You pushed me away with all that crazy shit. How can I possibly believe George Harrison is my father? How do you expect me to accept that? When I was a kid, I believed it all. I carried around that 8x10 photo from the *White Album* for years, telling all my friends, teachers at school, everybody, he was my dad. You know what they did when I showed them the photo?"

"I suppose they laughed at you."

"They called me a *love-child* and said my mom was a crazy hippie. And with a name like Sadie, in Myrtle Beach, I mean, it wasn't easy. You know how hard it was to make friends when I never even wanted to bring them to my own house. I was afraid you would start in on them about India like you did on me."

"I'm sorry, honey. What was I supposed to do? Lie?"

Sadie closed her eyes and then stood. "Yeah, Mom, that would have been perfect."

Mary Kay could never figure out where things went so wrong with her daughter. How something so beautiful had turned into something so ugly. Perhaps she should never have told Sadie about George. Mary Kay could hardly connect Rishikesh with her life now. But because of the light and her talent for forgetting, Mary Kay had trouble remembering most of the bad things of her life anyway. And when she did and the light was not with her, then a glass of red and a couple of Paxil helped ease those wrinkles out. Something she could count on, for her slip into darkness was always always the same. Mary Kay preferred the light when she could reach it, because the light left her refreshed.

Christopher Bundy

Paxil left her emptied out, and of not just the bad but the good too. But if her only option was the bad things and the sharp stabs of pain that came with them, then she chose the emptiness.

Sadie brought Mary Kay a glass of wine and put on a CD of quiet, almost angelic music, a woman's voice that settled both the room and Mary Kay—if only she had found that soothing music earlier. Sadie sat next to her on the couch. Her eyes were rimmed in black circles, tiny creases flowering at the edges. She's much too young to look so old, Mary Kay thought. Had she made her this way? Sadie picked up the baggie of pot and shook it.

"It's the kill. Want some more?"

"I'd better not."

"Yeah." She began rolling a joint. "Listen, I had a pretty good date and I'm feeling generous tonight. You want to talk, now's you're chance. I'm listening."

Mary Kay wanted Sadie to understand the magic she had experienced in Rishikesh, the magic she had never been able to explain to Sadie before her daughter shut down and refused to listen anymore. As a child, Sadie had sat transfixed whenever Mary Kay talked of India, a time when Sadie had asked about her father daily. Mary Kay showed her glossy black and white and color pictures inside big books on The Beatles, photos of India, George behind Baba and a crowd of others, all dressed in kurta pajamas, flowers in their long hair, smiles. But eventually Sadie wanted to know where he was *now*, what he was doing *now*, what he sounded like *now*. Did he smile a lot? Did he smoke cigarettes? Did he wear coveralls or a suit and a tie? Did he drive a big car? Did he smell like Mr. Palmer (one of the only dads she knew of and probably not the best of smells)? Did he shave like the dads on TV? Would he like the Orange Octopus ride at the Pavilion? Could he bodysurf or build a sandcastle as big as a doghouse?

Does he like chocolate cake?

It was a few days after Sadie had turned seven.

I'm sure he does. But why do you want to know if he likes chocolate cake?

It might be his birthday. So I could bake a cake, a chocolate one like I had for mine, and send it to him.

Sure, honey, he likes chocolate cake. But where would I send it?

This detail had failed to discourage Sadie and she baked the cake anyway, a mess of flour and cocoa and milk that she tired of when it didn't look like the photograph in the cookbook. When she forgot it in the oven and smoke began to leak from the door, Sadie had to run next door for Mr. Palmer because Mary Kay was in a deep sleep and couldn't be roused. And at the end of any story about Sadie's father, Mary Kay finally admitted to her daughter that for *right now* he was *not here*, but would be *one day*. Again and again she promised, until Sadie stopped listening, stopped asking, and stopped believing.

Even as a teenager, those troubling years in which Sadie disappeared for days at a time, her daughter had listened, even if she hadn't necessarily pretended to believe any longer. But once Sadie went to India to see for herself what sort of magic existed there and lost her fiancé Berdy to a riptide off the Goan coast, she finally stopped listening altogether.

"Fair enough. I want to tell you about Rishikesh."

And Mary Kay did.

"Everything changed once The Beatles got there. After three months with Baba and a family of others like myself, kids most of them from all over, Baba introduced all of us to The Beatles, who he had been seeing in England for months, teaching them transcendental meditation, the power of mantra, the teachings of Guru Dev: all of the things we believed could change the world. There was no one who hadn't heard of them by then. Yet, as much as I was in awe of these pop stars, it was Baba that I dreamed of, Baba that I believed in with all of my heart. The Beatles were something, sure, their arrival a grand to-do—and it was February because I remember the group celebrating George's birthday—an entourage of shabby celebrities with guitars and bright clothes, girlfriends and wives, journalists and hangers-on. Baba told us he would be busy for a while, his energies spent on the ambassadors of peace, new, flowering branches of his tree of knowledge. He would use their celebrity, he told us, to help spread his words of happiness, his blend of Western science and Eastern mysticism. While there was no need to shout his message, these young men would plant the seeds of his love much faster and to a greater audience—to the whole world in fact."

Mary Kay was wrapped in the love and stillness of Baba's home, her family of strangers closer to her than any people she had ever known. So she too saw these celebrities as more than rock stars: they were voices for Baba's message. Baba had even come directly to her, on his knees in her simple room, not bowing but sitting before her on a rug, with a question, his voice soft and high, almost like a child's or a woman's. Would she like to join him? he asked. Would she help him reveal the truth of his message to these young men?

That night, there was a big dinner for all of the guests. Normally, Mary Kay would not have been invited but Baba asked her to help serve. Even then she couldn't remember all of the names of the people there. Paul and Ringo she knew had left Rishikesh early. But there were other Beatle people, assistants and the sort, journalists, wives and girlfriends, the singer Donovan, Mia Farrow and her sister; there was a Beach Boy too, maybe more, she couldn't remember everyone, and a group of Americans and British young people like herself, there ostensibly to hear Baba's words, but spending more time at the arm of a Beatle or a Beach Boy. Not all, of course, but some. It didn't matter, they were there, and so many at Baba's table to receive his good news. After dinner, Baba left the room, saying he was tired and needed to rest for the next day's teachings, and the group grew louder, more restless in Baba's absence. Mary Kay remembered the smell of dope suddenly thick in the air, though drugs were forbidden in Baba's house. She remembered the sound of John Lennon's voice as he mocked Baba's laugh and bowed to the group for a giggle. *I am the Great Wok*, he joked. Others joined in, and it soon became like a circus. They were like school children when the teacher had left the room. Mary Kay couldn't believe they would be so rude when Baba had taken them in and tried to open their eyes to a peaceful way. All but George, who stood and left the room. When Mary Kay followed him, she found him pacing as he plucked at a song on his guitar, cigarette dangling from his mouth. He told her not to worry about the others. He understood Baba's message. Mary Kay didn't know what to say. Here was this huge celebrity, who looked so young, his hair grown long, but there was a genuineness in his face she did not see in the others. She was drawn to him beyond the celebrity who vanished as soon as he was away from everyone else.

When Baba found them in the garden, Mary Kay began to cry, upset that these bad-mannered rock stars and their hangers-on were mocking him behind his back; this great man who could teach them so much they had nothing but ridicule for. Baba only giggled, his high, gentle laugh comforting as always, and sat her down, George too.

We're all children in the eyes of God, he said. *So sometimes we must let ourselves be children. Sometimes we must play. Sometimes we must ease the pain in other ways.*

Baba brought out sliced mango on a plate. He encouraged them to eat.

Savor its sweetness, he said. *Like the mango, the meditation has a sweetness that you need only taste to appreciate its beauty.*

In his calming voice, he recited mantra over them. Within minutes, Mary Kay was awash in warmth, the sweetness of his song, the sadness in her heart gone too, a golden beam of light leading directly from him to her and out the top of her head, all the hurt rising to the sky. Mary Kay had no need for anything else. There was a purpose beyond her immediate understanding, he told her, a greater message to be born there. Baba put his hands on Mary Kay, removed her scarf, and asked her to lie down.

"There was such a peace in that garden," Mary Kay went on. "And with his hands on my face, along my arms and over my legs, I felt beautiful. You can't imagine the beauty I felt at his touch. Such warmth rolling over me in waves."

"Must've been one funny mango."

"Please, Sadie. You'll have plenty of time to make fun later. Let me finish."

Beside her, George lay on his mat and Baba ran his hands over him as well. Mary Kay could sense that he too felt Baba's warmth, his peace. She remembered feeling pleased he had told her the truth in the garden, just the two of them—he did get it after all and he thought enough of Mary Kay to tell her so. It made her happy. He was serious about learning the way and she was helping him, exactly as Baba had asked, which also made her happy. With this aura of happiness around her, with bliss their greatest and only goal there, she slept. Mary Kay woke the next morning in her room, fresh flowers over the bed covers; she felt as if she had been asleep for a hundred days. She was being celebrated, Baba told her at breakfast. There was a new branch on the tree, he said.

"I did not see George again." Mary Kay finished her wine, afraid to look Sadie in the eyes.

"Oh, Mom, I…"

"Baba was right. You, Sadie, were the new branch. You, Sadie Louise Keegan turned up eight months and two days later, always impatient, and full of fuss."

"That's a beautiful story, Mom, sort of. But, you know I can't accept that. You know that, right?"

Mary Kay recognized real sadness in her daughter's eyes, no longer the anger that had always fired her face, scarring it with deep lines much too early for a young woman.

"Listen, I don't doubt that something special happened there, that you found something wonderful and understand more about it than I ever will. But, there are some awfully big holes. And, frankly, it sounds like you're simply repressing something you didn't like for a nicer ending. It's alright though. It doesn't matter anymore. I'm not angry. I don't know what else to say. I'm not sure I can give you what you want. I don't even care anymore who my father is, was. It doesn't matter now. I'm thirty-three years old. It's too late for all that."

CALIFORNIA

From the moment she left Boston for Los Angeles, Mary Kay had done her best to believe that what she had done was right, trying to make Sadie understand the truth about her father, how she and George Harrison had been joined in body and spirit under Indian skies, a night of holy union. But it didn't count for much now. Sadie would rather it never happened at all, it seemed. Mary Kay had always believed that Sadie would be thrilled to know her father was such an icon. She thought it was a good thing. But Mary Kay had never known how to make it real for her daughter. And if not for all of the unanswered letters she had written to George—one a year for Sadie's thirty-three years—explaining who she was, where she lived and of course about Sadie too, Sadie might have understood. In over thirty years of letters both heartfelt and gracious, she had received not a single response, other than a restraining order from an Oxfordshire clerk of court. So Mary Kay had decided to live and let live. Sadie would always be her daughter, but she seemed to have little room in her life for her mother or her mother's story. Even if Mary Kay had put her best foot forward, her true foot, and stumbled a bit, she had done her best. Sadie had made it clear if she wanted any sort of relationship with her that Mary Kay would have to agree to not mention George Harrison, Baba or Rishikesh again. By Monday, Mary Kay had decided to make one last trip to California and Blue Jay Way—the melody of those three words enough to make her smile again—to say goodbye to George and start over with Sadie. And she tried to ignore the doubt creeping in behind her own story. After making plans to see Sadie again in the spring, Mary Kay took the train to the airport and had her flight home switched to Los Angeles. On the four-hour journey to the West coast, Mary Kay dreamed this time with only the help of a few glasses of red wine of California as a place where the sun always shone brighter.

BLUE JAY WAY

Mary Kay stood with a handful of hibiscus in the Hollywood Hills at 1 Blue Jay Way, once George's California home. She was ready to be done with her old life, ready to forget again. Now she and Sadie could both be free of suffering. It was true, just like Sadie said: George was dead, and so what Sadie knew of her father didn't matter much anymore. Mary Kay stood facing southeast looking over LA, the cityscape a silhouette behind the haze, and waited for an ocean breeze. Though she couldn't see water, she knew it was nearby, a whole new ocean with a whole new smell. Just like when she had left Rishikesh to birth and raise Sadie in another ashram further south in Kerala, George and the other Beatles back in England, Baba off on a tour to heal the world, and a polite if insistent suggestion from his aides that she raise her child elsewhere. When the ashram in Kerala fell apart over disagreements about how things should be run and its numbers dwindled, Mary Kay moved with her infant daughter to Myrtle Beach, then a rising oceanfront jewel along South Carolina's sandy coast, a town full of night air and the laughter of kids.

At first, Mary Kay had sought shelter in Norfolk with her parents, but they had other ideas for their unmarried daughter. They were clear that an infant would not fit in with their retirement. They would love their granddaughter and play grandma and grandpa when they could, but they had done their bit with children. Her cousin Emily invited Mary Kay to Myrtle Beach to live with her and her toddler son, where she found a job as a waitress at night and helped her cousin with rent and childcare during the day. Myrtle Beach: a good place to raise a little girl, she thought. It had turned out differently. Myrtle Beach had simply become a place to rest her feet and get ready to work for another day. *Sleep on it and in the morning you'll feel better.* A piece of her own mother's advice that proved to work for Mary Kay even if she needed help sometimes. Hadn't Baba taught her to leave the past, to unburden the body and mind from the ills of yesterday? Hadn't he said the past is like a winter skin that we must shed? Wasn't she doing that now? It was good to be in California; she knew the place, a song in her head that wouldn't let her forget.

It seemed right. Her suffering was that her life must remain a secret, a nothingness behind her. Mary Kay had waited there at Blue Jay Way once a year for George for fifteen years, waiting there in the same spot in the Hollywood Hills for him to arrive. She had even made a trip to England, waiting outside of his Friar Park estate with a sleeping bag and a picture of Sadie as an eight-year old—a favorite of Mary Kay's taken at the beach, her tan little girl smiling into the sun. Then came the restraining order and a warrant, nothing serious but she could never return to England. Sadie didn't know, but her mother had traveled. After that she drafted letters monthly, filling them with details of their time together in India, details that only he would know. He had to *get it*. Just like he had told her in Baba's garden the night of their spiritual union, just as a communal light had burned through their bodies in Rishikesh. Just as God had blessed them with a baby girl.

SEE A PENNY PICK IT UP

Two days later, Mary Kay prepared to leave LA and sat down for one last meal in a restaurant near the Forest Lawn Memorial Park after spending a day there looking for celebrity gravestones. Christmas was only a week away, so Mary Kay treated herself to turkey, mashed potatoes, green beans, cranberry sauce, and iced tea. In the booth behind her, a girl struggled to breastfeed her wiggling infant and read a book with one hand while she ate with the other. The girl was dressed in loose jeans and work boots, a wool overcoat over a sweatshirt, and a stocking cap pulled fast around her studded and ringed ears, though outside it was 65° and cloudless. Her face was drawn and she looked like she hadn't bathed in days.

"Need a hand?" Mary Kay turned and asked. "You know, while you eat."

"She won't sit still. All day she's like this. I just want five minutes to read my book," the girl answered. The orange paperback read in arched yellow letters *Breakfast of Champions.* Mary Kay didn't recognize the title, but she had never read much. It sounded like a self-help sort of book, one that gave you confidence and courage to go forward and succeed. Mary Kay had tried one of these books once—*First You Have to Row a Little Boat,* by a PhD in Family Healing. She reckoned that it was still underneath her bedside table, a crease at the beginning of "Chapter 3—Now You're Walking." As much as she had tried to absorb what the PhD was saying, she could hardly remember what she had read in the previous paragraphs and usually lost her place. After a while it became a chore and one evening she simply kicked the book under the bed and forgot about it. The book had not even been good for her insomnia, usually revving her nerves up to a jangle, as if something wanted to leap from her chest, so that she often tossed it to the floor with a sudden and puzzling twitch.

"What a pretty little girl." She smiled and leaned in to see the baby's face.

"Thanks." The young woman attempted a smile, but her face was clouded with weariness and other thoughts, half moons like bruises under tired brown eyes.

"Good book?"

"It's the only one I got. Weird and funny sort of. So long as it takes me someplace else."

"Hi there, sweetie, what's your name?" Mary Kay pursed her lips at the baby.

"Penny," the girl said.

"That's a pretty name."

"Thought it might be good luck."

"Well, sure it is. See a penny pick it up, all day long have good luck."

"Yeah, that's it."

"I have a daughter, too. Sadie. Quite a handful. Cried all the time when she was a baby."

"Penny's a good baby, most of the time. Just seems like I don't have any time to myself."

"Oh yeah. Sadie, you know, she's a special one. Got a special father too, but that's another story." Mary Kay held out her hands to the girl. "Mind if I hold your little good luck charm?"

"Huh?" The woman pulled the infant girl from her breast and closed her blouse, stood up and brushed crumbs from her lap.

"Your Penny, mind if I hold her. I've held a baby or two in my time."

"I guess not." The girl handed her baby over to Mary Kay.

"Hey there. Such a lucky little girl, aren't you. My Sadie was a real gift from God, I tell you, and Baba too. A child of nature, I called her."

The young mother had begun to eat hurriedly, scooping spoonfuls of mashed potatoes into her mouth, barely listening to Mary Kay.

"My, aren't you hungry. Baba, he taught me how to feed my soul so that I would never be hungry. To this day, I just don't need much food. Just a little nourishment for the soul, that's all."

"That's great. Food does it for me though." As the girl ate, Mary Kay rocked baby Penny in her arms, cooing and kissing.

Mary Kay hardly heard the girl, her attention focused on the baby. Sadie had been like this once, a little good luck charm. The young woman finished eating and stood, slipping on a dirty, torn daypack.

"Listen, do you mind watching Penny for me, just while I clean up a bit, get a moment to myself and stuff? I won't take long, I promise."

"Well, of course, she's such a doll, such a good baby. Aren't you Penny-girl? Maybe she'll bring an old lady some good luck. Isn't that right, little Penny? She's just beautiful, really. Such a good baby. Like I said, my Sadie, she would cry all night long. Never gave me a minute of peace. Not a *minute*."

"I guess. Listen, thanks, I mean it. I just need like a few minutes and I'll be right back."

"Don't say another thing. We'll be fine. I know how it is. My name's Mary Kay."

"Lily."

"Don't worry about a thing, Lily. Me and Penny'll get along just fine."

FOR A LITTLE WHILE

Outside the sun had begun to set a fuming orange and Mary Kay felt nervous, a stirring in her chest she couldn't quell. From the window by her bed in the Morrison Hotel overlooking Hope Street in downtown Los Angeles Mary Kay tried to find her point of light but she couldn't recall most of her mantra. Her eyes filled with sunspots as her thoughts drifted away from Baba and his words, whatever they had been. Mary Kay knew Sadie would never accept her story, never quite be the daughter she wished for. There were times even Mary Kay doubted what she knew. She did know that the day after her communion with Baba and George, the entire gang of celebrities, including George, had packed up and left. Disappeared without so much as a goodbye. Later she heard rumors that Baba had acted improperly with a woman in the ashram. Gossip surely, Mary Kay thought, brought on by fear of what they didn't understand and nothing but the kind of debris that newspapers everywhere thrived on. Words, words, words. So many words made Mary Kay tired and she placed her head down on the windowsill. She thought about sleep and how soon it might come, but when she reached into her purse for the familiar orange bottle, it rose without a rattle, empty.

"Surely, I have…"

She rummaged through her purse, a sincere belief that if she wished carefully enough and dug with enough earnestness she would find what she wanted. And when she did, she told herself to remember the ease with which she had given into the hope earlier in the day. How easy it was if she just let go of the worry a little. Things would happen. With a glass of Gallo from a bottle she had picked up on the way, Mary Kay swallowed two white pills, then another because, she reasoned, she was in a strange bed in a new place and needed her rest for whatever new adventure

God might offer her. Turning her face for the breeze outside, Mary Kay closed her eyes to the sinking sun the color of a peach where only a sliver of sunlight remained, certain that this time she smelled the ocean.

PLACE OF BEAUTY

J. K. Dane

Where the little girl sits is here, atop the hill, with a book stuck inside, a fragile book with a delicate voice, waiting for the chance to fly. The wind took the wildflowers from the hillside, picked them all, like a greedy child, pulled apart the petals while the girl turned so old she thought there was something wrong with death for not taking her away, already.

Come, she complained. She was tired from having worked all those years in the high school office, cranking the absentee list through the ditto machine, the names of the students she typed turning purple, the pages spit into a pile, students' names suspended, absent, in mid-air, hanging over the rooms like a fog, her shoes marring the shine on the wooden hallways, as the teachers stopped briefly their lectures to glare with one slant eye to the papers that poked their noses under the doorways, the absentee lists, delivered.

That was before she turned useless, forgetful, uncovering her skin, to stand naked, frowning at her reflection, wondering who was staring back at her, too ashamed when she was young to look for long even though her body was smooth, back then, and strong. Only when she was a little girl, before memories, did she touch herself unabashedly, sliding her fat fingers into her vagina and feeling around for what was inside.

Now and then, at this effete age, beyond memory, the nurses find her sitting on her bed, nylon hose around her ankles, shoes still on, skirt gone, underwear disappeared, sitting as if she were waiting for a train, except her hand is stuffed between her legs and the room smells so. Once when she thought herself old but was still so young, she found her daughter with legs spread, poking at that seed of a hole, and she chided her daughter who looked at her confused, unaware there was anything wrong, so the woman pulled the girl up by her arm and spanked her. The little girl cried and sucked her thumb, associating that new odor on her fingers with sorrow.

Outside, it snowed. Not on the flowerless hill, but in the back of the house where the little girl pressed her face to the window, gazing at the yard, as flat as a mirror, textured with sparkles. It doesn't matter which little girl - the old woman, or her daughter, the newborn baby, or the new mother - they all saw the snow the same way.

Back to the book that flew up into the sky from inside that little girl, the book that eventually fell, down, down, like a shot bird, tumbling. It landed and disappeared, swallowed by the snow, leaving nothing but a hole. An empty nothing filled with silence. She ran barefoot, terrified by the aching cold, disappointed to be ruining the perfect plane of snow rendered even more stunning by the hole made from the falling out of the sky and looked in and saw. The book was smiling.

She reached in and found it was made of watermelon sugar as if its creator took the mind and shook it, watching the words fall down through the midst like fake snow under a plastic dome, grabbing at the flakes two by two and hammering them down to the page, that's what this book was like, the one that grew inside her, retrieved after its interrupted flight, the one she hugged as she carefully stepped, one foot making a new track, the other retracing her last, creating a mystery for anyone who cared to peek over the fence and read what was written in the snow.

When the girl was a woman and mindful enough to believe in what she thought, she discovered the book was perfect nonsense. By then, she had slept with the book for years, sniffed it, as she did lovers, in and out of her bed, like a change of sheets she accepted them, expected them to show her something new about the world since the first and only one she needed had showed her something that no one else ever could, down by where the railroad tracks cross the river.

That was how she chose to live, young, middle aged, old, with men in her pocket, a book in her bed. One, she married. Couldn't even remember why. They square danced on the cement outside the public pool, the kids waiting for them on the bleachers, fidgeting bored as usual, but they, wife and husband, didn't care, relished it, man and woman, the only time they were truly happy together, her dress swaying around her knees, like a triangle chiming, his hair easing out of its studied style, slicked back with a comb and touch of Vaseline.

In the spring the snow melted and made a mess of things, a terrible mess, as the decaying woman said, her mouth tightening, cinched with a string, having long forgotten how she loved square dancing, her spine curving toward the mud as she walked the neighborhood visiting her grandchildren. She thought it a shame that they played barefoot in the street gutters with all those diseases. Here was her granddaughter, hair knotted, clothes ragged, with the current wrapping her ankles as she watched her leaf boat slip into the sewer. She ignored her grandmother's scolding, how she will never become a proper woman, never inherit her diamond ring, if that's how she cared to act, like a boy, playing in the filthy gutter.

It was the same time of year, a decade later, when the little girl became a dancer, put on a wedding dress she found in the cedar chest and performed in the university's gymnasium, a lament for that diamond ring and all it represented, already passed to her mother whose knuckles, too, were beginning to swell, like the grandmother's, like the grandmother's grandmother. She danced in the wedding dress for the sparse student crowd, certain that her grandmother had long forgotten the promise to never give her the ring since the hoary woman, by that time, couldn't remember whether it was summer or winter, often calling her granddaughter by her daughter's name.

Where the little girl sits is here on the hill where the flowers don't grow, the mirror reflecting gray hair. She squints, trying to see what she will look like as an elderly woman, not believing she will turn into her grandmother, day dreaming since she is so full of baby, she cries. The children crowd around her, demanding bread, milk, butter. She obliges and each night falls into bed exhausted, the baby keeping her awake, kicking at her belly. She's scared of all that is to come. Though it's happened before, all the way back to the beginning of time, she can't fathom that this giant growing inside will emerge through the coin-sized doorway of her vagina.

Once, she believed that she remembered life in the womb, dark days full of warmth and the coursing of her mother's blood, the rumbling journey through the stem of the birth canal. But her mother frowned and said that was impossible, so those memories broke apart and dissolved, her mother being the ultimate authority, wellspring of wisdom, object of security.

The first time she understood her mother to be fallible, a person with a history, was when her mother showed her that photograph, a casual gesture made while sifting through boxes. There was her mother, youthful and flawless, during her one great adventure as a hotel maid in the Cascades, wearing sunglasses, posing in a swimsuit, surrounded by cocky men, flexing their muscles. Her mother had never learned to swim, was terrified of the water, but risked drowning, her daughter realized, to go out in a canoe with them. She did it for those men she scarcely knew, men she would never see again, whose names she would forget, she risked tipping over and breathing water, sinking like a stone, because when the soft parts melt and come out between the legs there's no reason to what a woman will and will not do.

The photograph could not predict her future as a teacher, instructing the proper way to grip a pencil, gently reminding the children that "b" is bat and ball, not ball and bat, she lived vicariously, imagining that she was hovering over the seedlings of master poets. Her own dream of writing poetry had been soured, years before, by a single venomous comment, so she chose to do what educated women did, and while on break from the classroom, relished summer shade at the city pool, absconded in Victorian novels while her daughter learned breast stroke, back stroke, the crawl, a mother's sacrifice, so that her daughter unlike her, could learn to swim, this girl who had so much trouble learning to read, frustrated by that book she clutched, the words confusing her until she screamed, throwing it against the wall. How surprised, then, the mother was to open her daughter's diary, one summer evening, years later, when the girl was out, to read words woven like an ancestral basket, confident and intricate, she could not take her eyes from the looping cursive and read to the very last page, the secrets a daughter believes her mother will never discover.

In the dark, the mother waited, pressed into the corner of the couch, angry that her daughter had snuck off, already thinking herself a woman. Cicadas pulsed, marking the beats of her imagination. She was capable of visualizing accidents of the most horrific kind.

It was the boys from the neighborhood who had blindfolded the daughter and drove and drove, all of them laughing, out to the abandoned quarry. They led her to the edge. The rocks hurt her soft feet since the boys had left her shoes on the hood of the car so they wouldn't get wet. They told her to dive in. She heard splashing, trusted those handsome boys, repeating her mother's mistakes, held her breath and jumped.

She came up from beneath the silk-skinned lake, water cool enough to inhale rolling over the curves of her body, her long hair black as otter skin, stuck to her, making rivers around her ears, down her neck and shoulders. She opened her eyes and gasped. It was more beautiful than anything she had ever seen, the trees' secrets revealed in the moonlight, the water as kind as violets, the sky so dense with stars she could bite it. And did, splashing those boys, they all reveled in the surprise, the splendor penetrating to bone marrow.

The mother sat waiting, draped in the diary's hurtful words, thinking how impossible it was, her daughter still so much like the child she gave birth to, she cried, past midnight, and wiped her eyes when she heard the latch turn, the cautious footsteps, the girl dripping wet, having been out with the boys from the neighborhood, a mother knows, and she was mad because of all the things she never did, obedient child, all the words never written, left to rot, a woman in midlife, watching the clock, churning worries, no longer collecting admirers. Her daughter froze when she saw her, curled into the couch, and the mother sought revenge, called her daughter a slut since she knew exactly what occurs when water touches ebullient bodies, the velvet awakening of desires, a shyness tingling the breasts, she knew and yet had forgotten, trapped as she was in motherhood. Incensed, the daughter stepped off her mother's boat. She, the little girl, the old old woman, like her mother, like her grandmother before her, was relieved by her rebellion, launched from the maternal grasp of love.

Where the little girl sits is here, inside the fossilized skin, she admires herself in the mirror, giving herself permission now that death is near. Her hands like a newborn baby's, she can see right through to veins, tendons, bones. Her fingertips trace across her brow, around her eyes, over her cheeks to chin. Amazing. For generations that skin has delineated the border between then and now, contracting into frowns, expanding into smiles, the skin like earth's crust, creased into hills and valleys with every quaking concern, every gathering of clouds, every swell of wind.

She was afraid when rain came, tornados invading her dreams, spinning gray snakes with lightening fangs, nightmares given by her brothers who had told her that the sky falls when it thunders. Her father brought her out to the porch to watch the rain pouring, smacking every leaf, flooding every street, the rain so loud they had to yell to each other, she wanted to hide in the basement before the tornado came and spun her off to once upon a time, never to return again. They all ridiculed her and stayed on the porch to watch the sky empty until the dark clouds dissipated and the sun sighed on the afternoon horizon, the sidewalks sparkling. She could finally breathe, fear transformed to beauty.

Years later, new anxieties invaded her nights, rolling from side to side, always moist between her legs, her breasts round and milky, the belly taut, waiting in the dark for sleep to serenade her, until she imagined things she was ashamed of, things she never wanted to come true, her hands between her legs, under the covers, her husband snoring beside her while the leaves turned yellow and red. Finally, her womb undulated, the pain crescendoing, wave upon wave pounding at harbor's shore. She screamed and pushed, the sky kaleidoscoped and finally toppled, full womb made empty, a relief as palpable as fruit sprung from blossom, there upon her chest, diaphanous body, soft as dew, the bliss of a face never before seen. A baby girl is born.

She climbs the hill where the flowers used to bloom, book and baby cradled in her arms, still fresh from the womb. She stops, curious, surprised to find lying, the old woman long ago forgotten, vagina dry as paper, no longer recognizing the wind. Wizened and tired, she never again wants to scrub another dish, to sweep another floor, to care about time, or worry if the children are hungry. She blinks and sees a girl at her side, the old woman's eyes as empty as the newborn baby's. The girl lifts those translucent hands and places them upon the book, upon the breast, the heart beneath the skin and bone, stalling, starting, the quiet between the wheezing breaths growing longer, silence lingering, alone and naked, bones curling like the fallen leaves of autumn.

Where the aged woman sits is here, that little baby girl, so suddenly old, on the edge of the bed, atop the hill, face pressed to the window watching seasons circle, she warms her hands between her legs, insides like watermelon sugar, sweet and mellow, the very reason why the men loved her so and now gone, so long ago, now they're gone and she's almost joined them, gone to the hill where the flowers no longer grow, the book reincarnated, there inside that ancient woman who remembers the journey through the birth canal, again and for the very first time.

GRIFOLA FRONDOSA

Bryan Walpert

The first thing the closet man said surprised her. Not the first thing, but the first thing she remembered. It was not what she had expected to hear from a closet man. *Tell me what you imagine.*

The summer the mycologist moved in, Carol decided to deal with the bedroom closet. It had been bothering her since she bought the house the year before. The musty smell, the lack of organization, the lack of space, the horrible bi-fold doors that kept coming off their tracks so that she had to lean them against the wall. She wanted a walk-in with a door on hinges. She wanted her clothes arranged neatly by season, formality and color along double racks, high and low, a shoe rack the length of one closet wall, multiple level large shelves for boxes, bags. A variety of hats. She tried to imagine walking into the closet to her shocking reflection in a full-length mirror against the back wall.

The mycologist moved into the house in June. She had advertised in the paper for a housemate. She needed someone to help her pay the mortgage, to help to fund the closet build-out. It might also help having the place feel less empty. It was a four-bedroom, two-bath house, built in the late 60s, with a large eat-in kitchen, a living room with wood floors and a dining room off the living room. It was ranch-style, all on one floor, one of its appeals. It had a connected two-car garage where she did her laundry, a back patio overlooking a small backyard where she had planted a partly-successful vegetable garden (tomatoes refused to grow despite careful nurturing of seedlings in small pots in the kitchen). Her ad specified a non-smoker, preferably a mature professional. Carol was surprised when she heard the timbre of the mycologist's voice on her home voicemail; surprised at her own surprise. She had so fully constructed her imagined housemate as woman that she hadn't thought to specify gender in the advertisement. Sitting on one of the stools at her kitchen counter, she replayed the voicemail several times. It was too bland a message to tell her anything, but his voice was warm, the tone a familiar uncertainty; she could tell he was young. Carol walked around the house, imagining living with a man again. She summoned the smell of old running shoes left by the door in the kitchen, the sweat emanating from his clothes, the smell a man makes in the toilet, the unwiped splashes on the floor; she walked into the empty room she'd planned to offer and pictured the bed half-made, jeans and shirts scattered on a desk chair, a single dying houseplant on the windowsill. She made the long-distance call.

The mycologist told her he had been accepted as a doctoral student in biology at the university, where he would start in late August, though he had lined up some lab work in the department for the summer. He studied mushrooms. He was 28 years old, seven years younger than Carol, and a non-smoker.

"Do I count as professional?" he asked, laughing over the phone. "It does sometimes seem like I've become a professional student."

When he arrived a couple days later to meet her, Carol was surprised at her reaction, at how good-looking he was. Silly, she thought, to assume a mycologist would be nondescript or small or mousy or socially inept, an assumption she hadn't known she had made until it was overturned. He was close to 6-foot two; he was thin, almost skinny, and tanned. His hair was black and curly, grown too long; he would have to wear it shorter soon, by thirty—it was starting to recede. He had green eyes, a day's stubble, good teeth. He smelled just a little and not unpleasantly of sweat, as he walked past her into the house when she opened the door for him, his face flushed from jogging up her street (he'd been late) in the heat and humidity.

"There's no central air," Carol told him, wanting suddenly to reveal the worst about the house—the loud creaks of the floorboards, the whine of the old dryer, the occasional flooding in the basement, none of which she mentioned. "You'll need to buy a window unit if you want one."

"I don't mind," he said. The mycologist looked directly into Carol's eyes when they spoke; she felt it in her stomach.

Carol showed him the room, and what would be his bathroom, and the space in the garage. They agreed to a one-year lease. The handshake, which he initiated, was firm and dry.

Carol worked as a librarian at the same university as the mycologist. She had a master's degree, and had been working in libraries for eight years, in this one for three. Carol liked the library when it was quiet in the summer, and liked it in September when lines formed at the checkout desk and students roamed, sometimes desperately, for an available seat in front of a PC. Carol found pleasure in the scent of the books, the groan of the slow elevator, the hunt for a title, the everyday miracle of placing her hand, in a matter of minutes, on the spine of one particular volume among the more than a million on the shelves.

She assisted both students and faculty with research, mainly in the humanities, ran research classes for undergraduates. The job came with a faculty rank of assistant professor, which meant she had to undertake her own research. She chose an issue to do with library teaching and new technologies, which she plugged away at out of obligation, working at home for two hours most mornings to this end. But she preferred the other parts of her job. Research required an imaginative leap that she could not recognize in herself; the idea exhausted her. She wondered sometimes whether there was an irreconcilable difference between her role as a librarian and her role as researcher, a tension between the known and the unknown. The line between them seemed fragile, the thinnest membrane, but it existed, and she wondered whether one had to stand on one side or the other.

Carol had sent a broadcast email through the library seeking referrals to contractors. One of front desk clerks, Jenny, responded with a name. He had done good work on her house, Jenny said, and his rates were reasonable because he had only recently gone out on his own. Carol called his cell phone, got his voicemail, and left a message.

What you have to decide, the closet man said, *is whether to expand or to contract*. The closet man spoke in Zen koans, she thought. He wore Birkenstocks but smoked camels. He was like one of those boxes she'd draw in class when she was bored in high school—one minute you see it from the top, but look away and when you return you see it from the side. He stood in her bedroom, taking a tape measure to her closet, the walls of the room. He smelled faintly of his cigarettes. *Tell me what you imagine*, he said.

The mycologist moved in while she was at work; she'd
met him on the porch first thing with his copy of the
key. When she got home—early, about 3:30, to check on
him— he was standing in the kitchen, her Cheshire cat mug,
her favourite, in his hand, and staring into the backyard
through the window over the sink.

"Hedgehog," he said, pointing out the window. The
heat of the coffee had made the Cheshire cat disappear.

"In the middle of the day?"

"Mushroom. It's the common name of *Hydnum repandum*.
Also called Sweet Tooth," he said. "Coffee?" he asked,
pointing to the pot, half-full.

"I see you've made yourself at home," Carol said. The
tone was flat enough to be taken as satisfaction or rebuke,
both of which she felt. They walked into the dining room. Her
eyes involuntarily moved in the direction of his bedroom.

"Go ahead—take a look," he said.

Carol was mildly embarrassed but too curious to be
proud. His room was much neater than she imagined.
She took her time. A full bookcase (novels, biographies, a
surprisingly small number of books on fungus—e.g. *The
Missing Lineages: Phylogeny and Ecology of Endophytic and
Other Enigmatic Root-associated Fungi*; *The Triumph of the
Fungi: A Rotten History*; *Mycelium Running: How Mushrooms
Can Help Save the World*), a large rubber plant in a pot on
the floor, a wicker laundry basket, a Turkish area rug on
the bare floor, a simple wood desk and chair, the inevitable
framed print, though not one she recognized, and a queen-
size bed, not the futon she had envisioned.

"Does it meet your expectations?" he asked, standing
right behind her.

It was a comfortable bed, quite firm, she found out. Not
that week, but soon after that. There was no awkwardness
about it. She didn't sleep with him every night, just three or
four times a week, and always in his room, on the queen-size
bed that he had placed head towards the window, which he

left open, a small box fan propped on the sill. She wondered whether he understood that her room remained one portion of the house—and therefore of her—for now, at least, closed to him.

Carol first heard from the closet man a few weeks later when the phone rang on a Saturday morning while she and the mycologist were eating a late breakfast. "I'd nearly given up on you," she said. Carol had been distracted, had put off thinking about the closet. She realized she still wanted to do it. They agreed he would come out to look over the closet on Monday and work out an estimate.

When Carol had hung up the phone and returned to the kitchen table, to her coffee and the paper, she felt the mycologist looking at her. Before the phone call, he had been doing a crossword puzzle in an old issue of the Mycology Society of America newsletter, "Inoculum." She'd thought he was joking.

"Oh, it's real," he had said. "19 across: *Insect body part targeted by* Laboulbenia cristata *and* Rikia dentroiuli *fungi.* How embarrassing; I think I'd have to look that up."

"Are you serious?"

"Okay, here's an easier one. 44 down: *A term for the asexual form of fungi, usually bearing a different name from the sexual form.*"

But he was looking at her now, rapping the pencil slowly against the page. Of course. He would want to know who called—he'd heard only her end, saying she was still interested, agreeing to see him. It was the part about living with a man that she had forgotten. She understood that he didn't feel he had the right yet to ask. Soon, she knew—in a week or a month—he would feel he had that right. Carol experienced a hot wave of irritation; it was her business, her house. But this passed.

"My closet man," she said. "I'm redoing the one in my bedroom." It occurred to her belatedly that mentioning the bedroom closet would inevitably raise questions in his mind; it was an accidental invitation to him to consider that part of the house she had reserved, almost an implied obligation on her part, like mentioning a dinner party she was hosting to an acquaintance she did not wish to invite.

She would have to move out of her bedroom into the office. She hadn't thought of that. Is it necessary? The closet man said it was. Dust from sawing wood, from sanding the wood and the plaster on the wallboard. The smell of primer, of paint. If she gave him the house key, he would have it cleaned up and would be gone before she returned each day; but she couldn't sleep in her room. The dust would get into her sheets, would linger in the air, latch onto the walls, get into her hair and lungs. She considered this, breathing in parts of her closet, enclosing part of what would enclose all of her things.

Carol went shopping. It was for hats, though she didn't think about this directly. She kept it in the distance, touching it with her mind now and then as she drove to the mall, like probing a sore tooth. The mall was crowded, so she had to park at the outer edge of the lot and walk through the heat, feeling it above and also below, where it was drawn to the lot's black surface. The rush of cold air made her shiver when she opened the mall door. She stood before the map just inside, feeling herself cool, looking through the shop categories, planning her route from the entrance clockwise, upstairs then downstairs.

She decided on expansion. This meant encroaching on the space in the next room, the fourth bedroom, rather than building out into her bedroom, reducing its liveable space. Was this the right choice? *It says a lot about character,* the closet man said.

Carol and the mycologist got into a routine. She would return from work, and he would have made dinner. She bought the groceries. They never spoke about it. He would make omelettes for her on Saturday mornings. Once, as she drank her first cup of coffee, he went out into the yard, returned with the *Hydnum repandum*. She stood up, leaned against the door for the angle to watch, as he washed them, sliced them roughly, then sautéed them in olive oil in the pan, added the eggs. He saved a piece of mushroom, which he lifted directly to her lips. She took it from him with her hand and ate it in several bites. She would have assumed, if she'd paid attention to it in her yard, that the mushroom was poisonous, but, true to its name, it was sweet. It occurred to her to wonder at her own assumption that those were mutually exclusive categories.

Several nights a week they would lie together, afterwards, in his bed, on top of the sheets, the warm air from the box fan hardly dissipating the sweat.

"Tell me about your research," she said one of those nights, when it was too hot to sleep.

"What do you want to know?" He sounded surprised.

"I don't know. We haven't really talked about it. What fungus are you studying?"

"I'm currently interested in the interaction of *Phallus impudicus* and *Aminata vaginata*," he said, touching her thigh.

"Don't be an ass." She removed his hand.

"Okay. Cytotoxic effects of polysaccharides and other compounds in *Grifola frondosa*, among others," he said. "Is that helpful?"

He was being a patronizing shit. But she'd realized his research wasn't really what she was after. "I mean why fungus?"

"Why anything?" he said, turning onto his side to look at her; she turned her head and could see his profile in

Grifola Frondosa

what streetlight came through the window. "Why quarks or earthquakes or genes?"

"Something in particular must have attracted you to mushrooms."

"What color is your bedroom?"

She closed her eyes. "I see," she said.

In the mornings, before going to the library, Carol sat with her laptop in the narrow space between the desk and her bed or at the kitchen table, listening to the echoes of the closet man at work in her bedroom. The thrum of the electric saw; the scream of the sander; the scrape of what she imagined to be a putty knife. Hammering. She never heard him exclaim or curse.

Carol looked up *Grifola frondosa*. It turned out to be the Maitake mushroom. Was he kidding her? She did a search with "cytotoxic." There were promising trials using Maitake to treat breast, prostate, lung, liver and gastric cancers. She linked to studies in Brazil and Japan that suggested eating mushrooms regularly over the course of years reduces the risk of cancer, to another study that indicated certain mushrooms help boost immune systems that are suppressed by chemotherapy and radiotherapy treatment, and to a third that described a promising mushroom turnover recipe using the maitake, with a warning to pick these mushrooms only when they were young because as it aged *G. frondosa* grew acrid, unpalatable.

Carol had lived alone for a decade, since her marriage had ended. It had lasted three years. Since then she'd dated, if that was the word for it, but those few relationships tended to peter out in a few weeks or months. She knew she was not unattractive. Shoulder-length dark black hair, slim, casually pretty, blue eyes, still the right curves in a pair of jeans. But in a small town, pickings were few; fewer since she'd passed thirty, just as promised by the statistics young television reporters enjoyed trotting out around Valentine's day. There was always the drive to the city, but the idea exhausted and depressed her; the couple of times she had gone to singles events there, the two-hour drive made her feel a kind of obligation, even desperation, which led to bad decisions. She'd gradually gotten used to the idea of being alone; not the idea, really, but the condition, which was a set of actions and habits. She knew several women her age in the same situation, mainly academics who had spent years building careers, putting off marriages or sacrificing them, a couple of them with children from those marriages, and she spent time with them, though she did so less these days; the talk too often became bitter, and she felt something false in the camaraderie, felt that each of them hoped it was a club from which she would be the first to resign her membership.

Most recently, she'd started this past winter, as by a force of will, a bit of a crush on her doctor, a young, athletic and awkwardly beautiful man—awkward because he carried himself as though unaware of his beauty—to whom she was referred by her gynecologist. He returned from a vacation with a tan, a ring on his finger, and a photograph on his desk; she let go of the effort without much sense of disappointment. Best to keep it professional; no doubt there were rules, and he'd seen her body in the harsh light of the examining room, had touched her with rubber gloves, which he expertly tossed into the wastebasket as she dressed. Now, of course, the whole thing felt like melodrama. The doctor's office was in the city. About three weeks before putting the ad in the paper, she had made her third visit to this doctor in as many months.

"What's the verdict?" she asked, sitting beside his desk.

"Treatment," he said. "It's time to start."

Carol felt suddenly dizzy. She tried to breathe regularly. He had warned her this was in all likelihood coming. She had thought of it in the same way she thought of the end of summer when she was a child, a hazy notion, a place she'd have to visit someday, something someone else would have to deal with, a different Carol, a future Carol. She had been living as in the dark and knew it, wanted to be there; until now she hadn't realized how fragile that moment was, that it was not up to her when it ended.

The doctor touched her shoulder. "It's relatively early," he said. "Anything is still possible."

The closet man didn't mind if she stopped in to watch him work for awhile, so long as she wore a dust mask and goggles, which he loaned her. She admired the facility with which he worked, the lack of hesitation when he tore out a piece of wall board, the rhythmic precision with which he tapped a nail with the head of the hammer, then brought it down hard. He wore work boots now. She opened the two windows, loaned him a pedestal fan. Still, it was hot. He kept his shirt off. He was thin, his stomach and back more defined than she expected. *Wrought* was the word that came to her mind.

A mushroom, Carol was surprised to learn, is not the organism. The mushroom is produced by the mycelium, the body of the fungus, which is hidden below. Mycelia live for years and can spread over acres and acres, unseen. Mushrooms are delicate, their veil, cap, stem and gills mainly composed of water. They have a lifespan of several weeks, sometimes only days. A mushroom exists solely to produce sexually reproductive spores.

Carol knew that the closet man wiped the sweat from his forehead with his right hand, that he hammered with his left, that when he hit his thumb he placed the hammer gently on the ground, stood up, held the thumb and breathed, looking out the window. She knew he had a white van, without lettering. These are the things she did not know: his age, where he was born, his favorite foods, how he got into this business, what he thought of her decision to expand her closet, his relationship history.

Y our problem," her ex-husband had said towards the end, when they had given up counseling but not yet the addictive aesthetic of the counselor's vocabulary, "is that you're inaccessible."

By this, she understood him to mean that she had made "him inaccessible to her. She had told him plenty of things about herself—private things, embarrassing things—over the three years of marriage and the two when they were dating. She told him about the drugs she had taken (pot, hash, ecstasy, LSD twice, cocaine once and never again—all at college), her sexual history, the one time she slept with her freshman roommate, Hilary, something she had never told anyone. It wasn't revealing herself to him that was the problem. It was allowing him to reveal himself to her. It was what he wanted to share with her—his embarrassments, his fantasies—that she kept at a distance. He opened a door and beckoned her into a dim room; she stood on the stoop, under the porch light. He could not access himself through her; he could not see himself through her eyes, could not see himself revealed to her—and it is this part of her that she denied, the part of him, that he meant when he said she was inaccessible. All her own revelations, those she now deeply regretted making, could not make up for this intimacy. That they seemed unable to have children—when they thought they wanted to have children together—she knew seemed to him, whether he thought this through consciously or not, its physical manifestation.

"Fuck you," is what she had said in response. "I told you about Hilary."

Fungus, Carol learned, are not always destructive to their hosts. Some maintain a symbiotic relationship with, for example, the tree on which they grow, helping them to absorb water and minerals, to survive.

Naked, the closet man's body seemed to Carol to hum. There was dust around them. They lay where her bed used to be. It was just after 11 a.m. She was late for work. There were a hundred questions she wanted to ask him. They had grappled with each other's clothing, except for the closet man's shirt, which was already off, and her dust mask. He had stayed her hand. *Keep the mask on,* he'd said.

Carol knew it was a mistake after only a few bites of the omelette. Even the smell had bothered her, as the mycologist turned it in the pan, his back to her as she sat at the kitchen table. She dropped her fork, ran to the bathroom. She didn't vomit; just dry retching.

"Are you alright?" The mycologist stood in the doorway of the bathroom.

She nodded. "Are you poisoning me?"

He looked offended. "I'm not an idiot. They're the same mushrooms I used before."

She'd said it only as misdirection, as a joke. "I'm sorry. Of course."

He stepped aside so she could walk by. Her stomach felt suddenly empty. She returned to the kitchen, opened the window, tried a piece of the toast, unbuttered on a new plate. It settled her stomach, so she stuck with it.

She turned her head away when he tested a bite of his omelette. He noticed, moved his plate from the table to the counter. "Should I take you to a doctor?" he asked.

"I'm okay," she said.

It was at breakfast, not in bed, that the mycologist said, "It was because of my brother."

They had been reading the paper. He said it suddenly, as though he were reading to her from an interesting article.

"What was?" Even as she asked it, Carol knew where he was going.

"My interest in *G. frondosa*," he said. He pushed away his plate, streaked with butter and pieces of egg. "I had a younger brother when I was a kid. He died when he was eight years old. I was eleven."

It had been weeks since she had asked him. Carol wondered how often he thought of her question. She wondered why she had asked it—knew she would not have asked if she'd known the depths from which the answer would rise. She didn't want him to tell her. It was pushing its way inside her now, this picture of a curly-haired boy and his brother. She tightened her stomach, held it at bay.

"Poisoned mushrooms," she said.

He looked surprised. "No," the mycologist said. "Leukemia."

One of the most difficult decisions even for experts with regard to mushrooms, Carol learned, is which to pick. Of the 10,000 species in North America, she discovered, only 5 percent are known for certain to be either safe or toxic. Some mushrooms labeled safe in one edition of a field guide, such as *Tricholoma equestre*, have been reclassified as poisonous in another. It is surprisingly difficult, even for experts, to decide whether a mushroom is one variety or another, whether a mushroom will tickle your senses or send sudden pain through your belly.

The doctor said, "This makes things more complicated." It always makes things more complicated, Carol thought. It's just that what it is making more complicated is already more complicated.

"What are my options?" She had trouble even getting out the sentence. The word itself—*options*—felt alien in her mouth. It was sterile, hygienic, like the doctor's gloves and needles.

"The conventional wisdom has been to terminate," the doctor said. "That's been thought best for you and the baby. Chemotherapy can lead to birth defects. And it's hard on your body—we're poisoning you almost to death. Pregnancy is physically stressful. You won't be at your strongest when the drugs hit you."

"Conventional wisdom," she echoed.

The doctor had been leaning forward. He sat back in his chair. "Well, there is some tentative rethinking. More women are dealing with this now because they're having children later, and the evidence seems to suggest birth defects may not be as likely as we thought; being pregnant may not be as dangerous during treatment as we thought, either." He paused. "But we might have to put off treatment to the second trimester to give the baby its best shot, which is a risk for you; and no one knows the long-term effects on the child, even if it comes out with all of its fingers and toes. There's just a lot we don't know. Most of it we don't."

Expansion or contraction, Carol thought. She nearly laughed.

"We're talking shades of risk," the doctor continued, when Carol said nothing. "I can give you the statistics, if you think that will help. You'll have to make a decision soon. Things are at a delicate stage. You've got two clocks running now."

Carol spent quite a while in the hat stores at the mall. It was more complicated than she expected. She spoke with a friendly woman named Judith in one of them, who took her through the possibilities. No see-through hats, Judith advised, because they don't protect against the sun; and, of course, there is vanity to consider. The fit was a difficult call, given how much hair she had now. So Judith suggested she not buy too many, just a few to start, and those should be loose-fitting and adjustable. But Carol had trouble deciding on only one or two. She settled on a baseball cap, a wide-brimmed sun hat, a denim turban, and a khaki hat with vertical pleats, a wide cuff, and terry lining. She'd probably need to wear a cap underneath some hats to avoid irritating her scalp, Judith said, so Carol bought a wig cap. At the last minute, as Judith was ringing her up, Carol added a light blue sleeping cap.

When the closet man finished, he helped her to move the bed back into the room, told her to wait a day for the paint in the closet to dry. The electrician would come to connect the closet light on Monday. The closet man left two messages for her on Saturday, but Carol had not yet decided whether to return them. Saturday evening, she opened the closet door, took a step in and looked around. She sat right in the middle of closet floor. It was hard to tell without the overhead light. From where Carol sat, she barely heard the knock at her bedroom door, then a muffled voice. It was the mycologist. It sounded like, "Can I come in?" Or did she imagine it? She tried to imagine an answer. She sat in the fragile dark.

THE PET MORTICIAN

Rachel Furey

One and a half semesters into college, Riley decides to move back home for reasons she cannot tell her father and reasons that, fortunately, he does not ask about again after his initial calm questioning that yields no response from her. Maybe if her mother had not died the night she was born, Riley could tell her mother about the reasons; unfortunately, Riley long ago gave up even dreaming of seeing her mother's ghost. She also suspects her mother, if she were able to appear in some form or another, would not listen at all. People who are robbed of their lives early cannot be expected to understand those who wish to end their lives early. Still, Riley's mother has an ethereal quality that makes Riley feel as if she just might understand everything.

Riley's father offers her her old bedroom and a job at the library where he works, but Riley declines them both. She does not take the same near-orgasmic pleasure in dusting old encyclopedia sets that her father does, and she has no wishes of returning to the bedroom she was sure she would never live in again after graduating high school. Instead, she takes up residence in the basement—a cold concrete-floored room with a few small windows near the ceiling that grant a dismal streak of sunlight that just happens to match Riley's dismal outlook for the future. The chill of the cement floor tingles right up through Riley's slippers. With the lights off, the room is dark and hazy, and oddly comfortable in being so. Riley outfits the room with an old bean bag, two mattresses piled atop one another, a small chest of drawers for her clothes, and a small refrigerator. The only thing missing is a hobby to entertain her throughout the day.

Riley discovers that hobby when she leaves dinner early (her father made burnt macaroni and cheese) and now that dusk has set in, decides to go for a walk down the road. It is springtime and the road is practically a graveyard of amphibious life—limbs strewn from berm to berm. A pond lies only yards beyond the far berm and so many creatures are cut short in their journey to or from it. The blacktop is moist with both rain and bodily fluids. The discovery of Riley's hobby comes in the form of a three-legged salamander—one of the few survivors—struggling its way down the road. Riley bends and scoops the small orange salamander into her hands just as a car blazes past. She finds the creature's fourth leg—its left front one—bent beneath its abdomen and attempts to push it back into place, but has no success in doing so. The leg, probably clipped by a completely clueless driver, is limp. Riley knows her biology professor would have plenty of phrases for such a creature: *destined to die, easy prey, no longer capable of survival,* and *will never get a mate.*

"You will not die," Riley promptly tells the salamander. "Maybe out there where there are predators and mates unfairly discriminating against three-legged varieties of the species, but I will take you in." Riley scavenges an old fish tank from the attic, outfits it with moss and a small pool of water, and places the new friend inside. "I will name you Trooper," she says.

The next morning, Riley places a sign in front of the house: *Salamander Rehabilitation Center (see basement).*

A week later, when no one has stopped by, and Trooper has died (receiving a proper burial in the back yard for which Riley built a small coffin out of toothpicks and permanently straightened Trooper's limp leg with some airplane glue so that he could go to heaven proudly standing on all fours) Riley adds to the sign: *Salamander Rehabilitation/ Mortuary Preparation and Burial Center (see basement).*

A few days later, when Riley has two new salamanders she is attempting to rehabilitate (one owning only two legs and the other missing a substantial portion of its tail) and a toad (which seems to only have the problem of being so round it can't efficiently hop from one place to another) and still has not had any customers, she considers the other frequent victims of amphibian drive-bys and makes yet another change to the sign:

Salamander/Newt/Frog/ToadRehabilitation/Mortuary Preparation and Burial Center (please see basement!).

Two days later, a man comes in with a rabbit. His face is flushed, his hair a mess, and his T-shirt shows dark ovals at the armpits. He cradles a small white rabbit in his hands.

"Did you read the sign?" Riley asks.

"Yes," the man says, holding out the rabbit to her. He glances around the dim basement and seems to take all of it in—Riley's small collection of furniture and the group of terrariums lined against the far wall. "Do you have a license?" he asks.

"Do you have a Salamander/Newt/Frog/Toad?"

"No."

"My answer is the same as yours," Riley says. "I suppose those who put the time into earning a license do not feel they have the time for those smaller species that often fall victim to roadside blunders, lawn mowing accidents, or tortuous children. I do not have a license, but I have the time."

"My rabbit is sick," the man says. He pushes the rabbit toward Riley again.

"Rabbits are not on my sign," Riley says. "I cannot guarantee anything, but I will try."

"Ok," the man says.

Riley takes the rabbit in her hands and it doesn't move. Its ears are flat and its eyes closed. She runs a hand along its body and can't find a warm spot. "This isn't the result of tortuous children, is it?" she asks.

"No," the man says. "But I do have children. I haven't told them yet. They are expecting a healthy rabbit when they get home from school."

Riley cradles the rabbit in her hand and brings it up to her ear to listen for a heartbeat. The hairs tickle her earlobe and for a moment she thinks the creature alive, before realizing it is her that jumped and not the rabbit. "I am not an expert," Riley says. "But I am fairly certain the rabbit is dead."

The man shoves his large hands into his pockets and dips his head.

"Please don't cry," Riley says. "I don't have pet grief counselor on my sign yet." Though she suspects she might be able to manage were the creature a Salamander/Newt/Frog/Toad (she did all right coaching herself when Trooper passed). It is those mammalian species that people tend to get so connected with that an actual counseling degree might be in order.

"But you do mortuary preparation?" The man's eyes glow a little bit.

"Mortuary preparation and burial."

"Can you make the rabbit look alive?"

"What?"

"That's part of the mortuary preparation, right? Makeup? Can't you make it look alive just long enough so that I can get another rabbit that looks just like it? My children will blame me if they discover it has died. They think I feed it too many potato chips."

"How would I make the rabbit look alive?" Riley asks.

"I think that is your question to answer."

"Can't you just tell them it's sleeping?"

"They're on honor roll, they're a little smarter than that."

"I suppose the eyes would have to open," Riley says. "Give me a minute," she says, pushing the rabbit back into the man's hand.

She returns with two small sewing pins and one by one, pushes them against the top of the rabbit's eyelids, puncturing skin, and pushing deep into the fur until the pins lodge into more skin behind the rabbit's eyes. The rabbit doesn't even flinch. And the pins hold.

The man delightedly smiles. "That's good," he says. "The hair is so long you can't even see the pins."

"But I can't make it walk again," Riley says.

"It doesn't have to walk. It likes to hide inside its box sometimes, but if I can just get the head to stick out everything will be all right. Can you make its ears stand up?"

"I don't know," Riley says. "I suppose maybe with paperclips."

"Try."

Riley straightens two paperclips and places one in each of the rabbit's ears, lodging the clips in the eardrum and then allowing them to extend upward.

"I think that will do," the man says. He pushes a twenty into Riley's hands and then skips out of the room.

"You had a visitor today?" Riley's father says at dinner. They are having tofu burgers on wheat bread with lettuce and tomatoes.

"Yes." Riley eats only the bread, lettuce, and tomatoes.

"What did he want?"

"He brought a rabbit. I told him rabbits weren't on my sign. I told him where the veterinarian's office was."

"So he wasn't a real visitor?"

"Yes, he was real."

"Have you seen the paperclips that were holding my stacks of bills together?"

"No."

"Are you going to eat your burger?"

"No."

"You should eat your burger."

"I would eat it if it was real."

Four days later, a woman shows up with a hamster and Riley begins to doubt how many people who can actually read are left in the world.

"The sign-"

"I know," the woman says. "But Phil told me about what you did with his rabbit and it worked. He finally found a similar-looking rabbit a couple towns over and got the rabbit switched before his girls suspected anything."

"Did he give it a proper burial?"

"I don't know," says the woman. "But do you think you could work that same magic on my hamster? I'm not going to get Betsy a new one. I just want the time to introduce her to the idea of death before the hamster officially dies."

"But it *is* dead."

"But you can make it look differently, can't you?"

"I don't know," Riley says. "A hamster is smaller than a rabbit. It will be harder to do."

"You don't have to make the ears stand up," the woman says. "Just get the eyes open. That will be enough. You can't make it walk again, can you?"

Riley gives the woman an incredulous stare. "I cannot even get a fat toad to hop on a regular basis. Not even when I put it on a treadmill."

"That is unfortunate," says the woman. "Those creatures that are alive should be happy to be so."

"I guess," Riley says. She understands why the toad doesn't move; sometimes it is hard enough to simply exist.

"Take the hamster," the woman says, handing the creature to Riley. "I have errands to run. I will be back in an hour."

The hamster has a cowlick on the top of its head and Riley smoothes it over with her pointer finger. The hamster is the perfect size for Riley's hand and even dead, it provides her a strange source of comfort.

"I wonder what your final moments were like," she says out loud. "I wonder if you twitched in your wood shavings or if you just quietly passed on. How will I ever make you look alive again?"

Riley decides on threading a small needle and piece of string through each of the hamster's eyelids, tying a knot on the underside of the eyelid, and then tugging the string, weaving it through some loose skin on the back of the hamster's neck and then tying another knot. "You don't feel a thing, right?" A part of Riley still waits for the creature to scramble to life in the palm of her hand. But it does not.

Riley spends her last minutes before the woman returns lying on her bed with the hamster on her chest. She peers into its glassy black eyes as if she can peer into the afterlife. Is there still the small remnant of a soul inside there? Or is only the outer body left?

The woman is more pleased than Riley suspected. (Riley purposely did a semi-messy job so that the woman might change her mind and allow Riley to prepare the creature for a proper burial.) "This just might work," the woman says. "I picked up some books at the library. Your father helped me out. I think I will be able to prepare Betsy for death."

"Is that something you can really do? Is that something you can really prepare for?"

The woman laughs. "Of course," she says. Then she winks at Riley. "Especially when you know it's coming."

"Please come back," Riley says. "When you need someone to help prepare it for burial. I can do that. I can build a nice little coffin. Betsy can even paint it."

"Thanks," the woman says, gripping the hamster in her hand. "But I think this one might be small enough to flush."

Small enough to flush. That reminds Riley of *it*. Of the reason she left school. Part of what scared Riley was that she couldn't even be sure what had spurred *it*. Maybe it was the doddering of her drunk dorm mates, who sat in the hallway laughing to themselves and throwing up, though Riley well knew they would do it all over again next weekend. She would not, instead remaining that girl they failed to even acknowledge with a nod in passing. Maybe it had something to do with Riley's roommate's boyfriend, who was buried under the covers with Riley's roommate— both of them engaging in a chorus of orgasmic groans that Riley had not only never engaged in but was also terrified at the thought of. Maybe Riley's environmental science course, something she thought should be renamed *Doom and Gloom: 100 reasons you could die today and be ok with it*, played a part. Maybe that macaroni and cheese—so bad it made Riley miss her father's burnt version at home—had something to do with it. But none of these, nor all of them combined, provide any real justification for what Riley did that night, despite how many times she attempts to pull it together in her head.

She did it while her roommate and roommate's boyfriend groaned under the sheets. She did it with the remainder of her roommate's bottle of Advil—forty-seven capsules in all. Riley lasted an entire eight minutes before slipping down the hall past her vomiting dorm mates and sitting herself down in front of one of the toilets. She reached a finger all the way to the back of her throat, pushed it into one of her tonsils, and then watched as the capsules came sliding their way out in a stream of dinner remains. In the toilet water, they floated like buoys or life rafts and, momentarily, Riley felt the surge of being alive and the excitement of merely existing without the burden of existing in a phenomenal manner. But as soon as Riley flushed the toilet and the buoys were gone, that feeling vanished. Riley was only one of many girls who vomited in the bathroom that evening. She was, however, the only girl who knew she had to move out the next morning.

When Riley's father returns home from work, he descends the stairs and appears in front of Riley, who is squatted behind the large toad, trying to prod it into hopping. "I found it in the middle of the road," she explains to her father. "Wouldn't move. I had to carry it right out of there. It was like it was trying to kill itself or something."

"Mrs. Welster came into the library today," Riley's father says while he sits on the edge of her bed. "She said you seem to be in the business of making dead pets appear alive."

"I wouldn't call it a business. I've only done two." Riley sits Indian style on the cold floor. She pushes a pointer into the toad's behind and still it doesn't move.

"I am worried about you. The neighbors complained about that sign of yours but I told them there was no harm in rehabilitating the small creatures or even in helping aid in their journey to the next life. But if they find out about this—"

"They won't. I don't plan on changing the sign again. I'm all out of room anyway."

"You can't do this forever."

"This is true," Riley says. "None of us can do anything forever."

"Maybe that toad needs to be outside," Riley's father says. "Maybe then it will have a reason to jump. This room is cold and dark. You really should come upstairs."

"Who will watch over the toad if I take it outside? How do I know it won't go sit in the road again?"

"How do you know it will?

"I don't. But it's not a chance I can take." Riley glances at the small basement windows and sees that they are splattered with rain. "I need to check the road."

"It is dark and raining."

"Yes, that is why I need to check the road."

On the road, Riley finds another toad. This one is not large, but instead small and scrawny, perhaps because one of its back legs is limp—just simply dragging along behind it, a burden to tow. Riley moves the toad to the grass bordering the road and gives it a chance to hop away while she peels small salamanders and frogs from the road—carefully timing her extractions with the weak flow of traffic—and, in the back yard, digs a small hole for each of them, saying a small prayer—*May you find in heaven what you never found on Earth*—a full fourteen times.

When Riley is finished, the toad is still there and she scoops it into her hands. Goose bumps rise on her arms not because she can feel its heartbeat in her hand, but because even when she begins to squeeze it, the creature doesn't move.

"You are too passive," Riley whispers to it while she sets it in the tank with the other toad. "Neither of you know how to fight for your life."

Riley's father knocks on the basement door.

She tells him she is working.

In the next week, there are no more visitors to Riley's basement. A windstorm comes through and uproots the sign, carrying it off to a destination she does not know of. The toads stare at each other from opposite ends of the tank. Sometimes they near each other, but once they catch Riley looking at them, they move apart. The grassless patches of ground from the growing number of graves make the yard look like prairie dogs live there. Sometimes, at night, Riley pulls a stool up against the wall, turns off the light, and stands staring out those narrow windows. She stares at the road and tries to guess how many small bodies will be there and how many she will even be able to separate from the road. She wonders if any of them try to duck or swerve or if they well know what's coming and cross anyway. She wonders if they prepare themselves ahead of time. And if they even can.

One of those nights, when Riley is staring out the window and guessing the count is up to at least thirteen, the phone rings from upstairs and she goes to it. Her father is on the other end.

"I'm working late," he says. "We got some new books in. I want people to be able to check them out as soon as possible. We got a new one on salamanders. I ordered it just for you."

"Okay."

"Do you want me to bring the book home?"

"What?"

"The book on salamanders?"

"Oh. Yes."

"You will be okay until I get home?"

"Yes."

"I love you."

"I love you too."

When Riley returns to the basement, she hears gentle squeaks and turns to the toad terrarium. The new toad has clasped itself around the middle of the larger and shows no signs of letting go despite its limp back leg. Strings of eggs sit coiled on the mossy terrarium floor and the larger toad does not look so large now. Riley scoops up the strands of slippery eggs in one hand and the attached pair of toads in the other, and ascends the stairs as quickly as possible, making a jog for the pond just across the road. She loses some of the eggs on the way; they slip out from between her fingers, plummeting to the blacktop road she crosses. She places the rest in the pond, as well as the eagerly mating pair. Although Riley cannot see them, there must be many other toads in the pond. Their chorus is nearly deafening and it makes her scalp tingle.

She watches the toads for a time and then stands at the edge of the road, wondering if any of the creatures pause before crossing or just make a dash for it. She wonders if they are aware of the peril or if they just blindly jump into it. Riley watches the few cars fly past. There are not many of them. Just a blur of headlights now and then. Given the curve in the road, Riley knows her form must not be visible until the cars are nearly upon her. This would not be a bad moment to go on. She has just returned two toads and their hopeful eggs to the pond. Maybe that is enough life to balance everything out. She inches closer until she is standing atop the edge of the road. A car whizzes by, but it is traveling so near the middle of the road that Riley only catches the wind of it, making goose bumps rise up and down her legs. Another step. What would a mortician be able to do to her? Could he possibly make her beautiful? Could he make her more wonderful in death than in life? The groan of an engine sounds in the distance and Riley crosses her arms over chest as if this is one of those trust falls from the opening weekend of college. What they failed to tell her was that catching someone physically and emotionally are two different things and that no one can be trusted to do the latter. She closes her eyes and takes one more step into the road while the sound of the approaching car whirs in her ears. She only hopes that it is fast. And that her mother already has her arms out just waiting for her.

The sound of the engine grows louder before the brakes begin to screech and the car groans to a halt. It stops close enough to Riley for her to be able to feel its heat. When she opens her eyes, she sees her father poking his head out his window, his eyes wild with fear.

"How did you see me?" Riley asks. "How did you see me around the curve?"

Her father squeezes the steering wheel and bites at his lower lip. A thin line of tears rolls down the side of his cheek. "Get in the car," he says.

Riley doesn't move. She isn't sure if her feet still work.

Her father gets out of the car and picks her up in his arms, somehow managing it despite his thin build. He squeezes her at his chest the way he used to do when Riley fell off her bike or tripped down the stairs or got another nose bleed. He squeezes so hard that for a while Riley can't breathe and actually thinks she might go in her own father's arms. But she does not. Her father carries her back to the car and places her in the passenger's seat. In the driver's seat, he doesn't say a word. He doesn't drive. He only leaves his four-ways on and just keeps staring straight ahead. Headlights begin to appear behind them and the car slows, stops, and then honks.

"Dad," Riley says. "There is a car behind us."

"We are fine," he says. "They will go around us. We are not moving until we talk."

"Here?"

"Yes, here. I will not move this car until we have talked."

His eyes are bright and determined and his hands unmoving, despite the chorus of honks sounding behind them, a chorus of honks that drowns out the chatter of the toads in the pond, where new beings—small and vulnerable—are being sung to as they emerge and begin their struggle for life with no one to look after them. So many will get lost; it is easy to get lost. Beings looking after one another is a rare and delicate occurrence in this world. Had Riley's father not been the one coming around the corner… Had Riley's father not looked… Which must be his greatest fear? Riley feels a warm knot rise to her throat and cannot get the window down in time. Instead, she vomits right into her lap and the wetness soaks through her jeans. Her father pulls a napkin from the glove box and helps to wipe it from her thighs.

"I have all night," he says. "And those cars behind me do too. They just don't know it yet."

Riley stares at the small pool of vomit on the floor mat and looks for the lifeboats, but doesn't find them there.

"I almost died," she says. "Twice. I almost died twice. And it might happen again."

THE OTHER MAN

Molly McCaffrey

"What is it that you see in Danny anyway?" you ask me over dessert at the most expensive restaurant in College Park. The one the professors go to when they entertain visiting writers, the one all the other grad students think is too pricey to bother with—which, of course, makes it all the more appealing to you even though your credit card bills already eat half of your graduate stipend. Despite your record debt, you insist we find out what all the fuss is about, and for some reason I can never say no to you.

Our waiter thinks we are a real couple; he doesn't notice the way you look at *him*. And I have to admit we look good— no, great—together: you in your charcoal gray Calvin Klein sweater, the one that sets off your olive skin so well, and me in my black halter dress and Jimmy Choo slingbacks. It almost feels like we *are* in a real relationship, and I even think we might make it through the evening without a disagreement until the subject of Danny comes up.

After taking a moment to consider your next step, you continue: "Is it his status as a college dropout, his employ as a techie geek, or his wake-and-bake habit that you find so appealing?" You stop talking to scoop up the rest of the tiramisu we are sharing.

Sure, Danny is all you say he is, but that's just the surface stuff. What I like about Danny is that he *is* different. Maybe it is his lack of education and his drug habit, or maybe it is his thoughtfulness and his strangely possessive cat. Bottom line: he isn't like other guys. How many guys keep cats that want to scratch their lovers' eyes out? And even when he is high—which I admit is mostly all the time—Danny's eyes look as clear and blue as the kind of ocean you only see in travel brochures. When I look at him I think of dinner cruises and parasailing and Margaritaville, and even though I know they shouldn't, these images give me a sense of contentedness, of peace. But these are all things I can never share with you. On the other hand, I *can* tell Danny, and I do. And we joke around about going to one of those all-inclusive resorts and lazing on the beach in our own private cabana.

It is Danny's ability to do this with me—his ability to dream, to laugh—that makes me feel like I am getting the real him, not the notion of who he thinks he should be, the way it is with everyone else. I know you think it's time for me to move on. You've said as much. But I'm not interested in relocating when Danny feels so good.

"I guess he just seems real," I say, my words sounding more like a question than an answer.

You run your tongue across your upper lip, collecting the remaining sweetness, and give me a look I've seen too many times before. "But it's not *going* anywhere," you say as you dab your mouth with the cloth napkin, and I wonder why it is that you always talk about where *I'm* going rather than where *you* are right now. From the moment we met, you've been more interested in critiquing my choices than making your own. It was three years ago during an awkward graduate school orientation: me hovering by the snack table, afraid of saying the wrong thing, of sounding like a fraud;

The Other Man

you confidently moving from group to group with your jargon-heavy insights and analyses. I swooned over your vocabulary, your swagger, and I longed for the way you seemed at ease with every author discussed. Within a week, I was following you around, hoping your understanding, your credibility would rub off. Your constant critique seemed a small price to pay for your attention. But as long as we've known each other, I can't remember one time when we talked about *your* future. Sure, we talk in general terms—about what kind of guy you'd like to be with, about where you'd like to live after you finish school—but it is never about anything real or concrete because your whole life has become about abstract things: about the dissertation, about theory, about pedagogy. I can't even think of the last time you socialized with anyone besides me. By all rights, you are my best friend, and I love you in *that* way, that gay-best-friend way, but sometimes I think you want me to live so you don't have to.

The first time Danny convinced me to try Ecstasy with him, he refused to have sex. He mumbled something about it being too much.

"Too much?" I said, seeking clarification.

"Yeah, you know? *Too* much."

I laughed and thought about how you always talk about Danny's inability to articulate. He's no Joyce, you like to joke.

You know I've never been one of those people who does a lot of drugs—that's one of the reasons we could hang out. We agree that life itself is a better high than anything artificial. But I never pretended to be totally clean either, and I like to get stoned as much as the next person. But it took weeks for Danny to talk me into E. I won't lie to you about it now, though I hid it from you before: as clichéd as I know you'll think it sounds, it was simply amazing, it was phenomenal, it was the best sex I ever had with my pants on. When Danny lightly ran his hand along my arm, I felt it all the way down to my core. Of course, I couldn't tell you about it, with your codes and your ethics. But I secretly wished you could feel it too. And more than anything I wanted to tell you how much trust I felt for Danny after it was over.

After dinner that night, the tiramisu night, I lie on Danny's bed alone, thinking about your questions and tracing imaginary pictures on the ceiling. I know I should be thinking about where Danny and I are going, about how he always says he's not into the commitment thing, about how he never talks about who he dated before me, but instead I think of the way it felt the night he touched my arm, the goose bumps on my flesh. I know we don't make sense—he doesn't get Faulkner, and I don't understand code—but somehow we connect.

I don't notice Danny walk in the room until he speaks. "Are you thinking about *him* again?" he asks.

I roll away and put a pillow over my head so he won't see my face flush.

"The *other* man," he teases.

I laugh, and he pulls the pillow gently away. I look at his eyes and involuntarily think about snorkeling. He kisses me, and things progress as usual. Something about Danny makes me feel more comfortable being myself than I have ever felt before—as if there is nothing wrong with desiring sex or being naked, as if there are no rules. Things have never been better between us than they are that night, and for once, the cat lets us sleep in peace.

"But what do you talk about?" you ask over lunch a week later at a new pan-Asian place you found in the District. "You can't just fuck *all* the time." You pause and then add, "Or *can* he?"

"Isn't this the best green curry you've ever had?" I ask you.

You put your chopsticks down pointedly, set your hands on the edge of the table and lean in, your eyes goggling me like a happy hour drunk. I know you are trying to be amusing, but I also know you won't let it go.

"I don't know what we talk about," I offer. "What does anybody talk about? What do we talk about besides food and who's sleeping with whom in the department."

"We talk about fucking literature, that's what we talk about!" Your voice rises just enough to make me uncomfortable, and I look over my shoulder to see if anyone is listening. You ignore me and go on. "We talk about film, for Christ's sake. We talk about the beauty of art, or have you forgotten?"

I want to believe that you are right, that we only concern ourselves with such lofty matters, and a few years back, I would have bought it, but now, I know enough to understand that this is mostly a pose. "Speaking of film, what are we seeing this weekend?"

"Why don't you see a movie with *him*?"

"We *can't* see a movie together, remember? All we do is fuck."

"Oh, yes, I forgot." You snort and become distracted with collecting noodles on your chopsticks. I know I will have to give you a real answer sooner or later, so I think about the conversations Danny and I have shared—the ones that didn't revolve around Club Med. Some nights we climb out his apartment window and take the ladder up to the roof. We sit in rusty lawn chairs and try to find the stars behind the yellow haze of the city lights. Sometimes we talk, other times just look. All I know for sure is that it is there, on the tar roof of Danny's apartment, that I most like to wait for another night to pass.

"I don't know what we talk about," I say. "Sometimes we talk about what we want to be when we grow up, or how things are different than we imagined they would be."

"You mean, *he* talks about what he'll be when he grows up, and *you* say you'll wait for him."

"I'm not waiting for anything. I'm content with the status quo."

You snort again. "And by that, you mean the fucking?"

"Would you shut up about that?" I look around the restaurant as obviously as I can, hoping you'll honor my request.

"I'll say one thing," you add. "He must be fan*tas*tic in bed."

That weekend Danny and I go to a movie, or a film as he calls it. Danny says Hollywood movies are nothing more than product placement, and films are the things I see with you. Danny laughs a couple times, and I can tell he likes it because his body is slumped to one side the way it does when he first slides into a comfortable high. I smile and loop my arm around his. It feels nice to have someone to touch in the dark of the theater for a change.

When the movie ends, I grip Danny's arm, so he can't get up. I don't want to have to tell you that he failed our test. We both always say a guy isn't worthy if he can't sit through the credits. That not doing so demonstrates a lack of introspection.

When we walk out, I ask Danny what he thought.

"I don't know," he says with a grin that tells me he's trying to hide something. "It was entertaining and all, but what was the point?"

I think about how you would answer such a question, then compose my words as carefully as I can. "The point," I say, "is to show that reality is a construct, that nothing is actually real." In my own mouth, your words sound forced; my old feeling of fraudulence returns.

"Yeah, right," he says and looks away from me as if he's irritated, as if he'd rather be somewhere else. It's a look I haven't seen on him before.

The Other Man

"Didn't you at least like the use of a nonlinear chronology?"

"Why can't they just let a story be a story?" he asks. "It was a good story, wasn't it?"

"Yes, it was," I concede.

"So why not let the story speak for itself?"

"It's an artistic choice," I say, thinking this should be obvious.

"Sure, it's artistic," Danny says. "But it's nothing new. It's only innovative if it's never been done before."

I can't think of a reason to argue.

"Let's get out of here," he says as we approach his car. "Or wait a second! If the car is just a construct, then I guess we're not going anywhere, are we?"

"Very funny," I say and wait for him to open my door.

That Monday at school I tell you about my excursion with Danny. You listen attentively as I describe my impression of the imagistic direction and tell you how the lead actor made me so hot I couldn't wait to get back to Danny's place.

"And what did Danny think?" you ask when I finally stop rambling.

"Danny thought the film lacked innovation because the director was just emulating techniques we've seen so many times before." I want to sound convincing, so I add, "He thought it was derivative."

"Is that what *he* said?"

"Who?"

"Danny?" you ask. "Did he actually *say* 'the film lacked innovation'? And does he even know what the word *derivative* means?"

I don't answer. Instead I look over my shoulder to see who is rustling down the hallway. "Hi, Kara," I say as one of our fellow grad students walks by the open door of your office. For a moment I imagine what would happen if she just kept walking, if she went down the stairs and outside, never to return again. It's a thought I have been returning to a good deal lately. When I turn back to your probing face, I am suddenly aware that I am growing tired of your questions.

I speak to you in a whisper: "I don't want to talk about this anymore." I sense that I need to be as firm as possible, more explicit, if I am to avoid further interrogation, so I add, "I don't want to talk about Danny."

"I don't want to talk about him either," you say in a dismissive voice, as if I am one of your students. Your brusque manner surprises me. Even for you, it seems bitchier than usual. I sit back abruptly, and you go on before I can regain control of my emotions. "I don't think you should see him anymore. That's all there is to it. You might as well just end it."

I wonder if you are becoming the controlling and manipulative person everyone says you are. I think about what it is that makes you think you can tell me what to do. I say, "Just because you're in graduate school doesn't mean you're smart. Maybe you don't like him because he just *is* smart."

"No," you say matter-of-factly. "I don't like him because he's not veracious." You pause, as if waiting for me to consider your words. My mind goes directly to the place in my brain where I have hidden away my questions about whether or not I can trust Danny, the place where I put all the days I don't see him, the times he forgets to call. But I don't want to betray my insecurities, so I quickly disguise my unanswered questions with a look that feigns disapproval. You continue: "I simply don't want to see you get hurt. I care about you, that's all." Your voice has taken on that paternal tone I despise so much, and I feel the need to get away from you before anything else is said. I stand up, alerting you to my departure. I want to shove my empty chair at you, I want to injure you—not because of Danny or anything you've said, but because you and I don't make sense anymore. Instead, I just go.

When I leave school that afternoon, I go right to Danny's. He's working on a freelance job, debugging or something just as vexing. He takes the time to kiss me even though I have shown up unannounced. While he finishes, I lie on his bed and play mind games with the cat, teasing her with one of Danny's socks.

Later, Danny and I order chicken wings for dinner. We decide to eat on the roof, and when we finish I loft the bones into the alley without a thought to littering or consequences or anything else: my small rebellion. Danny asks what's wrong, but I can't tell him the truth because the last thing I want is for him to hate you, even though he's not that kind of guy. I can't lie either; you know I'm no good at that. "Maybe we could talk about it later," I say. Danny is good at taking hints, and he changes the subject, but that night things never feel right or easy like they usually do. And later, while Danny breathes deeply, I am unable to sustain sleep. I wake abruptly, with a jerk, certain the cat is working her magic, putting a spell over Danny and me and our dreams.

You and I don't talk for days. Three to be exact. This is how we always fight, so I don't worry about this altercation being any worse than normal, even though I wonder if it should be. The phone rings on Thursday, and I know it is you because of the time: ten minutes before three. You always call then, twenty minutes after your last class. I pick up on the first ring, just happy you've made contact. But you sound distant, and I realize that this time our wound hasn't healed on its own.

"Can you come over tomorrow night for dinner?" you ask.

"*You* are cooking?" I'm skeptical.

"Just come over and see." You barely say goodbye before hanging up.

I arrive at your house promptly at seven. I know you don't like it when people are late, and I want to put things right, so I am catering to your way of doing things: being on time, wearing the pashmina scarf you gave me for Christmas, and carrying a bottle of Pinot Noir.

You open the door as if you've seen me coming—even though your window doesn't face the street. It isn't until I get to the doorway that I sense you are not alone.

"Am I early?" I ask, confused by your lackadaisical demeanor.

Your mouth is pursed into a sour knot. Instead of answering, you jerk your head back, indicating something behind you. You haven't been on a date in years—no one's ever good enough for you—so I can hardly believe what I think you're trying to say.

I cross the room in a rush, stopping at the door of your bedroom. At almost the same moment that I see him, I realize what is happening; I know it is Danny who is there with you. Am I surprised to see him there? Not as much as you might think. I know you are trying to prove something to me—about his loyalty, about his sexuality, about who he really is.

Danny is asleep in your bed, his pale, hairless chest rising and falling with his breath. Even though his body is covered by the sheet, I can tell he's not wearing anything. It's a familiar sight, and if I try hard enough, I can almost pretend it's like any other day when I come out of the bathroom and find Danny asleep in his own apartment.

I walk over to the mattress, sitting on the edge. With just the tips of my fingers, I brush his shoulder. I know he won't respond; he's always been a deep sleeper. I can feel you watching me, wondering what I will do next, but I don't care about you anymore. I lift my legs to the surface of the bed and inch back into the curve of Danny's body, just as I've done before. Danny puts his arm on top of mine, and I shut my eyes. It feels as close to home as anything does these days. As I lie inside Danny's shell and wait for him to wake, I start to imagine what will happen next.

The funny thing is that I know your attempt to break things down would only make us stronger if I let it. Now I can see the parts of Danny I couldn't before. I understand that I can't cage him in any better than you can control me.

And it's thinking about the word control that makes me finally understand what I have to do.

So, no, I won't ride off into the sunset with Danny, but I won't do it with you either. Maybe I'll leave the world of abstract thought and unread manuscripts behind for good. Maybe I'll opt for something more real, something more mundane. Maybe I'll book passage on a Carnival cruise line and go all-out: play shuffleboard all day and drink Mai Tais all night. I'll gorge myself on the all-you-can-eat buffet and make friends with other swinging singles. But, don't worry, I won't ever forget you. I never could.

In fact, I'll be sure to send you a picture postcard—you know the kind with artificial-looking aquamarine waters and loopy cursive script. I know that you'll be embarrassed when it arrives in your postal box, that you'll wonder who might have glimpsed your name above the address as you clutch it against your well-toned chest. And just knowing that I've managed to put a tiny little scratch on the inscrutable image you project to the world will be enough for me.

Contributors

Dick Bentley, Amherst, MA
Dick Bentley's books, *Post-Freudian Dreaming* and *A General Theory of Desire*, are available on Amazon or at www.dickbentley.com. He attended Yale and the Vermont College of Fine Arts and his paintings, which he combined with graphic poetry, have been exhibited in New York and western Massachusetts. His fiction, poetry and memoirs have been published on three continents. Before teaching creative writing at the University of Massachusetts, he was an urban planner for inner-city housing, serving as Chief Planner for the Mayor's Office of Housing in Boston.

William Borden, Toyse City, TX
William Borden's novel *Dancing with Bears* was recently published by Livingston Press. His novel *Superstoe*, first published in the U.S. by Harper & Row and in England by Victor Gollancz, was reissued by Orloff Press in 1996. His short stories have won the PEN Syndicated Fiction Prize and The Writers Voice Fiction Competition and have been published in over 50 magazines and anthologies. The film adaptation of his play, *The Last Prostitute*, starring Sonia Braga, was shown on Lifetime Television and in Europe. His plays have won over 100 playwriting competitions and have had over 300 productions throughout the world. A Core Alumnus Playwright at The Playwrights' Center in Minneapolis, he was Fiction Editor of *The North Dakota Quarterly* 1986-2002 and is a member of PEN, The Dramatists Guild, ASCAP, and the Authors Guild.

Jane Bradley, Toledo, OH
Jane Bradley has published two books, and her stories have appeared in numerous journals including *The Literary Review*, *The Virginia Quarterly Review*, *The North American Review*, *Crazyhorse* and *Confrontation*. Her story collection *Power Lines* was listed as an "Editor's Choice" by the New York Times Book Review. Her novella *Living Doll* is used in many programs for professionals who work with emotionally disturbed children. She has received both NEA and Ohio Arts Council Fellowships for her work as well as three grants from the Arts Commission of Greater Toledo. Her screenwriting text *Screenwriting 101: Starting Small While Thinking Big* is forthcoming in 2009, and is currently circulating a new story collection and a novel. She teaches creative writing at the University of Toledo. Originally from the hills of Tennessee, she is still trying to adjust to the accent and the multitude of parking lots all around her in Toledo.

Christopher Bundy, Atlanta, GA
Christopher Bundy's stories and essays have appeared or are forthcoming in *Glimmer Train Stories*, *Ellery Queen Mystery Magazine*, *Atlanta Magazine*, *The Rambler*, *The Dos Passos Review*, and others. He is a founding editor of the journal *New South*.

Melody Clayton, Southport, NC
Melody Clayton is, by and large, a writer and member of the Horror Writer's Association. She is a graduate of the University of North Carolina at Wilmington with an M.F.A degree in creative writing. A collage artist, family party planner, as well as a master

gardener in training, Mrs. Clayton describes herself as "a jack of all trades, master of self delusion, self doubt, and self indulgence." She is currently at work on an award-winning novel.

Steve Cushman, Greensboro, NC
Steve Cushman has worked as an X-ray Technologist for the last fifteen years. He is the author of the novel *Portisville* and the short story collection, *Fracture City*. More information on Steve, and his writing, can be found at www.stevecushman.net.

J. K. Dane, Chippewa Falls, WI
J.K. Dane is a writer and artist residing in Chippewa Falls, Wisconsin where she may be seen riding her bicycle in a wig, evening gown, and rose colored glasses. She is a founding member of the Freaks and Geeks, Chippewa Falls Premiere Lunch Club, serving a variety of lentils, casseroles, and other oddities. She carries, among other necessities, a harmonica and bamboo flute. Her short story "Treading Water" was published in *Big Water*, Main Street Rag's 2008 Fiction Anthology.

Rayne Ayers Debski, Boiling Springs, PA
Rayne Debski's stories have been published in *Rose & Thorn*, *Thema*, and other journals. Her fiction has been selected for dramatic readings by theater groups in Albany and Philadelphia. She reads and writes in central Pennsylvania and is working on a collection of short stories.

Steve Fayer, Boston, MA

Steve Fayer's work as a documentary writer for PBS has been recognized with a national Emmy for *Eyes On The Prize* and a Writers' Guild of America Award for *George Wallace: Settin' The Woods On Fire.* He is also co-author of *Voices of Freedom,* a history of the civil rights movement, one of the New York Times "notable books of the year" (Bantam,1990). His fiction has recently appeared in *Bellevue Literary Review, Dos Passos Review, Natural Bridge, New York Stories, North American Review,* and *Saranac Review.*

Rachel Furey, Carbondale, IL

Rachel Furey grew up in upstate NY, received her BS from SUNY Brockport, and is currently completing her MFA at Southern Illinois University, where she also teaches. Her nonfiction has appeared in the *Press 53 Open Awards Anthology, Women's Basketball Magazine,* and the Twins and More edition of *Chicken Soup for the Soul.* She also placed as a finalist in last year's Charles Johnson Student Fiction Award and *Glimmer Train's* New Writers Short Story Contest. In addition to writing, Rachel enjoys the great outdoors and has spent time working with the Vermont Youth Conservation Corps, Southwest Conservation Corps and Gulf Coast Recovery Corps. In the fall, she plans to begin work on her PhD at Texas Tech University.

**Kathleen Gerard,
Township of Washington, NJ**
Kathleen Gerard has had her fiction and nonfiction widely published in literary journals and anthologies, as well as, broadcast on National Public Radio (NPR). Her fiction was awarded the *Perillo Prize* and was nominated for *Best New American Voices*, both national prizes in literature. *Sustaining Falls* is the headline story from a novel-in-stories of the same name, which is currently in search of a publisher.

Sam Howie, Spartanburg, SC
Sam Howie has published fiction and nonfiction in such periodicals as *Shenandoah, The Writer's Chronicle, Fiction International, Potomac Review,* and *Southern Humanities Review.* His work has been included in anthologies by Main Street Rag Press and Hub City Writers Project. Sam has served as Acting Director of Creative Writing at Converse College, where he currently teaches and directs the college's Young Writers Summer Workshop. He received his MFA in 2002 from Vermont College. His story collection *Rapture Practice* is forthcoming from Main Street Rag and available on the Main Street Rag Online Bookstore. He lives in Spartanburg, South Carolina with his wife, Margaret, and son, Jed.

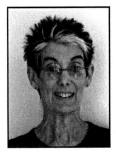

**Marilyn Harris Kriegle,
San Francisco, CA**
Marilyn Harris Kriegel has occupied a place on this planet for 70 years. During this time she has been married, divorced and married again. She raised one child who became an artist and schoolteacher in NYC. During the 60's, Ms Kriegel taught school and as president of her teacher's

union was instrumental in obtaining rights to collective bargaining for the profession. In the 70's she became a psychotherapist and was a pioneer in the human potential movement leading encounter groups around the world. In the 80's she was co-chair of Antioch West University's MA in Holistic Studies and co-authored a popular non-fiction book with her husband. In the 90's Ms Kriegel had a practice in couples counseling and dedicated herself to writing. In the 21st century, Ms Kriegel became a certified teacher of TriYoga and is currently a student in San Francisco State University's MFA program in Creative Writing.

Kerry Langan, Oberlin, OH

Kerry Langan's fiction has appeared in literary journals in the United States, Canada and Hong Kong. Her stories have appeared in *Other Voices, StoryQuarterly, Cimarron Review, American Literary Review, Thema, Rosebud, Phantasmagoria, Eureka Literary Review, Yuan Yang, The Antigonish Review, Fireweed* and many others. Her work is also included in the anthology, Families, The Frontline of Pluralism, and will appear in the forthcoming anthology, Solace in So Many Words. Her non-fiction has appeared in Working Mother.

Pat Lynch, Sacramento, CA

Pat Lynch has published in The New Press, Alimentum and Weber. She has written for the Sacramento News and Review and is currently working on a collection of short stories.

Contributors

Molly McCaffrey, Bowling Green, KY

Molly McCaffrey teaches creative writing at Western Kentucky University and works for Steel Toe Press. She received her Ph.D. from the University of Cincinnati and has served on the editorial staffs of *The Cincinnati Review*, *Oxford Magazine*, and *The G.W. Review*. Nominated for a 2008 Pushcart Prize, an AWP Intro Journals Award, and Scribner's Best of the Fiction Workshop, her work has also been recognized in the North Carolina State Brenda L. Smart Fiction contest and has appeared in *Vestal Review*, *Cairn*, *Gravity Hill*, *Antipodes*, *Word Salad*, and *Quirk*. In addition, she has a critical essay in the newly released *Gilmore Girls and the Politics of Identity*.

Ray Morrison, Winston-Salem, NC

Ray Morrison's stories have been published in more than a dozen journals and magazines, including *Ecotone*, *Night Train*, *Aethlon*, *Carve Magazine*, *Foliate Oak*, and others. He has twice won Honorable Mention in the Lorian Hemingway Short Fiction Competition. A practicing veterinarian, he lives, works, and writes in Winston-Salem, North Carolina where he shares his home with his wife, three children, and an ever-changing number of animals.

Dorene O'Brien, West Bloomfield, MI

Dorene O'Brien is a fiction writer and a teacher of creative writing at the College for Creative Studies and Wayne State University in Detroit. She has won numerous awards for her fiction, including the international Bridport Prize, *Red Rock Review's* Mark Twain Award for Short Fiction, the *New Millennium*

88

Writings Fiction Award and the *Chicago Tribune* Nelson Algren Award. She was also awarded a creative writing fellowship from the National Endowment for the Arts. Her short stories have appeared in the *Connecticut Review, The Chicago Tribune, Carve Magazine, Ellipsis, Passages North, Cimarron Review, Detroit Noir* and others. Her short story collection, *Voices of the Lost and Found*, features many of her prize-winning stories. Visit her at www.doreneobrien.com.

Cari Oleskewicz, Hagerstown, MD
Cari Oleskewicz's fiction, essays and opinion pieces have been published in *The Pedestal Magazine, Colere, Italian Cooking and Living, The Washington Post, The Baltimore Sun*, and *New York Magazine*, and her poetry has appeared online in *Unlikely Stories*. An essay has recently appeared in *Dog Blessings: Poems, Prose, and Prayers Celebrating our Relationships with Dogs* (published by New World Library, June Cotner, editor). Cari is currently working on a novel which keeps trying to morph into an epic poem. Follow Cari on Twitter (http://twitter.com/carilynn72) and look for her page on Facebook!

Daniel Pearlman, Providence, RI
Dan Pearlman's stories and novellas, most of them falling into the various "fantastic" genres, began appearing in 1987 in magazines and anthologies such as *Amazing Stories, The Silver Web, New England Review, Quarterly West, Semiotext(e) SF, Synergy, Simulations, Imaginings* (Pocket Books, 2003). His books of fiction to date are *The Final Dream & Other Fictons* (Permeable Press, 1995); a novel, *Black Flames* (White Pine Press, 1997: a twisted excursion into the Spanish Civil War); a second fiction collection, *The Best Known Man in the World & Other Misfits* (Aardwolf Press, 2001); and a science-fiction

novel, *Memini* (Prime Books, 2003). His work has received outstanding reviews in periodicals such as *Publishers Weekly*, *Booklist*, and the *Washington Post*. Though a native of New York City, he has lived with Lovecraft's ghost in Providence, RI, since 1984.

Charles Rammelkamp, Baltimore, MD
Charles Rammelkamp edits an online literary journal called *The Potomac* http://thepotomacjournal.com. His novel, *The Secretkeepers*, was published in 2004 by Red Hen Press, for whom he also edited a collection of essays on American cultural issues *Fake-City Syndrome*. In addition to a collection of short fiction, *A Better Tomorrow*, (PublishAmerica), he has published half a dozen poetry chapbooks, and a collection of poetry, *The Book of Life*, was published by March Street Press, which also published his other collection of short fiction, *Castleman in the Academy*, which contains eleven stories about a community college writing professor. For ten years, Rammelkamp was on the adjunct English dept. faculty at Essex Community College. He is also a staffwriter for several magazines and contributes a regular column on urban legends for *Mysteries Magazine*.

Nicole Louise Reid, Evansville, IN
Nicole Louise Reid is the author of the novel *In the Breeze of Passing Things* (MacAdam/Cage). Her stories have appeared in *The Southern Review*, *Quarterly West*, *Meridian*, *Black Warrior Review*, *Confrontation*, *turnrow*, *Crab Orchard Review*, and *Grain Magazine*. She is the winner of the 2001 Willamette Award in Fiction, and has also won awards from the Pirate's Alley William Faulkner Short Story Competition and the F. Scott Fitzgerald Literary Society. She teaches creative

writing at the University of Southern Indiana and is fiction editor of *Southern Indiana Review*.

Claude Clayton Smith, Ada, OH

Professor of English Emeritus at Ohio Northern University, Claude Clayton Smith is the author of a novel, two children's books, three books of nonfiction, four produced plays, and a variety of poetry, short fiction, essays and reviews. He holds a B.A. from Wesleyan, an M.A.T. from Yale, an M.F.A. in fiction from the Writers' Workshop at the University of Iowa, and a D.A. from Carnegie-Mellon. His books have been translated into five languages, including Russian and Chinese. He was the 2008 Claridge Writer in Residence at Illinois College. His latest book, forthcoming from Kent State University Press, is *Ohio Outback*.

Merry Speece, Columbus, OH

Merry Speece has published two chapbooks of poetry and has been a recipient of a state arts commission fellowship in prose. Her *Sisters Grimke Book of Days* (Oasis Books, England), which one reviewer called a prose poem, is a mixed-genre work of fragmented historical scholarship.

Steve Taylor, La Crescenta, CA

Steve Taylor teaches at Glendale College where he has won a whole bunch of teaching awards due to a system he worked out where the students do all the work and give him all the credit. Before that, he had a whole bunch of different jobs where he did all the work and someone else got all the credit. He likes the new system. He went to a lot of schools, such as UCLA, Columbia, and Claremont, and some even gave him impressive-sounding degrees, but his favorite was Vermont College because of all the trees. The stuff he writes has got him an L.A. Arts Council Literature Award, made him a finalist in the Katherine Anne Porter Prize and runner-up in the New Millennium Writings Awards, and won him the MSR Short Fiction Contest. Main Street Rag Published his short story collection *Cut Men* in 2005. Humoring him in this way has only increased his urge to write even more stuff.

**Bryan Walpert,
Palmerston North, New Zealand**
Bryan Walpert holds an MFA from the University of Maryland and PhD from the University of Denver. He won the 2007 Manhire Creative Science Writing Award-Fiction, and his first collection of short stories is forthcoming. His poems have appeared widely in such journals as *AGNI, Crab Orchard Review, Hayden's Ferry Review, Runes,* and *Tar River Poetry*; he won the 2007 James Wright Poetry Award from *Mid-American Review*. His first book of poems, *Etymology,*was published in February 2009 with Cinnamon Press. A recipient of a national Tertiary Teaching Excellence Award in New Zealand, he teaches creative writing at Massey University and is the poetry editor of the literary journal *Bravado*.

Dede Wilson, Charlotte, NC
Dede Wilson is the author of three books of poetry, *Glass,* finalist in the Persephone Press Competition, *Sea of Small Fears,* winner of the Main Street Rag Chapbook Competition, and *One Nightstand, The Main Street Rag*. Her short stories have been published by *Negative Capability* and in the *Nightshade Short Story Reader*. Her poems have appeared in many journals including *Spoon River Poetry Review, Carolina Quarterly, Tar River Poetry, Cream City Review, Poet Lore, Asheville Poetry Review, The Lyric, Poem* and the *New Orleans Poetry Review..*

She has been a Blumenthal Reader and was nominated for a Pushcart Prize. Two full-length manuscripts of poetry and a chapbook are seeking publishers.

Josh Woods, Carbondale, IL

Josh Woods is Editor of *The Versus Anthology* (Press 53, 2009), Associate Editor of *Surreal South '09* (Press 53, 2009), and Assistant Editor at *Crab Orchard Review*. His fiction won the 2008 Press 53 Open Awards Contest in Genre, in print through the book *Press 53 Open Awards Anthology*, and he is contributing fiction to *The Versus Anthology* and *Surreal South '09*. His non-fiction and book review works have appeared in *The Susquehanna Review*, *UE Magazine*, and *Crab Orchard Review*. He is currently enrolled in the MFA Fiction Program at Southern Illinois University at Carbondale, and he is at work finishing his first novel, in encyclopedia form, about paranormal pandemonium invading small-town Kentucky and the blue-collar machinist who stands in its way.

Lisa Zerkle, Charlotte, NC

Lisa Zerkle's poetry has appeared in *Crucible*, *The Main Street Rag*, *Thrift Poetic Arts*, and online at literarymama.com. She is a co-editor of *Kakalak: Anthology of Carolina Poetry*. In 2008, she wrote a monthly column for the *Charlotte Observer* as one of their Community Columnists. Lisa advises everyone who loves poetry to search out Sarah Lindsay's luminous new book, *Twigs & Knucklebones*. She lives in Charlotte, NC with her husband and their three children.